INTO THE DRAGON'S DEN

Book Two of the AXE DRUID Series

Written by CHRISTOPHER JOHNS

© 2019 Mountaindale Press. All rights reserved. No portion of this book may be reproduced in any form without permission from the publisher, except as permitted by US copyright law.

This is a work of fiction. Names, characters, places, and incidents either are the products of the author's imagination or are used fictitiously. Any resemblance to actual persons, living or dead, businesses, companies, events, or locales is entirely coincidental.

TABLE OF CONTENTS

Dedication 5
Acknowledgments.. 6
The Story so Far.. 7
Chapter One 10
Chapter Two 79
Chapter Three... 133
Chapter Four... 156
Chapter Five.. 172
Chapter Six 207
Chapter Seven... 234
Chapter Eight.. 257
Chapter Nine... 285
Chapter Ten 302
Chapter Eleven 319
Chapter Twelve... 350
Chapter Thirteen 378
Chapter Fourteen 387
Chapter Fifteen 400
Chapter Sixteen 420
Chapter Seventeen... 439
Chapter Eighteen 456
Chapter Nineteen... 468
Chapter Twenty 485
Chapter Twenty-One 500
Chapter Twenty-Two 519
Chapter Twenty-Three 537
Chapter Twenty-Four 563
Epilogue... 579
Afterword 582
About Christopher Johns 583

About Mountaindale Press 584
Mountaindale Press Titles 585
    GameLit and LitRPG 585
    Fantasy 586
Appendix 587
    The Good 587
    The Bad 591
    And The Ugly 592

Dedication

Dedicated in loving memory to Jaken "Warmecht" Fox.

I hope that, wherever you are, you see the lives you've touched and know that there many. I only hope that the one who matters knows who loved her as much as your friends always have. Little Moon, wherever you may be—Dad loved you, kiddo.

Acknowledgments

A special thanks to my amazing family, my loving fiancée, and my friends. Without all of you, this story would lose its meaning. Thank you.

To my son: Someday, may you walk these worlds as I have and feel your creativity flow as surely as mine did. My most precious gift I give to you is a view of worlds inside your mind and the imagination to walk there and find something of your own.

I love you, son.

The Story so Far

I still couldn't believe what just happened. One of my greatest friends had just disappeared in a plume of sulfurous smoke after a knock-down-drag-out battle with one of War's generals.

Sorry, War is this galactic assho–forgive my language–*being* who takes his vast armies across the cosmos and conquers one planet at a time to add to the fold before moving on to the next one in-line.

Know what? You guys know me by now, right? Let's let me have my fun and swear like the Marine I am, yeah?

Typically, each place he's gone to before, he's taken without much of a fight. I can't really speak on that myself because I still don't know all that is possible on the situation in the rest of the cosmos. Just that the gods here, led by Lady Radiance, are keeping him and the main host off of this world and away from Earth by extension. They had just enough juice to bring us here through a dream and are doing everything they can just to slow him down long enough to get rid of his vanguard and generals so that he stays out for good. They have this theory that if he can't collect a world in the line he's working in, he will just stop because of his own pride.

It hasn't been easy for them, and nearly all of their focus is needed, so they need us to hurry. With the magic of this realm and whatever the gods can spare, we've been hunting down War's scouts and generals who managed to get on to the world before Radiance and company knew what was going on. Luckily, that handicap leans even further in our direction because the Gods of this world based their civilizations and realities off Earth's most recent iterations of video games and the great galactic conqueror's people can't sense our presence the same way they can with the Brindollans.

Thank God—the *gods*—for that.

We had the opportunity when we first were brought to this world to choose an avatar, our physical manifestation here on Brindolla. That could have been any number of creatures and races.

Could I have chosen a human? Yes, but that's like asking someone with a lot of money to go out and get you a plain, bland, vanilla cake. And we all know that you want some of that good chocolate cake with the whipped cream icing and—*shit, I'm hungry now.* Regardless, I wasn't going to be a plain-Jane human when there were other options.

So I had chosen a Kitsune, an anthropomorphic fox person—fox-man—with glossy, raven-black fur and electric blue eyes. That had been all until my recent adventures in the realm of the Fae, where a Blood Rite made me a Celestial Kitsune. It wasn't too different from normal, except now, there are constellations of stars represented in my fur, and I have two tails, though the second tail had actually been awakened by another Kitsune druidess. But I didn't feel much like wagging them at this point.

On top of that, we even got to choose our classes and even take on some crafting classes as well. Me? Why, I'm a shapeshifting, spell-slinging Druid. Of course. Who turns even furrier thanks to a curse given to me by a crazy alpha Werewolf—but more on that later.

My friends and I—Bokaj, Jaken, Balmur, James, and Yohsuke—we've had some successes, gotten some major bruises, kicked some serious ass, and made friends with ancient and powerful beings and probably more than our fair share of enemies. Maybe. But hey, can't make an omelet without breaking a few eggs and punching a few faces, yeah? Wait, that's not right.

Or is it?

Whatever. This whole thing is confusing. Look—what you need to know is that we just took out one of the big guys, and now, shit has gone tits up. Fuck. This will not be pretty. Wish us luck.

Chapter One

Balmur was gone. POOF, cloud of sulfur-smelling smoke, and he was no more. Rowan, the physical body of Blight, one of the five generals War had sent ahead of his planetary raid, was now dead. To be honest, I didn't give a damn about the notifications blinking in the bottom left-hand corner of my vision. All that mattered was that my friend was gone.

I looked to my left and saw my other friends were walking toward me slowly. Some of them were nursing health potions to replenish their HP—hit points for the uninitiated—lost in our fight with the jackass.

"You guys catch what just happened to Balmur?" I asked. I scratched my chin, the fur rustling under my claw-tipped fingers.

I was doing my damnedest not to freak out—maybe this was a trick. Right? That was possible still.

Yohsuke, my brother-from-another-mother was the first to respond, "I caught a bit there at the end. I saw him disappear. You thinking what I'm thinking?"

His half-Drow-half-High-Elf gray skin glistened with a bit of sweat in the afternoon light. He wore a black cloak around most of his body but only raised the hood when needed. His white hair blew slightly in a cool breeze, and his yellow eyes flashed to our other friend.

"Think it was the Hells he was taken to?" James asked as he jogged over.

Fuck. I groaned mentally. *It hadn't been a trick*

James, called Aaron at home, was another friend from the Marine Corps that Erik—Yohsuke—had introduced me to.

It was on our way to hunt for the generals that we had found James the Dragon Elf sleeping in the cave entrance of a Goblin lair. His black scales provided the same protection for his body as our armor, and he seemed cool with that. His monk training had also given him some monstrous abilities and physical endurance. The man could take a hit.

"It sounds like it," I confirmed with a shake of my head. *Fuck.* "We've got a link to the Hells through you, right, Yoh? Can you ask him to get us there?"

"I can try." He nodded and began to step toward a shadowed alleyway. "I'll see what my asshole 'patron' thinks, the fucking piece of shit."

"Yo, where's Balmur, man?" a large, metal-clad figure asked as he stepped over to us.

Jaken, our resident tank and one of our healers, had chosen the Fae-Orc race, his almost-lilac-colored skin was hidden under the bulk of his mithral armor. His large sword and shield were strapped to his back, and his black hair would need to be put back in a ponytail as it was severely messed up and whipping about his face in the breeze. His black goatee and mustache were really quite dashing and made me wish I had deemed it fit to check into facial hair when I had been making my own avatar.

"We think he was teleported to the Hells," James answered before I could.

"He was WHAT?!" Our final party member had just poked his head around our seven-foot-tall Paladin, and he looked *pissed.*

Bokaj, the other Jake in our party, was a former coworker of mine and a friend I gamed with on occasion back at home. He had chosen an Ice Elf as his avatar's race. Lot of Elves in our party, yeah, I know. Wanna fight about it? He also happened to be our now-missing Rogue's, Balmur, best friend. The two had known each other for years and years, and it was starting to manifest in the Bokaj's obvious outrage at his friend's predicament.

"Look, man, we don't know for sure, but we think he could have been taken to hell. We really need to stop repeating ourselves like this. Give Yoh a minute to let us know what the demon knows, and we will try to make a plan." I tried to pat him on the shoulder, but he just stepped back and hugged his panther familiar Tmont.

The nearly full-grown black panther butted her head against his chest and eyed me knowingly. When she was smaller, she had a penchant for biting my tail. She had continued to do so until I threatened to beat her ass.

Kayda, come here, please, I thought to my own companion, well, familiar. The bond's a lot more in-depth than someone's bond with a pet. I could feel her presence—our bond—in my mind.

A second later, I heard a screech that sounded like a peal of thunder in the sky signaling her approach. A large azure and ice-blue bird dropped from the sky, her feathers ruffling in the wind. Her six-foot-tall frame touched down with a soft *thwumph*, and the Storm Roc cooed over me. Her feathers, the azure-colored ones, fluttered in a soft breeze, their color close to that of her lightning—it's blue as well—but her shimmering, lighter feathers were the color of ice and almost as cold at times. Some of them reminded me of icicles with how they were shaped, but as she looked me over head to toe to see if I was hurt, I could feel the warmth of her and her affection. After she was satisfied I didn't have any grievous injuries, she turned in Yohsuke's direction and hopped off toward the alleyway.

He stomped forth from his shadowed hiding place and waved Kayda away. Yohsuke had a special place in her heart because he had helped me rescue her from a raiding party full of Goblins.

"Fucker can't get us to the Hells." He growled. "It's beyond his means to get us all there, and he says we aren't strong enough yet to go there anyway. Though the two levels I just got went a long way to juicing me up. How about you guys? Any loot on the general?"

"General didn't drop shit," James spat. "Gave a ton of experience, though. Got me all the way to level 20."

I thought for a moment before speaking, "Let's allocate our points. Then we can try and find his base or whatever and raid it."

I opened my stats screen with a thought and looked it over. *Yes!* I thought with a clenched fist. Turns out killing the general had leveled me three times. Bittersweet as it was, levels would help us get Balmur back.

Name: Zekiel Erebos
Race: Celestial Kitsune
Level: 20
Strength: 40
Dexterity: 31
Constitution: 30
Intelligence: 45
Wisdom: 34
Charisma: 17
Unspent Attribute Points: 15

Trying to decide my best route from this point on would be a little difficult. The Druid class as a whole is a heavy hitter depending on how you build it, as most classes would be, but I wanted to be more of a utility to my friends. So far, I had been trying to be well rounded, filling into whatever the party needed me to do. I could help heal, do some serious physical damage, and blast the *hell* out of some people with magic. Didn't hurt that I had a familiar and I could shapeshift too, which was a great deal of fun and pretty deadly. For the other guy.

Before I decided to pour my points into some crazy stats and possibly screw myself over, I decided to look into my other notifications.

CONGRATULATIONS!

You have reached a milestone in your advancement and have unlocked the following abilities.

You may now have one additional animal companion or familiar.

Why had no one ever mentioned getting another familiar? Dinnia didn't have one. Was that because she hadn't found one that she wanted to take as a familiar, or was she waiting for the right time? Could she even take another? Too many questions.

Limitations on shape shifting abilities have been lifted slightly. You may use a form with the ability to fly. Flight time and ability will be calculated by constitution, dexterity, and strength. Newest limitation is set to non-mythical creatures. In example: the caster could not take the form of a dragon, phoenix, or roc of any sort until later in their advancement.

Interesting, I grumbled in my head. Honestly, the thought to fly had occurred to me, but I never found a bird cool enough to want to turn into, so I just kind of kept putting it off until I no longer thought of it. And non-mythical creatures are the new limit? How dope would that be to become a dragon? Moving on.

You have unlocked another tail, as a nine-tailed Kitsune. This tail will allow you to choose an extra spell to learn from current and past spell choices. Would you like to choose now?

I chose not to in hopes I unlocked other spells with my recent levels.

ABILITIES UNLOCKED

Teleport – The caster and a number of creatures equal to the caster's (intelligence divided by five) can travel to a place the caster has been before within a distance equal to the caster's (intelligence multiplied by ten) in miles from the spot where the spell is cast. Cost: 300 MP. Cooldown: 30 minutes. Range: 450 miles. Creature load: 9 creatures.

Snare – Caster summons the elements to hold one subject. Subjects with higher strength may only be hindered, while others may be unaffected completely with even higher strength—plan carefully. Cost: 50 MP. Cooldown: 1 minute. Range: 100 ft. Duration: 1 minute.

Lightning Storm – Caster summons a cylinder of electrical energy on a chosen point. 60 ft wide and 120 ft tall. Cost: 250 MP. Cooldown: 30 minutes. Range: 60 ft. Duration: 15 Seconds. Restriction: Can only be used outside.

Wind Step - Caster levitates as if walking on the very air we breath. Cost: 46 MP. Range: Touch. Cooldown: 3 minutes. Duration: 2 Minutes.

Oh, oh my giddy-great aunt! TELEPORT. It was all I could do not to scream aloud at the fact that I had *finally* gotten the one spell I had always wanted.

There are several different brands of goodies in a lot of games that need a little looking into, yeah? As to why the above are called 'abilities'? It's because I have the *ability* to cast them. It's an ability. Weapon abilities are kind of the same, but they are on a cooldown basis. You use them once, they cooldown, you can use them again. Some spell abilities have cooldowns and costs. Following? Me neither, but the ability to cast spells like this was important to me, especially as a Druid.

Don't get me wrong—I got spells, baby. I had Fox Fire, Lightning Bolt, Filgus' Flaming Blade, Winter's Blade, Regrowth, Mass Regrowth, Nature's Voice, Fireball, Nature's Path, Water Sphere, Heal, Diamond Skin, Blade Shift, Star Fall, and finally—Polymorph. All of those have a myriad of uses and have saved my neck more times than I cared to admit. Hell—they had saved my friends and I more times than I could count. I was packing.

But to be even more candid, I had some abilities that I had gotten from the Primordial Elementals too. One of which was Diamond Claws, the only kind of ability that carried over to my actual base physical form. The others I had to take on Elemental form to use.

But these? Holy crap. Teleport would speed travel times up so much it was ridiculous.

I could choose two of them, so I took that one—duh—and I also nabbed Lightning Storm. I went back to my tail option and chose Snare. That spell had a decent amount of utility to it, and I needed another crowd control spell. Wind step seemed unnecessary since I had the ability to fly now as a shapeshifter.

The next notification was one I hadn't expected at all.

CELESTIAL ABILITIES DISCOVERED

Shadow Blessing – The caster chooses one creature within range and gives them the ability to become one with shadows. Whether it is to assist in dodging attacks or sneaking, the shadows will help how they can. Cost: 50 MP. Cooldown: 5 minutes. Range: Touch. Duration: 20 minutes.

Star Blade – The stars themselves bless a weapon within range, causing it to deal holy damage. Cost: 25 MP. Cooldown:

None. Range: 30 ft. Duration: 1 hour or until dismissed (by caster or wielder).

Summon Celestial – A Higher Celestial being is brought forth to render aid at the request of the summoner. The nature of that request and the aid rendered may vary, and help is not always guaranteed. Cost: Full mana bar. Cooldown: 24 hours. Duration: Dependent on the request of the caster. Restrictions: Caster cannot request the Celestial become a familiar, stay in the Prime plane indefinitely, or sacrifice their power for the caster or any other creature in the form of experience.

These spells were endowed—meaning that they weren't choices. I just got them. Which I had to admit was pretty badass. That last spell sounded intriguing—the ability to call for aid. It would help, for sure. The cost was prohibitive so using it in combat would be out of the question unless in the most dire of circumstances. And even then as a last resort. The other spells, though? Those were going to be huge in the coming battles. If we ended up having to go to the Hells to get our friend, holy damage would serve us well.

With these spells came a heavier need for mana, and I was tempted to dump my stats into intelligence and wisdom. Hell, Yoh was probably going through a similar issue himself. His Spell Blade class ate mana and spit out ass whoopings. It was a problem that we loved having, because his mana usage was always the best. His strikes were the most effective because of his Spell Sniper ability. It let him target certain things and get critical strikes and—if he hit the head—potentially confuse enemies.

For me, though, I needed to be strong, fast, and able to sling spells. My ability to be a multi-purpose tool for the party was the key to keeping us relevant in a few areas. Granted, the party would do well without me—they're all much better gamers than I am. Strategy, luck, and skill, they had all that and more.

I provided support that kept us flush in a lot of situations, even if the others pulled my ass out of the fire more than I cared to admit.

With that in mind, I added a point to my wisdom. The next four went to my dexterity, five to strength, and five to intelligence. I felt a rush as my muscles bulged once quickly and seemed to thicken and strengthen even as I felt more lithe than before thanks to the points in my dexterity. I never felt any smarter or wiser, maybe a little itchy? I couldn't tell you.

I checked Kayda's stat page and was pleased to see that she had leveled up to fifteen. Three levels worth of points to play with—nine since she earned one point that was spent on a stat used most per level and three for me to spend—so I threw four points into her strength and five into her dexterity. Her other stats—constitution, intelligence, and wisdom—had gone up naturally by one point apiece, so the result looked good enough for now.

Name: Kayda
Race: Storm Roc
Level: 15
Strength: 20
Dexterity: 25
Constitution: 26
Intelligence: 15
Wisdom: 11
Charisma: 10
Unspent Attribute Points: 0

Normally, I would dump into her constitution and increase her health pool, but for now, her ability to throw down was what we needed most. Also, with her being large enough and strong enough, she may be able to carry someone other than me in my fox form.

I checked the spells she could learn, and I had to admit, the pickings seemed slim for her fifteenth level. One did seem interesting enough—Flash Freeze.

Flash Freeze – The caster touches one target and freezes them solid. Cost: 50 MP. Range: Touch. Cooldown: 1 minute.

That would be interesting to see in action. I could imagine her plopping down on some poor, unsuspecting Goblin, freezing it solid, and hauling it into the air before dropping it on some other schlub.

I stretched a bit, bending at the waist and putting my hands on the ground. Fighting was tense work, and I was still pissed off about that little boy having died. Rowan's death hadn't been painful enough to avenge the lad, in my opinion. That rage left me stiff all over, and it was a good, languorous stretch that would help me ease out of combat mode.

My tails caught in the breeze and rustled in the air. It felt good.

Look, man, I'm a fox—what do you expect?!

Once I finished, I went over to my friends as they seemed to be finishing up their own leveling.

"We good?" Jaken asked. He was bending and making circular motions with his arms like he was loosening up. "What's the tally on everyone's new skills, abilities, and what not?"

Skills are abilities that some of the martial classes get. James has a few that allowed him to use his ki in different ways. Jaken had skills that let him get the enemy's attention and keep it.

I filled the others in on the spells and Celestial abilities I had gotten for leveling up. Jaken also received the Summon Celestial spell, but his was likely from his service as a Paladin rather than mine being from a racial ability. I wondered if mine would be less powerful because of that, but it would have to wait.

Yohsuke got a self-buff that let him be harder to hit called Blur, a spell called Putrid Mind that confused the enemy, and another buff called Hell Blade to give two allies massive added fire damage to attacks. The last two were expensive casts at 100 MP apiece—the buff was per casting but definitely not bad to have.

Aside from our shared spell, Jaken chose a shield spell that summoned a "monster" to attack anyone in front of his shield. It was a touch thing, so they had to be right up on him, and the monster didn't leave the shield. It did, however, immobilize that target, so it took some damage away from him.

So, imagine a Goblin in front of his shield, he activates the spell, and a large mouth emerges from the shield and bites the Goblin, holding it in place and causing damage over time. Now, he has one less thing that can hit him.

He also got an instant heal and area of effect spell that healed allies and damaged foes called Radiant Burst. It took all his mana and only spread thirty feet from him, but all allies healed to full health in it, and enemies got damaged and knocked aside—so that's a win. The downside was that it takes *all* of his mana—no matter how high it goes—to cast no matter the amount he has. So that would be a last resort kind of deal, that and the long cooldown.

Not to mention—a resurrection spell.

These were crucial in a lot of role-playing games because, well, they bring people back to life. Though, with how things seemed to be going for us lately, I doubted we would have to use it, and none of us really wanted to entertain the thought of any of us actually biting the big one. Kind of like the last spell he had gotten, this took all his mana. Tack a full 100 HP on top of that, a cooldown of twenty-four hours, and that it only worked up to three minutes after the target died—and it was great news. Just a little rough to think about.

James took a pretty sweet ability called Sunder Armor; it allowed him to find the weak point in an enemy's armor and then crush it. It increased his damage output to that target and lowered their defense too. Ki Confusion, which caused his opponent to become confused, duh, but this was especially detrimental to spellcasters because it could cause the spells they cast to backfire. And finally, Elemental Channel, which covered his body in a specific element for different effects.

That last one sounded dope as hell and vaguely like my own elemental shapeshifting. I couldn't help but be a little proud.

Bokaj only took one new ability, Arrow Trap, which would trap one target in vines with one arrow for a little bit. What was really cool was that he unlocked a secondary class. The ever infamous, ever sexual and talented—Bard.

So with secondary classes, it was kind of a hit or miss requirement to get one. Weird—I know. But here's why, from what he seemed to be thinking and gathering. When you choose your starting class, it's automatically available, but in order to qualify for another class, you have to meet requirements. It looked like, for Bard, that you had to have a high amount of charisma, be able to cast some spells, and have some kind of bardic talent. Luckily, Bokaj was a musician back home on Earth, so he had all of that. The downside to it was that it seemed like it was mostly guesswork to get a class you wanted unless you knew someone who had done so previously.

But man, how about that Bard, eh?

Now, from the books I'd read and games I'd played back home, these guys were as much, if not more so, jacks-of-all-trades than my own class. They could do everything and with their charismatic skills, would look damned fine doing whatever they wanted. They also got some pretty sweet magical abilities and were adept at social maneuvering. More than a few villains and maybe some Dragons—just saying—had fallen prey to their sexy wiles.

The downside? We would need to find a trainer for him to be able to unlock the class and use it properly. It was there, he could see it, but he didn't have access to anything.

Having more than one class wasn't unheard of in a lot of games, especially tabletop games. My only complaint was not being able to do it myself. I'd have to try and figure out how to do so for myself and get a more badass class to pair with my already sexy Druid abilities and spells.

"Good?" Bokaj asked tersely. "Can we hurry up and go figure the fuck out how to get my best friend back now?"

Everyone nodded, and we turned to where we had left our Fae friends in an alley behind the house. As we walked, we spotted the citizens that had been taken in by Rowan, the general, and bent to his will. They had acted brainless and hostile—like those old-timey zombies limping at the heroes as they ran away. They lay in a pile; we'd had to fight and kill these ones, but for some reason, there were others lying lifelessly in the streets that we had to step around. It was daunting.

My thought was that they were probably either reanimated dead, or they had been enslaved to the point where they were brain dead. That was no life to live, and once this was all done and over with, I would try to honor them as best we could.

We grabbed the "emissaries" of the Unseelie Court and bid them follow us. They obeyed with nods. It was hard not to be angry with them. I knew they couldn't have helped us in that fight against the general, but still—they had been safe here in hiding while we risked our necks. And now my friend was gone? Fuck, man.

A red tinge began to cloud the edges of my vision, and I growled deeply as I willed the rage and Lycanthropic transformation away. While we had been in the Fae Realm, we had a fun run-in with a psychotic alpha Werewolf bent on trying to wrest control of the realm from the queens of the Seelie and Unseelie, and she had given me the "gift" of being a Werewolf. She died, unpleasantly. The thought made me bare my teeth in a grim smile.

"Let's try and take care of the people of the city first, man." Bokaj gestured to us all angrily as he lifted a large man up into a more comfortable position.

"We have to help these people," Jaken said, redundantly. "There has to be something—anything—we can do."

I closed my eyes in thought, then willed the spell I had in mind to activate.

A large rent opened in the air in front of me with the sound of tearing fabric, and golden light poured over us. A ten-foot-tall Greek statue stepped out. Well, it looked like it should be made of stone at least. The thing was *buff* with a capital Holy Shit! It had a halo of spun gold above tightly curled hair that looked like it could be blond. Golden wings spread behind it as far as fourteen feet to each side. The eyes were golden as well—I think I was beginning to see a theme.

"Summoner," it greeted me in a deep baritone, "what is it that I can do for you?"

It took me a moment to find the words that had barreled out of my head the second the very fabric of the universe tore open before me. Ah well, fuck it.

"Yes, hello." I searched for a name and floundered, so I cleared my throat and continued, "Yes. Please, if you would be so kind, heal all the citizens in this city."

Look, if you were in my place looking at a heavenly being such as this dude, you would stumble with words too. Stop judging me.

It stared at me for a moment in absolute silence, then kneeled down and put a hand to its ear and said, "Say your request once more, Summoner."

"I, uh, asked you to heal all the citizens in this city," I stated louder once more with a little more order in my tone. It reminded me of the orders we would get when I was a lance corporal in the Corps.

The being smiled and stood tall, its wings bursting forth from his back. "As you wish."

The being—*angel,* I thought to myself—snapped his fingers and a horn the size of my great axe appeared in his left hand. He raised it to his lips and blew mightily. The thunderous call lingered in the air after he stopped, and he smiled at the sky. Clouds of silver and gold began to formulate over the entirety of the sky above the buildings and land that we could see. Then a warm, soothing raindrop fell from the sky and tapped my arm. A smile crept unbidden to my face, and the urge to stand in the rain was more than a little difficult to fend off.

It was a gentle drizzle, really, but soon, all the people that we had left laying on the ground began to visibly relax.

"You aren't the first to use this power unselfishly for their very first summoning, and I hope you will not be the last. I am Samu, Torchbearer of the Seventeenth Celestial Squadron under

Lady Radiance Herself. You may call on me for anything that you need within the parameters of the spell, but know this—I was able to perform this miracle because the general is gone and the people here aren't dead, just locked away in their own minds and bodies. They will awaken in their own time. Doing this much was within my abilities, but it has cost me." He looked toward the heavens with concern. "Lady Radiance has needs of all her people to assist her and the other gods in keeping War thwarted, and unfortunately, I cannot do more for you at this time. Please, use this ability only when you have great need. Good luck and may Radiance guide you all."

There was the sound of tearing fabric once more, and the angel was gone. The citizens were none the wiser that I was aware of, and I wanted to try and keep it that way.

"Good thinking, man," Yohsuke whispered beside me. "Let's go see if we can't find some people who aren't still napping and get to wherever this asshat's been holed up."

We called out, looking for anyone for about ten minutes. Finally, a small child, a little girl who looked to be around five years old, looked out a window. Her tiny, blonde curls bounced as she watched us uncertainly. She kind of brought my son to mind, but I didn't want to think about him amongst all this carnage and anger.

Bokaj, as pissed off as he was about his friend being missing, was still the most charismatic person in the group, so he asked her which way Rowan had come from.

"The bad man?" she asked softly. "He's from the tower—that way. We don't go by the tower. Too many spooky people." A small tremble showed on her body, and with a sniffle she continued, "My friend was there too. He hasn't come to play with me since."

"Thanks, little one." Bokaj tried to smile at her, but she seemed to be able to tell it was forced and shrank back a little.

I threw her a coin to try and help her family a bit more. She simply looked at the platinum in awe and disappeared from the window.

We moved in the direction she had nodded and kept an eye out for more of the puppet city folk. The few we came across laid on the ground, no longer just drooling heaps lying there unblinking and unmoving. They were alive, obviously, but they were still semi-catatonic.

We tried to make the ones who had fallen awkwardly more comfortable, but other than that, we just left them and moved on. The more we passed, the more uncomfortable I felt. We were here to stop this galactic asswipe from taking this planet, then ours, but at what cost? These people were so low a level that they couldn't defend themselves. They needed us, and more people out there may be experiencing the same thing.

"Let's get to the tower. I'm happy we could help these folks, but we need to move." I sighed, my anger coming to the fore again.

The Fae-Orc nodded and held a fist out for me to bump. We continued on for another ten or fifteen minutes, finding hundreds more people laying in the large, expansive streets between shops, houses, and a tall tower carved into the side of the city's namesake—Maven Rock. The stone was as dark and ominous, but there were blue symbols etched into the side of it all the way up that stood out in stark relief against the black backdrop.

"Warded?" Yohsuke wondered as he stepped closer. He touched a rune, and it glowed briefly, but nothing happened.

"Maybe try the door of the tower?" I said in a hushed tone. Luckily, my mana had fully recovered by now.

Yohsuke nodded and tried the door—it was locked. Of course it was. It never could be that easy, could it?

Jaken stepped up next to the door and kneed the lock a couple times as quietly as he could. Then he got mad and booted it unceremoniously. The door flew open and banged against the stones inside, causing the group to check out our surroundings. Nothing stuck out, but being in the open here was not my idea of a fun time.

"Go, go go go," Yohsuke whispered harshly, and Jaken moved through the doorway.

Once we were all inside, the last person through shut the door, and we began to file up the stairs slowly, leaving the Fae to their own devices at the bottom. There was no telling if a minion of War was at the top of this tower, and them being this close would likely be a beacon to it. Better that they think they had time, right?

Balmur's presence was even more sorely missed; as a Rogue, he was our primary trap finder. Sure, Bokaj could, and he was, but he was no Rogue.

The traps we did find were runes that were inert and devoid of any power. They were drained and seemed to have been for a while.

"Think the cocky, smug bastard didn't care whether someone came at him or not?" Bokaj grumbled to the rest of us.

"Probably not—he was a fucking general, man," Yohsuke confirmed. "Better still check for traps, though."

In the next half an hour of slowly moving up the staircase with no rooms to speak of, we found nothing but an indignant spider in a windowsill and a single mirror halfway up. It was more for function than fashion—plain silver lining with sigils etched into the side and a reflective glass surface. We touched it, and nothing happened other than burning the ever-loving shit out of my poor fingers. Werewolf—gotta love the whole silver allergen thing. So other than being a shitty, annoying source of slow cardio, nothing of great import happened on that damn flight of stairs.

Once we arrived at the top, the door to the place was wide open. Bokaj finished checking the doorway for traps, and Yohsuke looked for any kinds of magic, but nothing stuck out.

Inside the room was a lavish interior that would've made me drool if I hadn't known that Rowan's stupid ass had been here recently. The stone floor sported multiple rugs and carpets of varying sizes and colors all over. A set of pillows and mats were piled off in a corner. There were doors carved into the stone with no visible marking as to what they could contain or what was behind them. There didn't seem to be anything of real monetary value in this area. It seemed to be a living room or a reception area, maybe a bedroom even.

We opted to try the doors from closest to farthest. So the closest door to us was on the left-hand side, closest to the pile of pillows and mats. The doors were all dark brown wood against the dark stone, so they stuck out, although what they were attached to, I had no idea.

Going with the theme, they were checked for traps. Nothing on this door, but the others did have something, so they were important enough to guard. Bokaj wasn't sure what the traps were, but he told us they were there, so I took his word even if the doors all looked the same to me.

Jaken shrugged his shield on to his left arm, brought his sword into his right hand, and had me open the door. With a cry, he brought the shield up and stepped into the room. When he put the shield down, he realized it was a chamber for ... undesirable acts needing a chamber pot. Nice.

"Smooth, poo Paladin," James teased a bit and clapped the Fae Orc on the shoulder.

"You can go through that shit first next time then, man," Jaken grumbled. Though he sounded angry, it was more a teasing gesture than anything. Jaken was a good dude like that—usually calm and friendly, almost always smiling or goofing off, and fiercely loyal. Gotta love friends like that.

The next door, we gave Jaken the nod, and James made some kind of remark along the lines of not needing a secondary toilet. We all chuckled.

"Focus, damn it," Bokaj grunted.

The rest of us settled.

It was out of character for him to be this way, but his best friend was quite possibly in hell, so it was understandable.

Jaken readied himself at the door while James grabbed the doorknob and looked to us. Yoh was off the side toward the right of the door with a hand on his Astral Adapters—they allowed him to condense his mana into sword blades. Bokaj stood out behind us in line-of-sight to the door with an arrow drawn and ready, while I brought up Jaken's rear. I was the only one almost as strong as our Paladin, so I was there to help him push if needed.

The door opened, and we tensed, then were surprised to find ourselves flying backward through a window opposite the door. I hit the window first, which hurt, and was able to try and push Jaken back and slow his momentum a bit. He was closer to the wall than me, but luckily for me, Kayda had been flying outside to try and be nearby. Unfortunately, there was no *way* she was going to be able to grab us both. *Or was there another way?* I thought to myself.

I flailed for a second before sending a call to Kayda and focused on a point below Jaken's falling form and cast my spell.

Vines burst from the wall and clutched at the falling, armored figure but couldn't seem to find purchase because he was too heavy and falling too fast.

As I began to despair at the damage Jaken would likely take—life-threatening damage—I heard him cry out in pain. The tip of an arrow burst from his chest and seemed to expand and sprout vines of its own. That brief pause in momentum was enough to allow my spell to take hold, and I turned my thoughts to myself.

I heard and felt Kayda closing on my position and shifted into my fox form. She caught me as gently as she could, but it still shaved off about a dozen HP. We were safe for now. My familiar brought me up to the window we had been shoved out of and tossed me to the window. My paws caught the opening and dug into the stone. I scrambled up then in a little breathlessly. I felt a hand snatch me by the tuft of the neck and tug, and I was inside. I shapeshifted back to my fox-man form and saw Yohsuke standing there looking angry, but he sighed in relief.

"We saw what you did, man." He smiled a bit. "Good shit. Let's pull him up real quick. There was a log trap in there."

I just nodded, and we pulled a rope out. It had been Bokaj's arrow that helped catch him, but the vine attached to the arrow wasn't strong enough to do much more. We lowered it and waited. Then Yohsuke smacked the wall.

"He's fucking trapped down there, goddamnit." He chuckled and grabbed his own rope out. I leaned out and recast my spell on the same spot before the first one could fail and drop him.

We lowered Yohsuke out the window with his feet in a set of stirrups we had tied into the rope. Once he got to the strung-up Paladin, I willed Snare to release, and he was free at last.

Once they were both safely indoors, we patted Jaken on the back in support, and I healed him up fully because we could have need of his mana if shit really hit the fan. I took a second to cast Regrowth on myself as well, ensuring I'd be up to full health in a minute. The arrow may have been meant to trap, but it was still a strong hit.

"Yeah, sorry about that." Bokaj grinned wolfishly. Jaken would never live this down, and the look on his face was priceless when he realized he had been shot.

"Come on then, let's go see what the hell this trap was." Jaken sighed tiredly when he saw the log. "My ass—shit hit like a freight train on steroids."

"Sure thing, target practice." James all but burst laughing at his own joke. The rest of us chuckled, and even Bokaj smiled.

When we turned toward the door, a log was in the doorway. It was just large enough to take up the majority of the doorway with chains that held it aloft. Upon touching the log, I just *knew* it had been enchanted to hit harder and faster than what would normally occur, and in the same vein, I knew that because of my Blood Rite from Maebe, Unseelie Queen and overall badass. Thanks to her gift, I felt more in tune with my magic and abilities. Like they were all more a part of me than what the world's video game-like mechanics and laws should allow.

Yes, the idea behind any game was that, once you gained a skill, ability, or spell, you could use it automatically as long as the prerequisites were met. Most of those were mana costs. I had yet to see one that had any other kind of prerequisite, but that didn't mean they weren't out there. With the spells and abilities I had been learning since coming to this world, the knowledge was fed into my mind and muscles directly. I just *knew* what to do. It was instinctive.

But like most games and life in general, you could theoretically know how to do something and still suck at it. It took time to master skills and abilities of a physical nature and thoughtful use of spells. Sure, I could sling spells fast and loose like some uber-talented Mage, but that wasn't my purpose. Nor was it me. A more planned approach with magic could be as disastrous to the enemy as a flurry of spells, if not more so. I had learned that from years of gaming at home and my new mission here.

Okay. You caught me. I lied. I like to play it fast and loose and get up close and personal with a lot of my enemies—specifically with my axe. The planning I do is more reactionary than I would like you to think. There—happy?

But lately, it felt ... *different.* More natural. I hadn't taken the time to look into it on my status screen, but I felt like it may have had something to do with my racial evolution. I could've been wrong, though—sure as hell wouldn't be the first time, and it definitely wouldn't be the last.

The chains came unhinged after Jaken took out a couple of pins, and the log crashed on to the ground. We dragged it out of the room while Bokaj checked for more traps. Nothing more stuck out to him right away. Cautiously, I led the way into the room.

The room was long with benches and shelves throughout, piles of gold and other odds and ends in one corner. Books, huge, leather-bound tomes, and other items sitting on the shelves. Looking up and seeing no more logs, I took another step into the room. I felt a prick on my shoulder, looked, and saw a small dart sticking out of my armor. It had only stung a little, and

I lost a couple points of health. A quick glance revealed more darts flying out of a row of holes in the corner of the ceiling.

I cast another spell I had never really thought to use, stupidly, and felt my skin grow cold for a moment, then warm. My fur and flesh had turned to diamond as Diamond Skin took effect—all incoming damage was halved. Better to get this over with as the duration was only three minutes. I cast Regrowth on myself, a spell that recovered 3 HP per second for thirty seconds. It would keep me from losing health for this stupid stunt. I began to sprint into the room, trying to dodge the darts and the thin, wooden pikes that began to thud into the ground as I moved.

"WHO THE FUCK CHECKED FOR TRAPS AGAIN?" I roared in anger.

I felt a large hand grab me by the scruff of the neck and pull me back. I yelped in outrage and surprise as Jaken's shield appeared over my head.

"You're supposed to let the tank do this, man." His normally surfer-like tone was all business as he noted the obstacles ahead. "You watch the front. There's no getting you back there now. If a pike comes up, try to break it before it stabs me."

I heard a muttered apology behind us, but we kept moving forward, slower now. Jaken protected me as best as he could, and I tried to break as many of the pikes as I could. Healing shield or not, I was still getting hit, jabbed, and poked at, and the darts were coming from different angles now.

"Try to find the switch to turn it off!" I hollered back to the group. "This shit hurts!"

Run into the romper-room, Zeke, I mentally growled at myself. *Play with the sharp objects. When will I learn?*

We finally hit the back end of the room after about thirty seconds of shuffling and destruction. I re-upped Regrowth on myself and then Jaken before looking back at my other friends. I felt three large thuds in my back and saw a debuff message pop up.

NOTIFICATION!

You have been poisoned. You will take 10 damage per second for 1 minute (damage multiplied by three for number of darts). Good luck!

"Poisoned?!" I cried in anger and disbelief. "Fuck me. Jaken, a little help here?"

"No, but I do have these." He reached out and made a gesture with his hand, and I saw a radiant, gold light gather around me once, then an ethereal white set of plate armor that almost mirrored the Paladin's own settled over my own armor. I looked over the buffs that he had given me and whistled.

Grace – Regenerates affected creature's health by 10 HP per second. Duration: 30 seconds.

Radiant Armor – Decreases damage taken by 10% and regenerates 7 HP per second. Duration: 20 seconds for Regen. 2 Minutes for damage decrease.

"Those mana efficient? No? Okay then, heal me when my health gets low. Without these buffs and regen spells, I'd flatline in ten seconds maybe? It's ten percent of my HP, so let's stick to heavier healing, and go from there."

"You got it, man." Jaken nodded and took out a couple health and mana potions. He slugged back the mana potion and passed the health ones to me. We would need to restock soon. Really soon. "If you have a heal, put it on Zeke. He's going to die without it."

Bokaj stepped up and threw a hand in my direction; green light enveloped my body, and my health jumped up ten percent. With my friends and me throwing constant heals on to my body, we were able to keep my health above zero. Made me appreciate the fact that we had healing capabilities other than our Paladin's a little more.

James poked his head around the corner and gave a thumb up. "Found it!" The deadly mechanical trap halted, everything going back to where it came except for the broken bits on the floor.

"Thanks, assholes." I grinned and affectionately threw them a rude gesture, which they returned in kind.

"Shut up, puto." Yohsuke grunted. "Got all this loot to look at. And you know how we feel about the loot."

"WE GET ALL THE LOOT!" James and I shouted together then laughed.

"Let's get this shit and get gone. Who wants to look at the money?" Jaken raised his hand, and Bokaj nodded him off toward the pile of coins. "Items? I'll take the shelf to the right front. You guys go take a shelf and see what's what."

This new side of our Ranger was a bit of a pain in the ass, but I understood. It was just so out of sorts for his usual personality, man. Oh well. Marines follow orders, and I could do that.

I walked over to the shelf near the rear of the room with the books and tomes. Every book I looked at told me the name and author on the spines. For the large part, they dealt with magical theories. The ones that caught my eye were compendiums on certain types of magical creatures. I nabbed the lightest two on creatures to look closer at later.

The items alongside them were some clockwork trinkets—think prototype watches and clocks but more in line with the steampunk trend. Although interesting and cool, they weren't complete or anywhere near useful enough; I left those alone.

One of the books was a spell book of some kind, like a personal one with a bunch of spells. The second I opened the book, my mind began to reel. Claws raked at my brain, and I couldn't think. Something was trying to grasp at my mind. If it hadn't been for Kayda shouting inside my head, I would've probably gone crazy. I threw the book away from me and began a spell to blast it, but as soon as it touched the floor, it began to burn with black flames, releasing an acrid rotten egg smell into the air.

James's hand hesitated and pulled away from a pointed hat. "We really need to stop touching things without checking them first."

Cautiously, we moved through and got what items we could that weren't worthless or cursed thanks to a quick glance over. Yohsuke seemed to be able to pick which ones were cursed because they seemed to radiate a sort of cold temperature, but it was hard for him to really relate, so we went with his gut on it.

According to Jaken's count, there were one hundred thousand gold pieces worth of gold, silver, and platinum pieces. We pocketed three thousand apiece and agreed to leave the rest to the city to use for repairs or to help the families of those who lost their life.

The items we collected, though, were very much magic oriented.

Pointed Wizard's Cap
+3 to spell casting, damage and focus.
+1 Defense
A cap created for a capricious and miserly wizard. He did not appreciate it.

That was a little odd that I hadn't seen those kinds of stats before.

"Yoh, you get what these mean?"

"Yeah, man, spell casting is a general term. It just means that the likelihood you screw up a spell during casting and go through potential backlash is slightly diminished." He pointed to the next bit. "Damage? Duh. And focus? Focus helps with things like spell sniper; it gives you a little more umph for your buck. These are small, but to someone like me, it would help."

Gloves of Casting
+2 to spell damage
+2 Defense
These gloves were made for a capricious and miserly wizard. He wore them once and didn't care for them.

Ring of Mana Storage
Capacity – 15 / 300 MP
The wearer of this ring can draw upon it until it is empty, before their own reserves run dry, or to augment their own mana pool.

Wand of Silence
4 uses of the spell Silence
Silence – The caster chooses one target and causes them to be unable to speak or cast spells with any spoken components for up to 30 seconds.

Those last two items were wild! Having that much extra mana would be a godsend, so we gave that to Jaken. Our strongest healer would need all the mana to be able to keep us all in fighting shape, even with me being able to help.

The wand would be the bane of any caster, though I had yet to know of any spells with verbal components that I had needed to use to cast. Maybe silence was purely a condition that just forced a caster to be unable to cast? That went to Bokaj since he would be the one most likely to have the time and distance to use it.

The hat and gloves went straight to Yohsuke, though he wasn't sure why I wouldn't take the gloves at least. I waggled my clawed fingers at him, and he grinned before slipping his own hands into the items.

I mean, yeah. He fights up close, and he's fast as all get out, but with Spell Sniper, the added damage and havoc he could wreak on the battlefield was simply too much to ignore. He fought from a distance at times, and it would all add damage to the DPS bucket.

"So what now?" I asked. "What do we do? Who do we go to get information?"

"We could try going back to Sunrise and seeing if they have a lead for us," Jaken suggested with a grimace.

"So, sit around with our thumbs up our asses while Balmur is having gods-knows-what done to him?" Bokaj shouted. "I don't fucking think so!"

Yohsuke, James, and Jaken looked uncomfortable, and I could see the anger in Bokaj's features begin to flare anew, so I stepped in front of him.

"Come on, man, let's go have a chat."

"We need to be out there getting Balmur back!" Bokaj shouted again, flinging his hand out towards the window.

I nodded as I took him by the arm and led him out of the room. Normally, he's pretty laid back. The first one to crack a joke. The first one to laugh. This whole thing was really getting to him, and I couldn't blame him; if it was Yoh who was missing, I don't think I'd be reacting any different.

"Look, man, I get it," I spoke softly, but firmly. "You're freaking out right now. Your best friend is gone, seemingly in a pinch, I get it. I know. But he's our friend too. And we are going to get him back. It is *going* to happen, but we need to be better prepared so that nothing like this happens again. We need to get stronger first."

"I know that, man." He sighed. "He's been my best friend since school. He and I know each other like brothers. He's somewhere right now... I need to get him back."

"And we will. Together." I bumped his shoulder with my fist and pulled him against my shoulder. "We're family, man. All we got. You, me, and the others. We are gonna get him back. But we can't do that if we are fighting and accusing each other of doing useless shit. Okay? This is what they want. They want us to fight with each other. Don't give them what they want."

He nodded, and I could finally see just how tired and defeated he was. His eyes were slightly bloodshot, and the worry lines were creeping next to his eyes and on his forehead. I could imagine the worry running through him. We all felt it.

I patted him on the back and left him standing there a moment to go grab the others and let them know that it was cool to come out now.

They filed out, Jaken first, then James and Yohsuke. They gathered around Bokaj and just let him have it. Jaken pulled him into a fierce hug that lifted the Ranger from his feet. James put a hand on his shoulder and just nodded quietly. Yohsuke stepped forward and gently punched him in the chest.

"He's top priority, man." He nodded. "Getting stronger and better loot is all that we gotta do to make that happen. So let's make it happen. Cool?"

"Sorry, guys." He looked down and scratched his head. Tmont rubbed herself against his legs and purred loudly.

I stepped over to him and smacked his arm softly. "Don't be sorry. Be stronger."

The third door was odd, a blank wall behind the door. We closed the door, opened it, and it was just wall. Weird, but the tower belonged to a Mage. I'm sure it had some kind of meaning, but at the moment, we were tired, pissed off, and just didn't give a fuck. We left the top of the tower the way it had been when we arrived, our looting aside, and walked toward the stairs.

Thinking about it and how we would likely be leaving, I called Kayda to the window and reached out to tap her wing as she coasted by. Her physical form dissipated into ebon-colored smoke and filtered into the collar around my neck. Much better.

James clapped his hands together eagerly. "Let's go talk to the emissaries and let them know that we will be going back to the village in hopes that we can get any information."

* * *

At the bottom of the stairwell, the Elves looked out the door through a small slit. No one seemed to have dared bother the tower since their miraculous recovery. Those who now sat up or stood and milled about were likely concerned more with their families and returning their lives to normalcy than looking for the cause of their freedom.

"I take it you had a better time finding your spoils above?" one of them said inquisitively as she eyed Yohsuke's new hat and gloves.

"Something to that effect." Yohsuke smiled and looked to me suggestively.

"What will you be doing now?" I asked, taking the hint.

"One of us will stay here," the speaker said. She pointed to the male Elf on her right, who bowed and stepped away. "The other two will make their way toward the larger Elven citadels toward the North where the High Elves rule. There we will begin our... representation of our Queen and her ideals."

"My name is Eroan Shalar, emissary to the Darkest Mother." The male she had motioned to bowed. "I am at your service, Lord Zekiel."

Lord? I thought to myself in surprise. "Uh, sure. So you're going to stay and lend a hand here then?"

"I will stay and lead these people, as they seem to be lacking in a leader now. This will be the first step toward our Darkest Queen's goals."

"Ho ho *hold the fuck UP.*" Jaken stepped forward and put a hand to the Elf's chest. "You're going to what?"

"I am simply going to offer my, and by extension, my Lady's, service and protection until such a time as they can lead themselves if they should choose to do so. I will not impede their ability to grow and prosper. The opposite, truly. But with an emphasis on gratitude to the Fae who helped lead them into standing back up on their feet so soon after tragedy befell their city." He motioned to his compatriots. "This is what we were sent here to do, Paladin. Do you intend to stop us and go back on your word to the Queen?"

"Do you mean them any harm?" he asked without giving any indication as to his answer.

"No. My Queen wants a strong people to act as her catalyst in this realm." His cultured voice quivered a bit, but he continued, "She desires footholds in this plane of existence. A wasteland of broken people and weaklings is not ideal."

Jaken took a moment to eye the Elf some more, then took his hand away and patted his shoulder. "Maebe seemed cool. So I guess it's okay. Just take care of them. There are some funds to get things going upstairs in one of the rooms."

The look on Eroan's face was panicked that someone other than me would use the Queen's name. I wasn't about to correct him. He was my friend and, by extension, hers. At least in my eyes. Of course, they hadn't seen the things that I had been privy to, except maybe Yohsuke, and only because she had introduced him to his demonic patron.

That had been another exceptionally bad time in my life, but it was over now.

I shivered slightly, remembering the horrors I had seen. I had watched her rip out one of her more disrespectful former captive's heart and stuff it into his mouth. Then she froze him solid, bleeding heart in his mouth—alive for however long it would take the ice to thaw. The last I had seen, he had been staring down, wild-eyed and terrified. All of this within the blink of an eye and with no remorse.

I'd also seen a softer side to her, the side that made me want to be her friend, her concern for her power base because it protected her people. Her love of art, even if it was kinda creepy and had resulted in countless frozen enemies and other such creatures. Her naivety at what it meant to have friends and her curiosity. Her dazzling intellect and observational skills. Of course, that had been before the whole heart thing—but hey, I'm not perfect myself. I shook myself from my reverie, focusing back on the matter at hand.

"I think that's as good as it'll get." I grunted. "How will you both get there?"

"We will walk." She smiled. "Telbareth and I are capable warriors, and we have a basic understanding of things here from books. We are also adept at disguise and woodcraft."

"Okay, what is your name?"

"Xelody, my Lord." She smiled sweetly and bowed her head respectfully. "I am to lead this expedition."

"Then we will leave you to it, Xelody, Telbareth, and Eroan. Should you need anything, send word to me through Maebe or send a letter to Sunrise Village. We will get it."

They nodded, bowed their heads, and stepped outside before the rest of us. We watched as they began to move through the people who remained in the street. As odd as they were to look at, these Fae beings in dark cloaks speaking to humans and the occasional Dwarf were surprisingly well received. People smiled back at them, grateful for whatever tender mercies they could give.

"Let's beat it before these guys start to come for us," Yohsuke suggested as more and more of the city's residents began rising stiffly from the ground.

I nodded, eager to move on myself. I never had been all that great with gratitude from strangers. Shit made me feel weird.

"I've got us. Come here." I closed my eyes and focused. As I touched the spell in my mind, I knew they would need to be touching me for it to transport us all. "Touch my shoulders, grab hands, hold wrists, whatever, but everybody has to touch."

I felt hands on each shoulder—one meaty and gauntleted, the other clawed and seemingly more delicate. I glanced and saw that everyone was good, so closed my eyes once more.

When I activated the spell, my map enlarged inside my mind, and I saw the places I could go. The radius I could go to was currently five hundred miles from my current position, so that left anywhere I had been to previously. I saw the place where I'd first met Kayda in the Lightning Mountains. Then I saw our destination—Sunrise Village.

I selected that location. The world left my feet, and a jarring force met my legs like I had just jumped off the ground for a moment and landed weird. I opened my eyes to survey our surroundings and was surprised to see that we were standing in the center of the village square.

One of the older bear Beast-kin blinked his eyes and started to sputter before crying out and hauling ass into the nearest building. A second later, Sir Willem Dillon followed him outside in his barkeep garb, a pair of sturdy, brown breeches tucked into black boots and a white shirt under a brown, stained apron.

The six-foot-tall human held a sword in his left hand and a shield in his right. His gray eyes were sparkling, even as they darted to and fro while he looked for the threat to his village. I had no doubt that he could whoop some serious ass if he wanted to because, even at his older age, he was still well muscled. Willem wore his gray hair pulled back into a ponytail with a small, reddish-gray beard. He'd be a handsome fucker too if it hadn't been for that badass scar along the right side of his face that started at his hairline and fell to his chin.

Don't let my jealousy color your decision on this, though, he's a handsome dude. Super nice guy. And as I was looking, his mustache game was *on point*. He had let it grow significantly since last we'd seen him. What did he use for that, I wonder.

Focus, you guys! Come on, I've got a story to tell.

"Well, I'll be." He smiled as he rushed at us. We shied away from the sword a bit, and the shield smacked against my right leg painfully, but he swung a hug on us anyway.

"It's the lads, Seamus!" He chuckled. "Radiance handpicked these boys. Wait, where's the wee one? And who is this strapping scaled person?"

"We have a lot to go over, man." Bokaj sighed.

"Well, come in!" He turned toward his tavern. "Come in and get some food and a drink. Tell me all about it."

So we did. We did exactly that. Sir Willem heaped our plates with food from his kitchens, the chef shaking Yohsuke's hand in greeting—happy that his favorite apprentice cook was back.

I couldn't speak for the others—as my mouth was full of this delicious food—so I listened as they recounted some of the events that had taken place since we'd last seen Willem.

It took a bit, and we stopped occasionally to answer a question here and there, but when we finished, our host stood and began to pace.

"...So all you know is that he was gone in a plume of sulfurous smoke and the general's snide remark?" he asked after a moment.

We nodded glumly. He paced some more, his right hand twirling the edge of his mustache in thought.

"Was a good thing you did for those people, by the way." He nodded my way. "Not a lot of folks do that. Maybe you ought to try the same thing once more? But this time, seek information? I never did, but this is a rather urgent matter in any case."

I looked at Jaken, and he shrugged. "Worth a shot I guess. I'll summon an angel and see what we can do."

"Better take it into the back of the tavern. Prying eyes are one thing, but an honest-to-goodness angel here may start quite a commotion."

We agreed and stepped into the back of his building. The ten-foot-tall fenced in area was well enough hidden for something so odd.

We signaled we were ready, and Jaken triggered the spell. There was a small, whumpf-like detonation, and a being of pure light stood before us. She—I assumed it was a she because of the flowing locks and obvious, womanly curves—stood waiting expectantly with her eyes on Jaken.

Sir Willem fell to a knee and bowed, but she didn't pay attention. She just watched Jaken.

"Hello," Jaken began. She cocked her head to the left a bit and seemed to decide that it was fine because her head went back to normal.

"Ask her if she knows a way to get to the Hells without dying," Bokaj suggested. Jaken echoed his question, and she seemed to consider for a long time before nodding her head.

"Can you tell us how to get there?" he asked hopefully.

She shook her head, then looked to the rest of us, then the ground. She nodded and knelt to the ground and began to draw something with her finger, the ground seeming to just disappear where she touched her fingers. After a moment, she stopped and considered her work before she must have decided it was good. She stood and clapped once before disappearing with a sucking sound.

"Fuck, man, that was weird," I mumbled.

"I've never seen a pure Celestial entity like that before," Willem spoke low in wonder.

"Is that what she was?" James asked. "She didn't seem all that helpful, what with the whole not-talking thing."

"Pure Celestial beings like that can't speak, or they would destroy any non-Celestials nearby who could hear them. Their voices are for the heavens alone, lad," pointing at the ground he continued, "but she did leave a clue."

"That there is the Celestial tongue," he said proudly. "Beautiful work, that."

"Can you read it?" Jaken and I asked together, only to groan when he shook his head no.

"Zeke, you stupid bitch." Yohsuke half laughed and half sighed. "Didn't Maebe give you a book on this shit?"

My palm moved of its own accord and struck my forehead. She had. It was a primer on the Celestial language. I hadn't had the chance to flip through it yet. I reached into my inventory and willed it into my hand. The small tome appeared in my palm. I knelt next to the symbol the Celestial being had carved.

It looked like a leaf with a branch behind it and two stars below it. It was so perfectly done that it could have been a natural part of the ground in the yard, having been there forever.

I looked through the words, definitions, and meanings, only to turn up nada. Irritated, I shut the book and stepped back into the tavern, asked to borrow some paper and charcoal to try and copy it. I placed the paper over the marking and began rubbing the charcoal over the piece until the relief of it was nearly identical.

From there, I took the paper and began to walk through the village. I asked as many people as would stop if they had ever seen a symbol like it, anything that might lead us to a clue of some kind. Finally, I worked my way over to the carpenter's building, her sign swaying gently in a slight breeze. I went to walk in, grasping the door by the handle and pulling to find it locked.

Not uncommon for that to happen. People took days off, and since coming here, I hadn't bothered to learn what the days of the week were—if there was even a "week" to be had.

I decided that it was time to go and meet Rowland—the black-bearded Dwarven blacksmith—for a chat and see if he knew what was going on with this rune or if he would know anyone who might.

I walked a few more minutes and spoke to more passers-by; one wolf Beast-kin swore up and down that it looked like a crest, but she couldn't be sure and had to hurry on because she needed to get to work. I thanked her with a gold coin for her time, and she gasped but took it with gratitude.

As I walked on, Rowland's squat-looking forge—a building made of wood in the front with a stone portion around the forge in the back—came into view. The back of the place was ringed with a tall fence, and clanging thuds of metal could be heard through the air as the Dwarf inside beat the hell from whatever it was he was making. I chuckled to myself as I thought about seeing him last time, piss-drunk and begging me to stay and make him another hammer.

I opened his door and stepped inside. Everything was much the same as I remembered. Weapons hung on racks along the walls and sat on shelves. The rhythmic clobbering of metal never stopped.

As I poked my head around the door frame into the forge itself, I was surprised to see a beefy-looking Dwarf, his blonde beard and hair plaited tightly with metal beads that reflected the glowing heat of the forge behind him. This wasn't Rowland—a black-haired and bearded Dwarf himself and definitely taller than my friend.

I waited patiently for him to finish his work, quenching the item he was working on in oil and setting it aside for a wiping down before I spoke. There had been no magic like I had seen Rowland using or skills that simply looked like magic to my untrained eyes. Just elbow grease.

"Excuse me," I spoke kind of loudly because I knew after hammering, his hearing may need a little time to return to normal.

"Wassat?" He grunted and turned to look at me. "Aye, looky here, fox—do nay sneak up on me again like 'at, or I'll be takin' yer tails."

"Forgive me, but the last time I was here, Rowland was the smith. Where is he?"

"Knowed me cousin, did ye?" he said in a low voice. He began stalking forward with his hammer in hand. "I suppose ye recognized him when he was layin' bleedin' at yer feet two nights past?"

"What?!" I growled in anger. "Where is he? Where is Sarah? What happened?"

He just kept stalking forward and fell into a low stance like he was about to spring at me, but I lunged forward and grabbed him by the leather apron he wore first.

"Tell me where my friends are!" I roared into his face, my vision blurring with red around the edges. I fought for control, barely winning.

To his credit, the Dwarf barely flinched and brought the hammer down to strike at me, but I just shook him a bit and displaced his aim so that it fell on my shoulder. I took roughly 40 HP worth of damage from it, but I didn't give a damn. If I started beating his ass in truth, I wouldn't get the answers I needed.

And I'd be Godsdamned if I was gonna lose another friend today.

"Zekiel?" A familiar voice from behind distracted me from exacting my vengeance on the little man.

I tossed him away from me and turned to see the dark-skinned Sarah. I rushed forward and began inspecting her at arm's length.

"What happened to your father?" I began asking.

"Da is hurting, bruised for sure, a few broken bones, and he's unconscious. The healer can't do much else for him." Shifting her gaze to the Dwarf, she continued, "Craglim, this is Zekiel. He's the one da' and I made the Blood Axe for. He's a friend."

The Dwarf brushed himself off indignantly and scowled at me, but I didn't give a shit. He could wait.

"Take me to him." I rounded on Sarah in full this time, taking her by the shoulder. Then a thought struck me. "Better yet, let's swing by the tavern and grab Jaken so he and I can look at him."

She winced, and I realized that I had accidentally grabbed her too hard. "Sorry about that."

I sent a mental call to my friends, and they agreed to meet us outside the tavern. We jogged to grab them, then took off to where the village healer's cottage was near the square but in the opposite direction of Sir Dillon's place. It was just that, a simple building made of roughly carved half logs stacked and nailed together with mortar between each slat. There was a porch with a person outside taking a drag from a pipe. As we approached, they stood and waved kindly.

"He's resting now, Sarah. You just left," the person said patiently. "He has not awakened since you brought him to me, and there is only time until he wakes up or not. The healing after that is up to his body."

"Is that all your skill will allow?" I asked. "Did you use any spells? How about healing potions? And what do you mean he hasn't woken up?"

"Well, Traveler, I do not have the affinity for magic that some others do. I am a mundane physician. I use medicine and knowledge of the body to heal. We did not wish to use potions as it has been a fight to set his broken bones and clean his wounds and because we did not know that they would help his injured mind."

"Jaken here is a Paladin of Radiance and has some powerful healing capabilities. Let him take a crack at healing his body," James suggested.

The healer considered it carefully, then nodded and beckoned for Jaken to follow. As they went inside, I turned to Sarah.

"Sarah, what the hell happened?"

"Someone found Da laying in an alley near the other inn on the outskirts of town beaten, bleeding, and unconscious." Her voice cracked slightly, but she caught it. "Barely alive, Zekiel. Da is the strongest person I've ever known, and they beat him nearly to death."

"Does anyone know what happened?" Yohsuke asked.

"A wee lass says that there were five of them, shouting and yelling at someone before the fight broke out. They saw a figure with black fur and a tail standing over his body just before running off after the rest of them. That last figure was the only one that was really seen."

"Motherfuckers!" I swore. "I'm gonna find out who the hell did this. You guys in?"

"A chance to work out some of my anger? I'll take two," Bokaj responded easily. The steely look in his eyes was telling.

James punched his open left palm and nodded along with Yohsuke who just smiled threateningly.

"Jaken will want in too. Rowland trained him in smithing." I nodded and began to think, to plot.

"There have been rumors in the last few days that people have been seeing things in the forest as well. Lights. Shapes. A hunter has disappeared, maybe others—I'm not certain."

I nodded. So this once peaceful village was now being targeted? But by who? War? A minion? I sure as fuck hoped it wasn't a general. We were in no shape to fight another one of those without Balmur.

We needed more information, and if there was something going on in the forest, I knew just who I could ask.

"Anyone know if Dinnia is around?" I asked.

"I don't know." Sarah shrugged. "I haven't heard anything about her here lately, and I don't really see her come into the village at all."

I nodded. Jaken came out of the cabin a moment later.

"I healed him." He sighed. "He's still out, but his body is set to rights. Maybe we can summon a Celestial again to heal him if he doesn't wake up again soon?"

"That sounds like a good idea, man," Bokaj clapped. "Why don't one of you guys go ahead and do that?"

"Hefty cooldown," Jaken said simply.

"Yeah, it's a twenty-four-hour cooldown. Neither of us can use it until tomorrow afternoon at the earliest. Not to mention, you all heard what Samu said, only in great need." I looked over at Sarah, the hope on her face easy to read. "We're going to do what we can for him, okay? Just let us try and get this sorted out."

I heard a derisive snort from behind me and turned to see Craglim walking up behind me.

"Ye'll likely get hurt out there, wee fox." He eyed me, then my friends. " I sees ye like to comport yerself with kin—Elves—bah. They do nay know to fight, I'm betting. Probably couldn't even hold an axe. Scrawny, the lot of you. I'll be gettin' at whoever brought me cousin low, do nay fret."

Yohsuke and James stepped up beside me, not to fight but ready.

Jaken held a hand out in front of the pair and glared at the Dwarf, who blatantly ignored him. Like it was beneath him to even notice the Paladin or his Fae-Orc avatar. Or his armor was hiding a lot of his body. I looked to be certain.

Yup. He wore his full mithral battle rattle, helm, and all, so he was covered head to foot in the badass light blue metal. Thank the Gods.

"I don't know what you're getting at, but we were the ones to free this forest of War's influence. We killed his minion. We killed his general. And if you don't chill the fuck out about my friends, I'm gonna do more than toss you."

"Bring it." He spat on the ground and splayed his hands wide in challenge.

"Craglim," Willem spoke as he walked up the road to our right, "They tell the truth. Rowland was one of the first to call them friend. They lost one of their own trying to fell a powerful foe and are well known to the Mugfist, Light Hand and Stone Hammer clans."

"Zeke and Jaken both follow the Way," James added.

"Good. All are equal along the Way." Craglim nodded but looked at us hard. "But that do nay mean I got to like either of ye. Or any of ye, for 'at matter. Me kin needs me—here I am. If yer gonna go and find the gutless worms, I'm comin'."

"No." Yohsuke snorted. "Fuck no. We can't trust you to watch our backs out there with Gods know who trying to kill us."

James nodded and flipped him the bird. Bokaj just watched coldly.

"Fine. You can come," I said, glancing coldly at my friends, "but if you slow us down, we leave you behind. If you get in the way, we tie your ass up and bring you back to the village and go on without you. You betray us or get my friends hurt in any way, and I will kill you myself."

All three of my tails flicked at the tip in annoyance, and I flattened my ears at the threat. I didn't give a shit if he believed it or not—it was what would happen. I'd had too many fucked up things happen to me and mine lately to let some bigoted Dwarf screw things up.

"I can agree to 'at." He grimaced as he looked us over. "I say the same of ye. Do nay get in me way. If I find proof ye had a hand in this, I'll brain ye meself. When yer ready to leave, I'll be at the forge. Do nay leave without me."

He turned and walked away after that, grumbling about the audacity of the Fae. He had no idea. I looked to my friends, and they stared back expectantly.

"He's going to fuck up whatever we try to do covertly anyway, intentionally or not. At least this way, we know where he is, and what he's up to."

"Respect," Bokaj said after a moment. He came over and bumped my knuckles with his.

"That's probably true, though I don't fucking like him," Yohsuke said.

"Me either," James added. "Fuck that guy."

"Same. But we need to keep him close just in case. I'm gonna go try and talk to the bears and see if they can tell me anything about what's going on in the forest. You guys can do what you need to—may want to restock on some potions and other consumables. I know I need some. There may be a stand in the square where they hawk stuff run by a teen and his little sister, may have an adult there too, but I don't know for sure. Be generous if you can. They were pretty cool last time. See you in a while."

I shifted into my fox form and took off into the forest. I bounded through the tree line and stopped by a large oak tree to check my map for the spot I wanted to go. It was largely grayed out, but the waterfall was easy enough to find. I placed a marker there and began to run. I followed my path, dodging in and out of trees and over brambles here and there with relative ease.

I took a moment to survey my surroundings before entering into the area around the lake and waterfall. I couldn't smell anything outside the normal scope of scents that I had caught on my way here—mice, voles, and other small prey animals. I caught the scent of a wolf and a faint scent of Sharo, Dinnia's panther companion. It was a little disconcerting that I hadn't scented a bear, but they could be leaving this area alone out of respect or maybe fear?

I shifted again into my Ursolon form, that of a twelve-foot-tall bear with brown fur and white stripes like a tiger. I easily weighed around twelve-hundred pounds, and it was all muscle, baby.

I stood in the center of the same area that my sparring match with Marin took place, then the battle with the pack of Insane Wolves attacked us. Then the fight between the corrupted bear and finally giving her her final request. My chest tightened at the thought of her dying, but it was how she wanted to go, how she deserved to go, and I had carried her sacrifice with me into battles that her protection had helped see me through.

I took a deep breath and let it go. This was no time to dwell. I reared up to my full height and roared as loudly and as long as I could. Then I shifted back into my fox-man form and waited.

After forty minutes, someone had come to investigate. I cast Nature's Voice, a spell that allowed me to speak with animals. A large bear with black fur and beady, black eyes cleared the foliage at a sprint. It saw me and came up short in surprise.

"Hello," I said simply.

"Hello, Friend of Bears." She snuffed the ground and followed it to me. "You heard that too?"

"That was me, sorry. I needed someone to take me to Queen Kyra. I have a favor to ask, and she may be able to help me. Can you take me there?"

She snuffed my chest before butting her head against it. "Yes. Follow me."

She turned, and I shifted into my fox form just to be safe. If someone saw my Ursolon form chasing after her, I could get fucked up. I mean, I was entering bear territory, and if a large animal was chasing my friends, I'd come in ready to beat ass, so fox it was for now.

We lumbered along for a good hour before coming to a halt outside a wooded hillside with a yawning cave mouth.

We stopped so I could shift into my fox-man form and recast Nature's Voice.

The inside of the cave was large enough that dozens of bears milled about with space to spare and greeted us as we stepped through the structure. A few snuffed at me before returning to their various activities. A popular one was feigning slumber.

"Hello, friend," greeted a light voice from up ahead.

Queen Kyra, her eight-foot bulk of light brown fur stood before me twenty feet away. Thayron, her mate and a dire bear with dark brown fur, raised his head and paw in greeting.

"It's good to see you, Kyra," I greeted her as we both closed the distance. I gave her a hug, and she patted me with both her paws. "I'm sad it can't be for a happier reason."

"Oh?" She tilted her head. "What is the nature of your visit then, friend?"

I filled her in on the rumor that I had heard. She scowled and called to the bear who brought me here. "Filbran, have you heard of these lights?"

"No, my Queen," she chuffed at the air, "but I will seek others to ask. Please, wait here, Friend of Bears."

I smiled at her. "Thank you."

She huffed and took off at a slow saunter, then cut right outside the cave mouth.

"You smell different." Thayron's breath blew across my ear. "Wrong. Like a different kind of predator."

I turned to see the great dire bear hovering close to me with his nose wrinkled as if it smelled something distasteful.

"A lot has happened since I last saw you," I admitted. "I'm... more than I once was. Let me see if I can explain."

I told them about how we had been exiled to the Fae Realm, then captured by the Werewolves there. They were led by Pastela, the crazy alpha who wanted her people to thrive and wanted to have perfect pure-bred babies with yours truly. She wanted to use those puppies and get to taking over the realm and all those who looked down on her and her people. Normally, I'm all for the underdog, but she had beaten the shit out of me when I wouldn't cooperate and then threatened my friends. Not to mention, she gave me the *gift* of lycanthropy. Even fantasy worlds had their communicable diseases.

Made me wonder if there was a shot for that? Fuck, I hate needles too. I'd be so screwed.

They listened quietly, though Thayron grumbled a little when I told him that the form he had gifted me was now less needed due to the Fae version of a bear. It acted kind of like an upgrade.

"What is this 'ursolon' creature like?" he asked curiously. "Is it big? Strong? Can you show us?"

"Yes, I am fascinated as well," Kyra agreed, "but we will need to discuss the Lycanthropy a bit more. Do you have it under control?"

I thought for a moment, then nodded. "I'm an alpha now since I killed Pastela. It makes it easier to control the change and rage that threaten me with it. Though, I don't know if there will be anything I need to worry about with the phases of the moon. She hadn't mentioned anything about it while I was there. It's a new moon now, and I haven't transformed to find out. Other than that, I feel in control."

"We will alert our sentries and scouts to an apex predator in the area and that they are not to engage with you unless you try to harm them." Kyra waved another bear who had been watching closely over and whispered to him. He glanced at me, and I smiled reassuringly before he scampered off. "I trust that if you feel you are a threat to anyone, you will take precautions?"

"Like, lock myself up?" I asked incredulously. Then I realized—she was thinking of the safety of her people and probably even the safety of the village as well.

She didn't know if I could keep the Werewolf and its cursed gift at bay, and looking at the concern and the musky scent emanating from her now, she was terrified.

"Yeah. I will. I'll have my friends make some chains and keep me under guard if I can't keep it under wraps."

"Thank you for understanding, friend Zekiel." Thayron bumped my chest with the back of his clawed paw gently. "That was a hard question to answer and harder still to ask. Come, show us this new form, and let us away from these unpleasant thoughts."

They stepped back respectfully before I shifted. I stood taller than the dire bear, and he growled in delight at seeing me.

The other bears that remained in the place came over and began to familiarize themselves with my scent. One even rubbed herself against me like a cat. She trundled off with other bears sniffing her along the way. I shifted back, much to the dismay of the bears around me.

"And are you stronger than a normal bear?" Kyra asked.

"I'm not sure," I replied teasingly. I was. A lot stronger, to be truthful. "I've got a good amount invested in my strength stats, so there's that. Having fought a few of them, it took a great deal of skill and effort to take one down. Imagine me behind those claws."

I waggled my eyebrows at him suggestively.

"Oh, I bet." Thayron chuckled. He brought out a large piece of meat and started to munch on it.

"Thayron, that's rude." Kyra huffed at him. "I know you eat when you get emotional, but he's still our guest."

"Yes, dear." He tossed the meat back behind him. "Forgive me, Zekiel."

I waved it away. Honestly, I'd prefer he not be hungry around me.

My guide came back into the cave huffing. "There have been reports of lights and strange movements in the south of our territory along the river, Majesty."

"Anything else?" the bear Queen asked. "No? Okay, I will dispatch a group to investigate. Then we will see what is going on."

"Actually, Kyra," I interjected, "why don't you leave that to my friends and I? We think that this may be a site for someone we want to investigate. A friend of mine was hurt, and a villager has been taken. We will take this; you keep your people safe. How does that sound?"

"Unacceptable," she said sternly. "Our neighbors are being attacked. If there is something I and my people can do—then we shall."

"Kyra!" I called out to her, and she looked back at me. "Look, I appreciate you wanting to help us out, but these people have us to help them."

Thayron grumbled from where he sat, scratching his rotund belly with three clawed digits. "And what, you come every time someone claims to see a snake?" He stood and padded closer until he looked me in the eyes. "We know of your purpose here, Druid. The Mother has told us. We are of a mind simply to help our neighbors and you by extension."

"If you would simply be as wise as I hope you to be, you would allow friends to aid you and these people in times to come, especially from friends such as us," Kyra rebuffed me softly, but the held disappointment was there. Like a kindly teacher or friend's mom who you adored, and you had caused their faith in you to be shaken.

Me, being the grown-ass man I was, powerful, strong, and independent, immediately broke down and muttered, "Yes, ma'am."

Kyra chuffed once and turned to walk toward the front of the cave. Thayron grabbed what was left of his meat and winked at me before trotting after her. A retinue of bears, five including the queen, stood outside when she was finished.

"What are you going to do?" I asked, trying to step in front of her path away. "You aren't going to go there yourself, are you? What about your people?"

"No, friend Zekiel." She giggled. "I am going to your village to speak with the leader there. I want to try to foster a better relationship between our peoples and offer what I can. You are perfectly capable of offering translational support, yes?"

I just stood there with my mouth opening and shutting as she trundled past me leisurely.

"Coming?" Thayron chuckled as he bumped my shoulder with his.

I sighed and transformed into my panther form and took the lead. I didn't know for sure if she knew how to get to Sunrise, but I did know that anyone seeing a group of bears coming toward the village was going to shit themselves. I beat feet, so I was well ahead of them, then left my scent along the path so they could follow me. Once I arrived in the village, I sent a call to my friends to meet me in the square. Then I sent a Message to Sir Dillon to bring whoever was in charge of the village to the square to meet with local royals. I took his chuckle in return to mean he would cooperate.

"Make way, folks!" I hollered as I shifted back into my normal form. "A bunch of important bears on the way through. Road's gotta be clear for them. Big meeting about to happen!"

The people seemed confused for a second but then began to line the sides of the street I had chosen to use. My friends arrived—all but Yohsuke who was busy perfecting his craft—and began to help call people out of the center of the roadway. Children cried out in wonder at the first sight of them— this pack of bears led by their queen, Kyra.

"Ma! That's a bear! A real, live bear!" a small human child whispered a little loudly. Her mother watched in both wonder and horror as Kyra looked directly at the child and began to sniff loudly.

"It's okay, ma'am," I advised her softly. I saw her clutch the child closer. "That's Kyra, she's Queen of Bears and has a cub much younger than your daughter. She would no sooner harm anyone in this village than I or my friends would without provocation. I swear it."

To help prove my point, I stepped over to her and knelt formally. Kyra chuckled, able to understand me since I had made it a point to top off my Nature's Voice spell when I got there, and nuzzled my forehead affectionately. "See?" I asked.

The child giggled uncontrollably and another, smaller child escaped his mom's shocked hand and toddled over to us. His eyes never left Kyra, even though his mother began to follow and whisper his name fiercely when she realized where he was heading. The human boy, probably two or so, mumbled at Kyra unintelligibly as children are wont to do, and she rewarded the child with a loving lick. He smiled and clapped after I snatched him up gently in my hands. His mother, a kindly looking woman, no longer seemed worried about his safety. She did her best at curtsying to Kyra. Kyra stood and bowed her head for a second in recognition and then motioned for me to relinquish the child to his mother. I did so.

She took the boy and began to whisper furiously at him. He began to make sorrowful noises, but they were out of earshot by the time he actually began crying in earnest.

I chuckled, thinking of all the times my son had started bawling when we took him from something he was enjoying. I returned to the present and began to move just in front of the procession, the other members of my party falling in around them as we went. The crowd gave a respectful berth as we moved through before closing in the gap behind us. After a few moments, we stood in the now-closed market square with what seemed like the whole town as witness.

"Tell me, travelers," said a humbly dressed man in his early thirties, "why are there bears in this humble village?"

He broke away from the crowd with Willem following closely behind with a sly smile. His features were handsome enough—chiseled jaw and brown eyes with long brown hair in a ponytail behind his head. His boots left almost no impression on the ground as he walked, though he was a well-muscled man.

"Forgive me, sir, I'm not familiar with you," I spoke respectfully. If this was who I thought it was, I wouldn't want to piss him off.

"You asked Sir Dillon to grab me," he smiled at my discomfort, "but no, you don't know me. My name is Sam Wildheart. I'm a hunter and trapper, but I'm also the mayor here in these parts. I try not to do too much in the way of 'governing', though. I find that people will treat each other well if you let them. And despite one unpleasant Gnomish man a while back—they've proven me right. Now, why is the Queen of Bears in this neck of the wood?"

"She has a... request for you," I said quietly. "If you would like, I'd encourage you to hear her out. Though privacy may work best, given the current happenings in the area around the village."

"I am aware, thank you." He clapped me on the shoulder and nodded to my friends. Then he looked to his citizens. "Sunrise! Blood of this village. I would ask that you trust me to work for your benefit as I always have. I will speak to the queen and see what is happening. Please, treat her and her retinue with the utmost respect. If you would, send for the butcher to bring fine meat and see about some honey. Berries too! Let us show our guests the hospitality of the people of Sunrise."

The crowd cheered and whistled as they sent runners this way and that. The bears tensed, but I waved them down a bit.

I motioned for them to follow me as I followed Sam to where he wanted us to go. It was just outside the village where we were alone near a small home with smoke coming out of the chimney. The windows inside were dimly lit, and I could see shadows moving around inside, but they made no move to come to the window.

"Here should be quiet enough for our purposes," he stated and turned back to the rest of us. "I understand you wanted to speak, Majesty? How can I help you?"

Through me, she expressed what she had in mind.

"She wishes to offer a mutually beneficial arrangement," I translated. He looked interested. "She says that her people will patrol the area around the village and protect your people if you will do her the favor of helping feed her people. She knows that you have people who hunt and fish. If you would help her people prepare for the winter, then she will see to it when you have need of her aid you shall have it."

"I think that can be arranged." The mayor smiled. "I would be more than happy to help with that myself. How about as a sign of good faith, we feed the bears we have here with us tonight, and I will see you back into the woods at first light?"

"I should like that greatly, friend Sam," Kyra said with a nod. So I continued speaking as she did, "We would be honored to receive your hospitality."

"Then let us go back to the square. Preparations should be well under way." Sam clapped his hands and motioned back for us to move along. "Derkaly, Shinda, and Sam Junior, come on out!"

The door to the small home opened, and two wild-looking Bear-kin children and a Bear-kin woman came outside. The older of the three came to Sam's side and curtsied to Kyra before telling her children to mind their manners. The children stopped and stared in open wonder at the bears before them. They were bear-like but had slightly more human in them. Their fur was shorter and their ursine features less defined.

"Hello, Your Majesty. I am Derkaly," greeted the elder Bear-kin. She pointed to her children, the eldest first. "This is Sam Junior, and this little ball of energy is his sister, Shinda."

Thayron was the first of the bear company to move toward the children, his hulking form easily dwarfing their own. "Do they speak our tongue Derkaly?"

She looked to him and nodded. "They are young yet, but they understand some. I have been teaching them where I can, but common is easiest for them. If you want to talk to them, I can translate for you."

"Please," he said gently. "I see you, little cubs, and I understand who and what you are. Your father seems a good man, and your mother a good woman. Tell me, do the others tease you? Make light of your heritage?"

The little boy listened as his mother spoke and he tried to respond in the language of the bear speaking to him. It was halting, but the meaning came across.

"Other children... not know," he said, trying to think of the words he would speak next. "Mother teach us bear ways, but they do not come easy. Other Bear-kin children call me... 'short-face'. Tease sister."

"I see," rumbled Thayron. He stood on his hind legs and towered over all of us. "Then they shall learn that that is not tolerated in bear society. That shall not do at all."

"No, it shall not," Kyra joined him. "Derkaly, you and the children are welcome among us and of course you, Sam. Let us go and make our hearts known to all. Shall we?"

"Come on, you two," Thayron grunted as he fell to all fours. "Hop on Uncle Thayron's back. I'll give you a ride."

The children made sounds of wonder, and Derkaly—with tears in her eyes—smiled at Sam. He nodded to the kids, who began to climb deftly up the Dire Bear's side and smiled at Thayron.

"Thank you," he said with a tired voice.

I passed the sentiment on to Thayron who was too busy trying to get the children to speak to him in bear to care about anything else.

We walked back to the sound of a fiddle being played lightly but lively in the center of town. Lanterns had been brought out, and a heavy table laden with meat, cheese, fruits, nuts, and all kinds of food stood in the middle. Kegs had been tapped, and a celebration looked ready to be underway.

Sam stood on a chair that was brought out for him to address the people.

"Let those of you gathered here today bare witness to a new union and a treaty between the Village of Sunrise and Queen Kyra, leader of the Bears to the East. For their protection from the dangers of the forest and the outside world, we will offer them food in preparation for their hibernations each year. It'll be good hunting, I'm sure! So, as we drink and feast tonight with our new-found friends, let us give thanks to them and to our older friends, those who rid the world of one of War's minions and Generals!"

As he finished speaking, all in attendance shouted in joy and began to clap.

"Let us not forget the one who was taken, though," Sir Dillon shouted from his place by the kegs of ale and mead. "Balmur fell for his friends and all our peoples. Let us share a moment of silent prayer to the Gods that they will see fit to bless him with strength until Zekiel, Yohsuke, Jaken, Bokaj, and James can rescue him from the depths of the Hells."

Every joyous face fell. Every clapping hand stilled. All around us stood in silence in memory of Balmur and his unknown sacrifice. Bokaj, to his credit, kept himself in check. He stood stock-still beside me. I put an encouraging hand on his shoulder and looked at him. He knew what was on my mind.

We would get him back somehow.

After a moment, Sam cleared his throat and raised a mug. "To Balmur."

Before everyone could lift their mugs, I stood solemnly and raised my own, raising my voice so that it would carry. "To those whose lives were lost in the fight with Rowan, and to the little boy whose life was taken in vain by an evil asshole. May they know peace."

We all lifted our various mugs, cups, and containers in the air and drank together. I saw some familiar faces in the crowd but didn't join them in their revelry after the toast. I needed to get away for a moment after that toast.

It was absolutely fucked what happened. Losing one of my friends like that, then coming back to this shit show? Rowland in a coma, someone taken and missing, and who knows what other fucked-up situations.

I watched the festivities from the shadows, just sulking a little. I watched as Thayron, still playing pony to the children, meandered over to a group of children, mostly Beast-kin with a few humans. I heard him grunting and growling angrily at them—saw their faces downcast in shame and fear—and felt that there was some hope for them still.

I continued my sullen vigil a while longer before I looked out into the night sky and saw an owl watching, which gave me an idea. I cast Nature's Voice again and called to it.

"Hey!" I whispered forcibly. I knew the owl could easily hear my from its spot a hundred feet away. "Can I talk to you for a second?"

It eyed me a moment longer before it fell from the branch it sat on and flapped my way. I held my hand out to it as a perch, but it landed on the roof to my right.

"Druid," came the light, breathy reply. "You called. What brings you to interrupt my hunt?"

"I was wondering if I could assume your form?" I asked. Now that I was closer to him, I could see him better.

His head, with feathers that looked like horned eyebrows over light yellow orbs, began to swivel back and forth as if searching for something. His small body of feathers looked almost solid in the darkness.

"What makes you think you are worthy of flight, Druid?" he asked with his head cocked to the side. It was a curious look on an owl.

"Because I don't want to hurt you to acquire it, and flying is the best way to hunt," I answered in a terse tone through my teeth. "My best friend, Kayda, is a Storm Roc, and she's taken me on a flight. It was lovely. I also used to fly where I came from. But mainly? It'll get you back to your hunting sooner."

"I suppose that is true." The owl sighed, then zoned in on something and looked back to me. "That's much too large. Never mind."

I looked and saw a large vole the size of a dachshund foraging in the tree line. I smiled and cast Ensnare on it. It squeaked in distress at not being able to move.

"Trade?" I motioned to it. "I caught you a meal. All you have to do is let me touch you for two minutes while you pick it clean. Hell, if you can't clean it yourself or don't want to, I'll tear the flesh off and feed you by hand. Does this seem agreeable?"

He seemed to think about it for a moment before shaking his feathers and flapping over to land near the vole. "If you will assist me, yes. This is more than I can eat myself, though."

"I'll find someone to help you out, don't worry." I summoned Kayda from the collar around my neck. The black gem pulsed once and dark smoke began to pour out of it until Kayda stood next to me in all her glory.

The owl fluttered his wings gracelessly, and the vole screamed, begging me to let it go. Kayda, hearing what was going on and seeing the animal snared acted first. She flared her wings and brought a talon down on to its head—killing it instantly.

"Mr. Owl, this is Kayda, my good friend." Kayda trilled and bobbed her head at him.

"I see you spoke truth, then." His voice quavered slightly. "Feed me and keep her from eating me—I will give you my form."

True to his word and mine because I had to feed him the vole, he gave me his form. A relatively good way to end the evening if I could say so myself. The festivities lasted a little longer, but I just headed back to my room after that. I was drained from the events of the day, and I needed to rest.

* * *

The mid-morning sun blazed high in the sky by the time I woke up. I stretched and washed my face and some of the more sensitive areas of my body with a basin of water that had been brought in at some point in the night. Feeling refreshed, I stepped out into the familiar hallway of Willem's tavern and toward the scent of food.

I walked out to find patrons in various stages of eating and daily life. I could smell eggs, bacon, toast, and other foods.

As soon as I walked into the room, Willem shepherded me to the mostly-empty bar and gave me a tall mug of cool water and shouted for a large plate of food.

"You missed quite the celebration last night, Zeke," he said with a concerned look.

"I know," I grumbled. "Just couldn't get my mind off the goings on around here and on our mission. I needed the time away to clear my head."

"Aye, and your heart." Willem clapped me affectionately on the shoulder. "I understand. Everything seemed to go over smoothly, though the mayor's wife did say that Kyra missed you when they were leaving this morning. She would have waited, but there was business to attend. Tell me, what will you do today?"

I thought for a moment. Yohsuke brought his and my own food out of the kitchen, and we bumped fists in greeting. He sat down next to me and dug into his own plate.

"I think today I'm going to go stock up on some mana and health potions of my own. I know the others were supposed to, but it never hurts to over prepare. Maybe grab some jewelry and other accessories to try and work on getting my enchanting leveled up some more. That free level will be helpful. Then see about scouting. If there's something to worry about in the forest, we need the intel." I shoveled another bite of the scrambled eggs Yohsuke had made for me into my mouth and chewed before asking, "You level up you cooking again?"

He grinned and nodded with his mouth full in reply, so I continued speaking and pointed from myself to Yoh.

"Besides, we don't know who is involved, and not everyone knows what animal forms I can take right now, so I could blend in better. I think I can handle that while you guys all prepare and Jaken gets Rowland taken care of."

"Well, I don't know how sneaky we can be when everyone here knows who we are, but I'm certain no one knows James. Other than the fact that he was with us." Yohsuke posed with a bit of bacon in hand. "Druid or not, you go outside, you'll have eyes on you, man."

"I acquired a form that may help with me being able to move about *relatively* unnoticed." I took a swig of water and stifled a yawn. "I found an owl last night and took that shape to use. It's just going to be a matter of whether anyone is looking for something minutely out of the norm, but I will have that covered. It'll be a simple in and out thing. If I find anything, I'll come back and let you all know what's going on and we can plan from there."

"Sounds good, man," Yohsuke said. He put his fork on the plate and slid off the chair. "I'll see if I can't figure out if anyone else has gone missing or just left without reason."

"Cool. I'm sure the others are doing what they can. I'll see you guys later. I'll send a Mental Message when I can to let you know I'm good." I handed him my plate.

"Sounds good, dude." He took the plate and walked it into the kitchen.

Willem was busy with another patron, so I left without a goodbye. If all went well, he would likely be helping us plan whatever happened next.

I went into the sunlight with a slight grin and turned my thoughts toward the task at hand. First, the potions. I swung a left and began to move toward the square and the wares for sale. As I arrived in the area, a crowd of people around the square gathered.

I heard some low grumbles and cries of disbelief before I heard the rest, "... And they will only be returned if the outsiders are sent home. This is a matter to be solved by the *true* chosen ones—sons and daughters of Brindolla."

I moved closer until I could see who was speaking; a thin pale-skinned woman with blonde hair and freckles was reading from a piece of parchment in her hands. Tears streamed down her face, and a large man stood behind her with a stoic but strained look.

"Your support and attempts to try and solve this issue on your own with these imposters at the helm are admirable, for certain, but they poison our world by being here. To protect them from the outsiders' influence and backward ways, we have graciously taken in the children of your humble village."

A low rumble escaped my throat, and the red rage of my anger rimmed my vision in an almost solid border. They had taken *all* of the children!? And now the were blackmailing the villagers with them to turn against us?

She began to sob uncontrollably as she tried to read the next portion, so the man took it and read it before he spoke, loudly for all to hear, "Please, think of the children."

I growled slightly louder and gritted my teeth as I fought against my urge to run off in search of them right then. That had been a not-so-subtle threat to the children that were taken or at least that's what the parchment implied.

"What would you all like to do?" I asked the crowd before me. They turned, the closest to me jumping in surprise and stared at me. "Who did they take?"

The man who had read the last words on the parchment stepped forward and spoke loudly, "My daughter and my son. You know of them. They sold you potions. You rescued my son from two men who were going to rob him and who knows what else. For that, you have my gratitude. They took several other children, from babies to some on the cusp of adulthood. All of them."

"I see." I sighed. This was getting complicated, quickly, but an idea hit me. "Well, then it is with hope that I tell you my friends and I have learned of a way to go home—in the North where the High Elves are. We will leave this evening, so that you may have your children back—hopefully. My deepest apologies to all of you, and my gratitude for your help and kindness. If it will put you better at ease, you can watch us go."

To my friends, I sent a telepathic call to all of them through our Telepathic Earrings, *Our kidnappers have upped the ante here, guys. They've taken children and teens hostage and won't return them until we are gone.*

What do we need to do? James asked back.

We make like we're going to leave, then we go get those kids back, man, Yohsuke explained before I could. Leave it to him to realize what I have planned before I can even say it.

I'm gonna take off and see about scouting. You guys get ready. No matter what happens, we move tonight.

After I filled them in on my lie, I nodded to the father. If I remembered correctly, he was the one who found the ingredients his wife used to make potions. He looked at me grimly while holding his wife's heaving shoulders and nodded back. At that point, I thought everyone just wanted me gone, so I forewent any of the potions I needed and walked to the tree line. The village was undergoing a major morale shift as parents shouted and tore down the streets shouting their children's names in vain. How had that many people been taken without so much as a clue?

Sure, there were all sorts of nasty creatures who took kids. Fae, changelings in particular, but they left their offspring behind usually. There were other creatures, lycanthropes, who ate anything that was nearby.

I cast Mental Message to Sam and let him know about the situation, "Are your kids okay?"

His response was the same as the others, "My children are gone too."

I sent him another spelled message, "I'm sorry, we will leave. Please, let the villagers know we will be gone this evening to go home."

There was no reply. Angry now, I marched for the forest.

Once I hit the vegetation and the trees, I shifted into my owl form, my body shrinking and becoming lighter everywhere. I ruffled my newly-formed black feathers with specs of gold and white throughout them and attempted to take off.

I flapped my wings mightily and fell to the ground anyway. I closed my eyes for a second and searched my mind for the sensations that Kayda had in flight. Watching her take off, it looked so effortless. I pumped my thin little, clawed legs and hopped into the air. I spread my wings and working the feathered appendages swiftly creating liftoff. It took some getting used to the thermals, the gusting currents of warm air that, from Kayda's memories, created lift that took less work to coast and glide on.

I could fly for a while before needing to rest, but it took some getting used to. All that work, fighting thermal flows and drafts to try and stay flying quickly. Luckily, my wings were about as silent as it gets in the forest.

I flew south for a while, heading in the direction that the bears had said they'd seen strange happenings in and was rewarded for my efforts. About an hour into the flight, I began to notice signs of struggle, some blood, and footprints. Half an hour later, I saw more and more tracks and signs of humanity in the trees. Then I saw what I was both hoping to find—and grim dread settled in my chest.

I referenced my map; more than fifteen miles from the village and under some kind of cloaking enchantments was a structure.

A small fortress with large wooden log walls lashed together with leather straps nailed tight and sharpened to points. The walls had a thin catwalk for archers and watchmen on the inside, and from where I was settled on a branch, I could see that there were four of them. I observed them for an hour. During that time, they stood at the four corners of the wall for ten minutes, then patrolled counterclockwise as soon as the first guard began to move. They paced to the next corner and stood for another ten minutes. From this distance, I couldn't tell their names or levels, but I could see that they were largely wolf Beast-kin.

Inside the walls were several tents, a pavilion that looked to be a dining area, and a fenced in area with a tarp over top. I couldn't tell who was in it, but the single guard at the gate in front of it made me think it was where the hostages were being held.

I waited until the next rotation before I took off into the air. I flew high into the sky, careful my shadow didn't cross the path of a guard and dropped like a rock into the middle of the camp. Just before I hit the ground, I spread my wings wide, hoping that I landed softly next to the central building.

I didn't. I overcompensated too much and caught a small thermal. It filled my wings and lifted me to the left where I smacked into a crate. It hurt, but I was whole. I eyed the guards that I could see, and while their ears had perked up, they weren't actively watching me.

I tried to listen for any snippets of conversation or anything I could but to no avail. Seemed the place was pretty against friendly conversation. Seeing only five guards, though, bolstered my hopes that this would be possible. Especially since at this close of a range, I could see that the guard at the gate of the tarp-structure was only level 13.

I looked to the other guards above and saw the highest there was level 14, and he was the one who always initiated the rotation. Seeing these guys made me think that there may be anywhere from five more guards to ten depending on how long the shifts for duty were.

Having stood watches like these when I was in the Marine Corp, it would stand to reason that a watch like this would last only as long as these men were capable of staying fresh. If they were well trained? It could be hours before the next shift change, but with as bored as these guys looked currently, it would likely be soon. As I watched for the next rotation, the guard at the door was replaced by one of the guards on the wall. Then he took that guard's spot.

Got it. There weren't many guards if they were doing that, and the likelihood that they had longer shifts was almost certain in my mind.

On the next rotation, I shot silently into the air once more to another branch and waited to see if the guards noted my movements. The highest level guard eyed my direction; he was too far to see his information, so I made a show of nestling and preening my feathers. After a moment of him watching me, he turned his attention elsewhere, and I stuck around and gave him a chance to glance at me a couple more times so I didn't seem too outside the norm. Though honestly, an owl outside around noon was a little odd to some. I couldn't be sure he was one of those people—so, we would call it at that. After the next shift that took his attention elsewhere, I moved on and went back to the inn.

Once I arrived, I landed in the fenced-in backyard and made my way inside. I sent a telepathic call to my friends through our earrings and gave them the skinny on what I had seen and told them we would need to strike tonight. Next, I cast Mental Message to Craglim and told him to come to the inn at dusk to "see us on our way" and to bring whatever he would need for the attack.

I made sure Sir Dillon was abreast of our planning and that he needed to placate the townsfolk as well as the mayor. He was to let them know that we knew we had to move on and find our way home.

After that, we waited at the healer's hut to see to Rowland when our cooldowns expired.

I summoned a Celestial to see about fixing what was wrong with Rowland. The being, who looked similar to the angel I had summoned before, took him into his arms and focused on him for a moment before kissing his forehead gently.

He glowed lightly for a moment, then the glow dissipated. The being laid him down without a word and with a nod.

Then he turned to me and warned, "No more summoning us for a while. The fight goes on, and we need our strength. In great need, we will come."

He left in a blinding flash of radiant light, unlike Samu had.

Now, I'm not saying he was trying to intimidate us—but it sure as fuck worked.

"I take it that means he's going to be alright?" James asked.

"I think so," Jaken said, almost as confused. "Maybe we ought to have the healer check him out?"

The healer came in and smiled. "I thought I would too. Hold on a moment."

They came over to stand beside Rowland and opened one eye to the light, then nodded. They checked his vitals and seemed satisfied before turning to us. "I think he is on the mend. I don't know what was done, but it seems to be helping. Only he knows when he will return to us, though, so I ask that you continue to let him rest here. And do not worry, I have heard of your plans to leave—I will see that his daughter is informed if I see her before the cousin does. Good luck to you all, and thank you."

"Come on, guys. Let's go get our things from the tavern and get ready." Bokaj stood and made a show of stretching. "Long journey ahead."

The healer stood and bowed their head. "I wish you all safe travels. Goodbye."

We left the hut and walked slowly through the village. More than one set of parents glared at us openly. Another set, a pair of bear Beast-kins, stopped us and thanked us for what we had done for this world so far. They wished us luck ahead and shook our hands. It was nice. This scene played out a couple more times before we entered the tavern.

Chapter Two

"Well, get ye goin' now." Craglim made a great show of ushering us out of the village. "Get ye gone so the good folk here can have their children back!" He waved back cheerfully at the sullen watchers. "I'll be walkin' em ta the edge o' the forest, so ye can have yer peace again."

He continued the charade for almost ten minutes as we left in a north-westerly direction. We had planned to travel this way for half an hour, then turn and walk toward the encampment, but with how boisterous and annoying the Dwarf was being, we only made it twenty minutes.

"Alright, you can shut the fuck up now." Yohsuke rounded on Craglim angrily. "You're just being a dick. Move as quickly and quietly as you can, and we won't leave your stupid ass behind."

I agreed wholeheartedly, and the Dwarf just chuckled at the angry Elf. His plate mail, treated with light leather padding under each plate to prevent noise, was really pretty quiet—perfect for stealth and defense, but the Dwarf in it was still an annoying fuckstick. I didn't want to give him the satisfaction of knowing I liked his gear. He carried his warhammer, a great-headed affair with a metal shaft and leather handle, in both hands and lagged behind us in the woods a ways. We didn't let him fall too far behind, but we didn't want him right up our asses either.

Like I said before, I don't fucking like him, Yohsuke reiterated for the third time in twenty minutes.

I know, man. We all don't, but he's a necessary evil. Now, about this place. Something is off. I scanned the area around us to be sure it was clear before continuing. *It's almost too poorly guarded. You all know the setup. What do you think we should do? I feel shitty for not thinking it a good idea to plan back at the tavern, but there were too many potential watchers. They would've guessed something was amiss*

Well, we could wait until they get to their corners. Bokaj could silence the one guarding the entrance to the tent, then we take out the guards on the wall at the same time. I mean, they are considerably weaker than we are. It shouldn't be too hard right? Jaken pointed out.

I had to admit—I agreed. I mean, it wouldn't be a cakewalk that was for sure. But still, our work would be cut out for us. Our only true mission was to get those kids out safely and get them home.

We walked on in silence, stopping when the world around us stilled, then continuing once we were sure the coast was clear.

Could we have just teleported there? Sure. If I wanted to go into hostile territory with a good chunk of my mana gone and without having the chance to see our surroundings first for optimal positions. So we walked. Was it boring and trivial? Sure. At times. But a necessary evil.

It took us into the early morning—I would have guessed around one or so, but I wasn't sure. We really took our time getting set up. Luckily, with the darkness having fallen, the enchantment seemed to be lifted. Maybe it recharged at night?

I could talk shop whenever. It was time to get these kids to safety.

We had Yohsuke set up on the north side of the place at the corner outside the range of sight of the wall. Then Jaken stood by outside the south and James to the east. I let Kayda out and hushed her mentally. She was going to stay at the west side and watch for trouble.

Having a stroke of brilliance and wanting to be sure of something, I approached Craglim about getting into my collar. It could hold one willing creature, so there was no reason it couldn't hold the Dwarf, right?

It took some convincing, something along the lines of, "Get in this fucking collar, or we tie you up, hang you from a tree, and leave your ass as a piñata for a whole bunch of things to hit and bite at."

"Wha's tha'?" He shook his head. "Fine, but if I miss the fightin', I'll ring yer bell."

Once he was tucked away, I shifted into my owl form and flew into the encampment to the spot I had landed earlier. I shifted back and let him back out. I clamped a furred hand over his mouth as he took a breath to start cursing. We were well hidden behind these crates, but the sound would attract unwanted attention.

I cast Mental Message and told him, "Shut the hell up or the children are dead and likely your family too because these guys won't stop until we're gone, and they don't seem to have any morals about how that happens."

He scowled and nodded. My mana recovered in a moment, then I shifted into my owl form and flew back out unnoticed. I repeated the process with Bokaj, putting him into the collar and transporting him. Once he was out of it, he nodded, and then we began. Everything happened at once.

Now! I whispered through our telepathic bond.

Bokaj pointed his Wand of Silence at the guard we could see on the ground, hit him, and I watched as Craglim sprinted straight at him. He began trying to shout, but no words cleared his throat.

I looked up in time to see the one on the north of the wall drop with an arrow in his back and a smoldering hole in his forehead. I heard a thud behind me and looked up to see James on top of the guard, taking his claws and shoving them into his victim's throat savagely.

Bokaj turned and fired two more arrows into the east corner guard, just as Jaken's sword shot into his chest. Kayda, last and certainly not least, flapped up, grabbed the final guard, and lifted him into the air with a tug. I threw a Winter's Blade at him. The spell, a sword the size of a longsword made wholly of ice, sailed into his chest, and Kayda dropped him before the projectile burst, causing blood and gore to splash to the ground. With a final thud, his head hit the ground from more than twenty feet up, his whole body crashing behind it. The audible crunch of a shattered neck was all that could be heard.

"He said you would come," said a voice that naggingly enough, sounded familiar. I looked to my right and walking out of the pavilion was a dear, old friend. "I didn't believe him, but he was right. Remember us, panther? Or are you a fox? The master said you were a Druid, but we didn't expect you to come as you had. Didn't expect you to come back to Sunrise. Druids don't normally care for cities, towns, and all that shite. But I do know what you are."

"Oh yeah?" I goaded. "What's that? I didn't know you had graduated from taking a kid's lunch money to kidnapping. Though it doesn't seem like a stretch."

The wolf Beast-kin growled menacingly. His gray fur covered by significantly nicer armor than last time. He had a nicer cudgel too. Last time I had seen him and his friend, they had been level 4—now, they were level 17 and way better armed. Not that I was worried. Ten more level 13 guards stepped out of the pavilion behind him. The flap opened, and I could smell the scent of food and wine. Some of them were armed with bows, the others armed with swords and axes.

"Yeah, you're stupid." He chuckled. "You would dare challenge the Children of Brindolla? Secure the children. If they get too close, slit a throat."

Three of the guards began to back toward the fenced in area with the tarp and gate, but they forgot to look for any enemies there. That was what Craglim was there to capitalize on. From his hiding spot by some of the crates next to the pen, he loosed a war cry and began to glow red, his eyes turning solid crimson. "Come an' get some, ye furry bastards!"

The rest of the game was up, and it was mayhem. Jaken kicked open the gates on his side of the fortress and bum-rushed the nearest guard with a shout and a crack of his shield across the man's face. He turned and beelined for his weapon, still stuck in the fallen guard from the catwalk.

Jaken, bud, get to the kids. They have priority. Drop some Star Burst on 'em, Yoh. I'm gonna get stupid here real fast. Stay away, all of you, I telepathically advised with our earrings and went to cast Fireball at the center of the group, but thought better of it. Instead, I cast Water Sphere.

To their credit, the guards moving forward tried to book it, but they weren't fast enough. The spell burst into existence, and several of the guards were sucked into it with the sound of water dripping. Four of them were immediately trapped, and a couple others tried to escape, but their limbs had been sucked into the watery tomb. I cast Lightning Bolt after that, Kayda doing the same and fried several of them. After that, a small ball of black mana fell into the center of the group and detonated with a large *THWUMPH!*

After the spell's detonation, arrows began to rain on the spot. The guards' bodies littered the ground. The only ones standing after the onslaught were Cudgel and his buddy, whose name I would never care to know.

We have to give this guy a name, right? I mean he's a complete asshole. Wait.

Perfect!

For the sake of clarity and because fuck him, let's call him Asshole.

The other two guards who were getting the shit kicked out of them near the cage were good with just Craglim and Jaken beating on them, and it looked like Bokaj was helping by firing arrows to foil their movements. It wasn't long before they were stepping over two broken men. They looked to be alive, I thought, but I wasn't sure.

Now, back to our regularly scheduled ass kicking contest.

Cudgel and Asshole were almost untouched—not a piece of fur singed from Yohsuke's spell, with just barely a drop of HP gone. And boy, were they *smiling*.

Wards? Yohsuke asked.

Probably enchantments too. I growled through our earrings. *Looks like strong ones at that. Magic resistance most likely. Melee from here.*

I summoned my great axe, Storm Caller, and planted my feet.

"That looks like a nice axe, fox." Cudgel pointed with his weapon. "Would look great on the mantle. Along with your head. Fodder didn't hold up the way we thought they would, but he didn't seem to care much about them anyway."

"I can't seem to remember," I planted the axe in the ground by the spike at the end, "was it you or Asshole there who pissed his pants when I sent you running last time?"

Asshole snarled and brought his longsword to bare on me. I snatched my weapon out of the dirt and whipped the handle between us, blocking his first slash.

Just as Asshole was about to disengage, a battering ram of fur hit him in the side and knocked him to the ground. Tmont had joined the party. She hissed and spit at him as he tried to raise his weapon to defend himself. The great cat would have none of it. She batted his arm down and slashed his armor and face. There was little damage being done.

I looked over to the side of the wall nearest Cudgel and smiled as I saw James perched on the catwalk.

James dropped on to the ground from above us and began to move in on Cudgel. The wolf seemed unthreatened as he pulled a bead out of his pocket and tossed it on the ground in front of the advancing Dragon Elf. James looked at it for a second, and when nothing happened, he stepped over it. As his foot cleared the bead, a large vine of ebony tore out of the ground and wrapped around his legs.

"Argh!" he shouted. "Fuck, this shit hurts!"

I stepped over and hacked at the base of the vine with my axe, having to trust that the others had my back. Last I saw, Yohsuke had been next to me, so I knew he would have me covered. Once James was free, a little lighter on health by 10%, I looked back to see that Cudgel had gone to try and aid his friend with Tmont.

The other two guards were moving now, barely conscious where Craglim and Jaken had left them. Seeing this, the wolf spoke a word as he tossed a bead at the two. Their health shot back up to full, and they leaped up from their backs to attack with more fervor than before.

"Look out!" Bokaj shouted from his overwatch position in a tree outside the wall.

Jaken turned in time to catch a sword on his shield and bat it away. The Dwarf rolled forward and tried to tumble into a fighting stance. It was... less than ideal. Probably a lot toward Dwarven grace. Sure.

"Kill them!" Cudgel shouted as he brought his weapon up for a strike on Tmont.

"I got him," James hissed at me. "Go help the others. Bokaj, on me!"

Bokaj rained down hate and arrows at the guards, bringing them down slowly with carefully aimed shots to vital places, then alternated his fire to Cudgel and back to try and distract him.

Whatever had healed the guards had amplified their resistance to physical damage. I activated Wind Scythe, my ability that allowed me to more accurately throw my great axe, and sent it careening at the guard in front of Jaken. The axe connected, and I activated another spell—Blade Shift, a spell that acted as a minor teleport with the caster's weapon as a focal point.

The world around me blurred, and suddenly, I had my weapon in my hand where it stuck from the guard's back. I put my hand on the back of his head and cast Lightning Bolt. His body went rigid for a moment. Then Jaken stabbed him in the throat with his sword. His body fell lifeless to the ground. Jaken punched my arm lightly before he and Craglim began to work on the final guard, and I turned my sights back on Cudgel and Asshole.

After casting a few of my spells, I was still sitting at 335 MP. So, what do I do?

Oh? You guessed it, right? Tell me you guessed bear. You did? Yes! Good job, boys and girls—become a giant, angry, fucking bear, of course.

I shifted into my Ursolon form and began to close on Asshole from behind as the wolf did his damnedest to fend off

Yohsuke's barrage of swipes with his Astral Blade. While he ducked under a swift slice for his throat and juked back a step, I was able to dig my paws under his arms and around his chest. I lifted him bodily and smashed him into the wall beside me to our left. The damage was negligible at best. These resistances were starting to get really fucking annoying.

I heard Cudgel shout, "You think you can just hurt me with that pathetic hammer, little half-man? Your mother hit harder than that!"

Craglim howled mightily, and a flash of red crossed the fear-struck eye of Asshole in my grip as he tried to scramble away from me. His back was to me still, so I smacked him in the side of the head facing me with my massive forehead, then roared for all I was worth in his face.

"You get that side!" Jaken ordered behind me, and more grunting and cackling laughter came from Cudgel as he continued to taunt and belittle his opponents.

I began inspecting his armor until I found what I was looking for—runes in the chest. They weren't ones I was familiar with, but I could guess that without the armor, he would be defenseless. He was struggling and kicking by this point, trying to escape the pressure on his back. He began to push, so I brought one of my serving platter-sized paws up and slapped his head against the wall. There was only a little damage done, but he was rattled, and I was still much stronger than him.

Back to the object of my discerning eye, though.

Sure, he was protected from damage by and large. That didn't mean I couldn't strip him of his armor. I took my right paw from his chest and began to feel along the sides of the leather chest piece for a seam or a buckle.

"Guch!" he choked. I had my left paw around his throat keeping pressure on him. He squirmed as he began to panic. "What are... you doin'?"

I opened my large jaws in front of his face and roared angrily. He gurgled as the pressure on his throat increased, but he stopped struggling as much. Finally, I found what I was searching for.

I sliced through the small leather clasp as if it were nothing thanks to my blessing from the Primordial Earth Elemental, Diamond Claws, and the chest piece loosened greatly.

"No, stop!" he tried to scream and kicked me hard in the chest. It hurt and did 10% of my health in damage, but a necessary evil.

I smacked him in the face until he struggled less, then switched paws and felt for the other strap on his armor. By this time I heard another shout behind me, rather than risk it, I kept looking. I found the other strap and snapped it.

I removed my paw and grabbed the edge of the chestpiece, removing it as he fell. My Diamond Claws pierced his fur and flesh with little resistance as I picked him back up. I turned around with him in my hand to find that my friends were holding their own against Cudgel. He was at three-quarters health. Jaken had taken some damage and was at about eighty percent health. James was hurt; another bead like the one that had held him earlier held him now, and he was trying to get it to let him go. He was a little over half health left.

Yohsuke and Bokaj were trying to land ranged attacks where they could, but Cudgel was deft at using Jaken as a shield.

Whoever had made their armor had been an exceptionally powerful enchanter with good materials.

"Hey, Cudgel!" Jaken shouted as the wolf tried to bare down on the trapped James. "Look who has your friend!"

"Like I would fall for th–" he started to retort but couldn't finish. I had thrown Asshole, and he hit him straight on.

They fell into a heap, and when Cudgel saw his friend's predicament, it was too late. Yohsuke and Bokaj filled him with so many arrows and astral bolts that he had no chance. By the time Cudgel fished a bead out of his pocket, Asshole was a pincushion, and we didn't let that happen. James snatched it out of his hand and threw it over the wall as far as he could. An explosion rocked the sky above us.

Jaken hauled the perforated wolf off his friend and tossed him toward Yoh and me.

He wasn't dead—but decidedly more porcupine than wolf at that moment. Cudgel made to try and help his friend, but James and Tmont blocked his path menacingly.

With me and Jaken serving as overwatch for him, Yohsuke bound Asshole's hands behind him with some rope just to be safe. He was too out of it due to pain to fight back and resist.

I shifted back, cast Mass Regrowth on my friends, and watched. The 150 MP cost for the spell sucked, but I had recovered a little while in Ursolon form.

"Now, you're next, little wolf," I said finally. He stared at his friend.

While he's distracted, hold him down and take off his armor. Quickly! I warned the others as they watched.

Jaken led my friends in the charge, smacking the wolf in the face and his friend in the shoulder. Before anything else happened, Jaken snatched Asshole by his shirt and hauled him off his friend, leaving the wolf exposed to us.

James finally managed to escape his vine prison and used a stunning Ki strike on Cudgel. While he was momentarily stunned, we grabbed him and held him down. His armor was identical to Asshole's, so finding the straps was easier this time.

We stripped him of his gear and tied him down.

"What are you going to do with me, you outsider scum!" He spat on the ground in front of us.

"Well, you can tell me what I want to know without me having to beat the shit out of you," Yohsuke replied almost cheerfully, "or—and this is the fun part—I get to beat the shit out of you. Well, what do you choose?"

"I'll die first," he growled.

"Well guys, you heard him." Yohsuke sighed dramatically. "He wants this ass whooping."

Well, while beating his ass would be delightful, he would just take it and die, doing what he had said he would. It would be a waste of time, and we couldn't afford that if any of the blood I had used to track them here wasn't theirs.

Those kids needed us, Balmur needed us because there was no way we were strong enough right now for the Hells, especially if these two fuckwits were any kind of example.

As I watched them pull the rest of Cudgel's armor off his body and my introspection reached a fever pitch, the red ring of my rage returned and pulsed enticingly.

Now, normally I'm a nice guy. I have my moments, sure—who doesn't? But these guys had *royally* pissed me off.

"There's no need to waste your time, brother," I said, patting him on the shoulder lightly. "They see us as monsters? Let's give them what they want, shall we?" Yoh looked at me in confusion before knowing dawned on his face, and the questions in his expression were ones I was going to have to deal with. "I'll be in control, but do me a favor? Hold my morals for a bit."

I reached into myself and pulled out the beast that had been peeking out of me every time I got angry since before our return from the Fae Realm. A flash of muted light later and I suddenly stood seven feet tall. My fur, half black and half white almost perfectly on each side with white on the left, black on the right. My Werewolf hybrid form was like this. I looked down at the quivering wolf before me and growled. Menacingly.

"If he won't tell us willingly, I could turn him and make him my bitch for the rest of his unnaturally long life." I stepped forward until I towered over Asshole, then reached down and grabbed the ropes that held him.

"Yo, Zeke, man, you good?" I heard James ask, but Yohsuke stepped over to him and shook his head.

Jaken was on high alert, and Bokaj was still in the trees, so I couldn't see him in my peripheral vision like the others.

I picked him up, and he began to scream. I cupped his lower jaw with my right hand and let my claws pierce his skin slightly. I looked over at Cudgel who watched with open-faced horror on his face.

"Speak, or I kill him," I said softly with no growl or anger. Just truth. "Why did you kidnap the children? What did you hope to gain? And who do you work for?"

"Mnff!" Asshole wept openly, but his jaws weren't able to move from my grasp. I felt a probing from Kayda through our connection, and I locked myself down tight. This needed to happen. I needed to be strong for this.

Cudgel clamped his jaws shut with an audible, final clack of teeth. I grimaced, looked at Asshole, and stared him in the eyes as I took my left hand and grasped him by the throat, lifting him higher into the air so that his body was between Cudgel and me.

The wolf in my grip struggled, and that excited the lycanthrope in me to no end, almost sickeningly gleeful to have something fighting us so. The red around my vision returned and threatened to take over, but I growled and fought it back.

I sighed, and with a roar of both anguish and rage, slammed my right hand through Asshole's body and tore his heart from the veins inside it. The floundering thing was held in my grasp on the other side of his corpse for all to see.

Jaken vomited. The others cursed vehemently, "Fuck, Zeke, fuck. Stop this, man."

"Go check on the kids, Jaken. James, go with him to see if the coast is clear there," I issued the order as the alpha would. No argument. No requests. Just orders.

They left quickly and ducked into the tarp-covered area.

I brought my right arm down, and the corpse slumped off of it to the ground with a sickening thud before I stalked closer to Cudgel. I leaned down close to his face and forced him to look me in the eyes by grabbing his lower jaw firmly with my bloodied hand.

"Tell me what we want to know, or I will do the same to you."

He looked me in the eyes, and I let him see that I had gone to that quiet place, that deep-dark of reality. He knew I would hold true to my word.

"We were ordered to if you ever came back," he said quickly. When he spoke, I let his jaw go, so he continued, "If you left, we would have kept our word, but we would have tried to turn the village and other places against you in hopes you would leave us. I don't know who we work for, but they are powerful. They gave us these items and taught us their ideals by letter. They told us the perfect way to gain strength quickly. For that, we didn't question them."

"Killing folk that don't hold to the ideals that we do." I motioned with my bloody hand for him to go on. "We receive missives, and they tell us where to go and hunt them down. And no, we burn them once we understand them."

I tossed the heart in my hand aside numbly, detaching myself from the action I had just performed.

"How many of you are there?" James asked as he walked toward us. "Kids are okay. Jake should be out in a minute or so."

"I don't know," he answered. He seemed to believe it.

"What was it you called yourselves?" Yohsuke asked.

"The Children of Brindolla." When we didn't interrupt him, he spoke with more venom, "We are the true saviors of this world. You have no stake here. You don't belong. You hurt our way of life by being here."

"I don't know who the fuck lied on us like that, but we're here to stop War and his fucking assholes so that our own world is safe. We want to be friends with you fucking people, but you did this. You brought this hate about—not us. We just want to go fucking home!" James spat on the ground and looked away, unable to control his emotions in the moment, it seemed.

"Liars!" Cudgel's eyes took on a zealous gleam. "We are the only ones capable of defeating War's hordes! The true Children of Brindolla! Not some pathetic outsiders." With the last sentence, he spat at my face, but I ducked it.

"I see." I growled. "Well then, anyone else have any questions?"

The others thought a moment, then shook their heads.

"Good, the–" Craglim bolted forward and stepped before me.

"I has a question." He stared at me as if he was daring me to stop him. "Who was it what hurt me kin? Rowland?"

The wolf actually smiled and spat again. James punched him in the side of the jaw, allowing him to speak, "Me and the other stronger guards. He was the most adamant and staunch supporter in the village other than the Paladin at the tavern. He needed to pay for his traitorous ways. He's probably dead by now, right?"

I began to laugh, so much so that I actually reverted to my fox-man form. He looked at me in confusion.

"Oh sorry." I tried to stop a moment to breathe. "It took that many of you filthy bastards to overpower him, and you *still* failed to kill him. They're all dead, and you feel like you can gloat? Rowland's fine, dickbag, but you won't be. Hey, Yoh, you still got my morals in hand, man?"

Yohsuke made a fist and clenched it tightly. "Yup."

"Excellent." I picked Cudgel up, then looked to Craglim. "I don't like you much, but Rowland is your family. You want to kill him, or you want me to?"

"I'd be likin' a crack at him first." He growled fiercely. "Iffin ye don' mind?"

I tossed Cudgel away from me and motioned for Craglim to take over. We watched as Craglim took his time breaking bits of the Wolf's body with his hammer, then taking the time to straighten the broken bits and hit them again.

Jaken had walked out just after the Dwarf had started his painful ministrations to the wolf.

"I'm going to go back in with the kids," Jaken stated after the first few whacks in his presence. "I feel like, while this is called for, I can't actively support it. He's unarmed. Let me know when we can go."

"You got it, man," I said dispassionately. "You wanna go with him, James? Just in case?"

"Yeah, man." He sighed almost in relief. "Don't take too long."

The wolf's HP was draining quickly enough, but the damage was blunt damage, and it was all to extremities. So there was no "life-threatening" damage to things like organs and whatnot. Still, that damage was adding up.

"Finish it, Craglim," Yohsuke ordered at last. "We need to get these kids back."

"I'll do no such thing!" he howled. "Hurt me kin! Rowland was a good smith. Good man. He didn't deserve tha' beatin'! He's gonna pay!"

"Either you finish it now, or I do," Bokaj said behind us on the wall. He hadn't made a noise coming over here and had an arrow nocked and aimed at Cudgel's head already.

The Dwarf looked outraged at the prospect of someone taking his kill, so he took a strong stance at the nearly unconscious wolf's head and stopped.

"Ye hurt me kin, Wolf," he spat, "but this be two-fold. You hurt me kin, and ye took'd those kids. I hope yer Gods will smile upon ye as the Mountain surely will me. This is the end of yer Way."

He brought his hammer up and arced it down perfectly. Gore splattered against Craglim's legs, and some had even found its way on to his face.

"Aye, thank ye, lads." He looked to those of us standing there. "Ye helped me avenge me kin. I'll not forget tha'."

"Don't mention it," I said. "Seriously. Don't tell Rowland. He's gonna be pissed enough as it is that someone ganged up on him and he didn't get a piece."

Craglim loosed a torrential bellow of a laugh, his hand smacking his stomach. "Hahaha, aye, tha' be true."

He looked at me funnily, but I left it alone. Grateful as he was or not, I was in no mood to piss around with him. The little fucker was annoying.

The experience was a decent drop in the bucket. The experience from the normal guards had been negligible at best, but Asshole and Cudgel had given a good chunk—around a hundred experience each for all of us, I assumed.

Yohsuke pulled Cudgel's pockets inside out, finding a single bead of orange, and slipped it into his inventory with a shrug. The armor and weapons we took because they looked like decent stock, some of the normal guards' armors were sliced, singed, and wet beyond repair it seemed, so we left those. Asshole and Cudgel's armors were still in great shape other than the straps being sliced through. We took them, even though it looked like the enchantments had been tied to the two wolf Beast-kin. Maybe we could have someone study them.

Another thing that was weird was that the information didn't pop up on our status screens when we touched things like normal items. Maybe we could have someone look at them at some point, but for now—other matters required our attention.

We went to check on the children with Jaken and James. The two of them stood in front of the gate like sentinels. The children seemed to have heard a bit of what happened outside and had begun to huddle together in fear. When the rest of us walked over, we had the Paladin and Monk call the kids outside.

I noted two friendly faces when I let the light from a freshly cast Fergus' Flame Blade shed over the area. The others seemed scared, but that was natural.

"Mr. Zeke!" A little blonde haired girl with pigtails and freckles sobbed. I looked over, and her older brother looked so relieved he might pass out. He let her go, and she began to sprint at me.

I caught her with my left arm and hefted her up into a hug. "Are you okay, little one? Did they hurt you?"

"No, they left the younger children alone." She looked to her brother and sniffed. "They talked to the older children for a while, though."

"They kept trying to teach us about their order," her brother said as he stood slowly. He held his stomach and limped toward us. "Those who didn't buy into it were punished for treason. I don't think any of us gave in."

The other older children were beaten and bruised, and more than a couple of them seemed uncomfortable in our presence.

Couldn't say that I blamed them. They had taken beatings for their faith in us and in their parents, and here I was with nothing good to tell them. They were safe now? They had been last time—at least we had thought they were, but this shit happened—and War's minions and generals were still out there somewhere. They weren't safe at all.

Jaken looked them over and began to mumble something beneath his breath. Then a large flash of radiant light and a wave of warmth swept over us. After the initial blindness and spots left our eyes, the children were all healed and so were we.

"What the fu–n was that?" Yohsuke nearly burst trying to correct himself before the children around us.

"Radiant Burst," Jaken muttered with a hand to his head, then turned to the children. "Hurts enemies, heals my friends. And guess what that makes all of you?!"

The children all cheered and began to laugh and clap.

"Let's get ye all home to yer mamas and papas afore they get to riotin'," Craglim said, clapping some of the children on their backs and ushering them outside.

With the path straight back to the village being as straight a line as possible and no real need for stealth, we made the walk in a few hours with rests where we could. The party was spread around the children to be sure that no one fell behind, and some of the older ones carried infants and toddlers, while we kept a lookout for anything that may attempt to stop us.

I cast a Mental Message to Sam, letting him know we were on our way.

"Wha– how, DEAR!" Sam's voice faded in my head. I blinked in confusion, then shrugged.

Moments later, we were in sight of the village, and all hell broke loose.

"The children!" a woman's cry rang out. "The children have returned!"

Children and villager alike clashed just inside the tree line. Sobs and words exchanged rang out in the area, and more voices raised behind them, letting us know that we weren't the only ones who had heard the news.

I noted Sam's children bolted straight to their mother and father as soon as they were in sight.

"Mama! Daddy!" the youngest one cried, almost taking his poor dad's nose off trying to kiss him. Pointing back to us, he cried, "They saved us from the bad people!"

I froze. I had almost forgotten about our little ruse. The villagers turned to us, and I couldn't see one look of anger or distrust. Sure, some of them looked worried—fuck, I know I would've been if my kid had been taken, but I didn't have it in me to see anyone in this town being a part of what just happened.

The man I had seen earlier, the herbalist who had read the final words on that horrid letter, left his wife to stand in front of us. He looked me in the eyes, steadily with his stoic face and held out his right hand.

I clasped his forearm with mine, and he pulled me into a bear hug so tight I thought I would take damage. "Thank you, mister. Thank you for saving our babies. You ever need anything—you ask. You come find me and mine, and we will have your back. I swear it to all the Gods."

"Your daughter and son—forgive me, I never learned their names—are good kids. They're friends of mine now." I smiled as he pulled back.

"Nora, Daisy, and Seth come here, please?" He held my wrist in his as he waved his family over. He pointed to his wife first, then his daughter and son. "This man is family now, ya hear? They all are. Thank him proper."

Little Daisy came over and hugged me fiercely. Her brother, a little more shy, grasped my wrist like his father had and smiled. His wife, Nora, just stood in front of me with her eyes downcast in thought.

"It's okay, ma'am," I said. "I know that it was because of us that the kids were taken, but we can't control those kinds of people, and we're still here for all of you."

She looked at her kids, then the rest of us, and nodded. "Thank you. All of you."

"You're welcome!" Jaken's big ass barged into the center of the group of parents, kids, and curious onlookers. "All of you, you are welcome! You don't have to thank us. All we ask for are two things. One, that you take care of your families. I have a little girl myself, and I know I would do nothing else but try and hurt the people responsible. They are gone! And with the bears helping to watch over you—you are safe!"

Jaken spread his arms wide as if in gracious acceptance.

The fuck are you doing, puto? Yohsuke asked through our earrings so we could all hear.

We need them to like us, and being selfish isn't going to help our cause. Look at them, man. They need to feel secure, and they need to lighten the mood—trust me.

The crowd cheered wildly. I saw some reflecting light in the area—eyes peered at us, and I saw one ursine head poke through the brush and sniff before they disappeared.

"The second thing is for you and your families to join us for a feast in two nights from now." People began to chatter quietly, but Jaken continued, "Let us welcome your loved ones back with a meal in their honor, and let us thank you for your service to this world!"

The crowd whispered and chattered excitedly, and I watched as Bokaj and Tmont slunk away while everyone else was distracted. There was a scowl of disgust on his face, and I could imagine that the delay, although well intentioned, was grating on his nerves. I couldn't blame him.

"On behalf of all of the residents here and those who may still be asleep," the purple and gold of the rising sun alighting on his mildly scratched face, Sam spoke with his arms raised in welcome, "we humbly accept your offer. Please, accept our sincerest thanks. Friends, no—FAMILY. You are all of our family now. Come, we must prepare! Go home! Love your families and know that you are safe!"

The crowd cheered again, and children danced and pranced around their parents as they flooded into the village and their homes to be together in private.

Sam, his wife, and kids stayed behind to watch over them as they left. Some of the families nodded. Another human woman promised us cookies and food any time. They looked at the families still making their way home, then Sam turned to us.

"Again, we cannot thank you enough," he said. He looked weary. His wife came over to us and hugged us each in turn. She was quiet, tears welling in her eyes, but she smiled nonetheless.

"You're fine, and you've got to go get some rest so you can be with your family properly." I clapped the mayor on his shoulder. "You both have to be exhausted. Get some rest and keep those kids close."

Sam nodded and tried to speak again, but he was interrupted.

"You don't have to thank us, man. Jaken said that." Yohsuke waved him and his thanks off. "He meant it. So do we. You guys took us in, taught us and made sure we were set. There's almost nothing we wouldn't do for you all."

Sam nodded and seemed to take that to heart, but before they could leave, we got together, and we each offered a hundred gold to the village. He could use that to pay for the food for the feast and also build some better defenses. He floundered with his thanks, but we cut him off before he could get too far. "Take it. No thanks needed. It is the right thing to do." He just stood there staring at us.

He did. Sir Dillon, looking bedraggled and half asleep, came to the edge of the village wearing a nightshirt and a pair of night pants. His sword and shield ready, he said, "Wha– what's happened? Is the village safe?"

We all laughed pretty hard for a few minutes. Then we returned to the tavern for the night. With that one bit of business off my heart and mind, I turned my thoughts to what Samu had said about more aid coming.

I tried and failed to turn my mind off after a bit, eventually falling into a fitful sleep.

* * *

I woke and started my normal routine. I shuffled down the hall and into the dining room for something to eat. Sir Dillon smiled at me warmly as he offered me a plate. I was the first one of our group in the room that morning,

"You'll be happy to know that Lady Radiance saw fit to grace me with word." He thumped the bar. "She said, 'aid has come' last night."

"Oh?" I said around a mouthful of eggs and biscuit. "Waph's tha'?"

"You will see." He chuckled and poured some cider into a cup. "Eat your food and be patient."

The rest of my friends, except Bokaj, wandered out of the hallway in bursts.

"Anyone seen Bokaj?" I posed as I lifted my fork to my lips once more with my final bite of food.

"I think he's out training right now," Willem answered. We looked his way, and he continued, "Hunters found arrows in trees around the area with crudely drawn targets and claw marks on the trees from a great cat."

"Makes sense, the idea that we would celebrate anything right now seemed to piss him off." Yohsuke turned an ire-filled gaze on me. "Speaking of pissed off—the fuck was that shit last night?"

I knew what he was talking about, and I had been wrestling with the answer since the kids had been found relatively safe. On the way back to the village, I hadn't had an answer. Now? I sure as fuck didn't. But I did know one thing.

"I did what had to be done." Even saying it had felt bitter. Like a lie.

"Yeah, and what Pastela did was necessary too, right?" he spat venomously. "As she beat the shit out of you, tortured you, and treated us like playthings for a couple days in the Fae Realm? She wasn't fuckin' wrong either, was she?"

"Dude, you know she was a monster," I shot back, my vision darkening with that same red veil of rage.

"That was some Pastela-level bullshit, and you *know* it." Yohsuke began to stand, and suddenly, I realized I was growling deeply in my chest. "You gonna turn and attack me, motherfucker?"

The others were standing now too. Jaken had a hold on my left arm, and James looked ready for a brawl.

I took a steadying breath, and the red faded slowly.

Yohsuke walked over to stand in front of me on my side of the table and muttered, "I 'held' your morals because I knew it was necessary at the time, but that shit was cold blooded. If we keep that shit up—we're no better than War's minions or the generals either."

Jaken's grip tightened considerably, painfully, around my arm. "We're better than them."

I nodded. "I start to lose it again and it isn't called for, or it's too callous–"

Yohsuke interrupted, "We'll beat your ass."

I had to laugh. "Thanks."

About this time, Bokaj walked in, grabbed a plate of food silently, and began to eat, tossing food to Tmont as he did. He ignored our greetings at first, but finally, an apple thrown at him from James brought him out of his reverie.

"Yeah?" He blinked at us, our questions plainly visible on our faces. "T and I were training last night. The whole prospect of this party thing pissed me off, and I needed to clear my head. I don't like it, but I get that it's a necessity to keep the goodwill of the village. Just don't take too long. We got a Dwarf to go save and some minions to kill and shit."

After a nod of agreement, I looked at the sunlight streaming through the windows and smacked the table. "Alright, time to see what this 'aid' is. Sir Dillon?"

"Well, he's asleep still probably." The older Paladin grinned at our disbelief. "Last room on the left, but it would be rude to wake him."

I looked at him, then looked at my friends, and bolted for the hallway. Bokaj tripped over Tmont trying to get off his bar stool. Yohsuke was fast, but Jaken shoved him playfully aside. James tried to push me into Jaken, but I shifted into my fox form and skittered into the hallway before shifting back.

At the end of the hallway on the left-hand side was a door that I had never noticed before. I leaped into the air and kicked it open, landing in a heap as the others followed me in, causing me to fall with their momentum.

"Huh, wha–" a groggy voice said from the bed.

In the bed was a blanketed form that began to move. A green-scaled head poked out and looked around. Draconic features dominated the face, but the voice sounded familiar. So familiar. Huh.... Wait. I looked at Yohsuke, then Jaken, and they looked from me, back to the figure.

"Nick?" The three of us asked at the same time.

The figure blinked lazily. "Weirdest dream ever."

"You bastard!" Yohsuke shouted. "Wake your cat-nappin' ass up, puto!"

"Get off me, you assholes." I grunted and started to try and stand. The rest of the group rolled to the side and began to stand on their own.

"Man, you sound a lot like my roommate." The figure yawned loudly. "Video games mechanics and some crazy blue light lady-voice. Fuckin' trippy."

The creature before me was, without a doubt, my roommate from home. Nick always spoke like this and liked his sleep. He and I had known each other for almost a decade, and when I had come home from the Marines and fell down on my luck, he was kind enough to take me in. We'd been like brothers since a little into our friendship, sharing the same sense of humor and interests, but that act of kindness had cemented it. It took a special person to take a friend in the way he had—and he'd done it without a second thought.

Jaken hung out with us regularly at our apartment, and we drank together. Yohsuke had heard Nick and I talking on more than one occasion, so he knew his voice.

As I got closer, I noted that his features along his cheeks, snout-like nose, and even around his royal-purple eyes were finer scaled. Seemed almost like green flesh. Around his ear holes and the sides of his face, the scales grew slightly larger and rougher. He didn't look quite human or Elven but more like a Dragon given a humanoid form.

His scales led to a mass of lime-green hair in a rather pointed widow's peak. As close as I was, I saw that the hair wasn't quite what I was used to seeing—it looked almost like even finer scales than on his face.

"Who are you guys?" he asked as he began to become a little more alert, "and why are you in my room?"

"This isn't your room, brotha," Jaken provided before I could. "You're on Brindolla. Welcome to the party!"

He looked confused. "Jake?!"

"Jaken, my man," The Fae-Orc grinned. "This is Zeke, Yohsuke, James, and Bokaj. We don't use our old names here—it may not be safe. Come get some food, and we will fill you in."

"Hold up." He sighed. "If we can't use our real names here, then call me Muu Ankiman. Just Muu. And lemme get dressed—kinda naked here."

"Clothes and shit are in the chest at the end of the bed." I pointed, and he stared at me as if I had horns. "What?"

"Fuckin' duh, dude." He waved us out. "Starting gear is almost always in the inventory or a large chest in the immediate area. Now, get out or get a show!"

We fled the room and went back out to the bar where Willem grinned at us. "Met your friend, I see?"

We all gave him a playfully dirty look. He smiled and went into the back to get some food ready for his latest guest. Ten minutes later, Muu walked out of the hallway. He wore a simple white shirt, brown breeches, black boots, and moved a little weirdly.

"What's wrong with you, man?" I asked.

"Do you have any idea how hard it is to move with a tail?" he asked exasperatedly and pointed to his own. It was only about mid-calf in length, thick at the base, and came to a rounded tip. It was the same color as his scales, and the bottom of it was a pale tan.

I grinned and pointed to my three. "You get used to it."

"Now, you don't see a Dragon Beast-kin very often!" Willem thumped the bar. He patted an empty stool and sat the food in front of it. "You'll be a curiosity to more than a few members of our village here, lad. Eat up! You'll need your strength."

"Yeah, you will." Yohsuke clapped him on the back. "Good to finally meet you, man. Hey, what class did you pick? And what weapon? What kind of stats are you working with?"

He was halfway through his food before he had even sat down fully. He finished chewing, then said, "Fighter. Status. Show Party." Then it was right back to eating.

Now, look—Muu is older than me by like a year or two, but the guy had been gaming since before he could fucking walk—so don't be shitting on your lovable main character here, okay?

The same little opaque screen that I saw when looking at my own stats flashed in front of my vision.

Name: Muu Ankiman
Race: Dragon Beast-kin
Level: 1
Strength: 15
Dexterity: 12
Constitution: 15
Intelligence: 15
Wisdom: 11
Charisma: 14
Unspent Attribute Points: 0

"Very nice." Yohsuke whistled.

"Cool," Jaken said, "but what weapon? You could probably do some magic too!"

By this time, he was almost to the end of his plate of food when he looked up. "Oh, sorry. Spear and Shield. I have them in my inventory, though they don't look too strong."

"You know how it goes, man," I said with a smile. "Basic gear for basic bitches. Why Fighter? I would have thought you would go Caster or Rogue."

"Oh, the blue light told me the party stats and classes before I chose my class." He shrugged. "After that, it seemed that melee damage and tanking were lacking, so I took what was needed. Though, the specifics I still don't know too much about. I thought it was just a dream—the same one I had been having for about a week or so."

"How come you never said anything, man?" I threw my arms out when I asked.

"You know how it is," he retorted. "You and I both have different schedules. By the time I wake up for the day, you've been at the gym for a couple hours already, and by the time I come home, I'm exhausted and want to relax. You're either asleep or gaming, so I just let it be. Besides, you have strange dreams all the time; why would I bother you about one I'm having?"

"That's fair." I sighed. "Well, let's go get you some equipment and some training. Any word on any kind of trainer for him Sir Dillon?"

"Willem, lad," he replied sternly. "After last night's escapades? You call me Willem. You're as much family to me now as the villagers here are, and I'll hear no argument from you, Jaken Warmecht. Now, as far as training goes, that's up to you all. The only Fighter in the village left when you lot arrived, and his services weren't needed."

"How do we teach him his skills then?" James asked. "Our trainers all helped us learn these things!"

"Fighters excel at martial combat," Willem began to explain. "They are weapon experts. All he needs is someone to teach him tactics, group fighting, and how to use his weapons competently. Jaken here is good with a shield, and Yohsuke has a weapon that acts as a spear I think? Other than that, you all know how to fight in this world. He may yet hold some surprises for all of you."

"Okay then, that settles it." I clapped my hands and rubbed them together. "We'll get you to the forge and get you twinked out. Then we will take you out for some training and see if there's anything that needs killing. Anyone else have any other plans?"

Pause. For those of you wondering, "twinked out" or the act of twinking a character is simply just getting them the best gear or better gear than what would typically be available for their level. Back to the story, yeah?

"Yo, you think I'm gonna miss this poor bastard's first few hours here getting his shit kicked in?" Yohsuke laughed a little as he clapped Muu on the back. "The fuck outta here. You're about to hate life, puto."

Muu groaned, and we all patted him and swatted at him playfully. As we were walking out, I heard a purr and then, "GRAAAAAGH FUCK!"

I turned to see Tmont had chomped on his tail. "Damn it, T." Bokaj smacked her rump, and she headbutted Muu playfully.

"I may not still be allergic to you," Muu shouted at the great cat as she skittered out the door, "but that doesn't mean you can bite my ass!"

"She's got a real thing for tails, man." I chuckled. "She's bitten mine too many times for me to count."

The rest of us stepped into the light of day; the village was bustling and more than a few of the citizens stopped what they were doing to wave hello. It wasn't them who made us gasp and wave, though. It was Rowland.

"Hail, travelers!" He strutted up to us, Craglim in tow. "Heard what ye did, ye brave, foolish idiots. Could've been killed, all o' ye. Who be this 'un?"

"Rowland, this is my friend and brother Muu." I smiled and clapped him on the back as I said his name. "We were on our way to your shop to see if you were back yet."

"I bet ye were." He walked through us with his eyes on Muu. "Good size, muscle tone. Tail looks limp, and he looks sheepish. Tell me, what are ye?"

"I'm a Fighter," Muu said uncertainly. "I'll be using a shield and spear. And heavy armor."

"A proper Fighter!" He guffawed and clapped enthusiastically. "Cousin, if me shop is in shambles, I'll skin ye—I swear it on the Mountain! I got work to do." With a wave beckoning us all forward, he said, "Come on then!"

The Dwarves bickered and barked at each other along the way to the blacksmith's forge.

"They always like this?" Muu asked in a whisper.

"No clue, but Craglim is an asshole, and Rowland is cool as fuck, so stay on his good side, yeah?" I replied in a low tone.

He nodded, then began to look around in absolute wonder. This world was new to him, so I couldn't blame him.

Ah, I remembered my first drink of the sweet nectar of Brindolla's sweet, sweet bosom of awesomeness. Sorry, was that weird? That was weird. I'll shut up.

Every now and again, he would ask one of us a question, and we would try to answer it if we could. One he asked was how Beast-kin came to be, but none of us had the slightest idea.

Once we arrived at the forge, all bets were off. Rowland found his forge in a state of meticulous care that he called, "Shite, but it will do."

They took measurements for Muu's armor. Once they had that, I had a few requests to make.

"Hey, Rowland," I began, and he looked my way. "Can you make him a really heavy spear? Not one that he can't lift, mind you—but one that is significantly heavier than a normal one? We want to try and train him as best as we can as fast as we can. His armor and shield need to be the same."

"Ah, that way he builds muscle and endurance faster?" The blacksmith grinned conspiringly. "Aye, I could do that. Don't need to be pretty, but functional?" I nodded. "Hmm. Give us to tomorrow around noon. Me worthless shite of a cousin will help too—aye, Craglim?"

"Help?" he shouted as if insulted. "I'll likely finish afore ye. Couldn't swing a hammer if it swung between yer legs, ye sorry excuse for an artisan. Master, my boot!"

"Oh aye, lad the hammer between me legs be on yer mind now?!" Rowland bellowed back. "Start tha' forge and let's see who hammers harder, me—or your MA!"

"Oh ye lit'le shite, I'll brain ye for tha'," Craglim threatened. "Take it those bastards knocked the sense from tha' ugly gob o' yers."

"Boys!" Jaken said, coming to stand between them. "Put your hammers away and bring out the *real* hammers. There's work to be done."

Craglim eyed Jaken for a moment, but Rowland broke the tension.

"Oh, but lad, ye never have seen me hammer." Rowland laughed at his own joke, and we all rolled our eyes.

* * *

"Again!" Jaken barked. "This time, let the block parry off the shield and not hit it directly. It shaves off the damage you take and will leave the opponent open to a counter attack."

Muu stood in the center of the clearing with the rest of us watching as Jaken took his sword and made a stabbing motion. They had been at it since we got here around noon, the shield being a little more nuanced than I thought. It was about mid-afternoon, possible approaching three our time?

Muu took the wooden shield in his left hand and shoved the incoming weapon away without it letting it sink into the wood like he had half-a-dozen times before, minimizing the impact.

"Yes!" James and I cheered.

"That's what I'm fuckin' saying, bro!" Jaken fist bumped Muu then went back to his place. "Now, imagine that there's a pulley system in your body. When you parry, you pull your shield arm in close and angle the blow away. Then you take your weapon and stab it forward at the same time. That's the next portion of the training. Let's have you parry a few more times since you seem to get the concept."

They did the same thing five times. Each time, the motion became more and more reflexive.

"Now, throw the spear in there too," I ordered. Jaken smiled and brought his own shield into his hand.

Muu parried Jaken's next attack and jabbed his spear forward, but it was a weak jab.

"If you're gonna do that, make sure you do it with some feeling." Yohsuke grunted. "Don't half-ass that shit, man. Mean. It."

"Right." Muu's shoulders slumped, and he looked to us. "I've never done any of this shit, man. You guys know I wasn't military. I don't have the experience."

"It's a little different from a bayonet, longer for sure, but the concept is the same." James pointed to the tip of the spear. "That pointy part goes into his fucking guts, and he dies. Then you scream 'cream corn' and move on."

"You scream that shit, and I will personally destroy you." I shot James a dirty look. "You know he doesn't fucking rate to say that."

Muu rolled his eyes, and Jaken took the opening he was presented. The Paladin swung his sword in a horizontal slash at Muu's shield arm. He parried the strike deftly and stabbed with his spear. The metal tip struck significantly harder than his last attempt.

"That's why we're doing what we're doing," Bokaj explained. "We have some experience, and it was hard won. So we're trying to give that to you without all the pain and suffering we had."

"And you just did that shit *on instinct*," I explained. "That's in only a few hours of training with us. Think of what we could do with you in a week? A month?"

He nodded. "That makes a lot of sense." He looked at the spear in his hand. "This feels too weird to use. It's too long."

It was seven-foot-long coarse wood with an eight-inch-long tip. Of course, it was fucking long.

"Let me try something then," I said. I stood and dusted myself off before I walked over to him and took the weapon in my hands.

Beginner's Spear
+2 to attacks
Please, do not use this as a spit for food.
Weight: 6 Lbs
A gift to the traveler from the Gods. Use it wisely.

"Bokaj, you think you could trim this?" I asked after inspecting it.

Bokaj dropped from the branch he was sitting on, took the weapon, and looked it over. "How does that sound, Muu? Where do you feel like you have the most control?"

Muu took his weapon, sat his shield down, and began to thrust his spear over and over. Eventually, he settled on a grip that felt good to him. He stabbed a few more times, then indicated that three feet from the tip of the weapon was where he felt he had the most control.

Bokaj took the weapon, found a decently sized log, and set to work with his saw. After he was finished, he handed the now four-and-a-half-foot weapon back, and Muu took a few swings with it to get a feel for it.

"Bring it, newb," Jaken taunted, taking a stance.

Muu took a deep breath with his eyes closed, then opened them and settled into a stance with his center of gravity low. He readied his shield and his adjusted weapon. Jaken sprung at him, stepping forward with his right foot and stabbing his sword forward. Muu parried the attack at the last second, then stabbed down at Jaken's chest faster than we had expected. Jaken managed to block, but Muu kept the attacks coming. With his shortened weapon, he could angle the attacks in different ways that made it more difficult to predict. He was forcing Jaken to step back step by step.

"Ease it off, Muu," I called.

I sent a Mental Message to Rowland, "Hey, Rowland, I know it's kind of weird, but we need the spear to be four and a half feet from the tip to the tail. Make it heavy."

"Aye, aye," I heard his voice respond. "Tomorrow. Noon. At the latest."

I smiled and continued to watch as the two in the center of the clearing began to trade blows and work on moving while fighting.

We spent another two hours working with Muu in the clearing before heading back to the tavern for food. The walk back was as easy as the walk there. During that time, we told him about some of what we had done since we'd arrived here. How we had cleansed the old ruined fort of War's Minion the Bone Dragon, then gone on to fight and kill the Goblins in their cave.

See, finding James in that cave had been interesting on its own, but then he said the monks had suggested clearing this place that turned out to be a Goblin dungeon. Wild, right? I thought so too until we had found and fought a Goblin King who whooped our collective asses as my group, James, Yoh, and I, waited for back up from Jaken, Balmur, and Bokaj.

Yeah, splitting the party was stupid, gimme a fucking break already, reader!

Muu's reactions were interesting. He'd gasp and mumble sounds of awe here and there. Then he began to ask us how skills and magic worked.

"It works the same way it does in video games, if that makes sense." Jaken paused to collect his thoughts, then continued, "When you learn how to do something, your body knows exactly what to do. The same with the spells and magic. It feels as if you have always known how to cast them."

I held a hand out before me and touched a large oak tree before casting Nature's Path. My being became one with the large tree, and I passed *through it* to a branch thick enough to hold my weight.

"Some classes use spells differently—duh, I know." I dropped to the ground with ease and motioned to the world around us. "We have our strengths and weaknesses. Like, for instance, I can't use the spells that Yoh knows because they're for his class specifically. Just like he could never do some of the things I could do."

"Wow." Muu breathed wide-eyed. "So, I understand what each of you *is* but not what you *do*. What does a Spell Blade do? Or a Druid? I know, in theory, what a Druid does, but I don't know here. And a Ranger? This is nuts! And I know Monks kick ass with martial arts and Paladins are holy warriors."

Yohsuke laughed and pulled out his Lightning Astral Adaptor. It looked like the hilt of a katana with yellow leather wrapped around the grip. He activated it, and black mana with white dots that looked like stars in the night sky erupted from the hilt.

"This is my weapon, it's called an Astral Blade." Yohsuke held it up so Muu could look at it. "It deals un-aspected magical damage, but this adaptor lets me channel my mana and give it lightning elemental damage if I choose. It can also become a spear if I choose, but I usually prefer my normal sword. I also cast spells and recently made a pact with a demon to gain more spells and power. So I guess that makes me a warlock too."

Muu looked to me next, and I shifted from my fox-man form to panther, then fox, to Ursolon, and back to full human. "My power lies with Mother Nature. I am her guardian. She allows me the forms of her children and elemental magic to deal damage. I was blessed by the Primordial Elementals of Earth, Fire, Water, and Air, so I can also assume elemental forms. They cost me mana and have a cooldown, though, so I'm not gonna do those right now. Also, I use a great axe as a weapon."

I equipped Storm Caller from my inventory and threw it at a small tree. It sliced cleanly through it, and then I summoned it back to my hand. It turned into lightning and returned like I was struck on the hand by a bolt of electricity. Then it returned to its normal shape.

Had to admit, among my friends, who were all so amazing at the things they did—it was super nice having someone looking at me in wonder as I showed off some of my abilities and spells.

Like that kid on the block who has the nicest new toy but has no idea how to actually use it? Yeah, that was me.

"I just have my handy-dandy bow and my trusty sidekick Tmont, tail bane," Bokaj said easily. He seemed to be cooling down from his worrying over his best friend. "Balmur, though, is a Rogue who can step through shadows and cast some spells. It's pretty damned brutal, man."

"Wooooah," Muu said in absolute awe. "That's so badass. I can't wait to see what I can do eventually! So when do we start power leveling me up?"

"We will get you trained for a week before we go out and start killing shit, man." Yohsuke held his hands out as if to slow the eager newbie down. "We need you to live through what is coming so you get the experience. Until then? We have you fight some basic shit and work with us."

"Sounds fair," Muu agreed. "So what's the deal with the heavy ass armor you're having made for me?"

"Stats can change from performing things like strength training and the like," James explained. "So it's possible to be much stronger than your level may allow."

"Right on," he said. "Let's see about some food. I'm starving!"

We laughed and headed for the tavern for a good meal and some quality time with alcohol. We had a couple drinks and told Muu about some more of our adventures. Before long, we retired for some sleep.

* * *

The following morning, I had to kick the door to Muu's room open to be sure he was awake. One thing to remember about him is that he's like a cat. He can sleep for more than twelve hours and still wake up exhausted. Never enough sleep for him.

"Wake up, newb!" I ordered boisterously. He groaned and got up. He was still wearing his clothes from yesterday. "We need to get some chow, then head to the market. We're going to get some stuff for you, then get your weapon. We'll do some light training this afternoon before the feast tonight. Bokaj and T are already out there somewhere training somehow, so let's go!"

"Free food?" Muu perked up at the prospect. "I like food. What kind of stuff do we need to get?"

"New clothes—you stank, bitch," Jaken teased as he was walking by. "Potions and all kinds of goodies, man. Wash up and let's go eat."

I showed him the wash basin. "Use this, and we'll be out in the dining room waiting with the food."

We finished our meal quickly and set out to see what we could find. It was just early enough in the morning that the vendors and hawkers were beginning to set up shop. Jaken decided to go check in with Rowland and see how the weapons and armor were coming—maybe give them a hand.

Muu once more looked at the world with wonder and awe. It was nice seeing someone so enthused by something that I seemed to be taking for granted lately.

I sighed at the thought, then remembered that I hadn't introduced someone very precious to me to Muu yet. "Hey, man, come here for a second."

"What's up, bud?" Muu asked. He was starting to master facial expressions, but the look on his face was a mix of oh shit and curiosity.

"Let me introduce you to my familiar and companion, Kayda." I touched the stone on the collar around my neck, and black smoke began to roil out of it.

Muu backed up a couple paces as Kayda in her full glory shrieked in joy at being released. She spread her wings wide and ruffled her feathers.

"WHAT IS THAT?!" Muu shrieked. He stood still for a moment in thought before hesitantly coming forward a single step, but I warded him off with a hand.

"Kayda, my love, this is a man who is very important to me, okay?" I pointed to him, and she regarded him with open curiosity. "He's like Uncle Yohsuke. You can be cool with him. He's going to be with us from now on."

She sent me a mental image of him and *Goblin?*

I tried—and failed—to stifle the laughing fit that I fell into at her question and the implication. "No, dear, he's not a Goblin. He's part Dragon and green. He's family."

Family. He touch? She looked from me to him and quirked her head to the side quizzically. *Pet?*

"She wants you to pet her," I translated, "but be careful, though. She's a Storm Roc. She could shock you or be really cold."

"Okay," he drew out the word as he sidled closer to her. "Hey there, girl. Kayda? Why does your name sound familiar? Name her after..?"

"Yeah, I named her after my son," I explained simply.

"Ah, that's why." He nodded and stuck his hand out toward her. Kayda, excited for a pat from people she could trust, threw her head against his hand. Muu flinched and yelped, "Ah!

You tell me to be easy, and she's just out here going for it. Pretty bird. Polly want a cracker?"

"She could kill you with a lightning bolt," Yohsuke said mildly from behind him. "Hey, bird!"

I hadn't seen him walk up, but Kayda had, and she was ecstatic to see him, especially because he smelled like fresh food. Supporting her running theory that when she saw him, she got to eat his food.

She hopped from where she was in front of Muu and almost knocked him down trying to get to her other uncle.

True to form, Yohsuke reached into his inventory and pulled out a leg of some kind of animal and put it in front of her. She pecked at it furiously, making cooing noises as she ate.

"Thanks for waiting for me while I finished up in the kitchen, fuckers."

"That's your familiar?" Muu whispered to me. "How the hell did you get her? And where do I find one?! Maybe not a bird, though."

"She's the only Storm Roc that I am aware of," I explained sadly. "Yoh and I found her during a quest. Her mother was mortally wounded and the rest of the clutch shattered. It took us a while to get her to hatch—we had to feed her a constant stream of electricity to have it happen before the mom died. She's been with me since. I told you that the other day, man. You forget it already?"

"Dude, new world? Magic, monsters? *Magic!* I could barely stop feeling myself up, let alone listen to every story. Give me some time to adjust, and I'll pay more attention." Muu eyed Kayda softly for a second, an odd look in his eyes. "Lost her mom? Well then, she's gonna be spoiled as shit. Just let me know when she's gonna be around, okay?" Muu spoke with a determined twinkle in his eye. I'd seen that look back home.

Now, I don't know about you, but the prospect of watching this majestic creature of the skies turn into a bird ripe for the Thanksgiving table made me shiver, y'all! I didn't even pay attention to that last bit.

And no—you sicko—not in anticipation. I would definitely be putting her ass on a diet. Gotta stay fit to fight. I was gonna get electrocuted. Damn it.

"Well, let's get you geared up and some stuff you'll need for our training and just general life here," I advised him. I grabbed his shoulder, and we were off.

"What about Kayda?"

"She's fine." I looked back at her, and I could feel her contentment. "She knows where I am and how to find me. Besides, Yohsuke will keep people from touching her uninvited. Last poor bastard who did that can't see her without twitching, she shocked him so bad."

"Remind me not to piss her off." Muu shivered.

"You won't need me to. She will let you know." I chuckled.

We came into the square, the morning light bouncing off trinkets and baubles. There was a small breeze, and people were still setting up. It took a moment, but we found a clothier, the one I had used before. Muu and I both bought clothes in our sizes. I bought enough to last two weeks. It wasn't like I couldn't put it all in my inventory. I kept it basic, though. Black or brown breeches and several colorful shirts. It wasn't expensive at all. I paid two gold with a tip included. Muu did the same with the money he got from his chest with his clothes and other items.

"A gold gets you a lot here," he said offhand when we were away from the happy vendor.

"Yeah, it does. My first weapon without the tip cost me about five gold, if I remember correctly." I waved to some children who had stopped to stare at us. "The people here are honest folk who work hard—they volunteered to take us in. We pay them well. I believe the exchange rate for money is a ten to one. So ten copper to a silver, so on and so forth. The rest of us have plenty of money, though, so your money will be no good for a while for things other than the very basic necessities."

"Thanks, man, I really appreciate it."

I showed him to some of the other vendors. I went over to the jeweler and browsed his wares. The seedy human stared at me hopefully and answered my questions readily. He sold me several gold rings, a gold bracelet, and a couple gold earrings. It cost me fifteen gold altogether. I tested the quality of each item and found them sufficient for the experiments I had in mind.

I took Muu to the potion stand and found the whole family waiting there, setting up.

"We wondered when you would be back, Uncle Zeke!" little Daisy shouted as we approached. "Who's your weird friend?"

"Daisy!" her mother and father reprimanded her hurriedly.

Muu, ever the character at home and in this life, stuck his tongue out at her, crossed his eyes, and made a funny noise while dancing. "I'm not weird, you are!" he teased.

The little blonde girl giggled in delight and rocketed out from behind the stand to play. While she chased Muu and grabbed at his tail, I went to speak to the rest of the family.

"Good morning," I shook the father's hand. "I'm sorry. In all the commotion last night, I learned the family's names but not yours or your surname."

He looked shocked for a moment, but it passed. "Forgive me, I'm Bryn Forrester. Can we interest you in any of our wares?"

"Why yes, yes you can." I grinned at him. "Your potions did me exceedingly well in my time here, and I was wondering if you had anything more powerful at hand?"

"For you?" Nora said with a sweet smile. "We normally sell our stock of these potions with the seller who goes to the cities within a week's journey, but we will happily sell you these ones. We could even take a commission for stronger ones if you would like to wait?"

She pulled a box of potions out from the bottom of the stall; there were thirty of them, small and in what looked like vials with wax sealed corks.

"Each one of these is a health potion of middling quality. The low-quality ones we sold you before heal twenty-five HP." She held a smaller vial up with a reddish-pink liquid inside—the old product. "These ones will heal fifty. We have similar ones of the mana potions, though we only have twenty of them right now."

The new potions looked to be more red and vibrant. The vial was slightly larger, now that I compared the two. The fifty would help, but it was kind of low. Then again, the potions were only to help in a time of actual great need. They were meant to augment healing from me, Jaken, and any ability the others had to replenish health.

"Okay, and what would you have the seller take for these?" I wondered. "After—I'm assuming—he takes his commission."

"We typically get five silvers for every sale of the low quality," she explained. "With the seller, he marks the price of the batch up so that we get close to the actual price of each potion."

"So, if these are twice as good, it would make sense to charge twice as much. So a gold apiece?"

She bit her lip and nodded. Her husband put a hand out to get my attention. "We would never dream of charging you full price again after what you did for us and for this village. We would happily take eight silver."

"No," I said resolutely. They looked mildly distressed, so I continued before they could interject, "What we did was what we would do for anyone taking care of us the way you all do. I will pay full price, and I will buy the lot of both."

Nora looked as if she was about to cry right then and there. She seemed like she was a crier. Bryn, though, seemed stunned.

"And I believe commissions were mentioned?" I asked hopefully. Nora nodded quietly, so I took the opportunity to press on, "What kind of potions could you make?"

"Ah, um. Well, it depends. I could make stronger versions of the health and mana potions given enough time to treat the ingredients and brew them correctly. I could make potions of strength, uh water breathing, resistance—though for a specific kind I need specific ingredients—and I could make other less... savory kinds of brews?"

"Like poisons?" My eyebrows shot up.

She panicked, and her arm began to flutter in my direction. "Don't say it out loud!" She looked around to see if anyone heard. "Reputable alchemists don't typically work with poisons and venoms. Bryn brings me things at times to strengthen my potions that, if used by a lesser alchemist, would kill someone. Over time, I worked out how to combine them in different ways to terrible effect, but I do not enjoy that work."

"Oh, I see. Well, my friends and I might have use for some of your most powerful... detrimental works if you would be able to create them?" I thought a moment, then added, "As well as some of the more powerful potions, and if you experiment and make something interesting, I would love to hear about it."

"Oh, Zekiel, you've made ours a very busy family." Bryn smiled. "Thank you."

I waved the thanks away. "It's all gonna keep me alive a little longer. How much do I owe you? Thirty for the health potions, twenty for the mana potions, and how much for the um, unmentionables?"

"Well, for my strongest stuff, I'd say maybe three gold for three vials? It would take a day or two for us to get them together and in applicators that will keep you from getting hurt while using them."

I dug into my coin pouch, dug out the fifty-three gold and handed it to Nora. Then I palmed another five gold to give them.

"Just in case money. If something gets made, three gold should cover it. The other two gold is a tip for you. This is a beneficial agreement, so please, keep this a secret, okay?"

Bryn shook my hand so hard, I thought he was going to pull my arm off. "Thank you, Zekiel. Thank you so much."

"My friends and family call me Zeke," I corrected him, "and unless I'm mistaken, I'm Uncle Zeke now. But the buying isn't over. Muu! Quit letting that little girl beat the crap out of you and come buy some potions, man."

I looked to find my friend laying on his back with the little girl trying to tickle him. He was squealing and yelling like he was terrified, "Help! She's crazy!"

Kayda called from the sky, her shadow settling above the prone form of Muu. Wisely, Daisy backed off, but Muu wasn't fast enough to escape the bird landing beside him. She pecked at him—gently—because she wanted to play too.

"Zeeeeeeke, the bird!" Muu shrieked. "Oh, god! Get the bird!"

"Get him birdy!" Daisy giggled in delight.

Kayda looked at her and sent me the image of her trying to tickle Muu. *Play?*

"Get him a little bit more, Daisy, don't worry—Kayda will help!" I called to her.

"There goes your Christmas gift, Judas!" Muu shouted. Kayda plunked a clawed foot on to his chest and spread her wings wide in victory. Muu stiffened like a statue. The whole of the square was keen to see what was going on, what with all the noise.

Daisy chose that moment to spring on to him and tickle him with extreme prejudice. After a few minutes of his shrieking and trying to reason with the two, it finally ended when he raised his hands.

"I can't! I give. I give up!" He gasped for air. "You win. I'll never disrespect Daisy again, and I'll feed the birds—BIRD—as often as she demands. Just get her off me!"

Kayda loosed a cry like thunder, and Daisy bolted behind her father. The Storm Roc gazed at the child in concern and hopped forward like a small bird on a branch.

Scared? She looked to me for help. I felt her remorse at scaring her little friend. I sent an image to her and suggested she give it a try. Kayda hopped forward one last time and held out her right clawed foot out closed.

I walked over to stand next to her and knelt down. I motioned for Daisy to come to me. It took some convincing from her father and mother. Finally, her brother Seth took her hand and walked her over.

"Kayda says that she's sorry she scared you." She gazed at the claw in worry. "Hold your hand out, and make a fist.

There you go, like that. Now, bump your fist with her claw. See? Easy! That means that you guys are buddies now."

Kayda ruffled her feathers, looked down at one of her wing feathers, and reached for it. She plucked it with her beak—the azure feather had a vein of cool light blue streaking through it—and offered it to her newest friend. Daisy took it gently and gave Kayda a hug for the gift.

I gave the Roc a gentle shove. "Go hunt. We will play with Muu some more later when we train."

She looked at the Dragon Beast-kin and sent me an image of a mouse shaking in fear. I laughed and shooed her off. She pecked me affectionately, then took to the sky.

"Thank you for getting rid of one of my tormentors," Muu grumbled playfully.

"Oh, don't worry, she'll be back later." He groaned. "Get some potions, and let's get a move on, man!"

"Okay, let's see what you have then?" he asked Nora, and she showed him the lower quality potions. He chose thirty HP potions, and we called it there as I shelled out the necessary funds.

By the time we were finished, the square had returned to normal, and we were on our way.

Hey, Zeke. They finished a little early. Come on over and grab these weapons, Jaken spoke into my head.

"Let's go get your weapons. Jaken just let me know they were ready," I related to Muu.

"How could you possibly know that?" He looked uncertain, then looked around to see if he could find Jaken.

I tapped my ear, and he gasped. "You can really hear that well?!"

Now, I'm usually one to be more playful, and believe me, I wanted to mess with him immensely. Oh, I did. But I let it go. Because I'm capable of being mature with a good sense of duty.

Ahem. Doody.

I had to laugh, "Hahah, no, man. The earring. It lets us speak to each other telepathically up to a mile away from each other."

"Oh, you motherfu–" I punched him lightly in the arm. "Ow!"

"Kids, man." I pointed behind us, and sure enough, there was a procession of about a dozen children trailing us.

He nodded, and we walked on in amicable silence. It wasn't long before we were standing in front of Rowland's forge. It was quieter than normal, but then I heard the shouting inside.

"No!" Craglim bellowed. "Ye'll no' claim victory over me cousin! I made that piece to perfection, that be certain. Ye only had to work the heavy iron for a bit!"

"Ye lost fair and square, and if ye don' like it, leave!" Rowland retorted. "Ye already insulted me friends, and if ye ever lay hands on me apprentice again, I'll wallop ye so bad yer mam won't even know ye!"

"Let's get in here, and mind the blond," I warned as I bolted into the building with Muu close behind.

I walked in to find Jaken holding Rowland by the shoulders and Craglim sporting his warhammer like he was about to swing it.

"The fuck is going on here?" I shouted. Both Dwarves looked at me; Craglim spat on the floor in my direction, then kicked dirt toward Rowland.

"He cheated, and he took an apprentice when there's good Dwarf folk here to take in." Craglim growled at Rowland. "Not tha' ye would know it, but it be only proper to teach a trade to the people best suited. Tha's DWARVES!"

"Fuck righ' off, ye worthless gob!" Rowland's face was near crimson and almost foaming at the mouth. "Leave me forge before yer shite shoddy work ruins me hard fough' business. Ye've lost yer Way, Craglim. Ye los' it, and I will nae help ye back if ye will be like tha'."

"I donnae want yer help if ye cannot help the Dwarves around ye to get ahead in life!" Craglim spat, and this time, it landed on Rowland. The enraged blacksmith fought even harder to escape Jaken's grasp, but the Paladin held fast.

I looked back at Muu. "Step out of the doorway. He's coming through fast." He nodded, and I shifted into my fox form.

I paced slowly around to Craglim's back, then shifted back to my fox-man form. I grabbed the Dwarf by the back of the neck and shifted my weight toward the door, throwing him as hard as I could. The door, door frame and some of the wall went with him, but he was outside.

I didn't stop there. I walked calmly outside and waited as he picked himself up and began to stalk forward. The red I was beginning to see at the edges of my vision informed me that I was starting to let the curse get the best of me once more.

Craglim began to ready his hammer, but I held up a hand. "You swing at me after touching one of my friends and insulting another in his own shop, I won't stop at injuring you. I know Fainne, your God and mine, would be mad I killed you—but I'm willing to bet he wouldn't be happy with you right now."

"Ye dare speak his name!" Craglim looked like he was close to popping a blood vessel. "Ye would hardly qualify fer his time, le' alone be worthy ta say his name!"

"He gifted me with my ability to engrave items with mana, and he also had the leader of the Light Hand Clan gift me with a deeper mana reservoir." I stepped forward. "I met him.

Spoke to him. He supports our cause so that we can protect assholes like you. Rowland said to leave, and I think you should."

The surly Dwarf cursed, picked up his warhammer, and sniffed at all of us. "Bah, I be on me way home, then. Good riddance."

"Looks like I'm going to owe you another new door, Rowland." I took in the damage to the door and smiled, remembering the last little asshole I tossed out of it—but more on that shit stain later.

Muu, Jaken, and I offered a very rude, one-finger salute to the little fucker as he walked off.

"Forgive him," Rowland growled. "He were raised by goats and jus' as hard headed."

"And ugly," Muu added.

Rowland rounded on the Dragon Beast-kin with a smile and a slap on the arm. "You. I *like* you. Bout time they had a proper brain working in the group."

"If Yohsuke heard you say that, he would be hurt, Rowland," I said teasingly.

"Milksop will nae drink me mead!" Rowland grumbled. "Boy has no brain or sense o' taste, I tell ye. Come on in, then. Time ta get yer gear."

We joined him inside, the bright light of the world behind us fading in heat and shade. The forge area was a mess. The anvil was knocked over, tools askew, and a broken hammer laid on the floor in the doorway.

"The hell happened in here?" I threw my hands at the mess. "And I heard something about him laying hands on you, Jaken?"

"He tried." The Fae-Orc grinned. "I *am* a tank, after all. It's my job to take the hate."

"Not the right kind of hate ye be wantin', lad," Rowland muttered. He easily tilted his anvil upright—it clanged back into position noisily. "The rest I can do on me own. In me own way. Here, Muu."

Rowland hoisted one item on to the table in the reception area of his shop. The weapons in here were left untouched. Dark-colored plate armor sat on the counter before us. It had clasps and straps to cinch it together and hold it tight.

"Ye'll be needing a thickly padded shirt to wear that beast," he warned. "Already sent word to the armorers, and they sent me some of their materials and said they'd send what ye need to the tavern for ye. They sent me their heaviest chain mail. I put tha' over a smaller, proper-sized chest piece. Then I fit and placed the outer shell to add to the weight of it. All told, it should weigh a great deal. It be unwieldy, but to train in? Perfect."

He showed Muu how to lift it, which was entertaining. It took ten minutes or so, but he finally got it. He moved around unsteadily for a moment, looked at us and said simply, "You guys are assholes."

"How much does it weigh?" I found it fascinating that this was something that could happen, to be honest.

"Hundred pounds," Muu said simply. "Like carrying a smaller, extra me. I hate it. What's next?"

The shield resembled a window pane. It was square and thick but bubbled out in the front. "Helps deflect blows if there's a bit of an angle to it," explained Rowland. "I made it of a thicker, heavier metal—cheap too as it's too hard for weapons. It be heavy, for certain. Luckily, I had some of this already started a week ago when I go' bored o' drinkin' swill."

Rowland chuckled fondly at the memory, I assumed, and grunted when Jaken coughed once.

"And the weapon?" Muu touched the shield but left it on the table for now.

"That one were a little more difficult," Rowland grumbled.

He went into the back of the shop and retrieved what he sought. He hauled out a large bundle under a sheet. Ah, Rowland and his sheets and unveilings. Gotta hand it to him—he did have a flair for the dramatic.

What he showed us was by far the strangest creation I had ever seen. The bottom of it resembled a two-liter pop bottle, forged to a metal haft connected to a sword with another sword in the center. If you were to set it on a table and looked directly at the tip of it—it would look like an X or a plus sign.

"Best design I could think up. Shite as he is as a person—Craglim forged a damned-fine training tool 'ere. I think ye should use it."

"It's so weird. Getting used to it will take time." Muu groaned.

"We have some of that," I reminded him gently. "That also gives Rowland and Sarah time to actually create an ideal weapon and shield for you."

"We will take your ideas, strengths, and weaknesses and get you well equipped for when we move out, okay?" Jaken put in. "Who knows when that will be. But we will work as hard as we can now, so you're ready in the future."

"Okay," Muu replied. "Let's go get this shit show started. Thanks, Rowland."

"Be sure to let me know how it all works for you!" he called as we were leaving. "Train well!"

Chapter Three

It only took us a bit to get to our training grounds after picking up the padded shirt for the armor. After that, we had Muu un-equip his armor and walk in his normal clothes so as not to waste time today. We wanted him to get used to it first.

Oh, you think I was gonna be all nice and let him take it off and not walk around like a newborn turtle? Well, you sure learned from that didn't you. It was hilarious.

We decided that anywhere he goes after the feast that night, he would wear the armor, and I would try to find some ankle weights too. Trying to train his legs would be a good idea.

We began as soon as we stepped into the clearing. He equipped his new gear once more and could hardly move. With the three items together, he was holding one hundred and seventy pounds on his upper body alone. Luckily, with his strength stat at fifteen, it was more bearable than not. He could make clunky, slow movements with everything.

So we started the training in earnest the same way we had the previous day. Jaken would attack, and Muu would defend. It was hard going. Out of every ten thrusts of Jaken's sword at a slow speed, Muu managed to only parry four. After an hour, it jumped to six. His endurance was good. It was exponentially better than it had been before coming to Brindolla—that was for sure.

Smoking, poor food choices, and other life choices hadn't been kind to the man's endurance at times. The couple visits to the gym had impressed me, but he didn't have the fortitude necessary to keep his body going the way I did. Exertion left him breathless, tired, and irritable.

We broke for water and to check on him. "You know, I think I know what I want to do with this class."

"Yeah?" I looked at him oddly. It took me to level 10 to figure out what I *truly* wanted out of my class. And I was still trying to figure it out.

"I want to be like a dragoon." He grinned at me. I'd seen this look before. "With all this weight training, think about how high I could jump!"

Dragoons, to us, are knights who are trained specifically to fight and kill Dragons. They usually wield some kind of spear or lance and, in a lot of games, jump insanely high to attack their enemies. They use the weight of their momentum and gravity to drive their piercing weapons into their foes from an advantageous position.

I'd be lying if I didn't think that was the baddest idea. In a good way.

"That does sound pretty sweet," Jaken admitted, "but I thought you wanted to help me tank?"

"I do. And I will, but the more I learn about what you guys do, the more I realize that I can do both if needed." Muu's sheepish grin gave way to the near-fanatic gleam in his eyes. "I think if a spell caster can make a greataxe work for him, I can help tank when needed. Right?"

"Yeah. You know we will have to increase the weight and have you practice jumping for that," I warned.

"Yeah!" Muu was excited now. I could hear his tail thumping the ground. "I can pour my stats into strength, dexterity, and constitution—I can jump higher and faster if those are beefier—and then take the fight to the enemy that way! Oh, but what about magic?"

"Dude, don't worry about magic." I waved the question away. "We have that covered and smothered. And besides, 150

MP as a Fighter? That's a lot, but we don't have a trainer for you right now. Besides, I can enchant things for you, and we can get you some good gear. Focus on what you want to do with your class, and let us take some of the pressure, okay?"

"Cool, man, cool." He looked around a bit. "So, this time while we are training, I want to try moving in this—full gear. Could you explain a little bit about what I can expect when leveling up?"

"Sure, man. You got it." I stood and helped pull him to his feet.

While he and Jaken paced around the clearing trading blows—Jaken raining them down and Muu attempting to block them—I spoke.

"Each level, you as a traveler receive five attribute points to spend as you see fit. Beginning at fifth level, you receive weapon proficiency points, specifically one per level. Now—move a little quicker next time, fucker, he almost got you—these points you can use to gain proficiency with a weapon. One point gets you the first tier of proficiency, two points the next. Sometimes, you will pick one weapon, like I did with the axe, and it will unlock the next kind of weapon, like the great axe."

Muu, slightly distracted, took a jab to the hip, and his health dropped by fifty percent. I cast Regrowth, and his HP began to refill. Jaken touched him, and his health replenished fully.

"Jesus, man, don't pull any punches on his account," I teased Jaken, who promptly flipped me the bird.

"So if I've got this straight," Muu panted and tried to wipe his brow, "I can be good at using any number of weapons?"

"Sure can," I answered, but I saw the skeptical look on his face and couldn't be prouder. "There's a drawback. Once you unlock a weapon tree, you can use those points to learn skills and abilities that someone using that weapon can learn. I have a few that I use all the time. They can be funky at times on cooldowns but completely worthwhile."

"That makes sense. So it would be a good idea to be proficient with one, maybe two weapons, then gather skills with those?" He tried to jab at Jaken with his weapon, but Muu just wasn't strong enough to move quickly just yet.

"It's a solid plan," Jaken advised. "I chose the sword and shield because I'm the tank and healer. With you though, all you need to worry about is parrying and fucking shit up. Just because you started with these weapons doesn't mean you have to stay with them once you hit five."

"Exactly right." I nodded. "Now, I want you to go ahead and jog ten laps around the clearing while I go cut some logs down for added flavor. Let's make this training our bitch."

As Jaken chased our newest member around, I went off to do what I said. Instead of risking Storm Caller, I brought out my blood axe. This weapon had seen me through some good fights. The massive head of it a foot and a half from point to point with a bladed pick on the opposite side and dark red wood along the haft with rigid metal strips to block attacks.

I found a few trees and began to chop them down. I activated Cleave, and my axe sailed clean through the tree on the first chop. I cut it into a more manageable size for me to drag back and began to do so. Then I thought better of it and just finished cutting the tree's trunk down into large pieces.

"Muu!" I shouted in a sing-song tone. "Oh, Muuuu!" Jaken and the requested party joined me a few moments later.

"Be a dear and drag back your knew training supplies?" I fluttered my eyelashes at him enticingly.

"You carry them back your own goddamn self, you fuck." He slid back with the same eye movement.

"No, seriously, we're gonna drag them back with rope. It's only, like, a three-minute walk from here," I said, waving his next set of quips away before they could start.

I pulled out a length of rope and tied it around the middle of the log for him to pull, then offered it to him. It took us a little less than half an hour to finish.

Because *someone* wanted to whine and complain about having to drag heavy things in their full battle rattle. It was heavy. Ha! You bet your ass it was.

Once we finished, we rested again, and I got started cutting a small enough chunk of wood for him to safely leap on to.

By the end of our training session that day, Muu had gained two points of strength and constitution and one point in dexterity.

At the feast that night, we ate, we danced, drank, and just basked in the unity of the village. Sarah even gave me a kiss on the cheek for helping bring everyone back. This caused Rowland to start in with more booze, singing and trying to get me to date his wee girly. We had a blast.

After that, the village began to plan a build for its new outer wall with wood that would be replaced with stone as soon as a good mason could be found. As they plotted to build, so did we. We would build our Fighter's confidence and skill as well as his attributes.

We had him running, jumping, carrying and dragging logs, and even fighting each of us by the end of the week. On our final day of training, he had gained another three points to strength, four to constitution, and six to dexterity. In our time training at the monastery with the monks who had trained James, we had each gained a few points to a few of our stats here and there, but his progress was insane.

In our fights, he could move his weapon swiftly and to the point that he could hit you in a given area from different angles—while parrying different attacks. He still got hit but not as much.

We had kept Rowland abreast of developments with his training and things Muu had in mind concerning his equipment. The Dwarf had been hard at work on his latest projects and seemed pleased with the results. He was putting the finishing touches on them on the final day of Muu's training, so we let him work and went to the tavern for the evening.

"Well, man," Jaken handed Muu a mug of ale, "how do you feel? You want to go out and start hunting with us?"

"Oh, uh, DUH?!" He spread his hands wide. "I've been getting my ass kicked nonstop. I wanna level up and help you guys get Balmur back. And kick some War ass!"

"Woah, there, lil fella." Yohsuke clapped the table. "You gotta walk before you fly. Okay?"

We all laughed.

"Hey, why don't we go try to find a trainer for you and Bokaj?" Jaken suggested. "That way, we know you aren't missing out on anything, and Bokaj gets the training he needs too."

"Yeah!" I took a swig of my water, then continued, "We can hunt on the way there if the area has monsters, and then we can branch out and try and get stronger too."

"And once he's up near our level, we can go and fuck up something big and get to where we need to be for our trip to the Hells?" Bokaj finished for us, his tone brooding still but better now that we had a more tangible time to leave. "We can go and get Balmur back."

The rest of us nodded. Bokaj had come a long way from the angry person he had been initially when Balmur had first disappeared. Still, everything he had done had served the purpose of driving us all forward. At least, when we saw him. He went training every chance he got, and when he was with us, he was driving Muu to push himself harder.

Bokaj looked at Muu. "If you slow us down, man..." He shook his head and seemed to think better of the statement or threat, as all of us turned our gazes on him. "Just be sure to keep up and do what we tell you."

"Hey, Willem?" I called to the bar-tending Paladin as I watched our Ranger. "Do you know where the Fighter trainer went and where we can find a Bard trainer?"

Willem looked confused a moment, then thoughtful—his eyebrows twitched a bit—and finally, he looked back up and spoke, "I think he lived in a city as a quartermaster for an army up north on the opposite side of the Lightning Mountains. Bard trainer?" We eyed him steadily, pointed to Bokaj, and he nodded his understanding "The city, I forget the name, is a larger one, so I imagine you could find a Bard there somewhere."

"Thank you!" we shouted. The patrons around the room eyed us curiously but knew we could be raucous, so they let us be.

The rest of our meal, we finalized our plans. Since we were the only two who had ever been there, Yohsuke and I would lead the way. Once we got to the mountain range, though, we were going to have to figure out what the hell to do. I could scout, sure, but that was risky outside of a forest as an owl.

Willem had said opposite side, but that didn't necessarily mean that we would be just going in a straight line.

"Well, once we get to a high point, can't we just look for the city?" Muu suggested.

"We can, yeah." I responded after some thought. "Push comes to shove, I can always teleport us back."

"You can TELEPORT?!" he hissed at me.

"Sure can. Anywhere I've been within five hundred miles," I smiled, "and before you suggest teleporting there, it's a big drain on my mana, and I don't want to have to deal with that cooldown. Also, this gives us a chance to get you some experience."

"That's fair, but *teleportation,* Zeke." He grabbed my arm and repeated the word in a creepy whisper, "Teleportation."

"Yup. That's what it is, man." I just shook my head. "Come on. Let's catch some z's. Big day ahead tomorrow. Also, let's go and grab you a mount tomorrow too."

"A mount?!" Muu shrieked. "I GET A MOUNT?!"

"Yo, I need one of those too!" James said as the rest of us walked back to our rooms.

* * *

We grabbed some more basic supplies for Muu on our way to the forge, just to be safe. Yohsuke promised to meet us at the stable when we sent him word. He was procuring travel food for us while Bokaj went to see if there was anything to be found in the square we may need. I also had him go check in with Nora to see if she had anything for me.

Once we arrived at Rowland's forge, Muu shoved through us and bolted through the door, shouting, "Where's that big baby with the hammer. SHIT!" *Clang. Clack.*

"Hold still, ye lit'le scaly shite. I'll only be whackin' ye the once today!" Rowland roared.

This was a new game that Muu had begun playing with the smith. He would walk in, say something completely fucked, and do his best to dodge his angry pursuer until we walked in. Today, we let Rowland take a few minutes.

"Ahhhh!" Muu screamed. "That was my tail, you fuzzy prick!"

"Let's get in there," Jaken snorted and walked through the door, "before Rowland actually beats the shit out of him."

Inside, Rowland had a struggling Muu by the arm and was about to wallop him with his favorite hammer. "Morning, the lo' o' ye!" He let go of Muu and turned our way.

"Took you guys long enough," Muu grumbled as he stood and brushed himself off.

"You know," I stepped leaned back against the door, "we could always go back outside. What do you think, Rowland?"

Taking the hint, Rowland grinned and snatched up his hammer. "Oh, aye, lad! I'll take another moment or two with this lit'le scaled heathen. Show him the Way proper, I will."

Those of us who knew Rowland well laughed—Muu groaned.

"Let's see what you made, man." I grinned after I finished catching my breath.

Watching him show us his goodies was always nice. Don't take that the wrong way. Too late? Okay. Moving on.

"Aye, I could do tha'. Come." Rowland patted Muu's shoulder affectionately. "Let me show ye what I did for ye."

Rowland pulled three bundles from beneath his countertop and set them gently on the wood. He pulled the largest bundle forward and took the cloth away.

Dark steel plate attached to chain links and a pair of plate leg pieces attached to leather leggings. The links were dyed green as close to his scale color as possible and linked together over a thin, leather, padded shirt.

"Leather will keep it from hittin' yer scales and making too much noise, though it'll still make noise," Rowland advised.

Next, he bared the shield. An interesting piece, as it was significantly smaller than the large one Muu had been using. It was also dark steel, oval in shape, and angled a lot more than the bubble shield before. There was also a slit in the front about an inch thick and as wide as the rim of the shield. There was a lever on the handle with a gap large enough for his fingers and a strap for his forearm.

"Put that on, lad," Rowland told the new owner. "Aye, strap it there. Point it away from us all, and pull that lever with yer fingers."

With a *schink*, a wide blade thrust from the slit I had seen before. From the tip to the shield, it was a foot long. It had a wide base and came down to a squared, sharp-pointed tip.

"Just as ye had requested, lad." Rowland grinned. "Took all me smithin' know-how. Even gave me a level to make it. The spear was fun, but I couldn't think o' how to make the same mechanism stick, so I went old-fashioned and wicked for ye. Hopin' ye like it."

"I'm sure I will, bud." Muu smiled and rubbed his hands together, the leather of the handle rubbing against the now-forming calluses there.

Rowland pulled the final sheet away, and I heard Muu gasp. He picked the weapon up and began to thrust it and swing it in practiced motions.

The spear tip—if it could be called that—wrapped around the shaft of the weapon for a good eight inches. Three wicked-looking ridges twisted into a triangular tip—there would be no slashing with this weapon, but it was beautiful. The whole thing was made of the same dark steel as the plate mail and the shield. There was a small, thick piece at the end of the weapon opposite the tip that was eight inches and almost bell-shaped with a curve and flat surface. With the tip and that bell thing at the end, the weapon was roughly four and a half feet long.

"This here be a good weapon. Solid made and hard fought, I tell ye." Rowland touched the piercing end of the weapon appreciatively. "This'll bleed a foe for quite some time, and with a twitch of the wrist, ye can have it out of 'em before a pint is gone in a good Dwarf's hands—I swear it."

"What's the thing at the end there, Rowland?" The way it moved made me think it was a blunt portion to strike with, but I could be wrong. Wouldn't be the first time.

"Counterbalance." He grunted as he watched Muu continue to flail it. "Weighs roughly as much as the tip of the weapon. If it be too top heavy, inaccurate to throw or thrust properly. Inefficient. I'll nae have that. If it were a traditional spear, the shaft would be wooden and the tip light—there's no need for a counterbalance when the shaft weighs as much as the actual weapon."

"Oh." I frowned appreciatively at the information and looked at the weapon in a new light.

"That, and ye can whack a noggin or two with it!" Rowland growled playfully and made a motion with his hammer like someone's head was beneath him.

"Atta boy, Rowland." Muu offered his knuckles to the Dwarf, and they bumped fists. "Let's get geared up and get going! I'm excited to use this stuff."

"Are ye headed out?" Rowland inquired. "If ye find any more ore or if ye meet a salesman in yer travels, get some ore or ingots, and I'll whip up some better gear. Me stock is running low. Unless you want to make a trip to Djurn Forge for me?"

I thought about that for a moment, but with how badly we needed to be moving on this—needed Muu stronger faster so that we could take off after Balmur, it wasn't feasible at the moment.

Sure. I could teleport there, theoretically speaking, but that would be something else to do other than go get our friend and kick some of War's minions' and generals' collective asses.

"If we get some time later, I just may." I bumped his fist with my own. "We need to get this guy in fighting shape, then ourselves a little higher so we can go and rescue Balmur. But if we do find any, I'll keep you in mind for certain."

A dark look passed over Rowland's face, and his eyes pierced mine. "Ye work hard, lad, all of ye. Best not to leave a living soul in the Hells for long. You bring me good materials, I'll hammer you what you need. Or you get it from the grandmasters in Djurn Forge. Ye mark me, I will help ye and yers how I can. On me Way, I swear tha' oath."

Muu, Jaken, James, and I looked at Rowland, and the gravity of his statement hit us all heavily. "We swear that we will do all that we can to get him back. You have our oath, and so does he."

Rowland nodded and looked us all over. He offered us all a solemn hug and pat on the back before we left. I tried to pay for Muu's weapons, but he wouldn't let me. Muu already had, and he wouldn't divulge how much it had been to make them.

We left with our thanks and told him we would stop back on our return. After Muu was sporting his new gear, we headed for our next destination.

On our way to the stable now, guys, I sent telepathically to Bokaj and Yohsuke.

I'm there waiting. Nora had some vials for you and specific instructions, Bokaj returned. *Yoh just got here too. He said to beat feet, puto.*

I laughed and explained it to the others. We moved as quickly as we could through the village without making people think there was trouble. When we arrived at the stable, a small stone home with an open barn on the left-hand side of it, Yohsuke and Bokaj greeted us. Yohsuke had already bought James his mount whistle, and I paid for Muu's. We paid full price this time as he had only one left after this.

As we had last time, the two of them blew into their whistles. A dense fog began to billow from James's whistle, a breeze blew his pant legs around wildly, and a monster rose from the ether in front of him. It looked like a Chinese Dragon, long, snake-like, floating body with a Dragon-like head. James reached up toward it, and a loud, bass rumble crept out of the creature's throat. James pulled his hand back slowly as he closed his eyes. With a few breaths, he began to glow with golden-white light that the creature seemed to find enticing. It wrapped itself around his feet, the large body coiling up to his chest, and it began to try and look into his closed eyes. The monk opened his eyes and smiled at the creature before offering his hand once more. It headbutted his hand and rubbed itself into his palm.

"Oh my god, that's what his does?" Muu whispered in shock.

"Blow it, and let's see what answers the call, man," Yohsuke urged.

Muu put the little whistle to his lips and blew for all he was worth. His shadow moved and rustled on the ground, then grew larger and larger. It grew until it was large enough to swallow almost all of us. I could see motion in it but couldn't make anything out until a snout burst from the dark pit. A black dire wolf that would have given my Ursolon form a run for its money hopped out of the inky pool and began to scent the air. It turned its glowing red eyes at Muu and bared its teeth—fangs that looked so sharp they could rend flesh were just inches away. A little drool fell from its gums and hit the ground, and the grass turned brown and gray almost instantly.

With a slight gasp and no regard for his own safety, Muu just stood there staring, until the one word he had been mouthing seemed to find purchase in his throat, "PUPPY!"

The dire wolf looked surprised and barked once when his summoner lunged forward with arms spread wide. The wolf tried to rear back, but Muu was surprisingly too fast. He had his hands clasped in a hug behind the wolf's neck and was scratching, petting, patting, and making baby noises at the poor beast.

"Who's a furry baby? You are, yes you are. I'm gonna love you and kiss you and call you Snugglebutt," Muu murmured into the beast's fur.

So, a note about Muu, as someone who is close to him. The dude is crazy about animals. He loves dogs, and he *hates* being told what to name things. He likes to play. So yeah, he's crazy. And I apologize for the hell that you, this poor creature, and the rest of us have to endure.

We hope he calms down—no promises though.

I cast Nature's Voice. "Hello, friend?" The dire wolf looked at me. "You seem a bit confused and uncomfortable. Can I help?"

"This is a strange place. Why does the lizard grab me so?" it whined. "I know not what a 'Snugglebutt' is, but it is not me. I am Nolorn, the Plague Wolf. I am a hunter. I do not... snuggle."

Muu looked rapt as the animal and I conversed, and I smacked him. "Let him go."

"What did he say?" Muu still had his death grip on the poor creature.

"He says his name is Nolorn," I translated. "He's a hunter, a Plague Wolf, and if he has to let the village idiot ride him with a stupid name, it's going to insult his honor. Now, let go!"

Hesitantly, the Fighter complied, and Nolorn shook his massive body. "Thank you. What kind of mind-addled lizard is this? Why am I here?"

"Well, he's my mount, and I say his name is Snugglebutt!" Muu reaffirmed. "And he will love me!"

The wolf grew more concerned, eyes shifting between me and Muu.

"You will treat him with dignity—and he can refuse to be your mount." Nolorn seemed to gather the gist of what was exchanged, but I still translated it.

"If I agree to let him call me this thing, will he stop trying to kill me?" Nolorn bared his teeth, and his tail dipped between his legs. "If I refuse to do this, that means another of my pack could be summoned, and I do not wish that."

"Look, Nolorn, he likes you," I tried to show him someone was willing to hear him out, "a lot more than perhaps he should. He's a really good guy. If you get to know him, you may not even mind the weird name. Give it a shot, okay?"

Nolorn seemed to puzzle over it for a moment, so I decided to sweeten the deal. "If you'll try to be his friend, I promise to translate for you if you have something you wish to say to him."

The Plague Wolf's large tail thumped against the air, and his teeth flashed again. "I find this agreeable. I will assist how I can."

"He's agreed to let you ride him, and he will try to be your friend." I paused a moment. "You can even continue with the funny name—but you have to show him respect. He is a proud hunter, and he could eat you."

Muu, deadpan and serious for the first time since he got here without a weapon in hand, looked at me, and I thought he was finally beginning to understand. Then softly, so as not to disturb the creature still in his arms, he said, "I deny your reality and substitute my own."

See? What did I tell you?!

Then he went back to petting the huge beast muttering, "Puuuuuppyyyyyy," as if it were a mantra. I couldn't tell if Nolorn was going to tear his head off or run away.

I cleared my throat and caught Muu's eyes with my own.

The near-homicidal look I fixed him with must have been enough for him to realize that the fun needed to end because he let go and patted the wolf on the head. "Come on, Frumpy-foot. Let's get out of here."

The Plague Wolf looked askance of me, and I simply shrugged. Who knew what was on his mind. We saddled the new mounts, and they allowed their riders on to their backs with little to no issue. I summoned Thor and bowed to him in greeting. He let me know that he would be happy to have me ride, and we were on our way.

We took our time on the way through the trees and foliage, letting Kayda fly and scout ahead from the sky. She didn't see much of interest, and the animals were smart enough to stay away from so many creatures who could be predatory. It also didn't help that I wouldn't call any of them to their deaths just to try and get some experience. Just because I could talk to the animals here didn't mean I wanted them to come to any harm.

No. We would turn our sights on things that deserved killing. War's people and anyone who stood in our way of getting Balmur back.

At the base of the mountain range, we dismissed our mounts, had a light lunch, and began to ascend the rocky terrain. We did so quietly for the most part. Bokaj would point out portions of rocky outcroppings that were unsafe and trails that were cold. The last time we, Yohsuke and I, had visited these mountains, we had been lucky to avoid these things, but now? It seemed like we were destined to have a little rougher of a climb coming our way.

Thinking back to that quest, the one that had brought Kayda into my life, made me realize what was here.

"Hey, guys," I said quietly. "Remember to keep an eye out for Goblins. There was a raiding party here that attacked Kayda's mom. Speaking of which, Kayda?" I felt her attention turn toward me from her new-found perch on a large boulder a dozen yards to our right. "Go fly for a bit, baby. Let us know if you see anything."

"Jesus, fuck!" Muu jumped when Kayda dipped close to the group and lifted into the air. "Warn me next time you let my personal nightmare out of the bag, okay?"

"What are you talking about, man?" Yohsuke smacked him lightly. "She wouldn't hurt you. She's family."

I thought back to his interactions with her before. The hesitancy. The screaming. Her likening him to a scared, shaking mouse. He hadn't truly been playing in the square when she came into the picture—he'd been afraid and had likely tried to suck it up to make sure Daisy would be okay. That Kayda wouldn't be seen as a monster.

"I don't know why, but I've always been afraid of birds," the green Dragon Beast-kin spoke with a shiver along his back that made his tail sway. "I don't know if it was from a movie I saw or the weird way that they can be cool one minute then flipping the fuck out the next—I don't know. But I hate them."

Muu saw the look of hurt on my face, and the rest of the party began to look at him oddly too. "Look, I'm not saying that I hate Kayda. I'm sure she's cool. She has been since I met her, but it's going to take work for me to get over this fear, man. I mean no offense."

"Right on, I get that," I said after a moment. I could understand. Hell, I knew people who had an unreasonable fear of all kinds of things. And Kayda was a big-ass bird. "I feel like shit for never having noticed before. But yeah, don't worry, man, I'll let you know when I bring Kayda around next time. If it helps, she does think you're interesting."

"Well, tell her I said, 'I know,' and let's get moving." Muu tried to smile, but I could tell he was a little shaken.

We left it at that and moved ever northward. Late that afternoon, we found a small cave to sleep in that night and keep us out of the wind. There weren't any tracks to be seen, animal or otherwise, so we assumed it was safe. The temperature dropped in the cave a bit, chilling us a little. Not that Bokaj gave a damn. The Ice Elf race meant he could be outside naked in a snowstorm and be comfortable.

The rest of us slept easily that night. Yohsuke and Bokaj took two of the four-hour watches since their Elven blood meant they only needed four hours in a trance-like state as a full rest. The plan for the following evening was for one of them to sit up with Muu and get him used to the watch rotation.

The next day, we climbed even higher. The plateau where we had found Kayda was looming closer. She hadn't gone toward it due to trying to keep an eye out for us, but she had thought about it.

She knew what I knew about the area thanks to my memories, and those memories weighed on her mind, filling her with a sense of both dread but determination as well. The weight of the emotion on her chest fell on mine as well, and it made it harder to breathe at times, but she deserved to know where she had come from, to see her former home outside of a memory tainted by the stress of trying to save her life.

After a couple hours of walking, we found it. It was just as I remembered, flat with rocky, glass-like protrusions from all the lightning striking the sand and stone in the area.

What I saw that was new were the huts that had been erected and now stood around the large stone walls of the perch the Lightning Roc had used as a nest. There must have been a dozen or so huts—I couldn't tell for certain due to our low vantage point and the large former shelter of the Lightning Roc. They appeared to be erected from wood and some scavenged branches from the trees below in the forest, tied together at the top by rough-spun rope, then held in place by stakes beaten into the rock somehow like it could be packed up and moved. Weird.

"Fuck, those things weren't here last time," Yohsuke spoke. His voice startled me, and I almost slipped on some loose gravel. Luckily, Jaken caught me, and only a little loose rock fell. The clattering was most likely lost in the wind, but it was good that he had caught me.

"Do we move on," James was looking as best as he could, but I doubted he could see anything, "or do we investigate?"

"I'll go owl and see what I can see." I stood back a bit and looked to my friends. "If it's Goblins, there could be some good experience here for Muu."

I looked to the sky and sent an order to Kayda to stay high up. There was no telling what was here, and with her HP, she wasn't the ideal scout for this. She understood, but her attention was all over the place.

"Bokaj—you help me cover Zeke," Yohsuke ordered quietly. "James, you got Muu. Both of you mind our six. No telling what is around here. Jaken, you got the swivel. Anything moves on our flanks, speak up."

Everyone but Muu nodded and went about what they could. Bokaj equipped his bow, and Yohsuke kept his eyes on a swivel for any signs of movement or hostility from the huts ahead.

Jaken turned his back and ducked down to watch the path we had used to climb up, and James took Muu by the arm and sat him down.

I lowered myself from our position and walked back down a ways before I jumped from the ledge and shifted mid-fall. My owl form came easily, and I glided down until I felt a wind thermal catch my feathers and lift me with a few beats of my silent wings.

As I came to an easy hundred feet above the little village, I could see that there were indeed more huts behind the large rock structure, but as I mounted the structure itself, I sensed no signs of life. No signs of a struggle. No heartbeats, no noises other than wind. I could smell that something disgusting had lived here, but the scent wasn't as fresh as I was expecting.

I dug up a bit more courage, then coasted down on the side of the stone structure that my friends could see, and landed on the ground. The huts had cloth doors of some heavy material, like horse blankets or winter blankets. I peeked into one of the open ones and saw more blankets on the ground and little odd baubles and trinkets of little value here and there. Still—no life, signs that life had been here sure.

I poked around a bit longer and kept finding much of the same.

I shifted back and waved for the rest of the group to join me. Jaken brought up the rear, while Yohsuke and James took the lead. Bokaj took the middle with his bow still at the ready with an arrow nocked, and Muu walked beside him.

"No signs of life," I explained. "Bokaj, you want to try and find a trail?"

"Honestly?" he asked quietly as he had Tmont sift through a hut. She came out and hissed at the whole thing. "Not really. Whatever this place belonged to isn't our concern since they aren't here. Whatever it was though, T hates them pretty fucking bad. We should probably move on."

"You think this wood is from the forest down there?" I asked as I stared at one of the huts.

He tapped the wood and examined it before shaking his head. "Nope. It's not dense enough. It'll stand the wind thanks to the stakes, but it's meant to be mobile I think."

"Don't you think it's a little odd, this whole place is a ghost town?" Yohsuke interjected. "No obvious signs of a struggle, no blood, no easy trail—just gone. That should freak all of us the fuck out. I mean, I ain't a bitch, but this has me a little nervous."

I nodded, the hair on the back of my neck and arms rose a bit. I didn't know if a Kitsune could get goose bumps, but it sure as hell felt like it.

"I'm usually one to suggest we have all our facts straight," Muu began. "So let's get out of here, right? I'd rather not see what respawning is like in this game."

We all looked at him for a moment, then it hit us—we hadn't told him that we weren't sure if we would come back.

Not it, said Bokaj mentally as he turned his back and began to move cautiously north.

Same. James patted Muu on the shoulder as he walked by.

Should probably be you and Jaken, Zeke, Yohsuke told us and began to follow the other two.

Jaken and I nodded to each other and looked at Muu, who seemed to be gathering that something was wrong.

"We need to talk, man," I said gently. "Come on. Let's walk."

"I'll watch our backs, Zeke. You go this first bit." Jaken fell back a few paces and began to look around.

"There are no guarantees that if we fall here, we come back," I explained. "The Gods say that they may be able to do something for us—but it's just talk until we know for sure. They say that if they can't bring us back here, they may be able to see our consciousness back to our world. Again—no promises. They don't know. So, while this world—this universe—is based on our video games and tabletop games, it's no game. We could die here. Forever."

"I have a spell that will bring someone back from the dead, but it only works up to three minutes after death, takes all my mana and a hundred HP, and it takes a full day to recharge," Jaken interjected from behind us. "Between all of us, we can keep you alive, but that's the skinny of it. So, try not to die."

"Fuck." The gravity of what he had just heard seemed heavy. His shoulders had drooped, and he trudged forward slowly, head hung low and his eyes half-lidded. "We could all die. I could never see my mom again. Some of my other friends—my family? There's no guarantee."

I pulled Muu into a side hug and spoke as gently and encouragingly as I could, "That's why the Gods here chose us. They knew we would fight tooth and nail for each other. None of us are going to let you die. Just like we know that you will do everything you can to save one of us."

He picked his head up and began to stride forward a little easier after hearing that. "That's why you've all been hard on me to train like you have?"

I nodded, and Jaken spoke for both of us, "The Gods sent you here to help us, and you will, but we need to be sure that the time we invest in you and ourselves is well spent. It's to help us get into the Hells and get Balmur back. Then we turn our sights on War's people. We've gotta stop them, man, or they'll come for Earth, and all our struggles here go to shit. You gotta be ready."

He stopped and stared at the ground a moment longer before looking back at us. "I'm glad you guys know all this. Let's get this shit over with and go get Balmur back."

"Attaboy!" Jaken fist bumped Muu, and they began to walk off ahead.

I sent a mental message to Kayda that it was okay for her to go and mourn her mother's loss now. Her appreciation and trepidation hit me together, and I had to stop to fight the dizziness that came with those emotions. I closed our bond a little, like turning a water nozzle down and watching a torrent become a trickle. I watched her physically dive from the cloud cover and descend on the structure. With it being abandoned, I wasn't worried for her safety.

I worried for her heart.

Chapter Four

We stopped about a twenty-minute hike from the site of the abandoned village and the Lightning Roc nest to rest and plan. Whatever had stayed there had been more intelligent than Goblins. Could they have been nomads?

"You know if there is an area with that many huts and hovels that there's likely a large group of potential enemies roaming around here," Muu spoke the thoughts we all had. "Do you guys have anything that could do well in a group fight?"

A few of us chuckled, I answered, "Well, take a seat, man. A few of us can put a collective hurt on a *lot* of people. I think between myself, Yohsuke, and Bokaj, we have enough AoE damage to need a really big stick to shake at it. Nah mean?"

He grinned. "Good. Because we're gonna need it. I can feel it."

"Oh?" Jaken raised his eyebrows. "You feelin' it now?"

Muu nodded, and we all laughed a bit more. Yohsuke threw a rock at him half-heartedly. "Feel that, puto?"

I had to admit, the thrill of a potential fight was enticing. I had been itching to stretch my muscles once more in a good fight, but the fact that Muu of all people was telling us he felt a fight coming was a bit unsettling.

"Let's get serious, damn it." Bokaj was busy checking the arrows in the quiver on his hip.

Yohsuke shook his head in exasperation. "Let's gear up for this shit then. I'm gonna throw Star Burst into my Ring of Storing. What about you guys?"

"Well, I can throw mana into my ring." Jaken focused on his ring for a moment, and the ring began to pulse steadily with blue light, then stopped. Jaken held his head a bit from the effort, so I cast Regrowth on him to help. He smiled in appreciation at me.

"I'm gonna go ahead and cast Star Fall into mine," I informed the others. "Let's take some prep time and get you some more enchanted arrows, Bokaj?"

"Wait," Muu said, throwing his hands out as if to halt the conversation. "You mean you can enchant shit and you haven't given me some sweet-ass power-ups?!" He looked at me as if I had stabbed him with his favorite knife. "You betray me, sir."

"Dude, you've literally never asked." I held my hands out to my sides in a display of openness.

His eyes narrowed at me dangerously, and it made me smile wider.

I couldn't help teasing him, "Look, I can't get you one of the earrings that I have because it's outside what I can do for my level, but there are things I can do. And again, you never asked. I didn't want to shove your nose in it."

"IF I COULD MAKE MAGIC HAPPEN, YOU WOULDN'T HAVE TO!" he whispered vehemently. He seemed to be getting that stakes were higher here, so volume could be an issue. I had to admit—I was proud.

"You'd never shut the fuck up," I said with a grin. "Let me take care of Bokaj and our weaponry first—then I'll work on your shit. Cool?"

"If it's amazing? Sure. Fucker." He huffed and sat down next to me. "I'm watching *all* of this fuckery."

"Whatever, dude." I chuckled and made a gimme motion at Bokaj. He forked over five more mithral arrows, and I got to work.

I'd done this process before, making arrows of storing. The concept was about the same as a Ring of Storing—the spell is stored into the metal portion of the arrow until impact releases it. The impact acts the same as the intent and focus needed to activate a spell stored in a ring. I copied the ring on my finger almost exactly line for line but included a pentagram that was almost closed. I put the spell I wanted inside, then sealed it with the necessary mana.

After half an hour of focus and explanation to Muu after each arrow was complete, I handed Bokaj three Arrows of Fireball, one Arrow of Star Fall, and an Arrow of Mass Regrowth. The last one I wasn't too sure about how it would work. I know for me, it allowed me to heal up to so many creatures around me for a bit and gave a decent amount of regeneration. It was an experimental one. I *hoped* that it would work the same as the spell—you cast it, and any ally in the sixty-foot radius is healed.

But experiments can fail at times too. Here's hoping we didn't need it. The enchanting had gone smoothly too. Much more so that it had initially—maybe I was getting the hang of it? Maybe the Celestial blood rite was affecting that kind of magical skill as well. We would see over time.

The spells left the arrows looking all the same, so to tell the difference, Bokaj painted the shafts with a little paint he had from his woodworking kit. The Fireballs were red, duh, Star Fall black, and Mass Regrowth was yellow. Easy enough to tell apart, but he said he would pack them at the back of his quiver on his hip so he could actually know for certain where they were.

I looked at Muu critically—he *had* been respectful and let me work until I finished each arrow, then he asked his questions.

"What are you thinking enchantment-wise?" I asked with a friendly sigh.

"Well, what kind of enchantments can you do?" he wondered. His hand had wondered to his chin, the little scale-goatee scritching with his clawed-fingertips moving through them.

"Take everything you know about enchanting in other games," he looked excited as I spoke, "and toss it into the fire." He actually groaned at that. "On Brindolla, what counts when enchanting is intent, focus, engraving, and mana. Inside those four things, my ability to enchant is pretty unlimited. Granted, I'm not the most powerful enchanter—not even close—but what I can do is helpful."

"Right on," he said with a nod. He closed his eyes for a moment. "Okay, can you give my weapon elemental damage? Make it so I can jump higher? How about a defense boost to my shield? Oh! Or maybe a dampener?"

"Woah!" I waved in front of him. "Pump the brakes, man. What was that last thing you said?"

"Dampener?" I motioned for him to continue with the idea. "Oh, yeah. So if I have to take an attack or parry, it dampens the force of the hit I take."

That's actually a pretty cool fucking idea. I smiled at him. How would I do that though? *But wait, would that affect the damage done by the blade inside it? Would that dampen the force generated by the inner mechanism?*

These were questions I couldn't really think to answer myself. Maybe if I confined it to the upper portion of the item? But would the enchantment work well if it were in such close proximity to another? There were too many variables for me to be completely comfortable with that level of complexity on an item that could save my friend's life.

"Let's worry about that one after I can talk to Shellica." He looked confused. "She's the crazy, old Dwarf who trained me in enchanting when we were in Djurn Forge. I may make a trip to see her soon. For now, let's see about getting those other enchantments going, yeah?"

He doffed his breastplate, and I got to thinking about the design I would engrave into it. But I didn't want it to be visible for anyone to see and get an idea of what it would do, so I put the engraving on the inside near the neckline.

As skillful as I was, I did let my mana recharge between jobs. My wisdom was high enough that after a little over a minute, I was back to full from all that work.

I closed my eyes and reached for the mana within me. I brought it in a line from what represented my mana pool near my navel to my finger. I envisioned the design in my head and began pushing the mana forward out of my body steadily. While my eyes were closed, I could sense the drain on my MP, represented by a blue bar. It was steady, but the cost was low, so I wasn't worried. I pressed the design, a simple feather repeated five times with each pointed tip of the quill faced inward, almost like a star.

Once I was finished with that, I took a moment to pull out of myself and focus my intent. I willed the armor to be lighter, as light as the feathers I imagined those in the engraving would weigh. Once I had that thought firmly in place in my mind, I began to channel my mana into the engraving. Around 200 MP filled it, and I pushed no further. There was no reason to, and after a week of getting my ass handed to me for doing just that, I had learned to trust my instincts. Or get whacked by said crazy Dwarf.

I hated her whacking me. Get your mind out of the gutter.

I repeated the process for his padded plate breeches with the same engraving. This time I had to flip up one of the plates and engrave it under there. The symbol worked fine, and the desired enchantment took.

I let him throw the items back on. Each one now had the **_feather_** identifier before the rest of the item. It significantly lowered the weight of his armor. Both items total only weighed eight pounds. I took his boots; they were hearty leather with nothing really all that spectacular about them. The soles were thick though, and that was enough for me.

"Hey, Jaken," I called the Paladin over. "You have any thin metal plates small enough to cover this sole from just above the bottom and a little way up? So that his movement won't be hampered?"

Jaken took the boot and eyed it for a minute. "I have some small pieces of leftover metal I thought were cool. Think you could melt them? If you can act as the forge, I'd be happy to try and hammer them into a usable shape. You have a desired thickness?"

"Yeah, let's go for no less than maybe an eighth of an inch?" I thought for a moment, then added, "They don't have to be long or too wide. Maybe about an inch and a half squared?"

He nodded, reached into his inventory, and pulled a few rock-like pebbles of iron out. "This work?"

"You have anything that may conduct magic better?" I asked. There was no need to beat around the bush here. "Copper, mithral, ebon?"

He nodded and reached into his inventory and grabbed a couple nuggets of some kind of whitish metal I hadn't seen before.

"This is something I found at Granda's forge." He showed it to me. "I think he called it 'Spell Steel?' They don't like working with it unless they have to because the process to forge it is complicated. I didn't think of it because they hated it.

They let me have some though because I was such a hard worker—and I thought it was cool as shit." He chuckled.

"What's the forging process like?" Muu asked, taking an interest in the metal.

"Well," Jaken took it in his hand and closed his eyes as if trying to recall, "it takes a lot of heat, a lot, then cools down quickly, so no one but a grandmaster level smith can form anything worthwhile out of it with any sort of efficient or reliable results. Also, you can't hammer it all that hard because when it heats, it's a little more fragile. It's as close to ideal as some metals for enchanting, but it's hellish to forge and costly to find. Not to mention the amount of money it would take to actually have a weapon formed from it."

Muu looked at Jaken as if he had a horn growing out of his forehead. "Ballpark estimate?" he asked in a hushed tone.

"For a dagger?" He rubbed his chin, mumbled a bit, then looked at Muu and said simply, "Probably around three hundred gold. Give or take."

"Jesus fucking hell!" James spat his drink out. "Fuck that. An actual weapon? That shit would be expensive as FUCK."

I thought about the price of my axe if it had been made with that material and shivered. Oh hell no. I mean, sure, as a Druid, I was drooling for material like that, and honestly, we could likely afford it. But just *knowing* that that had been a ballpark estimate was troubling. My first great axe had been about five gold. Storm Caller? Around a hundred, and I had supplied the main materials! Fuck, man.

"Alright, let me see if I can get it heated for you, and we can try and get it into position." I took the first nugget from him and stuck it into my palm.

I focused on the vision of flame in a forge, then brought the mana into my palm. I felt the metal take the heat, and after two minutes of steady heating, I sat it on the ground for Jaken to hammer. He tapped it to check the heat, then handed it back. "Hotter."

"Very well then," I mumbled. I poured more mana into the palm of my hand. This time, I brought the image of lava streams inside my mind. I felt the Mark of Flame, the blessing that the Primordial Flame Elemental had bestowed upon me, begin to pulse. That never happened. I almost lost my focus, but it seemed benign enough, so I continued pouring mana into the Spell Steel nugget. If I let something like that bother me, Shellica would have hurled a hammer at me if she could find one.

After working through most of my mana and having to wave my palm off multiple times, we were able to make two almost identical squares of metal thick enough for me to engrave. Jaken had lightly hammered—tapped really—until they were close to the shape I had in mind.

Rather than engrave them while they were outside the boots, I took the two boots and sat them in front of me. Taking a single clawed forefinger, I began to dig out a shallow square in both just above the heels in the thickest part of the leather sole. The layers were glued together, thick and grimy on the inside, but this was a portion that was never supposed to be seen, so it didn't bother me.

Once the now-cooled pieces fit snugly in place, I heated the leather and metal together so that they became fused, and I also smoothed any hammer marks or small imperfections with heat—like a little bit of welding on my part. I let them cool for a moment once more as I tried to think of how I would engrave the metal. I had limited space, so I had to be precise.

I grinned at the idea that began to settle in my mind, and it was simple enough that I could accomplish my goal and still tease my friend. I brought the image into my mind and settled into a better-seated position. Then I began engraving the outline of a frog as if seen from above. After that, I included three bars, like an upside down WiFi signal beneath the legs. I repeated the process for the second boot.

After they were both done, I enchanted them for jumping, just as Muu had suggested. When they were done, I was surprised by how well the enchantment had taken. It had cost me 100 MP per boot, but the results were stellar.

Frog Boots
+ 20 feet to a forward jump, + 12 feet to an upward leap. All impact from leaping or jumping while wearing these boots is lessened by 85%.
When these boots are worn, the wearer takes the phrase—"If you're feeling froggy, leap," to heart.
Enchanted by Journeyman Enchanter Zekiel Erebos.

"Holy fuck, man!" Muu gushed as he held the items and looked at the stats. "These are insane!"

"Some of my best work, man," I replied with a grin. After all the enchanting I had done, my level in the craft had gone up by one, so I was currently level 28 in enchanting.

In another twelve levels, I'd go up a level overall. So, if I were to get to level 40, right at that moment, my total level would be upped to level 21, as if I had earned that experience in a fight or through questing.

"Well, let's see what you can do, man?" Jaken encouraged.

"But what about my weapon?" Muu asked, flashing the short spear forward.

"You don't need that to fucking jump, fool." Yohsuke growled. "Let Zeke rest, man. He's been working himself over for you, and you haven't even said thanks yet."

"Shit, man." Muu turned on me and frowned. "I'm sorry—thank you."

"Jump, motherfucker!" I smiled good-naturedly. "That'll be thanks enough. I'll take your spear once you show off a bit."

He tapped on his boots and grinned, his sharp teeth shining. "Let's see how high I can go."

He squatted down a little bit, then pushed his hands up and pushed with his legs. He leaped an easy twenty feet into the air. He landed with an audible grunt and then grinned at us. "I didn't even try that hard that time."

"Leap forward!" James urged. "Like, long-jump style."

Muu nodded and set his feet in much the same way and propelled his body forward as hard as he could. He skidded to a stop thirty-two feet away and began to throw his arms around like crazy trying to keep his balance.

"Oh, dude," I whispered in awe to the others. "If we don't use that for an attack, we are *shitty* gamers."

I looked over in time to see Jaken and Yohsuke nodding. James stood in stunned silence, and Bokaj just grinned as he looked on.

I made a grabbing sign for Muu's weapon, and he got the idea. He jogged back and handed it to me. It felt odd in my hands, but it wasn't a great axe, so I couldn't complain.

"What kind of enchantment were you thinking?" I wondered. "I know you said elemental, but there are elements to choose from and, well, now you know what I can do. If you want to try some shit—we can try some shit."

Muu seemed to start thinking, then began to frown. Then he closed his eyes and began to scratch his head. Finally, he looked me in the eyes and said, "I have no clue. I know that, theoretically speaking, you could do pretty much whatever you want. What would you suggest?"

I thought a moment. That was a good question. After another minute of thinking, I got an idea.

"Well, we all have racial abilities," I began. I pointed to Bokaj. "Bokaj can cover his weapon in ice for an attack to potentially freeze an enemy. Balmur can cover his weapons in flames. Yoh can fully recover his MP once per day. And I'm pretty sure I saw James cover his fists and claws in acid."

"Don't forget, I can come back to life once per day," Jaken interjected. When the rest of us looked at him in alarm, he shrugged. "It's an Orc thing."

"Where the fuck was this information?!" James growled at Jaken threateningly.

Had to admit—I wanted to know too. He'd been holding out on us! Fuck. Maybe having a new guy in the group was useful after all. And I swear to all the Gods in Brindolla if you don't stop saying, '*you never asked*,' I will turn this story around so fast!

Too far? Too far. Cool. Sorry.

"Well what about you, Zeke?" Muu wondered.

"Zeke can see hidden things. I think I heard him call it True Sight?" I nodded at Yohsuke to confirm his statement. "Not to mention, he has his tails."

"Right," I agreed. "So, what is it that makes your race special? What special ability do you have that you could incorporate?"

Muu opened his stat screen and began to tinker a moment before answering, "Sheera's Venom? It says that the user can imbue his weapons and attacks with venom for one minute. It has a twenty-four hour cooldown."

"That's cool as shit, dude," James said. "Dragons are *dope*."

The two Dragons of the group bumped fists and chuckled conspiratorially.

"That's pretty fucking cool, I agree." I put a hand to my head and began to think. "Okay, so you use venom. Does it say anything about your weapon being protected from that venom? How about if I make your weapon envenomed? Oh! That reminds me, Bokaj, Nora had something for me, right?"

"Yeah, man, you just forgot to actually grab it from me," he explained. He reached into his inventory, pulled out a small box, and handed it to me with the attached note. "She said to read the note before you do *anything* with this box."

"That's fair," I mumbled as I opened it up and read it aloud.

Zekiel,

I included two of the most potent products I could in such a short amount of time. If you intend to use these poisons on any kind of weapons, know that they will cause the weapon to erode—not the way acid would but no less seriously. If you treat the weapon with the white powder I have included, it will allow you one safe use of the poison in the bright green stoppered vial. If you use the black powder for the yellow stoppered vial, it will provide the same result. The green will cause a burst of poison damage in one go and may cause the target to become confused. The yellow causes the target to take damage over time and may lower their speed. You have enough powder and poison for two uses of each. <u>Do not</u> *mix the two or confuse the powders. Either could result in a rather... nasty bit of business.*

—Your friend.

"That's not cryptic," I muttered. "Okay, so we have poisons." I began to tap my head in thought. "Maybe we can use one of them for your weapon?"

"Could you do that?" Muu wondered. "It says that you only have two uses of each. How would you make that work?"

"Well, and this is me spitballing here," I began, "I could make a protective barrier, like the ring of storing, that is designed to keep the poison there. After that, I add a portion of the powder, then the vial, and lock it in place. With that, the poison could be there forever or for a certain amount of time. There's no telling how it will work or *if* it will work. And honestly speaking, it could backfire, and you would have no enchantment for your weapon. It won't be safe, and honestly? I would rather wait until we are in a safer environment to experiment like that. At least that way we can commission another weapon if I fuck up."

Muu looked disappointed, but he seemed to understand. "Could you maybe make it armor piercing? Extra sharp?"

"Lemme see what I can do for ya," I said and began to think of ways to enhance his weapon.

It was already a wicked weapon. I had no doubts that it would easily cause a bleeding effect just from how it was made. Armor piercing? That would be lovely, but was there something... more I could give it? Piercing was necessary. That was kind of the point with spears. Pun... mildly intended.

It would be nice to have it come back, maybe? Like Storm Caller did for me, but it didn't have the raw elemental power that my weapon did. Though, I was sure that I could probably do it with a certain range. Besides, having him throw his weapon and call it back would be a little more practical with him as low leveled as he is for right now.

Fuck it, may as well try, I thought to myself.

I looked down at the tip of the spear and began to outline a drill-like etching into the metal at the tip. I finished that with more than enough mana to spare, then began to channel mana into it with drilling through armor in mind, watching the cruel tip of the spear puncture armor as it would part flesh like a hot knife through butter. That took a majority of the mana I had, so I sat for about two minutes to regain all my mana for the other engraving I had in mind.

Moving to the handle, just above the leather grip, I began to engrave a shooting star, complete with tail. The star portion itself was a pentagram. It was a small thing, two inches long from tip to tip, but I made the engraving slightly deeper than I normally would. The MP cost for that engraving was trivial, and by this point, my mana was just about full—literally points away. I recovered 360 MP per minute thanks to my thirty-five points in wisdom.

It seems ridiculous, right? Like, with that much mana, you could do so much! Well, that 360 MP is divided by twelve five-second intervals. So every five seconds, six one-hundreths of my mana returns to me—or 30 MP for those of us who are bad at math. So every five seconds for a minute to get that back. Now, I have 500 MP total. That's almost a minute and a half to get the full thing back.

Out of combat? Not an issue. In the middle of a brawl where my friends and I were fighting for our lives? That's a long-ass time.

As I focused on what I wanted the weapon to do, I began concentrating on the stars in the sky at night, like the ones I had seen across Maebe's arms and face.

The thought of the Unseelie Queen made me blush slightly, but I kept pushing the images I saw in my mind's eye to get back on track.

Like the stars that were present in my own fur, I saw the motion of the falling stars, the comets. The heavens themselves moved, and they moved so *fast*. As I poured my mana into the weapon, I saw that speed, and I held it fast in my mind's eye. I used *all* of my mana for this enchantment, and it left me with an unbearable headache.

"There." I groaned and tossed it to him. "Pick it up and throw it." He looked at me like I was dumb. "What the fuck did I just tell you to do?!"

He jumped at my sudden outburst, bent to pick up the weapon, and threw it away from him like a javelin. As soon as it landed in the ground, *in the ground*. The tip was buried in the stone solidly, and with that, I told him what to do next.

"Close your eyes, hold out your hand, and *will* the weapon to return to your hand." Enough of my mana had returned by now that I cast Regrowth, and the headache began to dull.

"Look, man, it's not that far away, I can just go ge–" Muu began, but the look I hit him with shut him up, and he did as he was told.

After a moment of concentration, nothing happened, and I sighed. "Don't think about it happening. *See it* happening. Will it to happen."

Muu looked withered but sighed, closed his eyes, and then thrust his palm forward with his fingers skyward. The weapon disappeared in a blur of light scattered darkness and reappeared in his grip.

"AH!" he accidentally shrieked. He paused for a moment before finally whispering fiercely toward us, "*I'm a fucking Jed–*"

No! No. Not me, copyright ninja. No. Move along.

We couldn't hold our laughter at the fact that he had actually called himself that in all seriousness, so we all had a good, long belly laugh at his expense. He didn't give a shit, though. He just took his time throwing it and calling it to him again. Each time it came back, he would gasp in delight and stomp his feet a bit.

"Yo, man." Yohsuke patted my shoulder. "What did you do?"

"I gave it a bit more juice than I meant to," I grumbled, "but I figured—if he can throw it and not have to worry about going to get it—he'd be safer. So, ta-da?"

"That's fucking dope, man." Yoh bumped my shoulder with his fist. "Might need to do that for all of us, haha."

I grinned at him and said simply, "Maybe. If you keep cooking as good as you do—you'll be the first one to get a lil something."

Chapter Five

We walked for another mile or so after our rest, and all was relatively clear. There were game trails, and we even saw a mountain goat in the distance who watched us dispassionately as it grazed on what it could find.

As we headed northward, the cloudy skies shifting lazily to gray and overcast, our eyes fell on a cave in the mid-afternoon sunlight. It would have been just another place to avoid except that, well, to be honest, I didn't want to. I could feel the dark entrance, only thirteen feet wide and twice as tall, *calling* to me.

"God, I need to be *in* you," Muu muttered. I looked over to see him staring at the cave. The others were looking at us oddly, but I didn't really care.

"You guys okay?" Yohsuke's eyebrows were furrowed beneath his hood as he looked at the two of us. "You look... off."

"I want to go into that cave," Muu said, and I nodded.

"Why?" Jaken asked. James stood off to my right.

"There could be loot in there," I whispered in a hushed tone. That thought grew more tangible when I swore I saw something shiny inside the entrance, just to the rear in the shadows. Though, to be honest, I couldn't even begin to make out what was past the entrance.

"Dude, it's just a cave," Bokaj explained. "There's not shit in there. Well, maybe a mountain lion or something."

"Let's just go in and check," Muu tried to reason with the others. "If there's nothing in there, then we know. We move on, but if there is, we kill it, and I get to level up, right?"

James cleared his throat and looked at the others. "Yeah, I wanna go in."

The others seemed to mull it over for a moment, but I was already crouched, walking toward the cave mouth. I couldn't wait for them to either decide or not. I *had* to know what was in there. I had to.

Now, my good sense leaves me often, but fuck, this cave was just hitting all the right buttons for me.

As I neared the cave entrance, the fur on the back of my neck and scalp rose, then fell back down as quickly as it had occurred. I looked around, and as I walked through the entrance, I was no longer entranced. That pissed me off because I just *knew* something had wanted us to come in here. I felt Kayda's mourning reach its peak, and her sadness washed over me, almost forcing me to my knees. Tears formed in my eyes and fell softly into my fur. I cut off our tie for the time being so I could do some exploring.

What I found was enough to make my instincts worthwhile. Recalling boot camp-level instincts, ones that had been damned near beaten into us, I raised my left arm and waved to my friends to come join me, then patted the air by my hip to tell them to walk softly. Muu didn't understand, but Yohsuke grabbed him and had him walk slowly. I looked to my left and realized the Bokaj was there with his bow at the ready.

Dude was taking on a seriously badass rob the rich and give to the poor kind of vibe for me with this dark and broody thing he had going for him.

That was fucking stupid, man, he used the earring to talk to me.

Well, there goes my previous thoughts.

As the others joined us, they saw what I had seen. Twelve sleeping creatures that looked like taller, stronger Goblins. They each had a crude weapon near their prone bodies.

Leave it to you to find a bunch of sleeping enemies. We're too far out to see the levels. Anyone want to sneak closer for a look? Jaken grumbled into my mind.

Yohsuke whispered softly to Muu to pass on what we were saying. Getting him an earring was going to have to be a thing.

Yeah, I will. Bokaj began to move cautiously forward with Tmont on his heels, watching the sleeping forms. It was a thirty yard sneak before he sent back, *level 12s, all of them.*

What do you wanna bet these are the owners of the huts? Yohsuke put forth as he began to slowly move forward.

We're gonna let Muu have the finishing touch on these guys, right? Should we AoE or go one at a time? I asked. I looked over the bodies, my sight uninhibited by the darkness, but the back of the cave was still cloaked in shadow.

Let me survey the area a bit more before we start raining death, Bokaj told us all as he moved through the sleeping figures toward the back. *Looks like there's a couple tunnels in here. I'm not seeing anything down them, though. It smells like shit and piss in here. Couldn't they go outside at least?*

Who cares? James groaned dramatically. *This place could be a dungeon. Let's kill them and check it out! Places to go, monsters to kill, levels to gain. Let's get to getting.*

You all ready? Yohsuke asked. He had shuffled as close as he dared. *Let's save the magic. Zeke, let Muu know that when one of us gets one of them low enough. He moves in for the kill.*

I nodded, then moved cautiously over to Muu and whispered, "If it has low health, you stab it. Stay close to me, and head on a swivel. No risks."

He gave me a thumb up and looked forward. We began to cross the distance slowly and carefully. I brought out Storm Caller and brought it above the creature's head, then moved it to the body itself. I pointed at Muu, to my head, his spear then the creature's head.

I gave a final glance to the party around me, standing over various sleeping forms ready to strike. All of them were within easy distance for Muu to get to quickly.

I repositioned myself, brought my weapon up, then down on the creature brutally. Even as it grunted, Muu stabbed his spear into the side of its head and finished it. Then he moved to the creatures before Jaken, Yohsuke, James, and the one that Bokaj had fired two arrows into lazily. Each one took one or two strikes from Muu to perish, then the others were alerted to our presence.

Muu stepped behind Jaken just as one stood. Muu flanked the Paladin, then came about on his shield side where he wouldn't be in the way. I looked and saw that his level had risen by one.

Disappointing, but he was here with us, and the experience was going to be skewed because of it. I also had to wonder if there was some kind of penalty to his growth because we were basically doing the majority of the work?

Back to paying attention.

Jaken hacked the arm off the creature in front of him, the club falling with it. It stared in disbelief at the subtraction from its being, then died when Muu thrust his spear through the top of its head.

James couldn't risk holding himself back as one of the green-skinned creatures tried to get to the green Dragon Beast-kin. He hit it hard enough that it crumpled to the ground dead.

As I looked at their taller frames, I had to admit I had heard of creatures like this back home in my reading. Hobgoblins? As the thought made itself known, the name bar above each creature shifted into **Hobgoblin**.

Gotta love this world.

After a moment of more careful fighting, all of the creatures we had attacked were dead. Though the final one had hardly put up a fight at all—it opted to just yell as loudly as it could in anger.

Muu was looting the corpses happily, so we left him to that and moved forward to look at the rear of the cave.

There were three tunnels. One that smelled almost entirely of feces and urine, the middle, and right, which smelled like the hobgoblins. I was going to suggest that we check out the rest of the place when I felt a small rumble shake the ground.

I looked to the others, and they were backing away from the origin of the shaking—the right hallway. As we backed away, more hobgoblins began to flood into sight.

"Kill them while they're funneling in!" Jaken shouted and rushed to stand between the tunnel mouth and us.

I saw Bokaj bring out an arrow, notch it, and loosed before shouting, "Fireball!" The concussion of the blast of flames rocked us, and it was a little harder to hear for a moment. Things sounded muffled. He sent another in. Notifications for experience flooded my field of vision, but there was still movement in the tunnel.

Yohsuke threw a bolt of astral and starlight into the hall, and a second later, another grenade-like blast erupted as his Star Burst detonated.

I let the others take care of the enemy in that tunnel and looked into the middle tunnel. I couldn't see anything, and I hoped nothing would come. Another burst of light and heat from the right tunnel let me know that Bokaj had used another Fireball Arrow.

"They're stopping!" James alerted us. "Jaken, get the hate, man! Get them to come to us."

"I'll try." Jaken's muffled voice reached my ears, and I saw him step into the tunnel. A burst of red aura covered his armor. "Come and get some, bitches!"

A cacophonous cry of outrage greeted him, and I saw another host of hobgoblins surge from the shadows in the back of the tunnel. They scrambled and clawed at each other to reach their prey first. An arrow hit one in the chest and the heavens opened a rent in the air above them and poured down raining stars. Star Fall Arrow was spent. Yohsuke threw another Star Burst. The damage of the combined spells shattered the enemies, and all was finally still.

"Oh thank the Gods that's over." I sighed in relief.

"I do not appreciate you slaughtering my army," replied a cool, masculine voice.

I turned to find a mostly nude man, his skin milky in color from the waist up, then red from the waist down. His muscles were toned and appealing. His facial features were appeasing, and the horns protruding from his head curved up and back over his head almost like slicked-back hair. He wore nothing but a loincloth that covered him, and looking at him, even with my True Sight, was confusing, to say the least. His demonic features, appealing visage, and the confusion I was feeling could mean that he was probably an incubus.

Look, boys and squirrels—I like to read a lot, okay? And a lot of the better books introduce the idea of some kind of sexy, powerful demonic figure to entice the good guy or girl, and it's not hard to see that this dude was clearly that.

Why are you looking at me that way? Don't judge my reading choices.

It didn't help that he had Muu by the throat.

The fuck is that thing, and where the fuck did it come from?! Jaken shouted into our minds.

Incubus, Yohsuke actually spat when he repeated my thought

My friend didn't dare move for fear of making the creature holding him decide he was worth killing. He had leveled up to four in all the commotion.

"How were we to know that they were your army, Incubus?" I tried to reason. I could just make out his level.

Incubus level 26

"You weren't." He waved the question away with his free hand. "They were merely my protection and a snack. The spell on the entrance was meant to entice anything mildly intelligent to come in. Though your Elven-blooded friends had no issues resisting my charm."

The clawed finger to Muu's throat slid along it teasingly. "This one is very curious about what goes on in these realms. He wasn't hard to lure away either."

"Look, let him go, and we will happily just leave you here, alone and in peace. I swear it," Jaken swore. He stepped forward a little more to get in front of the rest of us, and the Incubus tightened his grip on Muu's throat threateningly.

"Ah-ah." He wagged his finger at the Paladin. "No. You will be my new slaves and meals until I am strong enough to move along unimpeded. If you move, I will kill him."

Fuck him, Bokaj—you ready? I growled through our telepathic connection.

Bet your ass, came his cold reply.

I looked at Muu and saw him realize what would happen. There was fear in his body and then recognition. He began to struggle slightly.

"Look, your friend knows what will happen if you displease me," the Incubus purred in delight. He leaned down a little and whispered into Muu's ear. He went rigid, then threw his shielded hand up, and the Incubus gripped the arm and rested the shield against his chest.

"I *love* it when prey struggles." The creature's red eyes dilated, and he purred low in his throat.

"Good," Muu grunted and squeezed his hand, pulling the lever in his grip.

The blade burst from the shield and into the Incubus's throat, doing a measly five percent damage; it must have been a critical hit with how far apart in levels they were from each other. The creature squeezed and threw his assailant away from him. Jaken triggered Radiant Burst, saving Muu's life in the nick of time.

The rest of us were on our foe in a heartbeat. Three arrows burst from the Incubus's chest, and it dropped another twenty percent. It reached forward and blasted at Bokaj with fire that James took the brunt of the damage from, redirected the flow of the hit, and hammer fisted the creature in the side of the head. It knocked him into Yohsuke, who brought his Astral Blade into its back with a roar.

"Don't you EVER threaten my family again!" The feral roar leapt from my throat as I brought Storm Caller on to his open shoulder. I activated Cleave and struck a second time, then pulled back, tossed my axe behind me, and grasped his head in my hands and *squeezed.*

"Aahhhh!" it cried. I didn't care. The red ringing my vision began to throb wildly, and I cast Lightning Bolt into his head. A few more Ki-empowered strikes from James and some Astral Blade swipes from Yohsuke saw the fucker to ten percent.

We held him down, punching lightly to keep him distracted as Jaken brought over Muu. The newest member of our party stood there, still as stone, watching as the struggling form beneath us tried to get him to help.

"Please, I will not harm you, just—ah!—LET GO!" it shrieked.

"Muu, he's yours man," Bokaj prodded gently. "Stab him to your heart's content."

"Get some, man." Jaken smacked the now-biting fanged mouth of the Incubus as he tried to encourage Muu, "You got this."

Muu took a straddling position over the prone figure, stared into the creature's eyes, and he lifted his weapon wordlessly.

"No! I'll give you anything! Anything you want!" The Incubus pleaded wildly.

"Wait!" Bokaj barked, pulling us from our animosity slightly. "Tell us what's going on in the Hells and how you got here."

"I was approached by one of the newest members of a new order in the Hells, called War Path. They offered me power and all the souls I could corrupt on the Prime so long as I sowed as much discord and chaos as I could while I was here. It's a prospect that seems to be catching on with the lesser demons. Some of the more powerful demons are thinking of joining them as well, but there are bureaucracies to observe."

He eyed Yohsuke. "You understand that."

"Take us to the Hells," Bokaj ordered the Incubus.

"No." Muu shrugged and raised his spear, and my grip tightened significantly. "I can't! It was a one-way trip. The stronger demons, someone almost as powerful as a duke of Hell sends us to a random place. I'm not strong enough to return on my own, let alone someone else! Don't stab me, please!"

"Tell us more about the guys at the top of this order," I growled. "Have you heard any word about someone trying to take over?"

The Incubus balked at the question, so James punched him in his pretty face, and he spat blood.

"No one knows much, but some of the other Lords and Ladies of Hell hate them for tampering with the power structure. There was a rumor that one of them was sending a mortal into *negotiation circle*—vicious and fiery little thing—and challenging others for their servants. I was a free party, so I was approached by a scout of some sort."

"Where did they come from?" Jaken asked, and Bokaj shot him a look.

"No one knows. They just showed up, and people started following them with their sweet, sweet promise of defiling this plane." It licked its lips. "I've given you much. Release me."

I felt a tickle in the back of my mind that made my vision blur a little, but James smacked the Incubus again.

"What about the vicious little thing can you tell us? What negotiations are you talking about?" Bokaj was shaking now, his face a mask of anger and worry.

"I gave you the information! Release ME!" He struggled as best as he could but couldn't free himself.

Muu looked him in the eyes with a cold smile and said, "I love it when my prey struggles."

The creature stopped struggling long enough for a flash of sickening green attacks from Muu's spear and shield blade. He furiously slashed and cut and stabbed as quickly as possible.

The attacks weren't much, even paired with the venom of what I assumed was his racial ability, but the spots he was raining them down on eventually killed the Incubus with the critical damage and the rest of us beating the creature into submission.

Finally, the Incubus expired, and I watched as Muu's level leaped to eight.

Bokaj sat back, numbly watching the proceedings. He was obviously not here, and I thought I knew why. Balmur could still be alive, but we were no closer to getting to him, and War's general in the Hells was up to some serious shit.

"Nice, man!" I exclaimed, trying to lighten the mood a little. "We really need to work on those one-liners, though."

Muu grinned at me, then fell to his ass with his head in his hands. I watched as his shoulders began to shake, heard him sniffle, and the quiet sobs began to rack his body as he wept.

The others sympathized but looked uncomfortable.

If I had to venture a guess, this was his first real confrontation with mortality. Sure, family passes. Friends do too. But this was so much more visceral. I can't say that I blamed him or found his reaction to be something that would make me think less of him.

We had all been here at some point. Mine came the day I stepped on the yellow footprints at Parris Island, the first time I ever truly realized that I could end up having to take a life. It had taken what little youthful ignorance and innocence I'd had and thrown it away.

I squatted down next to him and patted his shoulder comfortingly. "We're here for you, man. Take your time. Actually, let's clear the bodies away into that tunnel. Then we can just sleep here tonight. No sense in going out into any more shit, yeah?"

He just kept crying. That was okay. As I stood and began to relay my thoughts to the others, a clap of thunder followed by lightning rocked us all. I looked outside, and rain began to fall from the sky in thick sheets.

Definitely wasn't going anywhere for a bit, so we got to work. We looted what we could from the bodies on the ground. None of the clubs or simple weapons were worth anything other than firewood and a stopper for water at the entrance to the cave. There were some copper and silver pieces strewn throughout the inventories of the dead. The same for the bodies in the tunnel, burned and singed as they were. The middle tunnel led to a large chamber with a pile of rags and fronds that looked like a bed.

There were all kinds of... unmentionable stuff on the coverings. We left that alone, and there was nothing of interest in the rest of the room, so we dragged the bodies in the tunnel that we could move in here.

The other tunnels were as interesting as the first—not. The one on the left was where we found the remains of several mountain goats and the right where we found the stench of bodily waste in the form of a communal bathroom.

It was a shit pile. Literally. I gagged, threw up all over the place, and left. I contemplated just blowing the shit out of the tunnel and caving it in, but James said it could be a bad idea.

The Incubus dropped an interesting couple items that I was fairly certain a couple people in the group would fight over.

Elrow's Horns

+ 3 to Charisma

Horns taken from the Incubus Elrow. A slightly customizable item that attaches with a thought to the wearers head—so dashing.

Given to the former owner at birth by his mare.

That was cool. It was a set of horns that looked exactly like those that had been on his head. After a moment of quiet, heated argument, finally, Bokaj just shouted, "I told you I don't fucking want them!"

The Ranger stormed over to the small barrier we had erected to try and stunt the rainwater a bit and keep it out of here.

The item went to Yohsuke after that because the rest of us had no use for charisma. He put it on and began to cackle as they shifted into what he wanted them to be. They slid to the sides of his forehead near his temples at the edge of his hairline, then curved slight back along the side of his head at an angle. They bent slightly up and away from the ears, thick near the base and coming to a pointed tip near the back of his head. As they settled, the color shifted from black to a dusting of red at the base to a pure black an inch above that and all the way back.

"Bow before me, fools!" He growled. "I am one step closer to matching that which you already know me to be. I am the overlord! Bow and scrape as you please. You shall all be henceforth known as my vassals."

We chuckled at his ludicrous outburst—it was a persona that he had in the Marine Corps. He loved that one game with the demon overlord who was a badass. It kind of stuck because he was a badass gamer. So, every now and then, this side of him would peek out to play. It was entertaining as hell. Other times, our enemies found it highly intimidating.

The next item was pretty cool as well; it looked like a barb—long and wickedly sharp—that looked like it could attach to something.

Lady Finger
+ 4 to attack
Requirement: Must be worn on a tail
Although the name may be confusing—this is not something that a lady would find at all tasteful.
Crafted in the third level of the Hells by a surly demon.

With myself and Muu, that made two of us with tails. My own were mainly aesthetic. They were awesome as fuck, don't get me wrong, but they lacked the muscle and control to actually attack anyone outright. Unless you counted smacking someone in the face with them. I could do that shit all day.

"Hey, Muu, your tail is kind of thick, man," I began as I held the item out to him. "You think you could use this?"

"Nope," he said almost dismissively. When I just looked at him like he was crazy, he elaborated, "My tail isn't that long, and I don't have the control with it that I would like to use it effectively. Besides, I don't want someone at my back close enough to have to use it. At least not until I'm good enough to fight on my own."

"That's fair," Bokaj grunted from his spot by the barrier where he was brooding. "Hey, what about T? Think she could use it?"

I thought about it for a second. Could animal companions use weapons like this?

"You want to ask her?" I offered the weapon to him. "I don't want to interfere with your cat, man."

He nodded, and I slid it on the ground to him. It skittered and bounced before reaching him.

Speaking of, I opened my bond with Kayda and found her soaring the skies of the storm, trying to work off her anger. Our minds melded a bit, and she saw what had happened.

Okay? Her question was simple, but the complexity behind it with the accompanying visions was insane. She meant all of us.

We're okay, love. Be safe, and keep an eye out for us. She agreed, and I turned my eyes back to Bokaj and the Lady Finger.

He took it and looked it over before turning to his panther pet. "Hey, Tmont, you wanna throw this on your ass? Stab some things?"

She huffed mightily, looked at him for a moment longer with her tail flicking back and forth lazily, then got up and wandered over to him. She bumped her head off his leg, sniffed the weapon, and growled at it.

"Come on, T," Bokaj reasoned with her. "It'll help you protect me. You want that, right?"

I could hear the rise in pitch of her growl into an agitated yowl, but she seemed to acquiesce that it was her wish. She offered her tail, and the item slid on to it—then shrank to fit snugly. And Tmont went apeshit. She hissed, spat, and tried to run away from her tail as the weapon flailed wildly behind her.

"Sweet *vengeance*!" I howled in delight. The cat yowled in my general direction, and I smiled even harder.

* * *

We spent the night going over what happened during the fight, explaining our positions and combative tactics to Muu so that he could learn our thought processes. He seemed to be getting everything. Yohsuke was making dinner while we spoke.

"Hey, man, seven levels in one day! That's nuts!" Jaken said in a lull. "What are you going to do with the points?"

Muu pulled up his stats and began to tinker. Finally, he decided on spending his points trying to even himself out. Of the thirty-five points he received for leveling up that many times, he put ten into strength, eleven into dexterity, and fourteen into constitution. That got him to an even thirty in strength and dexterity and thirty-five in constitution. Already better than me health wise and very close to the rest of us in total HP.

"Cool, man." I nodded. "Now, what will you do with your proficiency points? With the three you got, I imagine you could get the spear tree open and your short spear, too—maybe even an attack."

"Hmmm." He poured over his stats for a moment, found what he was looking for, then looked at me quickly. "Did you say three?"

"Yeah, man," I explained patiently. "We all get a point for every level above five."

"Dude, I have nine," he informed us.

The rest of the group perked up and got closer. "No fucking way, dude," Yohsuke muttered. "How?"

"Think it could be because he's a Fighter?" James proposed. "I mean, it makes sense. Fighters aren't really magic oriented in a lot of games, so they have to have something to give them an edge, right?"

That did make sense, now that it was explained Barney style like that.

"Okay," I said slowly. "What are you thinking of doing with them, man? It's your choice."

"Do they go away if I don't use them in a certain amount of time?" Muu asked.

"Nope." I shrugged. "I got past five before I figured out I even had them."

"Okay, I'll purchase what I need," he made some selections quickly, "then save the rest for when I meet another Fighter for some advice on what to do with the rest. What kind of build I want."

"That's a good idea," Yohsuke said as he stirred the food he had begun preparing. The pot above the flame was starting to boil, and he added some seasoning. "It never hurts to seek advice, but never forget this—this is *your* life. You do it how you want to do it and no other way. Not for me," he pointed at me, "him, or any other motherfucker but you."

Muu nodded and seemed to fold into himself in thought. We ate a good meal that night, some soup that Yohsuke had brought the ingredients for. I don't know what kind of meat that had been, but damn, it was good.

Muu and James opted to take the first watches, and I would take the last. I looked at Muu in concern, his eyes on the outside of the cave as he watched the rain fall. Deep in thought, as he was, I knew he likely wasn't really okay. I'd have to talk to him later.

As I laid down, my flame mark pulsed again, throbbing like it had earlier. This was so weird. I closed my eyes and tried to go to sleep in my sleeping bag on my bedroll.

As I fell into slumber, I felt heat. It started in the center of my being and radiated outward. It was comforting at first, the nurturing warmth of a beloved pet sleeping next to you in bed— or a loved one's warm chest. Then it grew steadily hotter, like a space heater. Then to the roaring heat of a raging flame. I opened my eyes. Something had to be wrong and found that I wasn't where I had been. I was standing in a room made wholly of flame.

The room seemed to breathe and wasn't adorned with anything that I could discern. It was just fire.

Forgive me, Druid, but this was the only way for me to reach you.

It had been hard for me to realize that the great flame before me wasn't a wall but a great elemental. But the voice sounded familiar. So familiar.

"You're the Primordial Flame Elemental, aren't you?" I asked. The heat was becoming more and more abrasive. I held my arm up in an attempt to ward the heat away.

I am. Forgive me, little flame, I cannot make my spirit burn lower for your comfort. Attend me, and I will make my visit brief.

"Please, what can I do for you?"

One of my children, a small flame like yourself, is lost in the winter lands of the Prime Realm. Find it and care for it for me until it is strong enough to come home on its own, or it decides to walk its own path.

"A small flame?" I queried. "An elemental?"

No, a creature born of fire and will. A small, chaotic creature of my realm. It will take the form of an animal that it has encountered. I do not know what that will be, but it is in the North. I can feel him, and with your connection to me, you will too. There are those who are seeking to take him and keep him as a source of raw power, corrupting his light and fire. Do not allow this to happen. Do this for me, and I will bless you further still.

"Okay," I said simply. Sure, this was a big deal, and the way he made it sound, there were other forces at work, but he had helped me immensely, and he seemed like a cool dude. "I'd be happy to help, but can you tell me if you can help my friends and I get into the Hells? Our friend is there, and we need to get him back. We're on a time crunch, I think."

The flame wall bent and crackled brightly and louder than before.

You are not ready to venture to the Hells—none of you are. They will corrupt you and consume you. You must be stronger. Better prepared. I will help with that how I can. Help my child, and I will make you stronger.

I thought for a moment before agreeing. If a Primordial Elemental, likely an equivalent to a god, knows we weren't ready, we would need to be stronger for certain. I nodded mutely, and the flames' intensity leaped into me for a searing second.

Thank you for proving my initial judgment sound. Burn bright, little flame.

The crackling sound of the Primordial Flame's voice began to fade, and I felt someone shaking me awake. I looked up to see James.

That hadn't been a dream—it was a vision, and the quest I'd received proved it.

QUEST ALERT!

A Small Flame in a Snowstorm – The Primordial Flame Elemental has requested that you find the small flame in the winter lands of the Prime Realm.

Rewards – 2,000 EXP, unknown.

"Hey, man, you got next watch." He looked at me for a moment then shook his hand. "You good? You're burning up."

I dismissed the notification that was flashing in front of me to look at in a bit. I glanced at my sweat-slick body and wiped some of the moisture from my forehead and started to stand and stretch. "Yeah, bud. You get some more rest if you need it. Or do what you gotta do. I know you don't need much rest."

"Thanks, man." He smiled, went to his things, and began to meditate.

I rolled my bedroll up and packed my things, like my axe and pillow. I opted to stand my watch with my back to the cave wall by the entrance in my Ursolon form.

The two thousand experience was a damned nice chunk toward my next level. Ten percent of it at least. And the unknown portion was interesting. I'd do it for the experience and as a favor to the Flame. But hey—gotta love it when cool shit can happen right?

I shifted back into my fox-man form and called to Kayda outside.

She shuffled her feathers and observed our surroundings before resting her eyes on me next to the cave mouth. I jerked back in surprise, and she tilted her head at me.

"Go fly, my love." I patted her head. "Let me know if you see anything strange, okay?"

She cocked her head the other direction and touched the top of my head twice with her wing before hopping out of the cave mouth and taking off. Smart-ass bird.

After I was sure she was gone and the others were either asleep or preoccupied, I cast a spell I hadn't yet—Shadow Speak.

Shadow Speak is a spell that Queen Maebe had passed to me so that she and I could communicate with each other. It was helpful as one of her chosen champions in this realm and as her friend. One of her only friends, in fact. I liked to think she thought of the others as more than acquaintances, but I couldn't be fully certain.

As I cast it, I watched the shadows next to me congeal and begin to mold into the face of the person I was contacting.

"Hi, Maebe," I said as she finally fully formed.

Her figure was of pure shadow but still appealing—an hourglass shape with the outline of her angular cheeks and her large, pointed ears that stuck straight out and back from the sides of her head. I could see slightly darker pools of shadow in her eyes and mouth. She was smiling.

"Hello, Zekiel." Her musical voice reached my ears, and I was overcome with joy.

Look, she may not be much to look at right now, but Maebe was gorgeous. Intelligent. Thoughtful. Deadly.

That last one was terrifying, but she hadn't really ever threatened me outright, and you know what they say about men and women right? Behind every man is a strong-ass woman.

They don't say that? Well, they fuckin' should, man.

I stood and stepped forward to try and pull the small shadow into my arms, but the cool shadows that greeted me in return were enough to chill me.

I'd spent nights sharing her bed—ALL PG, I SWEAR! Don't you gimme that look. Despite the fact that she's the reigning Queen of Winter and Darkness, she could be warm. Delightful, even.

Touching her now and not feeling that warmth in this alien place was almost as unsettling as learning my friends and I could die here.

That was an exaggeration—I had a crush, happy? I got the hots for the gorgeous, likely homicidal Fae Queen.

At least I have good taste.

"Would that I could return your embrace, dear friend," she said sadly, "but tell me of what has transpired. I have heard from my emissaries that your mission was a success and your loss. I am deeply sorry. What have you been up to? How long has it been since you thought to inform me of your days?"

I wanted to say that I thought of it daily, that I wanted to see her and spend more time with her than the few days we had in her realm, but there were other things to say.

"He's not dead," I said hurriedly. "We've been working with another friend from my other life who came to us after Balmur was taken—we believe to the Hells. We are currently trying to track down information and help our friend level as we gather our strength."

Maebe's shadow looked at me, and I could see stiffness in her shoulders as she stepped closer to me. "I will do all that I can to help from my side of the veil. Please, do keep me informed. And I will contact you as well. It has only been a day here since you left. Maybe I could contact you every few hours in my realm?"

I grinned like an idiot. "So, every day or couple days my time? I would like that." I scratched behind my right ear. "Uhm, you know, is Samir capable of speaking this way? Or could you talk to him?"

"I suppose I could attempt to contact him," she said wearily. "Why? Do you have need of the Fae?"

"I was more interested in seeing if I could come and see you at some point in the near future," I said with a little bit of hope. "I don't have a way to right now, but I think there has to be a way to traverse the veil at will if you can do it by being banished."

"You would risk his displeasure for this?" She seemed puzzled.

"He said we couldn't come back without his permission," I said, recalling the conversation. "That means he must have been open to the idea of it. I mean, he's the very embodiment of the Fae Realm. If the rest of you are bound by your words and oaths—he has to be as well. Right?"

"If you think this is so, then I will see to trying to gain an audience." She nodded. "Why is it you would ask this, though?"

"Because I want to see you again," I said simply. I felt my cheeks burned a little, but I wouldn't be dissuaded. Not bashful.

"I would like to see you as well." She smiled again, her ears dipped a bit, and the cool shadows pressed against my arm. "You have been away from here long enough to make me miss our conversations. I miss the one person whom I can speak with the easiest. Not to mention, you are entertaining."

"I'll do what I can to try and find a way to you," I said. "Maybe I can find someone who can teach me a spell to teleport there."

"You may find such a thing," she said. "Go and become stronger, my friend. Be safe."

"You too." And I watched as her form began to fade and coalesce back into the shadows of the floor and walls.

I spent the rest of the shift watching over my friends in quiet thought over what had just transpired. Was I falling for someone here? And why did it have to be with a Fae queen who had no qualms taking a life?

The heart was weird, man. Could I really make any kind of judgments against her when I had also torn a person's heart out of their chest in front of an enemy to make a point? Then threw the body on the ground coldly enough that my friends had thrown up and almost beat my ass.

Now? Yeah, now I had no leg to stand on, and then there was the fact that she was so awesome otherwise that now, it didn't matter. I was okay with that.

I made a mental check in with Kayda; she was fine, and since we had found the threat, she had taken the liberty of looking for the city we were trying to find. It was north and a little to the west of our current position.

She hadn't wanted to go too far from us with an unknown threat possibly being in the area, but now we were cool.

As soon as the others woke, I started the conversation on my mind, "Listen, this isn't easy for me to say, but I think we should see other people."

The others just looked at me, bleary-eyed and confused. Muu chewed his food, swallowed, then flipped me the bird.

"You aren't getting rid of me, fucker." Yohsuke grunted as he dished some eggs on to a plate for me. "What's going on in that big-ass dome of yours, though. I thought I heard you talking to someone."

"Maebe. I was telling her about what happened," I explained, "but seriously, we do need to talk about what's coming. I had a visit from the guy who gave me this." I presented my palm and pointed to the flame symbol tattooed there. "He needs me to find one of his creatures and protect it long enough for it to decide what it wants to do. I get a good chunk of experience and an unknown reward."

"So what's the issue, man?" Muu said around his food. He swallowed before continuing, "Let's go get the little candle and be on our way to my training!"

"It's in the north somewhere, in the winter lands," I explained. "I think that means in the north where there's snow all the time, and that means it's going to be much farther than you can go without proper training from another Fighter. And Bokaj without a Bard instructor, and yeah, I know he's a fucking tough guy now—but we need to capitalize on that class I think somehow. I'm thinking that we have one of two options."

Bokaj held a hand up. "You think that he and I should hit the city while you guys go further north to find this thing."

"Or we try and convince the two trainers to come with us," I added. "I mean, we could easily pay for them to join us for a while so that you guys can get some training in, but that's up to them and you. I don't want to take the risk in harming your abilities."

"I like the second one," James put in. He had his plate clean already. Marines—we put food away fast, man. "If we can stay together, that would be best. At least if it's an option," he finished.

"Yeah," Yohsuke said simply. "The whole 'splitting the party thing' worked for us once, but we almost got our asses handed to us. That shit ain't sat, and if we can avoid it, let's do that."

"Agreed," Jaken grunted. "Can't have you almost dying like you did last time."

"Okay." I threw my hands up in surrender. "Let's try finding them and convincing them to come with us. I don't know what we're looking at as far as who is competing with us finding this thing, but they are power hungry, so let's get a move on."

We packed up our things, did a last check of the cave—nothing in the final tunnel except a bed of straw, and the middle was just a larger cavern for the hobgoblins to sleep in.

As we were leaving, Kayda was closer to us now. I looked at Muu. "Kayda is coming back. I can see if she wants to go back in the collar for now, but she's gonna be here."

He paled a bit but nodded his head. As we walked, Kayda crested the side of the mountain a little way off to the north and landed with a thud next to me.

"Do you want to take a rest in the collar?" I asked, and she promptly replied, *No.* "Then will you keep scouting our trail down?"

She spread her wings and flapped into the air. Yohsuke whistled at her and tossed her a few pieces of bacon that she snatched up happily. She took off with haste and then sent me something that made me smile.

Goblin okay? She showed me an image of Muu looking pointedly away from her and keeping his distance.

I looked to him and asked, "Hey, Kayda wants to know if you're okay, Goblin?"

"I'm not a Goblin!" he shouted up at her and shook his fist.

She shrieked into the air, a sound of thunder and fury and flapped his way a bit.

"Shit-fuck!" He scrambled away from her, and she flew away.

Goblin okay, she cooed to me in my mind again.

"Oh, dude." I chuckled at him. "You just gave her free reign to fuck with you when she thinks you're sad."

Muu began grumbling about birds and everything else he could call the Storm Roc. We traveled as quickly as we could down the mountain in a northwesterly fashion.

As we walked around the bend in the trail, spires of stone rising still above us, we crested the ridge over the mountain. Over the ridge, we began to see the city. That's what it was—a big-ass city. From miles away, I would say it was massive. As we got closer, the walls built high into the sky with towers watching over them and guards aplenty came into easier view.

There was a gate large enough to fit two carts side by side that a large line of people were standing at. It took us easily twenty minutes in the line to figure out what was going on. They were searching each person who came through and talking to them.

Hey, don't look now, Zeke, but people are staring at you, Bokaj told me through our earrings.

One guy said tails at least twice, Jaken added.

I had been so distracted by the gate and gaining entry to the city that I hadn't seen the people around us staring so intently and listening intently as their friends whispered to them softly.

Dragons just got muttered at least three times, make it four, James put in.

I nodded to them, and we kept minding our business as we waited in line. Once we reached the front, the four guards stopping people stopped us.

"Declare yourselves, your business, and any wares you may wish to sell while in our fine city," the eldest looking guard commanded in a bored tone.

One of the younger ones in a matching set of leather armor colored gold and red with a tabard of a lion over the front dipped a quill in ink and positioned it over what most likely was a ledger.

A small note for everyone, some of us, when given the option to choose our names, had chosen surnames. Others had not. We weren't sure if there were ways to see those things undeclared, so we decided to be honest.

Bokaj stepped forward and spoke up, "We are Bokaj, Yohsuke, Jaken Warmecht, Muu Ankiman, Zekiel Erebos, and James Bautista." The younger guard scribbled furiously as he spoke. "We come looking for training before passing through. No wares to declare, though we aren't against helping the local economy. Know any good stores where we might get supplies for the cold up north?"

The young guard kept writing, but the other two had taken an interest in the conversation. The one off to the right looked to be human with plain features, stubble, and an easy grin, spoke first, "You lot could always check with the clothiers strewn about. Some are nicer than others, though you look as though you could afford anywhere with the armor these folks and yourself are wearin'."

He looked over to the female guard, a hard-eyed woman with a deep tan and incredible bearing. She had her hands on a pair of short swords at her hips, but she attempted a friendly smile.

"Where would you reckon they go for gear, Til?" the guard asked.

"Could try Fulk's Finery in the rich district, though I'm not sure you'll want to go there sporting those tails." She nodded to my tails. "Been a bounty on animal tails 'round here of late, and yours look mighty nice."

"Do the guards typically allow that kind of thing to happen?" I asked carefully. She smiled coldly and shook her head. "Do the guards have issues with people defending themselves? Say, if they were attacked?"

The eldest guards harrumphed and wagged a finger. "You better not mean to cause trouble in this fair city. The Guard at Lindyburg would give such a person due process, furbody or not. Get in, before I see you out myself!"

The other guards seemed to find the insult funny because they laughed. The younger guard's laugh came a little nervously, though, as if he were uncomfortable with it all. We walked by, and I'm pretty sure I felt a little wind on one of my tails. I ignored it and kept walking with my friends.

Inside the thick walls were buildings with thick streets between them. It was a small market inside the gates, some people opting to start selling right away, and buyers were everywhere. We left the madness of it all behind as quickly as possible.

We found an alleyway clear of prying eyes for me to go into and shapeshift into my human form—a dark-skinned man of the same height and build as my fox-man form.

"That's better," I grumbled. "Let's go find an inn before dark and work on finding those trainers."

After asking a few people where we needed to go to find a decent inn, they pointed us to the western portion of the city and a place called the Mercenaries March Inn.

When we got there, it looked like a warehouse that had been converted into an inn. We walked through the double doors, dodging patrons with ale and mead outside singing boisterously just before dusk set in.

The inside had a ceiling the was twelve feet from the floor, well-lit with crystals and windows with the fading light outside coming in. The tables and chairs inside were well made and left plenty of room between for passage to and from the bar area. There were six bartenders, as the bar was a full square with two entrances to get in. The people here seemed to be human by majority, but there were a few other races present. I spied a few Orcs and Half-Orcs off in the corner farthest from the door. Some Dwarves were strewn about, drinking and comparing weapons and armor. I even spied a couple of Elves.

"Howdy, folks!" greeted one of the humans from behind the bar. "What can we do for ye?" He had a bald head, a short brownish-red beard, and a genuinely friendly disposition.

"Well, we could use a few rooms," Jaken said, "and also some information, if you could part with it?"

"Well, the rooms are available, though we do ask that you bunk two to a room to save on space. This is one of the more popular inns for fighting folk, and they do travel through often." He poured a drink, took a long pull from it, and winked at us. "Thirsty work this. Anyway, one room is three silver, meal service is another silver, and booze? Oh, we got booze, friends. Now, what kind of information are ye looking for?"

Bokaj moved up to the bar and pulled a stool out for himself. "Gimme a round, and I'll fill you in. And some food would be appreciated. For my friends too. Water for the cloaked one, though."

Yohsuke's cloaked form waved once, and the bartender nodded, not thinking anything of the request.

The bartender moved around and began filling glasses and whistled for a server. A teenager with gangly limbs and stray whiskers on his chin came over and took our order for food.

Bokaj took a swig of the drink in front of him and sighed contentedly. He looked at the bartender and began with, "You have anyone in here who could train my friend here in his class? And do you know where I could find a Bard to train me?"

The man moved over to Muu, looked him over, and began to think for a moment before replying, "Several mercenaries here are trained Fighters, though not all of 'em are the best at training newbies. I'd recommend asking Zhavron—he's one of the Orcs over yonder—about some training. He hasn't had steady work for a while. He was sick when his company left to go on a mission. He might be interested if the price is right."

"Giledt!" a patron down the bar growled. A menacing, shirtless human man with big, beefy arms glared at the bartender. "I asked for me drink too longs 'go."

"Piss up a rope, tiny." Giledt waved dismissively at the huge man. "Ye were cut off. Ye know the rules."

"Fuck yer rules." The man started to try and come back into the bar area. "I'll gets it meself."

The bartender smiled at us reassuringly and winked one last time as he said, "One moment."

He moved toward the man who was busy trying to fill a tankard with ale but couldn't seem to figure out the mechanism. Giledt strode easily up to him, waving and smiling at the customers along the way. Some just shook their heads, the others just grinned and began to slam money on the table.

When Giledt got to the man, Tiny, he tapped him on the shoulder, then grabbed a mug with his right hand. The warrior looked up at him and spat, "Wha'? You're too busy to get me drink. So I'll gets it. Piss off, you weak little fuck."

"Ye were warned." Giledt punched the man in the face with the glass mug in his right hand and shattered it in his cheek. The bartender grabbed the now-stunned man's arm, threw it over his shoulder, then hip tossed Tiny on to the ground. He dragged him out from behind the bar and proceeded to punch the man until he passed out.

Giledt strolled back, collected a coin as a token of favor from some of the patrons, and finally stopped back at us. His fist was bloodied after he rinsed it in water from a pitcher. Jaken reached out and touched his shoulder, and the man glowed gold a moment.

"Well thank ye, stranger, mighty kind of ye." He reached out and shook Jaken's hand. "I wouldn't recommend doing any other kinds of magic out in public. Especially near the guards. Magic use is a criminal offense round these here parts." He flexed his fixed hand and smiled. "I hate it when people walk behind my bar. Now, forgive me—where was I?"

I ginned, "You were about to tell us if you knew where to find a Bard to train Bokaj here."

"Bokaj? What an odd name. Well, friend if ye wanna learn music, there's probably some in the richer parts o' town. Though where exactly I couldn't tell ye."

"Hey, we appreciate your help." Bokaj smiled. "How about those rooms?" He offered a few gold for meals, drinks and a down payment on a couple days at the inn and a tip.

"Come on Muu, let's see about going to find this Zhavron guy." I gestured to the Orcs and got up to go.

Giledt stopped us with a thump on the bar. "Never go to someone else's table without a drink, especially not here. Ye take one for ye and one for them. To not take a drink with ye is to say that yer lookin' for trouble, okay?"

"Thanks, man." I took the drinks from him. "My name is Zeke. This is my friend Muu. We'll be back."

He smiled and sent us off with a nod.

I mean Marine protocol was similar at times, so I couldn't blame the guy for giving me the extra drink, but if I had been fleeced a drink—he'd get an ear full.

We went toward the rear of the dining area and found a group of Orcs sitting together. A few of them seemed interested in us but weren't going to speak to us first.

"Hey, we were wondering if Zhavron was here?" Muu asked, clearly too impatient to care about the mood.

Several Orcs' eyes darted toward an older-looking Orc hunched over a mug. He hadn't noticed us yet, but we stepped over and sat in front of him.

"What do you want with me, human and Dragon?" quested the wizened but still strong bass voice.

"I was wondering if you would be able to train a new Fighter?" Muu asked. "I've had some experience fighting, but I don't know everything I should."

"Feh," he grunted. "Of course. Why not talk to any one of the other Fighters in this place? All of them would be able to tell you how to spend your points and swing your sword like any other gruberancht out there just as easily."

"Because," Muu continued, "who wants to just swing a sword or stab with a spear and not have form or technique behind it. Anyone can wave a sword around and call themselves a Fighter with enough points. What I want is true skill. Could you teach me that?"

The old Orc stood slowly, his hulking form—shrunken with age—rising above both of us. His scarred limbs crossed in front of his chest, and he eyed us both.

"What is your weapon of choice," he asked, then continued, "and how have you squandered your points?"

Muu smiled. "I used one to unlock the spear tree, then one to unlock the short spear sub-tree. Other than that, I have seven more."

Zhavron flinched as if he had been struck. "So many?"

"Is it uncommon for a Fighter to have so many points?" I asked quickly. Had the Gods blessed Muu that much?

"It is uncommon for an inexperienced Fighter to show that restraint and sound judgment." He uncrossed his arms and looked at the young warrior before him with a new respect. "You want to train with an old codger like me? Fine. Let's share that drink and go over what will come."

"We have a stipulation," I warned as we sat together. "We cannot stay long—we have something important to do that requires we travel north. Could you train him on the go?"

The Orc began to think and mull over the question as he eyed Muu. "You'll be an attentive student? Train daily and listen to lessons as we travel?"

"You got it." Muu grinned.

"Who knows, you may be able to train all of us a little," I supplied with a smile.

"That'll cost extra." He grunted and hefted the mug before him. "How long will we be traveling?"

"We aren't sure." I shrugged. "Do you have a rate?"

Zhavron shook his head. "I will come along. I will allot my price once our time together is finished. The more I train, the higher the price. Though," he looked at Muu again, "I'd be willing to give a discount seeing as though my student seems apt. You supply food, shelter, and alcohol."

"You buy your own booze," I haggled, "and we will provide the other things. And the other things, within reason. If we think we're being cheated, we will give you what we think you were worth. Sound good?"

He frowned, then grinned a toothy grin that made his chipped and scarred tusks flashed down to the base of his gums. "Can't blame a guy for trying, can you?"

"Certainly can't." I grinned and held my mug up before me. "To a good relationship."

"Aye. A good relationship." He toasted with Muu and I. "When do we leave?"

"As soon as we can," I stated. "We need to find a Bard to train my friend over there." I pointed to Bokaj who happened to see and waved to us. "You wouldn't happen to know a Bard, would you?"

He laughed for a moment. "What mercenary group brings a Bard who would cheat them out of their coin and all the prettiest ladies?"

"That's fair," Muu observed.

I wasn't going to be the guy who told the trainer about Bokaj seducing a lizardmen chieftain—the lady had been so much bigger than him. The weird part? He wasn't even a Bard in training then.

"Let's get some sleep then," I advised. "We can look tomorrow and go shopping for cold weather gear." I looked at Zhavron. "You have cold weather gear? Hat, gloves, and whatnot."

The grizzled warrior shook his head. I nodded. "You will tomorrow. We will be up early enough. Meet us here in the morning. You staying here?" He pointed at a room directly above him. "Good. See you in the morning for breakfast then, Zhavron."

Chapter Six

We woke up, had breakfast with Zhavron, and then moved out for the day. Zhavron was pretty knowledgeable about the city, and the place we were going to was close, according to him.

He led us through the streets filled with mercenaries of all shapes and sizes. Which reminded me, "Hey, Zhavron, is there a place for magic users here? I know Giledt said they don't like magic used in public but–"

"No," he answered swiftly before looking around. "This city takes to martial prowess and that only. They frown on magic users and any caught doing any kind of magic in public are dealt with as criminals."

"Oh fuck, why?" Jaken asked in a hushed tone.

"Magic users assassinated the late governor here." He stopped, not looking around as much. "He was a well-loved man. The populous didn't take well to that and neither did his widow, the lady Governor. After that, the Mages were tracked down and beaten to death. It is a taboo thing to talk about. I take it you are a magic user?"

I nodded with Jaken, but I spoke quietly, "But I can pass as a warrior with my weapon choice."

"I suggest you refrain from using magic here then." He pointed to a building. "There is the place. High society folks get Bards, but the best ones do not look like they do magic. You would do well to look here in the richer section of the city."

"A sound plan," James observed as we walked into Filk's Finery.

The outside of the building itself was posh, bordering on pompous with bright colors, fabric, and designs. Inside, the interior was as fiercely decorated as the outside. The proprietor, a small halfling woman with mousy features and thick glasses, her hair in a messy bun, and some kind of small pipe in her hand, waved at us.

"Come in!" she purred at us. "Come inside, darlings."

She hopped up on to the stool she was sitting on to look at us. "Oh, mercenaries! How I do love those broad shoulders and interesting stories. I will let you know now the cheapest thing I have here cost a gold, but you will be the sexiest one in formation—I promise you. Now, what can Kitty get for you?"

Bokaj was about to speak when she noticed him and leaped on to her counter to look down at him, "You."

She began to lift his arms and look over him as he tried to speak. She grabbed his face in her small hands and squished his cheeks so he was quiet.

"Don't speak, darling. Let Kitty work." She began to look over him again at speed. She cupped, massaged, and grasped to the point that I was fairly certain I needed an adult— and he needed an intervention.

"Ma'am, we just need gear for the c–" I began, but she threw her pipe hand in my direction.

"Do not interrupt Kitty when the Muses sing!" She looked back at Bokaj, his face still clasped in her hand. "You are beautiful, darling." She slapped his cheek with her other hand. "I do you for a discount. I do not do this. You will be fierce. You will be cold. You. Will. Be."

She turned away from him, clutched her hand to her chest, and her right wrist flew to her forehead before she spoke again, "Beautiful."

I snorted aloud and had to cough mightily to cover the sound after her head whipped my way.

"Thank you, but I don't really need anything made for myself," Bokaj tried gently to let her down.

"You do not understand. I design for you, you take the clothing offered—you adore me for the masterful job I do—or they buy nothing. Because I *sell* them nothing."

Seems like we're stuck, dude, Yohsuke said into our minds.

She probably has the best gear in the city. See if you can get us a discount and ask about good cold gear, I told him.

"You raise a very valid point," Bokaj said. "Tell you what, I'll do that for you. I'll even spread your name when I wear it, but I'll do that only if you extend the discount to my friends too."

"You are very charismatic, darling," The halfling purred as she puffed thoughtfully on her pipe. "I will do this. I will allow you to choose from last year's winter selection at a reduced price, but I will design the *full* outfit. I design all night. Three days."

Bokaj shook his head. "We leave sooner than that. Can you do tomorrow morning?"

"You expect a masterpiece by tomorrow morning?!" she cried, aghast. "No. I can do two days."

Bokaj turned the charm on eleven or some high-ass number because what he said next had even me all kinds of attracted.

"Aren't you the best designer in the city?" he asked, to which she nodded. "Don't you think you could put together the best outfit anyone has ever seen almost overnight? I bet you could," he took her hand and pulled her a little closer, "I bet you could do a lot of things in one night."

There. A warm, familiar sensation at the base of my skull in the back. That familiar feeling from the Incubus? How? Was that Bokaj?

Kitty blushed deep crimson, then smiled. "Oh, you know nothing, Snow Elf. Nothing. This is a challenge. Yes, I see that now. My best creation in so little time. I will call in my apprentices. Tonight—we create *Life!*"

"I'm certain you won't let me down." Bokaj kissed her hand sweetly. "Goodbye and good luck."

We walked out of the place as Kitty was scrambling to find parchment and a quill, calling, "Frieda! Bentel! Go and fetch the others. We have work to do!"

As soon as we were outside, we all stopped and took Bokaj to the side of the building.

"What the fuck was that, man?" I whispered harshly.

"I was just trying to be charming," he said defensively. "She would have taken too long otherwise."

"Look, man, that's all well and good—the discount is boss, but if you're gonna do that shit," Yohsuke looked around before continuing, "warn us. I'm pretty sure I speak for all of us when I say that made all of us a little uncomfortable."

"What are you talking about?" He looked to the rest of us for some kind of clue.

"Dude, it wasn't just her that you were hitting with all that schmooze," Jaken explained. "It was all of us. We all felt that shit. It was... weird."

He looked to the rest of us who were nodding, and even Zhavron spoke up, "See what I said about them taking the best women? And he's had no training? I would hate to travel with him trained."

"Okay, I'll give a heads up next time." He shrugged. "Sorry, y'all. I was just trying to help."

"It's cool. Just be more careful. Okay?" I said with a sigh. He nodded, and we turned away to try and find somewhere to start looking for a Bard to give him the training he needed.

After looking for an hour, we were near giving up when we happened across a poster written about a performance that night. Someone called Pharazulla was singing at a high-class inn called the Blooming Ruby that Zhavron said was near the governor's mansion.

"Really tough place to get into from what I hear." Zhavron closed his eyes while thinking. "What I recall overhearing was that you have to be dressed up nice."

"We can do that. Svartlan gave us all some finer clothes to wear," James said. "Though we don't all need to go, do we?"

"Yeah, some of us could sit this one out," I agreed. "I'll go. I enjoy a good show. Who wants to sit out."

Everyone else but Muu raised their hands. The rest of us looked at him, and he shrugged, "What? I'm not afraid to party."

We all laughed, and Muu and I went right back into Fulk's to talk to Kitty.

As we walked back in, there were at least eight young women of various states and sizes and two young men scrambling around the room, grabbing cloth and designs from the racks of raw materials. Kitty's formerly artful messy bun was now truly messy, and she looked a little frazzled as she manned the helm of the ship she ran.

She saw us and shouted, "Ah, Kitty's tormentors return. Thank them for the rush on this project babies, for Kitty will allow *no rest* this evening." The people in the place truly looked murderous at that moment. "We just came in to see if you had anything nice and already made for my friend here to wear tonight?"

"Where do you take Kitty's art?" the little woman asked as her eyes narrowed.

"The Blooming Ruby?" Muu said.

Kitty seemed to like the idea as she began moving toward the back room, then looked back at her apprentices and shouted, "Why are Kitty's babies still?! Get to work!"

There was a flurry of motion and a cacophonous cry of, "Yes, mother."

They worked in silence otherwise unless communication was needed—then it was terse and whispered.

A moment later, Kitty careened into the room with an outfit in a bag and said, "Two gold and you leave me alone to my work right now."

I paid her, and we left the place so fast I was sure the workers inside hadn't noticed our departure.

We walked back out to the others and motioned for all of us to get the fuck out right quick. It would be hairy for us if they caught us in the area after we said we would leave them alone.

We went back to the Marching Mercenaries and grabbed some more food. We had no need of weapons or other armor, though Bokaj was interested in going to the lumberyard to pick up some supplies that he could use to make some odds and ends he had been thinking about.

Zhavron agreed to take him in the time we had before the show. It started in a couple hours, so we had plenty of time to bullshit and work on some things before we needed to get ready.

I took out the rings that I had bought from the jeweler in Sunrise. They were cheaper made trinkets, nothing like what we had found or the level of quality made by the Light Hand Clan in Djurn Forge, but they were adequate. There were no precious gems to use in them either, so that was a moot point. I could probably find a jeweler here to work with, but that was simply more time wasted when I had some right here with me.

Besides, they were mainly for me to use to grow my trade and for Muu as he would benefit the most. I could get better things for him from Shellica and her folks if absolutely needed. Especially if we were going into Gods knew what in the Hells. We might all need to upgrade if that's the case.

I pulled out a ring and engraved several connected shields into it with minimal drain on my MP. I sat it down, then began the next ring, engraved that with little hearts and plus signs next to it. The almost-universal symbol for healing. After that was finished, I went back to the first ring and began to fill it with my intent and mana.

I focused on protection, shielding the wearer from damage, assisting in defense. It took 200 MP, but it was worth it. I did the same with the second ring, focusing my intent on recovery, wounds healing like my Regrowth spell.

Defense Ring
+ 4 to defense
Ring created by Journeyman Jeweler Similian and enchanted by Journeyman Enchanter Zekiel Erebos.

Ring of Regrowth
Wearer heals up to 20 HP on the initial use and 1 HP per second for 30 seconds after.
Mana cost: 10 MP
Ring created by Journeyman Jeweler Similian and enchanted by Journeyman Enchanter Zekiel Erebos.

The second ring was pretty awesome. With the mana cost, Muu could use it at least fifteen times or more before his mana bottomed out. Though with his low mana regeneration from a low wisdom score, it would be hard on him. The total cost for the second ring was 300 MP, ten times what it cost for me to cast the spell myself.

I allowed my mana to recover over the next couple minutes as I thought more about the kinds of items I wanted to create. I set the other rings back in my inventory—I would take requests or odd ideas from the group for those.

I brought out the bracelet and stared at it for a moment. I could try and make something that would give more defense. I could also go with a similar design as James' and my elemental items and reduce any kind of elemental damage that Muu took, but I wasn't confident I was good enough yet to do anything more than protect him from a campfire or a puddle—let alone the sheer destruction a wizard, Mage, or sorcerer could dish out.

No. This needed a specific function. Something that would help give him even the slightest advantage until it could be upgraded or replaced. What about blur? Could I make Muu move faster? Not like a generalized haste that would envelop his whole body, similar to what James could do. But maybe just isolated to the arm?

No. There's the chance that it could cause him to overextend and leave an opening for an opponent. We couldn't risk that at this stage. Not with him still learning.

I looked through my spells and abilities. Could I...? Maybe... Shit. I mean, I really needed to see about upping my imagination here. There was nothing to confine me! Why was I having trouble with something so seemingly simple? It was his job to assist in melee damage, right? So, what did that leave? Doing. Damage. The kind of damage was almost irrelevant. So, that left me with fewer options, but then again—there were so many!

I could enchant the bracelet to allow him to imbue his weapon with fire damage, ice damage, lightning—whatever! All I had to do was decide. But I wasn't sure how his weapon would react to the stress of it, and that left too much to chance.

There was a chance it would ruin even a well-made weapon.

Maybe I could help him to actually just throw it harder? Yeah, that could work!

I took the bracelet in my hands and focused on the image I wanted to engrave into the item. As I looked at it, the bands were held together by a clasp and a hinge that made it into an almost-solid piece when clasped together. It would fit him fine. On both sides, the inner portion that touched his skin—not the outer—I engraved a javelin in flight with a ring around the front and the same motion symbols I used for his jumping boots.

Once that was complete, I focused on what I wanted the bracelet to actually do—which was to make Muu be able to throw his weapon harder and faster than what he already could on his own. I had seen him throw it a few times lazily, and it had gone pretty far without the help. I saw the weapon leaving his grip to fly straight and true, but I envisioned it moving faster. So much faster and harder—hitting the target hard enough to shatter stone.

I poured my mana into the engraving. I poured and kept pouring. I filled the engraving almost to the brim before I got the feeling that if I didn't stop, it would be too much. I had full MP before I started feeding the enchantment mana. Now I was down to my last 25 MP—meaning it had required a whooping 475 MP to hit full. What the fuck had I created?! The spear had taken all of my mana and that had been able to damned near teleport the item to his hand.

It must have been awesome, because I was rewarded with another level in enchanting, bumping me up to level 29.

Thrower's Wrist

+ 4 to strength of thrown weapons, + 5 speed to thrown weapons

When a weapon is thrown by the wearer, it will move at greater speeds, distances, and with more power than is capable by normal means. Be careful if you decide to throw something at a friend without thinking.

Charges – 3 per day. Each charge returns the following morning.

Bracelet created by Journeyman Jeweler Similian and enchanted by Journeyman Enchanter Zekiel Erebos.

Hot damn! I whistled to myself. *Not the first charge-type item we have seen, Bokaj's Silence Wand being the first. Still cool as fuck!*

I decided to leave everything else as they were—back into my inventory they went. I then went to see about giving these to Muu. Then I thought better of it and decided to get myself a bath after catching an errant waft of my own stank hit me. I stashed the items then stepped out into the hallway to go downstairs and speak with the barkeep about bathing.

It was Giledt who helped me track down a bathhouse. "Yeah, it's right down the street, outside, and to the left at the door. It's the third building from the left with the steam above the door. Mention you're staying with us, and they'll treat you good."

He smiled at me as I nodded and wandered off outside and followed his directions. I saw the steam coming from a vent above the door pointing down in front of it, and I walked in through it. I felt grimy after that, like my pores were open to the grime and I wanted—needed—to bathe now.

As my eyes adjusted to the dim light, I could make out a desk with a small man behind it with a broad smile and an easy-going attitude and a single door off to our right. His features were tanned, a large nose, muscular build, and dark hair over his brown eyes. He wore a simple pair of brown shorts and a white shirt with a slit down the middle to show his toned core and chest. When he spoke, his voice sounded almost Italian to me.

"Welcome to the Steam Palace where all of your problems can—hopefully—be solved with a good bath." He pointed to himself and bowed slightly at the waist. "I am Remy. How can I assist you today, sir?"

"Well, Giledt at the Marching Mercenaries sent me. He said you would be able to help me get exactly what you offer—a good bath."

Remy's smile seemed to grow even wider. "And that you shall, sir. That you shall. Tell me," he began to busy himself behind the counter, "what kind of scent would you prefer? Do you wish for restorative oils to be added? Do you need *assistance* bathing?"

I blushed a little at the implication and smiled despite myself. I'm not a prude—I know that sex work is a thing and that there's nothing wrong with someone doing what they want so long as they actually *want* to be doing that. I know that there is a huge rabbit hole that could be gone down here, but for tonight—I figured I could handle myself.

"Thank you for the offer, but no." I smiled back. "I think I can handle myself. I would like to try the oils though, and if I could have a lighter scent, not so heavy on the perfume?"

"Ah!" Remy clapped and dropped to a knee behind the counter. He popped back up with a small basket that held two lidded containers, a towel, and some sandals. "Follow me then, good sir. I shall run you through our special treatment suite and then show you how to operate the equipment so that you have the best experience possible."

Gotta love the level of commitment to the guy's job. As he walked ahead of me, he tossed open the door, then waited for me to pass through. Once I was inside, he locked the door and continued further along.

"Why did you lock the door?" I wondered aloud.

"Ah, to keep out unwanted guests, my good sir," he replied with the smile he seemed to wear permanently. "The first section of the experience takes a guide to do and is a one-person use kind of thing. This keeps intruders out of that process."

I'd be lying if I said that my senses didn't go into overdrive trying to figure out if this was an attack. All I could smell were oils, incenses, and lotions. I could also smell different body scents that in this area were strongest. I stopped scenting the air but turned my other senses out. I heard different voices, some having conversations, others singing, others doing... well, more aerobic things—let's put it that way.

Other than that, I heard nothing. I saw the grimy boot prints, mud and what not on the floor before me and gathered that others had come this way before. I could stow my paranoia for now and let Remy do his job.

We entered a locker room area where Remy motioned to a curtained off area. "You can undress back there. There will be a towel waiting that you can use for modesty. Your valuables like rings and the like you can, of course, store in your inventory. If you would like any clothes laundered, we will do so for a modest fee. I will wait for you right here. Take your time."

I nodded and went behind the thick, white curtain and undressed. I put all my rings, my collar, and other items into my inventory. I pulled out several bundles of dirty clothes and put them in a basket on the floor. I found the extremely large towel that he had spoken about and wrapped it around my waist. I stepped out from behind the curtain. Remy stood with his back slightly turned but saw the motion and waved for me to follow him again.

We went into another room through the doorway, and I was surprised to see what looked to be indoor plumbing. There were metallic pipes with nozzles and small crystal gauges.

"This is our steam room," Remy spoke as he began turning nozzles in a specific direction here and there. He pointed to a spot on the floor. "If you would stand right there. A small burst of steam will spill over you, opening your skin and getting that filth out of your body. After that, we will have a heated shower of water over here." He indicated another spot off to his right. "Then we will proceed to the bathing area."

I stood on the first spot and nodded to him. The steam that came from the vent further opened the pores along my upper body, and I felt a little better. I stepped over to the shower area, took the towel away from my hips, and felt warm water cascade over my body, rinsing away some of the grime.

"Here you are, good sir." Remy's voice brought me out of the bliss I had begun to feel. He handed me a brush with a dollop of some kind of liquid on the bristles. "Scrub the grime away. This is only the beginning of your time here. Enjoy."

I heard the door open and close, Remy walking back the way we had come in as I cleaned my chest first

I cleaned the rest of myself as thoroughly as I could, dunked my head under the hot water and rinsed, then grabbed my towel. The rush of water over my head had been so ni–

"Please, good sir, do not dry," a feminine voice spoke behind me.

I turned to see a tall, well-built woman with the same kind of outfit that Remy had worn on. She had thick, corded muscles along her shoulders, arms, and powerful looking legs. Her Orcish features were softer than some of the males that I had seen previously. Her fiery orange hair swept into her left eye in a limp mohawk, and she watched me with the other blue orb. The green in her skin seemed almost like sea foam, and she smiled the same as he had.

"I am Vrawn." She bowed slightly at the waist. "Master Remy had to go back to the desk to deal with another customer. He asked that I see to the rest of your stay with us. Come, I will show you to your suite for the length of your bathing experience."

She motioned for me to follow and I did so. She was easily a foot taller than I was, but she moved so gracefully. Like a dancer. It was beautiful to behold. She held the basket that Remy had been carrying in front of her with both hands crossed before it.

She brought me into a hallway with doors on each side. The majority of the sounds I had heard previously were coming from here, but some of the more boisterous ones seemed to have subsided. I was taken past all the doors in the first hall, then into another adjoining hall at the end where we turned to our left and went into the third door.

Inside, there was a table with fruits of all kinds, some I didn't even recognize. Which, let's be honest, wasn't hard in a new world. There was also a chair behind a copper-colored tub with piping hot water.

"Please, good sir." Vrawn gestured to the tub. "If you would. Once you are in, we will begin your treatment."

I shrugged, then completely dropped my towel and climbed into the tub. The water was just this side of too hot, which was the absolute best kind of water to me. I let my body sink until I dunked my head when a large shadow crossed over. I came up quickly, on the alert as water streamed down.

Vrawn held her arms out and away from herself in a display of non-aggression while she spoke, "This happens often with you fighter types. Do not worry. I mean you no harm. This is a neutral place. We are here to serve. Relax, please."

Her face was serene, and she was surprisingly calming. I felt no malice, no ill intent. I decided to try and relax, but I used my earring to tell my friends where I was and what was going on.

Wolf calls from Jaken and Bokaj greeted me, but I felt safer that they knew where I was. The others just gave half-hearted affirmatives.

"Relax, good sir," she murmured as she began to work my shoulders in her grasp, kneading and rolling the muscles until I let the tension flee from my body. After a few minutes of massaging, she began to pour a softly scented liquid into the water that began to cloy the air. It tickled my senses and helped me relax even more. The water began to drain away, leaving me nude but covered in the oil.

"Uh, Vrawn?" I spoke, and her head appeared over my shoulder. "Is this normal?"

"Yes, good sir. This is the oil that we massage into the skin. It sticks to you with heat, then when we massage it in, it grabs dirts and grime and pulls it from the skin. Then we apply the other liquid in the other container. This causes a reaction with the oil that will purify it from your body. After that, we give you a rinse, fill the tub with more water, and you can take your pick of scents to cover yourself with that will stay for longer than average."

She pulled a chain, and two other women joined us in the room. One was human with a bald head, green eyes, soft—

but pretty— features, and thin frame wearing what seemed to be the uniform of the day here. The other was an Elf with golden skin, long, flowing, blonde hair and regal features. Her eyes were red, like a ruby, and her physique was that of a runner's—athletic and streamlined.

"May I introduce Odessa and Elnaril to you, good sir." Vrawn motioned first to the human, then to the Elf. "They will assist me in purifying your body unless you find them unsuitable?"

"No, please." I started to sit up, but Vrawn held me down gently. "They are fine. It's just a massage and a bath."

That last bit was more for me than anyone else in the room. Again, I knew this was their job. I had no problem with that, but strangers touching me had always made me feel self-conscious. I had to work through this.

They gathered around me. Vrawn worked my back and shoulders as the tallest, then Elnaril massaged my chest and stomach with Odessa working from my hips down.

I, uh, I didn't squeak when a certain hands-on Elf got a little *too* thorough. You're hearing things.

The rest of the bathing experience consisted of the rinse and the fragrance, a light, slightly citrus scent, being massaged into my skin once more.

While the professionals were at work, I drifted into my thoughts.

A lot had happened since we had fought that Incubus. A lot of information given. Balmur was alive and somehow being used to fight for servants? Maybe. We weren't ready to get into the Hells yet, but we had a quest to get some good experience. We would try to get Bokaj his trainer so that we could have that avenue open to us, if we could. We had a heading. More than we'd had previously flailing in the dark, hoping for leads.

With proper planning, hard work, and some serious teamwork, we could do this. Just had to hone the blades we had now how we could.

I felt the hands kneading my neck drift to my skull and then to my ears, and my left leg thumped against the inside of the tub. My eyes burst open in worry that someone had noticed.

The ladies seemed to be ignoring it, and that was so tip-worthy.

All said and done, it was two hours of being pampered that I hadn't known in either life. Not that I would have been truly comfortable at home with all this.

After we were finished, I was patted dry and dressed in the clothes that Svartlan, Maebe's personal tailor, had made for me.

The clothes themselves were finely made. There was a metallic blue tunic with a deep V in the neckline that accentuated the stark contrast between my dark skin and electric blue eyes. The top hung to mid-quad on me, and I wore it over a pair of black leather breeches that felt so soft and made no noise. I tucked the breeches into my boots, then put the black leather belt in the pack around my hips loosely. It was more for fashion than for practical use, but it felt good to look good.

We walked back out into another hallway outside a door hidden by a wall that gave the illusion of there being only one entrance to the room. At the end of the hall was a door that led into another illusionary wall behind Remy's desk.

"Ah!" He clapped his hands and spread them wide. "Good sir! How was your treatment? Did you find our services adequate?"

"More than, Remy." I smiled. The other girls had left us once their portion of the job had been concluded, though they had looked a little sad when they had been leaving. "How much do I owe you?"

Vrawn stepped forward and spoke, "He partook in the bath, massage, purification, and a light citrus perfume oil. He was a perfect gentleman, refused our other services politely."

I looked at her in surprise, but Remy seemed more than satisfied.

"Very well, for the whole process—excluding the courtesan services—it will be five gold," Remy said with a small, sad smile.

"And if I had partaken of the services?" I asked warily as I withdrew the necessary money from my inventory.

"It would have been another five gold per courtesan," Remy replied easily enough. "They, of course, would be reimbursed with the lion's share of it."

"Meaning?" I quested.

"Meaning, we would keep the majority," Vrawn explained. When I looked at her curiously, she smiled, flashing dainty tusks. "It would be five gold total, a gold to the house for the first sale of the night, which would have been you for all of us. Then we keep what we make after that including the four gold you paid after. It is a lucrative system when our customers are interested."

"So, to make sure I understand," I swept my hand to Remy first, "out of the fifteen gold total for their services, you— the house—would get three," he nodded and smiled, "and the girls would keep four. Then any other sales they made tonight would be theirs to keep?"

"That is correct." Remy nodded with his easy grin.

I pulled three more gold out for Remy, then looked to Vrawn. "Here, if you will give my regards to Odessa and Elnaril." I handed her twelve more gold.

The large Orc woman smiled genuinely and pulled me into an embrace I thought would crush me. "Thank you, kind sir."

She leaned back far enough to meet my surprised gaze, then planted a surprisingly soft kiss on my cheek before the titan of a woman walked away.

Remy laughed deeply, and I turned toward him. He waved at my face. "She does not do that. Most men do not wish to be with her because she is so..." He seemed to be searching for the word, so I suggested intimidating. "Yes! They are intimidated by her immense size and musculature. I believe you are the first to pay her for being who she is and not who she has to pretend to be."

"Huh," I said with genuine surprise. She had seemed so nice. "Well, I'm on my way out of town tomorrow possibly. So, forgive my needing to be away, but I have a crucial appointment tonight."

"Very well, good sir." Remy smiled again and bowed. "Never forget that you are always a welcome guest in the Steam Palace. Good day!"

I went back to the inn and met up with Muu. He was wearing a black doublet with brown breeches and a white undershirt. His boots, the brown ones he had been wearing this whole time, had been cleaned and treated.

"Looking good, man!" I greeted him. "Nice duds."

"Same to you, buddy." He started looking me over. "Where did you get those?"

"Same guy who made my armor," I explained. "Remember us explaining what happened while we were in the Fae Realm? Svartlan, the Orc? Yeah, he made these. This is my first time wearing them. Gotta say—I'm digging the look."

"Me too, brohaim," Bokaj agreed from my left at the stairs.

He walked toward us in a deep purple tunic that was cut diagonally at the bottom, belted to his waist with a thick, gray leather belt with soft fur on it. He wore black breeches with gray boots that matched the belt.

"*Damn.*" I had to whistle at him. We all laughed. "We ready to split? Weapons in inventories just in case?"

They nodded, and we set off. Bokaj had gotten the skinny on where we needed to go to get to the Blooming Ruby. We followed Bokaj to a building that looked like a straight-up castle. The outside had a moat around it that was six feet wide, and I didn't know how deep; the outer wall had a large rose painted on it with a deep-crimson ruby at the center.

It seemed a little gaudy, but hey—you know how rich people do.

There were two "guards" standing watch at the gate that we spoke with on the way in. They looked booted, had next to no bearing, and the true guards were on top of the wall to the building with heavy crossbows not fucking around. Soon as we stepped on the wood, there was a bolt trained on my chest, and I saw the other guard eye us steadily.

We must have looked good enough because they didn't stop us. We walked across the sturdy planks of wood toward the door. There was another faux guard, this one a human woman who took us to a table at the front of the house.

A human server came and took our orders for food and drinks while soft music played. I was plenty sure I wouldn't be touching the fish because fuck fish. The steak that we all ordered sounded to die for. Our food came and went, the potatoes with the steak had been drizzled with a sauce that was so good, I'd had to use the bread to sop it up and savor it more.

The flavor had reminded me of caramelized onion with some honey drizzled over it, garlic, and some thyme, but there was a taste I couldn't identify it at all that lent it a sweet, smokey tang.

The people watching us nearby could see this was something the lower classes would do, and I heard one call me, "a savage", but the wait staff left us alone.

After the meal had been served, the show began. The lights in the place, a crystal chandelier that gave a soft, white light dimmed lower, and a darkness overtook the crowd. A shimmering light flared in a balcony above us and reflected on to the stage to the right side of the building in front of us where a woman in a black dress that flared a bit past her legs stood with her back turned to us.

Her outline in the light was tall with black hair that seemed to sparkle a bit, and she was toned like a dancer. A light melody, playful and building, began from musicians outside the light. It reached a swelling note, and her voice began. A breathy, low, and seductive tone carried over all of us. I couldn't take my eyes away or pay attention to the world around me.

"A sweet summer breeze brought me to my knees and I saw you..." She turned around slowly, letting the audience catch her made-up face with smokey-looking eyes glancing at each of them in passing. *"You lit up my night, made me feel alright—yes it's... true."*

She began to sway, her arms and body shifting to the beating pulse of the rhythm. As she continued to sing about this mysterious summer lover, the crowd began to clap to the beat as she swayed across the stage. At the conclusion of the song, the lover had gone and so had her will, but then she found her fall knight, and there the song ended.

A small man came on stage as the lights began to brighten slowly. "Ladies and gentlemen, the lovely Pharazulla!"

Now that the harsh lighting wasn't in her face, I could make some of her features out. Her cheeks were soft and girlish in a pretty way, and her hazel eyes were flashing in the light. Her lips, drawn from smiling, looked a little thin, but her teeth were dazzling, and her skin was oddly pale. I could also make out the small points in her ears. A Half-Elf maybe?

"Thank you, all of you," she spoke, and her voice was still pretty bewitching. "Your adoration is so wonderful. I would like to thank my wonderful hostess, the lady Governor. May she reign forever!"

The crowd cheered and anyone with a drink near toasted to the statement.

With the show completed, the place began to take on a different air, and the music livened up a bit.

"Ladies and gentlemen, that concludes this evening's entertainment!" the little man said solemnly. "Please, do feel free to mix about and dance if you should feel so inclined. Lady Pharazulla will be taking interviews shortly after she rests her voice."

Man. Rich people, huh? I looked around the room and saw that this didn't upset any of the folks around us in the slightest. That led me to believe this sort of performance was commonplace. Expensive food, drink, and a song by a hot lady?

She seemed to be running quite the racket if this was all her idea.

"Interviews?" Muu asked in a soft voice. We watched as Pharazulla left the stage and went into a small hallway behind it to the left. "We need to see her first."

Bokaj and I agreed, and as dancers took to the stage area and waiters moved tables to accommodate more—we made our way toward that hall.

"Stop!" The small man who had been on stage waddled toward us. I realized, belatedly, that the man was a Gnome. "That area is off limits until I say so."

Bokaj turned on the charm with a wink to us as he turned. "Sir, you don't understand. I've come a *very* long way from the tribes of the north to find my long lost cousin, a half-Elven maiden who sings exactly the way she does. Please, you simply *have* to let me speak to her."

Bokaj took a knee in front of the little man and continued before he could interrupt, "I'm the last heir to the chiefdom, and it was my father's wish that all his kin be brought to him as he lay dying." Here his eyes began to water. "Please, sir. Please help grant a dying man's wish." As he said the last bit, he cupped the gnome's hands in his, and I heard a discreet tinkle of coins being exchanged. "Please?"

The gnome looked into his hands and jumped at what he saw before clearing his voice a couple of times. "Well... I suppose we cannot keep a dying man waiting, can we? Come along."

Nicely done, man, I congratulated him mentally.

He threw a grin over his shoulder at me and then looked forward to follow the gnome. He led us down a hallway with one door to our right near the beginning of the hall and then a door at the rear on the left. That was the door we stopped in front of.

The man knocked smartly, then spoke, "Madame Pharazulla, you have a guest who needs to speak to you most urgently regarding a matter of great import."

"Uh, one moment!" the lady called. "I'll be right there. I am changing!"

It sounded... off to me at best. As if she were stalling. We heard a series of grunts and thumps a slight whisper that I couldn't catch the words, then nothing. The looks on my friends' faces said the same thing, but we couldn't push into the place without alerting the man with us.

A moment later, a frazzled—but dressed—Pharazulla opened the door and poked her head around. "Ahem. Yes, who may I have the pleasure of addressing so soon after my performance?"

"I am Bokaj, my lady, and it is most important that I speak to you," my friend said with a slight bow from his waist and a hand over his stomach.

"Forgive me, but I do not know you, sir," Pharazulla said cautiously.

"You wouldn't, Lady Pharazulla," Bokaj said as if his world were crumbling. "That is the very fact I came to remedy. Please, if you would but give me a moment?"

"Fine, stranger, you may join me." She stepped slowly from the door. "You may go, mister manager. I will see to them quickly. If I need help, I will shout."

"Quite well." The gnome eyed us a moment more, then scurried off.

The door opened and allowed the three of us in before shutting swiftly. The room was as long as the hallway and was larger than you would think. It was lavish, smartly decorated with a huge bed in the center.

"Quite impressive—using bribery and charismatic charm against an imbecile like him," our hostess observed dryly as she moved away from entry area toward the bed. "I felt why you did, though I didn't hear everything. That and money would be the only things to make the house manager break his own protocol. Why have you come?"

"I need someone to train me to be a Bard," Bokaj stated flatly, dropping the charade. "You were the only one we could find quickly. From what I could see—and feel—you must be a good one."

"I am," she said simply, "and you were right to come and find me, but why do you not have time?"

"We have an urgent quest that will see us leaving town in the morning, just after we get cold weather gear," Bokaj informed her. "We travel north."

"Why?" she queried again, her interest seemingly piqued.

"Reasons," I replied sternly. "You will be paid for your time," I caught a stray scent and looked just over her shoulder, "protected and safe."

I sent a telepathic message to Bokaj with our earrings, *Hey, bad guy in the back, directly behind her, slightly hidden by the drapes. Has a crossbow.*

When you out him, he's gonna fire, Bokaj warned.

Then you'd better be faster with all that training you do without us, I finished and trusted he would be able to do what I knew he was capable of.

"What makes you think I cannot do that myself?" She arched an eyebrow.

"The man standing behind you by the window with a crossbow aimed at your back for one," I informed her.

The man panicked and fired off a bolt that hit an opaque burst of energy that appeared around Pharazulla. An arrow struck the man in the chest, then another and another, dropping his health chunk by chunk. Finally, my great axe struck him, and his health completely fell.

The Bard gasped as the weapon turned to lightning and returned to my grasp. Muu, slightly panicked, took a second to collect himself and then sighed in relief.

"How did you...?" she began, but I put out a hand.

"We can protect you," Bokaj reiterated for me. "Join us, get away from here and whoever is trying to kill you, and we will promise you payment and your life."

She seemed to think a moment, put her hands to her temples, and sat on the bed.

"What do you say?" Muu offered his hand to her.

"No," she replied. "I'm sorry, but I cannot go with you. My reasons are my own, but I will not leave. Not right now. You'll have to find someone else."

The hair on my body stood on end as a wave of whatever it was that Bokaj brought to bare on people when he was trying to convince them to do things rose around us.

"Please, come with us," he said in a clipped tone.

Pharazulla's gaze went blank as she stood and began to walk forward toward him. His look of concentration fell and gave way to one of victory.

As soon as she was within reach, her hand snaked out and slapped Bokaj across the cheek smartly. He looked at her in disbelief.

"You will need to be a *much* stronger person to ever have a hope of charming me, child," she spat. "Especially as untrained as you are."

"Come on, B," I grunted. "Let's get out of here."

I tugged on his arm and motioned for Muu to come on too. As we left the room, the Gnome who had brought us back was there with some important-looking folks. When we cleared the building, moat and all, Bokaj stopped in his tracks.

"We need to convince her to come," he said, temper starting to flare. "We need someone to train me."

"Yeah, we do," I agreed but continued, "Somewhere else. She's not coming, and I'm pretty sure if we tried to make her, the whole city would come down on us. Besides, time is not on our side. We need to get this quest out of the way, and we're competing with somebody trying to get there before us. We can try and find a Bard elsewhere."

"She does seem like the kind to try and fuck us," Muu observed, "and not even in a fun way."

Despite the tension in our conversation, we found ourselves chuckling.

I looked Bokaj straight in his eyes. "Look, man, this quest could give us an in with the Elementals, and that could be good for us. Plus, there's a good chance we may have to fight over the target. Good EXP in the meantime, and we find a better trainer. What do you say?"

He mulled it over for a moment, then nodded. "Okay, man. We get our shit and get gone tomorrow morning."

I clapped him on the shoulder, and we headed back to the inn for the night and some well-needed rest. Maebe spoke through Shadow Speak with me for a while. She hadn't been able to do anything other than petition Samir for me to be able to return with no response, and she felt I should know. After that, we simply sat in each other's company for a while until I fell asleep and the spell fizzled.

Chapter Seven

I rose early in the morning and wandered downstairs after packing to enjoy breakfast. As I cleared the stairs and looked to the bar, I found Vrawn wearing a nice lilac dress sitting with Giledt. In the dress, she looked almost dainty. It was a lovely look. She looked to be enjoying the conversation, but when she saw me, her eyes lit up a little.

"Good sir!" she greeted me with a wave. As I walked over, she produced a bundle from her own inventory. "You were in such a hurry last night that you forgot your clothes that we had laundered for you. I recalled you saying that you were leaving this morning, and Remy told me you had been recommended to us by Giledt."

She smiled at the barkeep who grinned back knowingly. "He's a friend from another time."

I took the clothes from her with a grateful smile and put them into my inventory. "Thank you, Vrawn! You're a lifesaver. And please, call me Zeke. You aren't at work. I love that color on you—the dress looks great."

Giledt smiled at me with his usual grin and motioned to the seat beside him. "Care for a seat, friend? Can have the kitchen cook up some chow for you, maybe treat the lovely lady to breakfast in appreciation?"

"You got it, Giledt—you the man." I grinned at him. I turned back to Vrawn quickly to check, "If that's okay with you?"

"I would be honored, Zeke." She spoke my name as if testing it. When I smiled at her, she repeated the gesture. This morning, her hair was swept out of her left eye and behind her pointed ear. Both eyes locked on me. "I know that you said you had enjoyed yourself last evening, but I wanted to be sure that you truly had?"

"Oh, absolutely!" I waved her concerns aside. "I've never had a massage like that before. Ever. And you were so nice to me, a complete stranger. I had nothing to complain about, and I wouldn't ever bad mouth someone who takes care of me like you did. So, thank you very much."

"It is always my pleasure, good–" I gave her a look with raised eyebrows, and she blushed. "Forgive me, *Zeke.*"

"Better." I took a water that Giledt offered us both and listened as my friends noisily made their way downstairs. "Here come my companions. This should be fun. Try not to let them tease too much, and if they bother you, let me know."

She nodded once, and I turned to face them. "Hey, guys!"

"Yo," Yohsuke grunted as he plopped down.

"Howdy," Jaken said. James waved at us and sat beside Yohsuke.

Bokaj plopped down next to Vrawn with an easy grin. "Hello, I'm Bokaj."

"Vrawn," she replied and bowed slightly. "It is a pleasure."

"Where's Muu?" I asked. Bokaj held up a hand to still us, and then I heard a sudden cry of anger and outrage.

Muu shot out of their room with Tmont barreling closely behind.

"Get the cat!" Muu shouted, much to our amusement and the ire of the hungover patrons around us. "Fuck! Bad kitty! Not the TAIL!" He howled as she gave it one final nip and slinked over to Bokaj's side.

Muu, wearing only his small pants and breathing heavily, stood staring at Bokaj with near murder in his gaze.

"That's a very hairy alarm clock," I observed playfully, "and thank god I don't need that wake up call.

"I hate it!" he shouted. I noted a few of the mercenaries around us groan. "There's not even a pun to describe how much I hate cats."

He stomped back upstairs and slammed the door. Bokaj flipped a gold to Giledt by way of apology, and we were served our food.

Dude, who's the dress? Bokaj asked.

She's a worker over at the Steam Palace that I went to last night. She took care of me. As soon as I said it, I blushed furiously.

The boys all went, "Ooooooooooh!" in damned near unison, and poor Vrawn was so confused.

"Nothing to see here. I'm just gonna go die," I grumbled as I put my head on the bar.

"I would not like that," Vrawn said, a little distress in her voice. "You were the model customer—better than. Serving you was my deepest pleasure."

"WOAH!" James hollered. The rest of the peanut gallery gave high fives, and my cheeks should've been on fire.

I'll kill you all! I roared through our earrings, and that just made things worse.

"Thank you, Vrawn," I said tiredly. "Please, let's enjoy our meal. Ignore them."

She laughed, her rumbling giggle catching Giledt's attention. He smiled and passed me a wink, and I really wanted to just Fireball the whole damned room at that moment.

Zhavron walked down the stairs with a bag and scratched his stomach as he eyed us.

After we ate, we bid Giledt and Vrawn goodbye. I thanked her again for bringing me my clothes. She reached down with her powerful, gentle hands and pulled me into a hug once more.

"Be safe, Zeke," she whispered in my right ear. I gave her a squeeze around her ribs and looked up to respond but didn't get the chance.

She ducked her head toward me so quickly that I couldn't react and pressed her surprisingly soft lips against mine in a chaste kiss. She brought her face from mine, blushing furiously, her cheeks a slight purple color, and she smiled once more. "Good luck."

Giledt clapped in delight, and even Zhavron grinned. I willed myself to smile back as more color crept into my face. That had been enough to cause all kinds of reactions.

The most obnoxious one being my friends whooping and acting the fool behind me. I waved goodbye, and we shuffled away. I saw Giledt pat a nervous looking Vrawn mid back and give her a thumb up. Zhavron just shook his head and gave me a little push on the shoulder, jarring me out of my stupor.

"Come on, lover boy," the grizzled Fighter ordered.

As we stepped into the sunlight of the street and the citizens moved around us, I was a little more conscious of eyes than before. Whether it was the heat, the heat in my face, or the fact that my friends were still dogging on me—I'm not sure.

I endured the jeers and good-natured teasing that lasted until we got to Kitty's place and we walked in. A frazzled Kitty and her exhausted looking apprentices waited with a simple parcel on the counter.

"Ah, you have returned to Kitty, darling." Her pipe lit up, and smoke filled the air before her. "Your clothes are ready. Henrique! Gather last year's winter line of coats."

One of the male apprentices leaped from his place to comply and brought out a rack on wheels. There were furs, thick jackets, and coats that looked really nice. The simpler ones were still good quality, and after I put a gray cloak with white fur beneath on my shoulders, I knew I had struck gold.

The others gathered appropriate clothing, cloaks, and other needed gear. I even made sure that Zhavron was taken care of. The old Orc picked the simplest looking thing he could find, and I tossed her three gold for our things. The others paid their own fees, and Bokaj tried to hand Kitty some money, but she slapped him again.

"You wear my clothing," she ordered pointing at the package. "You will find a reason to look superb, and you will wear it. Mention my name. Always. Be gone from me. I must mourn."

She began to pout dramatically as we left. The apprentices looked pissed, but they had probably gotten some good experience. I hoped. We made our way toward the north gate with Zhavron leading us. The crowds and people looking at us weirdly, but we probably just looked like a bunch of mercenaries on our way to a job.

As we left the gates, after declaring we were leaving to the guards, we heard a familiar voice to our right. I looked over, and Pharazulla sat in the shade of a tree just off the roadway.

"Took you long enough," she complained. She wore simple riding clothes compared to the nice clothing she had worn last night.

"I thought you weren't interested in coming along," Bokaj said. I looked at him and could see he was wary. "You had things to do."

"I did," she replied simply. "Now I don't, and it looks like you still need a trainer, as obviously, none of you are Bards."

That was oddly convenient, Bokaj growled to the rest of us. *Zeke, you see anyone around hiding? I don't see anyone who could be a threat.*

I scanned the area around here, the tree, everywhere as openly as I could so she would see me being weary. *Nothing and no one.*

"Rate of pay changes for the convenience," Bokaj warned, "and you pull your weight in a fight."

"Fine," she said. She motioned behind her, and a spectral horse appeared. She mounted up and rode towards us gracefully.

That reminded me, "Zhavron, do you have a mount?"

Zhavron smiled, put his fingers to his lips and whistled sharply and loudly. After a moment, a loud crash sounded from behind us at the gate, and a large animal sped our way.

As it came closer, the animal became a large wolf, roughly the size of Muu's mount. It skidded to a halt next to its master and began to pant at him in joy.

"Meet Norla." He reached out and scratched behind the massive wolf's left ear, and it fell to its ass and began to thump the ground with a leg. He hopped on to the creature's back easily. "Good girl."

The rest of us summoned our own mounts, Zhavron made observations about each and even told Muu he was a little jealous of his mount. "Wouldn't trade Norla for him, though. She's smart as a whip, this one."

"How did you come along such a spectacular horse?" I heard Pharazulla speak from behind me.

"Thor?" He whinnied upon hearing his name. "He's been with me for quite some time. I think he has something to do with my being favored by the lightning element and my companion."

"You have many companions," she said dryly.

"Not them, my familiar." I looked over to Muu. "Kayda's coming!"

"WHERE?!" He ducked in his saddle. His mount growled threateningly, and Muu breathed easier. "It's okay, Tickle Tail. Don't worry."

I summoned Kayda from my necklace, and she took flight almost immediately.

"Her?!" Pharazulla spoke in wonder. "She is why?"

"I can't tell for sure, but it seems like the best reason," I answered honestly.

We traveled at a good pace for most of the day. Zhavron learned more about Muu, his fighting style, and instincts in the fights that he had so far.

Pharazulla made sure to do the same with Bokaj, though the conversation was bent more toward getting to know what he had used his high charisma for, how often he did so, and the types of spells he could perform.

That evening when we stopped for dinner and bed, we watched as Muu underwent drills orchestrated by Zhavron. The old Orc brought out a longsword and stood before him. What took place was a pretty one-sided exchange of blows. Zhavron didn't hold back, and though he was strong for a level 8, Muu stood no chance against the experienced Fighter.

"You have decent instincts, but you are over eager," Zhavron scolded. "You must be either more patient or far more aggressive. That way your opponent will not be able to mount a proper defense."

They worked for an hour or more; the rest of us were content to watch.

The first watch that night was me, then Yohsuke, then Muu while Bokaj trained with Pharazulla.

Over the next few days, the sun smiled down on us, and the reasonable temperatures left us all comfortable enough. We grew more accustomed to having the two natives with us throughout that time. Pharazulla's approach to training was much more theory based, but by the end of the fifth day—and as the snow clouds began to show on the horizon—things began to truly take effect.

"Hey!" Bokaj said after we had been riding most of the day and had just stopped. "I got the first Bard spell!"

"Was it Charm?" Pharazulla asked politely as she stretched lazily. Bokaj nodded. "Good. This means you are ready to learn other things. Hurry and finish the strange instrument you have been working on while on your watches."

The rest of us looked at him curiously when he pulled out a long, wooden object that resembled a guitar. The neck was finished, and the body was beginning to take shape.

"You play guitar, bro?" Yohsuke asked. "Oh yeah! You did mention being in a band."

"Yup!" Bokaj pulled out his woodworking equipment and set to work.

As time continued to pass, both students quickly began to pick up their skills. By the next night, Muu could—somewhat—hold his own against the wily veteran, Zhavron.

After a particularly rough bout of fighting, Zhavron clapped his student on the back and asked, "Now, what kind of fighting style did you say you wanted again? 'Dragown?'"

"Drag*oon*," Muu corrected with a smile. "I want to be able to fight up close, sure, but I want gravity to help me hurt things that are fucking with us, ya know?"

"No," Zhavron replied gruffly, "but far be it from me to try and convince you otherwise. Now, look at the trees you have available to you and see what you can get."

"Hmmmm." Muu considered his status screen for a moment. "Thrust, Armor Pierce, Launch, and Bleed."

"Well, you could invest in all of them if you wanted. You have the points." Zhavron thought a moment. "You have some good weapons and armor enchantments."

At enchantments, I perked up. "He's about to have some better shit. Here." I reached into my inventory and gave him the two rings and the bracelet.

"Jesus CHRIST, dude!" he shouted in wonder. "These are fucking insane!"

"Thank you. Sorry, I forgot to give them to you sooner. I figured if I did so in the city, it could draw attention to us, and then I didn't want you to rely on them too much in training," I replied with a smile on my face. It felt so much better to be back in my Fox-man form. My tails swished behind me in pleasure.

"No, thank *you*," Muu stressed as he pointed my way.

Zhavron nodded. "I can see that being meant for the best, but if we had been attacked, I would have preferred he had them to not having them. What was the old saying? 'I would rather have and not need, than not have and need'? You see what I mean?"

I took the rebuff stoically and nodded. I was going to have to dig my head out of my ass sometime.

After a moment of thought, Muu looked at Zhavron and asked, "Can I talk to you and Zeke for a moment?"

Zhavron looked at him steadily and then to me. When I shrugged, the older Orc stood and walked a couple dozen yards away from the camp with Muu and me in tow.

"What's up, bud?" I tried to mask my concern with a cheerful demeanor, but I couldn't be sure it was believable.

"Well, I know from experience that it's rude to ask a warrior or a soldier if they've ever killed anyone." He looked at me. "I learned that from you. So I won't ask, but..." he looked to Zhavron, and I could see the beginnings of tears in his eyes, "but I have. It was my first, then second. Then so many more and they were all helpless. They couldn't do anything, man! And I murdered them!"

"Muu, if you had let them have even the slightest chance, they would have murdered *you*." I reached over and put a hand on his shoulder. "You did what was needed. What was necessary for us to survive. For you to survive."

"Sit down, boy," Zhavron ordered, then looked at me. "Best explain it so I can understand."

"We found a cave on our way to Lindyburg that was enchanted to make people *want* to come in," I recounted. "When we went in, we found some sleeping, low-level hobgoblins. We—the others and I—would hit them while they were asleep, and he would deliver the final blow."

"Mighty efficient," he observed with raised brows.

"Then we were attacked by a legion of them," I continued. "They were coming from a single tunnel, and we were able to funnel them and use magic to keep them at bay. It was a slaughter. While we were distracted, an Incubus six levels higher than us took Muu hostage. He was going to try and make us all his slaves-slash-food."

Zhavron looked to Muu, who was looking away, tears starting to fall as the story continued.

I couldn't blame him for what he was thinking or feeling, but it was odd to see my friend crying like this. So I kept explaining.

"The creature wasn't expecting Muu, significantly fewer in levels, to actually fight back, and he caught the demon by surprise. After that, we ganged up on him until he was close to dead, interrogated him, then held him down while Muu stabbed him to death."

"See?!" Muu threw his arms up and leaped to his feet. "Each time, the enemy was damned near defenseless! I had to have someone *hold them down* to be able to do shit!"

Zhavron looked at Muu with patience in his gaze and said, "Sit."

"And now, when I close my eyes at night, I can hear that demon pleading—begging—for me to stop." Muu began to pace in a tight back and forth route. "I can *see him*."

"SIT!" Zhavron barked the order at Muu, and even I jumped.

The command brought him out of it, and he sat down quickly.

"What you did—what you *had* to do—was out of necessity," Zhavron began, and as Muu opened his mouth to interrupt, the veteran Fighter growled at him, "Stow it. You will listen now."

Muu's jaw clacked shut.

"Listen close." Zhavron closed his eyes as if to see what he was saying. "When I was a young Orc, I was proud. Strong. I had trained my body from the time I could walk to be a proud warrior like my father. I would walk with him in the plains, searching for anything to prove myself to him. I started fights—won some and lost some—that I would never really remember why I started them."

Zhavron raised his hands in the air. "When it was time for me to choose my path in the tribe, I chose to become a Fighter. It's what I had known all my life, what I was most proud of. Until this point, I had not taken a life for anything other than sustenance or protection and never sentient."

Muu and I listened, enraptured. I had always loved listening to stories from my elders.

"Shortly after my training, I was level 3 or so at the time, we were attacked by a band of Gulfcots. Vicious creatures. Built like Trolls but much smarter and cunning. There was a score of them, and they set on us when we had just made camp. Took us all hostage, made us fight each other for sport."

A dark, haunted look crept over his face. He began to breathe slightly heavier, and his still closed eyes clenched shut. His hands had fallen into his lap and clenched tightly.

"Days turned into weeks, and by the end of it all," Zhavron's voice broke, and his lips pulled away from his teeth in pain, "my father had saved me from having to fight, by defeating the others before they started making us fight to the death. The first fight was the favorite—my father—against the weakling. They figured it would be a slaughter. Entertaining enough to drink to at least, for the first time—they had finally grown complacent as father said they would. We put on a good show—distracting enough to allow the others in our patrol to gather their wits and escape their bonds, but as it lasted longer, they grew suspicious."

Zhavron opened his eyes and waited until Muu looked him in the eye to continue, "My father threw himself on my sword so that the Gulfcots would be too distracted claiming their winnings from each other to see the freed prisoners gathering weapons. As the other Orcs began cutting into them, a scouting party from our tribe and a neighboring Elven tribe came upon us. Together, they destroyed those heartless bastards."

And there, as we watched, this grizzled, scarred Orc put his head in his hands, and his shoulders shook. He looked up, tears pouring down his cheeks, and he smiled.

"I stayed there, frozen, holding my dying father in my arms as he whispered the words, 'necessary sacrifice,' over and over until his eyes went cold."

Fuck, man. I couldn't imagine that shit. Not even in the slightest. I had some shit in my past, for sure—but that?! Jesus.

"Now, I will never say that the pain you feel right now is less." Zhavron motioned toward Muu. "I'm certain that Zeke will be able to tell you about his own first time. The first is always the hardest, and you will always carry that pain with you. However, what your friends did for you—and what you will inevitably do for them—will sometimes require that necessary sacrifice."

Zhavron stood, walked over to Muu, knelt in front of him, and said softly, "Do not become numb to this pain, but use it to forge yourself into the weapon you need to be to protect what you hold dearest."

I nodded, a tear coming to my own eyes. I could do some amazing shit. Fuck, I had decapitated a lizardman in a single stroke during a fight to the death, but that was some deep, thoughtful advice.

Muu nodded, sniffled, and looked his trainer in the eye and said simply, "Thank you."

Zhavron patted him, and that was all we said for the rest of the night. I think, if I was being honest, that was all that needed saying.

As I fell asleep that night, I felt the pulse of heat in my palm, and the burn of the fire tattoo entered my dream. I was once more in the realm of flame with the Primordial Flame Elemental looking down upon me.

Little flame, you have done well to come this far and so swiftly. I will help you in finding the one you seek. He has found his shape now, and it would have been much harder to seek on your own. The crackling and popping in my mind registering as words.

I felt a searing in my palm and grunted to try and keep from screaming.

This will help you feel for the direction you need to travel, it explained.

"Thank you." I rubbed my palm for a moment before I asked, "You said that others were seeking it?"

Yes, they seek dominion over the elements. With this creature, they will have what they need to begin their work in earnest. Why they have chosen my domain to begin their experiments, I do not know. Our time is at a close, little flame. Hurry.

The realm of flame faded, and the dawning light of the sun on Brindolla began to shine. Once again, I was sweating, and my hand felt like it was going to burn away for nothing. I looked at it, and the fur around it was singed and the skin blistered.

I cast Regrowth and watched the skin begin to settle. The singed fur was still there, but it would grow out.

I watched as the others began to come to in silence. Muu looked surprisingly refreshed, groggy, but like he had less weighing on his soul.

We ate a hearty breakfast that day, courtesy of Bokaj who had spotted a large ox during the night that looked good enough to eat. Luckily, the ingredients would keep because he had frozen them with his ability. Yohsuke, his cooking ever-fucking-phenomenal, had cooked up enough and salted it that we had plenty left over to offer to Zhavron's mount so she wouldn't have to hunt for herself.

"Why is that," Muu asked one morning as she returned with a bloody hare in her jaws, "that she needs to hunt and our mounts don't?"

"Your mounts are summoned from elsewhere, and while they are here, they don't truly exist unless you have a special class skill that even I do not hold." Zhavron patted the great wolf lovingly. "Mounted fighting is hard to master and only one class, Cavalier, seems to be able to fight on a summoned mount. Norla exists here because I raised her from the time she was a puppy to be my mount and friend. She must eat."

After that, I spoke to everyone about my dream and held my palm out toward the north. I felt warmth, like sticking my hand close to a candle, come over my hand. As I moved it away, the temperature cooled.

"I guess we have to go that way." The others trusted what I had to say and began to pack up. As we readied our mounts, I heard a voice—several voices and the beating of hooves—coming from the direction we had been traveling away from Lindyburg.

I turned to see what the commotion was about when light reflected off some armor. I saw the red and gold, then heard Pharazulla curse quietly.

I turned toward her. "What the fuck did you do?"

She looked at me, and I felt slightly off. "I've done nothing wrong. They are assassins like the one you killed when we met."

"I see." I shook my head and put my mind back to what was at hand.

"What are they doing here?" I heard Bokaj ask, as if through a fog.

"Isn't it obvious?" Pharazulla spat. "They've come to kill me. They will kill us all if we don't stop them."

She was right. She was *so* right. I shook my head to get the last drudges of post-meal laziness out of me and took stock.

There were five of them total, and they abhorred magi users, so they couldn't have any casters with them. I saw one with a bow, and the others looked like they had crossbows. My friends were off their mounts still, and they looked about as ready as they were going to be.

We couldn't let the element of surprise go to waste. As the assassins came close enough to be in range, I lined up my shot as best I could and cast Fireball. A streak of orange and black shot toward them, and as it hit the lead rider—it detonated.

In the confusion, I felt a hand on my neck running their fingers through my fur and then everything was lost to me.

The chaos that ensued was nothing short of a blur. I didn't remember anything. Just screams and pain.

As I came to, I realized I was at half health and healing slowly.

"Yo, Zeke." Yohsuke and Bokaj's heads swam into my vision above me.

My dazed mind began to swim. "What happened?"

"We were going to ask you the same thing, motherfucker," Yohsuke growled. "What the hell happened? Why did you attack us?"

I sat up quickly and fell straight back down. "What?!"

"Yeah, man, you fireballed those guards to shit, then cast Lightning Storm on them." Bokaj warded Yohsuke away from me so he could explain. "After that, Pharazulla came over and patted you on the shoulder... oh fuck."

He groaned and helped me to my feet slowly.

"She fucking rolled him!" Bokaj shouted.

"She what?" Jaken hollered. He was a good sixty feet away from us, kneeling over Muu's prone form, and Zhavron stood guard behind him with his longsword drawn and a dirk in his left hand.

"She cast some kind of spell on him that made him do some shit he wouldn't normally do. She told me about it. I think she called it Bend Will?" He threw an arrow that he had had in hand. "Can make people do some nasty shit."

"Dude, do you remember what happened?" James asked. He was limping slightly.

I thought for a moment. "I remember her saying... the people coming at us were assassins. They were going to kill us? That's all."

"Nothing else?" Yohsuke tested. "You don't remember coming at me with your axe? Setting Kayda free and telling her to 'get us?' Casting Lightning Bolt at Muu?"

"Why would I ever do any of that?!" I challenged him. "You guys are my fucking family! I would never hurt any of you. Where's Kayda?"

I heard a shuffle from behind me and turned to see my familiar. Her chest feathers were burned, and I could feel her pain now that I was aware of her presence.

What the hell had happened? "You all okay?"

"Check on the fucking bird," Yoh growled as he shoved me roughly toward her. "We can chat after."

"Baby, what happened?" I rushed over to her and cast Regrowth. I could put my own humiliation and shame aside for the moment. The others were okay for now, I think, but she needed me.

She opened our link wide and showed me as best she could from where she had come in. The series of images, sounds, and Kayda's emotions played in my mind.

I saw myself from her eyes, emotionless and spoke in a monotone, *"Kayda, get them."*

Me walking toward Yohsuke and James with Storm Caller in hand. Muu jumping in front of me, then flying away after a shock of electricity.

Father? Father sick? I heard her cry. She knew I would never hurt my friends. She tried desperately to plead with me, but it was like our connection had been gone.

Even though she knew I wasn't myself, she didn't want to hurt me. She wouldn't, but just because she wouldn't hurt me didn't mean that she didn't want to help my friends.

Zhavron shouted for me to snap out of it. James hit me hard enough to drive me to a knee, then tried to shake me out of it. I used his distraction to drive my diamond-like claws into the flesh above his knee and throw him away from me. Jaken cast a heal at him, and the vision shifted to a view from above us.

Kayda watched in horror as I threw my weapon as hard as I could at Jaken, it traveled so fast and knocked him back near Muu, who was starting to stand. She watched me raise my hand toward them, and she dove.

As the pain and confusion cleared my mind, I hugged her.

I looked at my friends, my brothers, and I tried to bring the words racing through my mind to bare. I wanted to shout that I hadn't been myself. That it wasn't me in control, but they didn't seem to care right now.

"I'm sorry," I groaned to them. Then to Kayda, I whispered, "I'm so sorry. That wasn't me. Kayda, I'm so sorry."

Better now? Not mad? She sent me images of me smiling and happy with my friends.

"No, baby." I cast Regrowth on her again. "I'm not mad. I'm all better." I looked at my friends. "Where is she?!"

"Don't you fucking yell at us," Muu groaned.

"She's gone, man." Bokaj sighed. "Sometime during the fighting, she mounted up and split. I could try and track her down, but conveniently enough, her spectral mount doesn't leave tracks."

"Fuck!" I yelled as loudly as I could. The red that signaled the beginnings of my curse began to ring my vision, and I had to focus on my breathing to keep from transforming.

She hurt my friends, and she *used me to do it*. I wanted blood. I would make what I did to Asshole look like a children's cartoon when I got my claws on her.

As I seethed in impotent rage and despair, the others were moving.

"Bokaj." Yohsuke waved him over to the rest of party, all of them having gathered around Muu who was still sitting on the ground.

I stayed near Kayda's side as they spoke for a few minutes quietly. It was hard to resist the urge to walk over, but after I had been used as a pawn like that—I couldn't blame them for being distrustful of me right now.

Finally, Zhavron came over and shooed me over to the group, staying with Kayda.

"Look," I began, "I don't know what the hell happened, but I am so sorry. I shouldn't have gotten affected that easy, man. I fucked up. If you're mad, I get it. I could have killed you all." I looked straight at Muu. "Fuck, I almost *did* kill you."

"Would you shut up, you sappy bitch?" Yohsuke grinned. "We believe you. Bokaj explained it all to us. Even proved it with his charm spell. Did you know that Muu–"

"OKAY!" Muu shouted. "Okay. He gets it. Got it? Cool. Shut the fuck up there, loose lips. Shit."

I wanted to know, but I could respect his privacy for now. Maybe I could tempt him with another item later? For now, I would take solace in my frie– family being okay.

We all laughed a little bit. I cast Mass Regrowth on everyone. It felt better.

"Get that damn bird over here." Muu grunted as he stood. "I got some shit to say."

I cocked my head but sent a mental call to her as requested. She hopped over happily enough. I guess that Zhavron had been feeding her bits of meat because she was content now.

Muu pushed through the others the stand in front of her, and she looked at him oddly.

"Zeke, you translate," Muu ordered.

"She speaks English, asshat." I rolled my eyes.

"Translate for *her*." He flipped me the bird and then went back to looking at my familiar. "You remember what you did?"

She ruffled her feathers and popped her head down, then back up in a nod.

"Yeah, well so do I." He stepped forward and threw his arms around her in a hug. "You saved me."

Uncle Goblin. She looked at me and cocked her head to the right. *Safe? Better?* She sent me images that she had shared through my memories. Seeing him hit so hard by the burden of those deaths.

"She wants to know if her Uncle Goblin is better now," I translated. He looked at me oddly, so I explained. "She sees my memories and mind. We share them every time she comes out of the collar. She knew you were hurting. Hell, she probably knew before I did."

He looked her fully in the face. "I'm okay now, tweetie. Thank you."

She pressed her forehead to the side of his face lovingly.

"Can't believe you let her call you Goblin." Yohsuke laughed.

"She can call me sprinklenuts for all I care," Muu retorted. "She saved me from having to go home to a shitty bed and back to work. I may not like birds, but she's cool by me now."

"Hey!" I blurted. "Don't teach her that!"

Kayda looked to me, and she shared an image of the top of Muu's head and the word, *Sprinkled..uts?*

"You mother*fuckers*!" I groaned. "No, baby. He's Uncle Goblin. You can only call him that."

Why? she chirruped curiously as she looked to the rest of the smiling people around us.

"Because it's weird and not his name, love," I stated firmly. I looked to the others. "We cool?"

"Yeah, man," James said, "but if you ever do some Bourne shit like that again, I won't go easy on you."

I nodded and looked to Jaken who shrugged before responding, "You know me, man. I can't do with the whole grudge shit on family. You know I got your back. That wasn't you."

Muu just flipped me off playfully and patted me on the shoulder. "We're good."

Yohsuke pulled me off to the side. "Look, man, I'm sorry about thinking you would ever do some shit like that on your own."

"Hey, don't worry about it." I looked at him, his features drawn tight. "If I had to take a wild guess—you were the one who brought me down, right?"

Now, if I had to pick anyone to bring me down, it was Yoh. Dude knew me better than almost anyone, and he was one of the better gamers I had ever known in my life. It would really chafe my ass if it was someone else.

"No." Yohsuke shook his head. "Zhavron clobbered you over the head before I could get to you. Which saved me from having to do something I'm sure I would probably hate myself for."

Well. Here comes the fucking baby powder. Goddamnit.

"Look, Yoh." I grabbed his shoulder and looked him in the eye. "I know you were thinking about going home." He eyed me a little more seriously. "Don't you fucking look at me like that, dick. I know you miss your wife. Wanting to be sure the party was cool. I understand. I'm not mad, and I don't blame you."

"Good. Because I can't do that until I make sure that traitorous bitch pays for almost costing me my brother."

I nodded. "Let's see what we can find on those guards. Maybe they have orders."

We took the time to relieve the singed dead of their belongings. We found a few gold between them, some travel rations, and water. There was a wanted photo of Pharazulla, an accurate drawing of her with a reward of one thousand gold for her return alive for crimes against the Governess of Lindyburg smoldering in a pocket that we found.

I reached out and willed Storm Caller to return to my hand; the bolt of lightning landed in my palm, and I put the weapon away. It was time for us to continue moving toward our objective.

We could try to find that wanted criminal when we were at full strength. Maybe between generals, but not right now. My revenge could wait. We would continue moving forward and try to get ready for the Hells and getting Balmur back. She would get hers.

Chapter Eight

After traveling for a couple more days at a decent pace, snow began to fall in truth. The wind and the plains gave way to snow banks and freezing sleet, and as the third day in this environment began to wind down, I could see the others beginning to slow down.

Our cold weather gear kept us warm for the most part. Those of us with reptilian blood were more affected. If this kept up, I was going to have to create... Fuck.

"Stop!" I shouted. "Let's camp here for the night guys."

"What are you talking about, man?" Jaken asked. "We still have at least two more hours of bright day. We can easily make camp then."

"Look at Muu and James!" Both figures looked like they were going to fall out of their saddles. They seemed stiff and lethargic—as if they were under the effects of some kind of slow spell. "We need to set them to rights before we can even think of moving on."

Jaken smacked his forehead with his palm. "I should've thought about that."

"We all should have," Bokaj grunted at us.

We stopped moving and began to clear the snow out of the way, so our presence wouldn't melt the snow and ruin things. We got a fire going, and I pulled out two of the un-enchanted rings and began to engrave them with a symbol of a hearth, a blanket, and the outline of the sun in quick succession.

I focused my intent on a warm, sunny day, the heat of a warm hearth, and the toasty feeling of spending a cold night under a thick blanket. With those thoughts firmly in place, I fed mana into the items.

Two hundred mana total later, I had two new and useful items.

Ring of Delightful Warmth

Wearer no longer feels the bite of the cold.

With this ring, it feels as if the wearer is near a warm fire. It keeps you comfy, but a blizzard would be enough to freeze you solid—so be careful!

Ring created by Journeyman Jeweler Similian and enchanted by Journeyman Enchanter Zekiel Erebos.

I walked over to the two of our cold-blooded friends and slipped one of them on to James' finger. The effect was immediate. James looked around, then down at the ring and then smiled.

"Thanks, man." He bumped my fist with his in gratitude.

I turned to Muu, who sat on the ground that we had just cleared and knelt in front of him.

"Here you go, bud." I placed the ring on his left hand's index finger, and as I prepared to stand, I felt a hand on my shoulder. I looked up to see Muu looking at me sadly.

"If that's how you're gonna propose to me," he smiled softly, "my answer is no. I'm a classy broad, and I deserve to be dazzled. You gotta at least buy me dinner first." He then winked at me, then whispered, "I expect fireworks."

I laughed hard enough that I fell on my ass and just stayed there laughing for a minute.

"You love me, bitch," Muu teased as he stood and began to move about the camp, seeing where he could help.

"Sorry, guys," I looked at the two of them. "I thought that you might be able to get through the cold because of not being truly fully reptilian. I thought that the coats would be enough. My bad."

Muu shrugged, and James waved it away. "I thought so too, but it's not just on you man. All together on this shit."

Just to check our route, I held my hand up. The last few days, the heat had risen in intensity the further we traveled north. Now, it was northwest of our position, and my hand felt like I had thrown it on to a hot skillet. I hissed in pain and pulled my hand close.

"I have good news, guys," I spoke out loud. "I think we're close to where we need to go, but getting there at night may not be a good idea."

"Good!" James groaned as he shook his joints loose. "Fuck this place."

Muu grinned and said, "I wonder what we're looking for!"

"If you got time to wonder about meaningless things like that." Zhavron popped up from behind him as if from nowhere. "You've got time to practice your technique."

"AHHH!" Muu shrieked in surprise. "Don't sneak up on me like that!"

"Get to it, two hundred thrusts," Zhavron ordered mercilessly. "Zeke, you too. Get over here and do two hundred chops."

I groaned. Since my being used as a distraction had almost killed everyone, part of showing my sincerity in being sorry was training alongside Muu. And Zhavron was a cruel taskmaster.

"We stop early, we train harder," Zhavron growled. "And no using that weapon lightening ability either. If you do, you do twice as many."

Feather Axe allowed me to lighten the weight of my axe so that it weighed next to nothing. I made the stupid mistake of doing it the day previously. I had ended up having to run and do every maneuver more than two hundred times. I was still sore from it.

I brought Storm Caller to my hands and began my training. I focused on precision and continual motion rather than going quickly.

Remembering what my drill instructors used to tell me, "Slow is smooth, smooth is fast. Perfect practice makes perfect action."

All the bastard needed was Smokey Bear, and he'd remind me of some of my own drill instructors. I shivered at the thought.

"So," I began as I continued my repetitions, "I'm fairly certain this is a group we're going up against. These guys want to move in on the Fire Prime's domain for some reason, and if they think they can handle moving in on a primal force of nature like that—they have to have some serious magic in their corner."

"You said that shit, man." Yohsuke waved it away. "We haven't had to deal with casters before—other than you—so we may be walking into some shit here."

"That's why I said something," I shot back. "We need to prepare."

Zhavron nodded his head. "You do." He stepped up beside me. "Too low. Bring your axe up two inches. You're leaving yourself dangerously open to attack. What you need is a Mage killer."

Jaken looked over at him from where he was setting up a tent. "A what?"

"Mage killer," Zhavron reiterated. He smacked Muu when his shield arm got lazy. "A Fighter designed specifically to combat Mages."

Bokaj sidled closer. "Go on."

"They typically get into close range and make it harder for them to cast their spells. They have skills and abilities that allow them to null magic of those they attack." Zhavron closed his eyes and concentrated. "They are rare, but it isn't impossible to learn how to do it."

Zhavron was instantly next to me and swung his meaty fist into my rib cage on my right side. As I coughed and fell to a knee, he grabbed my shoulder. "What did I tell you about leaving an opening?"

"Fucking asshole," I growled.

"You're paying me for this." He grinned, his tusks showed a little more. "Do not forget that."

"Oh, I won't." I groaned and took to my feet again. "You know where we can find someone to teach one of us?"

"Not up north." He shrugged. "Magic is much more prevalent up here because of the High Elves and their experiments. Those who excel at combating magic are run out of town or worse. Though, one of you may be more apt for it already."

James raised his hand. "I take it that means me?"

"Quite possibly." Zhavron smiled. "You can use your ki in some pretty interesting ways. It wouldn't be too hard to see you using it to move through a Mage's shields or get out of spell effect ranges quickly. It just takes practice from what I understand."

Zhavron looked at me, then James. "Cast Snare on James."

I flinched, then did as I was told. Roots and vines with thorns grew beneath James's legs and latched on to him. He grunted in pain and looked to Zhavron.

"Get out," The Orc said simply with a gesture.

James began to grab at the vines holding him, and his arms became stuck. "Fuck!"

"You aren't using your greatest weapon, James," Zhavron chided.

"Yeah, but if I use the Bladed Limb ability I have, it takes a lot of my ki and doesn't last that long," James grunted with the vines moving further up.

I ended the spell, and he fell to his ass.

Zhavron hit me in the ribs again. "You will listen to my commands, and you will only do as I say. I did not tell you to end your spell. James," he looked over at James, "stand and think of what you can do. Zekiel, cast it again."

I obeyed but had some *seriously* mutinous thoughts about this. I had already attacked them once this week. Wasn't that enough, you asshat?!

James was wrapped in the spell again. "You will deal with this pain until you can learn what you need to do in order to escape it." Zhavron snapped his fingers at Muu and me to resume our sets.

Every minute, I recast the spell. After fifteen minutes, I finished my chops, and I had to begin going through horizontal slashes. After five more castings, James roared in frustration just as the spell ended and I raised my hand to cast it again. As the spell released, James was gone, instead three feet to the right of his original position.

"Finally!" Zhavron clapped. "You are thick headed, son. That is what I was trying to teach you."

"You weren't teaching me shit!" James spat. "You said, 'in order to escape', and I couldn't think of one."

"And what is the best way to escape a trap?" Zhavron asked to no one in particular. When no one answered, he pointed at the spell reaching and grasping for anything to grasp. "It's not to get caught in the first place!"

James looked as if he was about to start swinging in that moment.

"Practice the katas the monks taught you, and reflect on what it is you need to watch and listen for when fighting spell casters," Zhavron ordered. James didn't move fast enough, and the veteran Fighter barked, "Did I stutter?!"

"You keep treating us like boots, and I'll hit you so hard you'll fucking start to," James barked right back. "Yeah, you may have seen some shit, but me, Zeke, and Yoh did our fucking time. We don't have to be treated like shit anymore."

"Yeah, I have to agree," Yohsuke said. "I don't like it. For a newb like Muu—no offense, man—" Muu gestured that it didn't bother him. "But we didn't sign up to be treated like shit. Zeke earned it, a little, but us? Nah. Chill the fuck out."

"I am hard on you all because you will need it for what is to come." Zhavron sighed. He motioned for us to stop. "Muu's ability has truly improved. The rest of you can always use improvement, and I see a serious lack of motivation to do so. You've become complacent. Why?"

"Because we have to focus on this damned quest!" Jaken spoke up rather loudly. "And trying to get Muu caught up to us. He's not a burden, he's learning the same as us, but the longer it takes for him to catch up to us and for us to get stronger—the harder it feels like it'll be to get Balmur back!"

The rest of us were stunned silent. So he continued to fill the void.

"So, we trust that whatever we are doing up here is going to give us some kind of clue as to how to get that powerful." He spat, stood up, and advanced on Zhavron. "The Gods are working their asses off, and so have we. This is hard on us, draining and exhausting because we have to be the ones to fight this whole world's problems for them! But we wanted to do that together! What kind of thanks do we get? Our friend kidnapped and sent to the Hells because we killed some really powerful asshole. Then the children of the village that took us in were kidnapped so they could be used to blackmail said village."

He clenched his fists and began to shake in rage. "It seems to be that everywhere we go, we end up costing someone their freedom or their life!" Tears began to fall from his eyes. "But we keep going because we have people counting on us at home. We get our shit pushed in constantly, but somehow, we keep pulling through. We took a big L on that last general, even if we won, and now one of our friends is paying the price. So yeah, we're a little pissed off and down on ourselves. You want to paint the target on your ass for a good kicking? Cool—because we could all use the stress relief."

I put Storm Caller away and stepped over to him. "Hey, come on, bud. You know we're doing what we can. He doesn't know any of this. That's not his fault, and it isn't ours. He's just trying to help in his own way, ya know?"

Jaken ran a gloved hand under his eyes, then his nose angrily, then looked back to Zhavron. "We're under a lot of pressure for shit we can't really discuss. We aren't at our best right now, but we will be. We just have to focus. Come on—let's eat then get some shut-eye. I'll take first watch."

We spent the rest of the night in quiet contemplation, a few of us—myself included—gave Jaken a comforting pat on the back. He just sat there, eyes on the horizon.

The following morning, we had a large hot breakfast of sausages, eggs, and toast with warm tea. The food went a great way toward improving our dour mood. As we were getting ready to leave the site of our camp, Zhavron stopped us to say something.

"If you would like to pay me, I can be on my way," he supplied. When no one moved, he spoke again, "I did not mean to insult you or make light of the things that you have done so far. Obviously, it has left you haunted and hurt. I thought it complacency, and for that, you have my apologies. I sense the potential in you all—and I wouldn't see it squandered. If you'll have me, I'll join you for the next leg of your journey. If not, I would hope we could part ways as friends, and I could have your forgiveness."

Jaken spoke for us, "Get on Norla and ride with us, man. Just take it easier on the rest of us."

"You're right, too." I shrugged when the others eyed me. "We all need to toughen up. I'll be joining you more often for training."

Zhavron nodded assent to me.

James walked over to Zhavron and offered his hand. "I appreciate you being cool about last night. I shouldn't have snapped at you like that."

"Don't worry about it, James." The veteran grinned. "I can be a bit of a Ruktoft."

"What's that mean?" Muu asked curiously.

"Well, it's Orcish," Zhavron explained. "It loosely translates to the hole of a man's," he pointed to his nether region, "you know."

"Oh!" Muu's eyes lit up. "We have a word for that too!"

"What's that?" Zhavron queried.

Yohsuke laughed. "It's 'dickhead' and believe me, we can all be dickheads."

We all laughed harder and saddled up. I checked our path and felt the heat in my palm a little further west than it had been last night.

"Looks like the creature is on the move," I informed the others. I looked at Thor and cast Nature's Voice. "We need to haul ass today, bud."

"I haul only you, Druid," he replied smartly, "but if you mean that we should make haste—I can provide this."

I grinned. "Let us make haste then, good friend."

Thor reared, his forelegs clawing at the air, and as soon as his feet touched the ground we took off in a hurry. The snow was rough on his movement, but we seemed to be making good pace.

By the afternoon, we were in sight of a large line of fir trees, and my hand was boiling every time I held it forward.

"Closer to the trees," Bokaj called. "You guys see that?"

I looked but couldn't make anything out but snow and tree, but if he saw something—I believed him.

Call it out, brother, I spoke to him through our earrings. *What do you see with your special eyes?*

"Wolves and some huge thing that they look like they're trying to bring down." I looked over to see him begin standing in his saddle as we moved forward. "There are some other smaller figures coming up behind them."

"Probably what we're looking for. Get ready!" Jaken said. "I'll take the front. Muu, you bring up the rear and try to snipe anything that looks like it's casting a spell. James, beat wholesale ass on anything that has magic."

"Got it!" Muu brought his short spear into hand and got it ready. "Onward, Nolorn! We have ass to kick!"

Nolorn, the Plague Wolf Muu was mounted on, brayed and howled one long note that Norla chorused into the distance.

"Fuck, there goes the surprise," James cursed.

"They know we're here. Something else is coming out of the snow!" Bokaj informed us. "Get ready!"

"James, you beat caster ass," Yohsuke ordered. "Zeke, let's kick some snowmen face in."

I roared into the distance. The wolves had no idea what we were doing, but as we came closer, I saw what we were looking for. There was a smaller wolf that looked to be red and orange against the snow, and the other wolves, white with patches of gray along their pelts, fought to protect it from whatever that large white thing was.

As they came into view, I cast Nature's Voice and yelled, "We're here to help you!"

The alpha at the front of the pack looked at us and howled to us, "A welcome friend, Druid!"

I stood and leaped from the saddle into the air and shapeshifted into my owl form and flapped to a point above the snow creature. It was too distracted by the wolves baying at it to see me above it. The Mages, however, began to shout and curse. I shifted into my fox form and began to drop, then shifted into my hulking Ursolon form and dropped properly.

I swiped and roared at the creature I landed on; its cold body hurt a little as I hit it, but the snow gave way to claw and tooth easily. Or so I thought. Its health bar began to refill steadily as I gnawed on its shoulder. I shoved it toward the trees and shifted back.

Upon closer inspection, I saw the snow beneath it begin to cascade up its body to seal the wounds I had made. Its level wasn't visible to me either.

"The snow creatures heal!" I shouted to the others.

"See if you can melt it!" Muu replied from the rear.

I looked over and watched him launch his spear at one of the casters, a little man with a balding pate and brown robes on. It hit hard enough to pierce straight through him to the counterbalance and James appeared next to him almost instantly. James kicked the man in the throat and fell on him with clawed hands stabbing like blades covered in golden energy.

The snow creature tried to plow into me as I was distracted, but I leaped out of the way.

"Jaken, get in front of me," I roared. "Zhavron, help the others with the casters." I turned my head to the wolves behind me. "Friends, please keep them distracted while I charge this spell. When I give the word—run far."

The alpha of the pack nodded his head. "Thren, Fear, Rilk, and Skyla—to the Druid. The rest of you, protect the flame."

Four wolves, one larger than the alpha, stood in front of me protectively. They snarled at the snow creature. Jaken joined them and gave me a brief nod before I began to charge my spell. Kayda called overhead, and I heard the sound of lightning crashing into the snow and heartfelt cursing.

I could charge the spell for fifteen seconds and hoped it was enough. Just before the final pulse, I shouted, "MOVE!"

The wolves scattered and fled behind me, Jaken dropped to his knee and hid behind his shield.

The spell shot from my hand on the third pulse and hit the snow creature. The shot pierced the snowy chest a little, then an inferno burst from it that melted the snow within a sixty-foot radius. It was all just gone, and the only remains of the creature was a puddle.

Jaken, his shield slightly blackened from the blast, stood and shouted, "Nice shot!"

"Thanks." I grinned.

"What?!" He looked confused. I shook my head and pointed to the next one and the other casters. There were four more of them, and they were lobbing spells at us now. They weren't big ones, yet. A ball of flame, not to be confused with my spell, flew my way and a red and orange blur leaped in front of me. It was the fire wolf.

It took the spell in its jaws and shook it apart like a piece of meat in, well... a wolf's mouth.

It seemed to grow a little, looked at me, and nodded. The pain in my hand was unbearable at this point.

I felt the heat reach toward my mind but ignored it. I looked over and watched as Yohsuke cast his Star Burst spell and blew the hell out of the other snow creature then began swinging his Astral Blade through it rapidly.

Kayda dipped close to one of the casters and tapped it with a wing. They froze with a stunned look before a blue ring appeared around them, and they moved once more. Fuck.

I heard one of my friends cry out and turned around in time to watch in horror as all four remaining casters turned on James and cast different elemental spells. One cast fire, another earth, water, and then the last cast some kind of wind blade at him. He wasn't fast enough to get out of the way of all of them and got caught by three. The earth spell simply grazed his left foot as he fell and his HP bar fell dangerously low.

I got him! I growled at the others mentally.

I bolted forward, inside my sixty-foot range and hit him with Heal. 100 HP filled his bar, and some of his more serious wounds began to close.

He stood, and the rest of us got to work. The four of the Mages had backed closer to the wooded area and began to close in on themselves.

We surrounded them in a wide circle. *Don't get too close to each other,* Yohsuke warned. *That makes an easier target.*

I looked at Muu who stood fifteen feet away and cleared my throat. He looked at me, and I made a sly throwing motion at my waist and waggled my eyebrows at him.

His reptilian features hardened and he looked at the people we were surrounding. There was an older man, a young one who looked to be in his early twenties. The two others were female and looked like they were in their mid-thirties. All of them had the same brown robes on, and their fingers and mouths moved as they began to cast a spell in unison.

Muu brought his arm up. Then he threw his spear. Where we were was a short way away, but it fell before it reached any of them. The two that had seen the throw looked at the weapon, then the thrower, who began to rotate his arm as if injured. They began to look toward the other threats, namely Jaken who began to pulse red like a beacon.

Suddenly, the spear was back in Muu's hand, and he *launched* it like he had before. The black streak glowed a sickly green and hurtled toward the old man. Just as it was an inch away, it thudded against an opaque bubble that formed around the casters.

"Motherfuckers!" Muu grumbled angrily. He held his hand out, and his weapon returned.

"You have no hopes of harming us now," the old man spoke smugly. His voice was wizened and a little light. His strong, bulbous nose and wrinkled features sagged, but he smiled a toothless smile. "Give us the elemental creature, and we will be gone. None of you will have to die for killing Horace. Just let us capture the creature, and his sacrifice would be worthwhile."

"Not happening," Jaken spoke aloud. In our minds he said, *Is there any way we can get in there?*

It took all four of them casting that thing together, man, Yohsuke answered. *I highly doubt it.*

I thought for a moment, then said, *If you guys can keep them distracted, I can see about burrowing under?*

Thing looks like it's a bubble, man. I don't know if you can do it. James put in.

I kicked the snow in frustration. *We could always beat the shit out of the shield and see if it cracks?*

I don't think that'll be bright, Zeke. They put enough mana into that thing to make it a pain in the ass to break down, for sure, Yohsuke explained. *Especially if it stopped Muu's fuckin' Zeus canon. They'd nuke us if we got too close.*

Think we could charm one of them? Bokaj asked. *I can do that now.*

It's a spell. I doubt it would go through the shield, but if you want to try it, be careful. Yohsuke crossed his arms loosely.

I called to Kayda through our connection, *Steer clear, dearest. Watch for an opportunity if you can, but keep an eye out for others.*

She called once more and flew higher.

Bokaj stepped closer and began to speak with his arms to his sides in a non-threatening gesture, "You guys want the wolf, right? Let's talk about it. What do you want it for?"

"Our birthright as Man," the elder said. "We, the Order of the Prime, believe it is our duty to understand, restrain and control the elements, rather than leave them to their chaotic and unpredictable natures."

"Why would you want to do that?" Bokaj wondered.

"The order was founded by humans for the advancement of magic, and the betterment of mankind," one of the women spoke. This one had red hair and hawkish features. "If we can bring the elemental realms to heel, we can grow that much more powerful. Think of all the different kinds of magic we could study and improve!"

I saw the others in my party grimace at what we were hearing. They wanted what I had currently, but they wanted to control all of it rather than allow the elementals to be separate beings with autonomy and choice.

"So, you want to bring the elements under your command." Bokaj nodded. "What was that about mankind? Does that include my kind? As I understand it, the High Elves are already pretty magically dominant here."

"They waste their time and squander their gifts," the young man spat. "They were the ones who sought to end humans using magic. The lesser races? The beasts and other creatures? We did that! We created them, gave them life."

"Introduced them to slavery," Muu shouted as he began to step forward. "Hundreds of years, your wizards and sorcerers made and kept Beast-kin of all kinds and enslaved them. Zhavron told me all about it. How you made them your personal armies. It was when the Elves stepped in and showed us that the tethers you had over us were wrong that we were able to assert ourselves."

"Shut up, filth!" the young man spat. "You do not get to speak ill of your betters."

"Hey, hey, this is my conversation," Bokaj said. He was close enough to touch the barrier now. "So, why, after all this time, have you gone looking for these things? These elemental beasts?"

"They are the key to understanding the elemental realms and how to control them," the elder spoke again, motioning for the boy to be quiet. "The veil between these realms has been thinning in certain parts of the world where these creatures come through. We can track them, capture them, and study them."

"I see, that doesn't sound so bad." Bokaj shrugged. "You guys seem to be doing this for what, purely academic purposes? Pursuing the advancement of magic, right?" The casters nodded, though the younger man looked pissed. "I can do a little magic too. Do you think I could join this order?"

"You are not the kind of magic user we would let in," the young man answered smartly.

"No, I really can do magic," Bokaj rolled up his sleeves and settled into his position a bit. He closed his eyes, then smiled and looked at one of the women, the redhead. "You want to see it, right?"

She answered him breathlessly, "Yes, I would like that a great deal."

My grip tightened on my weapon, and I saw Yohsuke's hand clench at his side. Muu stopped moving forward and let his hands go to his sides in a forced attempt to look less hostile. The wolves began to inch forward cautiously. If one of the casters looked their way, they stopped moving.

The young man looked at the redhead strangely, and Bokaj snapped his fingers to get their attention. "You do too, right?" The other woman looked at him as if he were repugnant. "But this one requires a volunteer." He looked at the red-headed caster and winked. "Come help me."

Three things happened at once. The young man roared, "No!" and he lunged forward. The woman's hand slid through the barrier into Bokaj's hand.

"Drop the spell," I heard Bokaj whisper.

The barrier dropped, and all hell broke loose. A drove of twenty wolves fell on the older caster before he knew what was happening. His screams and attempts to cast any kind of spell foiled when the alpha tore his throat out.

"Kill the other members of the Order," Bokaj whispered to the redhead.

She turned and began to mouth a spell at the other woman who had her hands full with Jaken and Yohsuke.

James went after the young man, who suddenly stepped away from the fray and began to mouth something.

I took Storm Caller, activated Cleave and Wind Scythe, then belted the weapon at him. He smiled, then disappeared. The weapon sailed through the spot where he had been standing, and I called it back to me. Between the lightning spear that shot from the redhead's hands and the ass beating she was taking from my other friends, the other caster stood no chance.

Within seconds, she was dead, and so was the old man who the wolves had overwhelmed. The other caster stood there, motionless.

"What about her?" James asked as he walked back over to us. "Can we ask her questions."

"No," Bokaj said simply. "I get two orders per spell. Those were it, though I thought that racist fucker was going to be fighting us."

"What spell was that, man?" Yohsuke asked.

"It was Charm at first, and all that requires is that they are close enough to see me," he explained. "The closer the better. They become fascinated and are more friendly. Likelier to do as I ask, but within something that they might be more inclined to do. The other was what Pharazulla used on Zeke— Bend Will. It makes the target do things they wouldn't normally do, even if it's something that they outright wouldn't do, like fight their friends."

"She taught you that?" I gasped.

"No." He shook his head and spread his hands. "She taught me Charm. Bend Will was a spell that once the class became fully available, I acquired it. I guessed Bards are squishy and convincing people to fight for you would be a good idea. Even against their friends. Sucks I can only do it once a day."

"Shit," Muu said in wonder. "Well, what do we do with her?"

We looked at him somberly, and finally, Zhavron spoke up, "Necessary sacrifices."

"Ah." Muu's face fell. "One of them already escaped. So we have to tie up loose ends, right?"

I put my hand on his shoulder. "Yes, but you don't have to do it, man."

"No," Muu said with a shrug that pushed my hand away. "No. I need to do this. I need to forge myself anew. Become the weapon which protects my friends."

I shook my head. "That's honorable, man, but seriously, you don't have to."

Cold lanced through me, and as I looked down, I saw a jagged spear of pure ice sticking out of my stomach covered in crimson and gore.

"Zeke!" Muu roared.

He juked around my body and accidentally shouldered me into a turn and tumble. I watched as if I was in slow motion as Muu dove on top of the now free Mage. Punching her once. Twice with his shield.

I felt radiant energy engulf me, and Muu growled, "I'll kill you for that!"

Muu put his shield above her chest, over her heart and brought his spear back and thrust with everything he had. He triggered his shield's blade at the same time, and her health plummeted. He twisted the short spear and pulled it out viciously.

Her body shuddered and lifted briefly off the ground before falling, her health falling with it.

Muu sighed, then looked at us. "Level 9 and then some. Zeke okay?"

I felt a very odd sensation as someone jerked the spear from my body and another wave of healing hit me. I stood slowly, then we all stepped forward to give him some comfort as he spent his stat points.

"Druid," I heard the alpha behind me. Now that combat was over, I could get a good look at him. His fur was pure white, and his eye—the other was a scar—was cool blue. His tail was high as he addressed me with the pack stood arrayed in a fan with him at the base.

"Alpha," I greeted him with a nod. "Thank you for your assistance. Without you, that could have gone poorly, but why were you here?"

"The Mother sent us," he replied. The wolves behind him wagged their tails three times when he referred to Mother Nature. "She felt the weakening and then the tear of the veil that allowed the flame passage to our forest. When we found it, the snow hurt it to even move. We nurtured it to health, then let it join us for a bit. She bid us protect it from the creatures here, but the humans were a surprise she had not known of."

He looked back at his pack. All the wolves lowered their tails and crouched a bit. He looked back to me and my friends.

"You saved many of my pack," he said with his head held high. "What do you call yourself, Druid?"

"My name is Zekiel Erebos."

"The Mother speaks highly of you," the alpha remarked. The other wolves gathered around me as they gathered my scent. A couple of them growled deeply the closer they got, the largest among them being the most fervent.

"Moon Touched," he growled. "Back, all of you."

The rest of the pack backed off.

"You better have that shit on lock Zeke," Yohsuke quipped. "Wolf boy that you are, they ought to like you."

"Rilk," the alpha barked. The largest wolf backed down slightly but kept his eyes on me. "The Mother has told us of him, and if he's Moon Touched, he has proven he isn't driven by the beast. Can you not feel his presence?"

Several of the other smaller wolves muttered the word alpha.

"I'm an alpha in my own right." I looked down at them. "You've done my friends and I a huge favor by helping us with all of this. I'm no threat. Promise."

The burning in my palm returned two-fold and I hissed in agony. The wolf was close again, his orange eyes on me. The heat reached for my mind once more, and this time, I let it come.

I rocked back on my heels as I felt the whisper of flames across my mind, the voice of the Primordial Flame Elemental whispered through the core of my being.

Touch the creature you see before you, I heard the crackle of flame inside my head. As I locked eyes with the Flame Wolf, the crackle continued, *Complete the quest, and gain your reward, little flame.*

I reached out to the Flame Wolf, his orange eyes locked on mine, and he trudged forward. The heat became more and more unbearable until I was grunting, tears forming in my eyes. Then his head touched my hand, and the burning stopped suddenly. The creature was gone.

QUEST COMPLETED: A Small Flame in a Snowstorm – The Primordial Flame Elemental has requested that you find the small flame in the winter lands of the Prime Realm.

Rewards – 2,000 EXP, unknown.

I felt the rush of the EXP hitting me letting me know that I had leveled up along with the others, then I felt something else. I gathered from the stirring in my body and mind that I wasn't entirely alone. At least, not the way I had been.

He has seen your strength, little flame, but is not yet strong enough to return to my realm, The Primordial Flame explained. *Will you safeguard him until he is strong enough to return to my side?*

QUEST ALERT!

Enkindle the Elemental Beast – The Primordial Flame has asked you to oversee the growth of the Flame Wolf until it is strong enough to return to him.

Reward – 3,000 EXP, unknown.

Will you accept: Yes/No?

Another damned unknown reward? Fuck! I accepted readily and felt a bloom of heat in my chest.

LEVEL UP!

You are now level 21!

CONGRATULATIONS!

Blessing of Fire deepened – You are now friendly to all beings from the Elemental Plane of Fire. Spells and abilities unlocked! Elemental Tinkering (Fire), Heart Flame, Burning Familiar.

Boy, was this like Christmas or *what?!* I used my screen to look over the new abilities I had earned.

Elemental Tinkering (Fire) – Flames now heed your command unlike they had before, and new spells can be created and discovered within the proper elemental realm. Be warned that mana is consumed at a higher rate while tinkering with a spell or discovering a new spell.

Heart Flame – Your body has become home to an elemental soul. You become more resistant to fire damage as host. Your body burns hotter. Your ability to manipulate flame becomes more instinctual.

Those were beyond cool as all hell. I looked at the spell I had unlocked with it.

Burning Familiar – The elemental soul inside you takes corporeal form at your command. Takes place of a familiar, if the summoner has a familiar already—and no ability to take multiple familiars—they must choose. Number of Familiar positions available 0/2. Cost: 50 MP. Cooldown: N/A.

Zero of two familiar positions? Wha– oh! *That must mean that Kayda and the new beast each count as one,* I thought to myself. So until I made him strong enough to go home, he was stuck with me.

You may name him, little flame. He will heed your word as if it were my own, the Primordial Flame Elemental's voice whispered through my head. I got the distinct idea that it could be the proximity of the elemental creature or that the quest was completed.

I flexed my will and summoned the Flame Wolf into being. Fifty mana drained away, and I watched as a burst of flame saw the creature sitting at my side.

"Woah," I heard Muu whisper. "What the fuck is going on?"

"Beats the shit out of me," James grunted. "Better him than me. He's gotta feed them all."

I thought for a moment, taking him in visually. His paws burned lightly, and his skin was charcoal black with bits of red and gray near the top of his body in a line. His head looked like a normal wolf's, but it was red and orange with blue undertones near his eyes that offset the orange of his irises.

"I think I'll call you, Coal," I said as I leaned down to touch him. He was warm, like a normal dog. He leaned into my hand as I pet him and it was a comforting feeling. My palm burned sharply, and I held it up to look at it.

The flame symbol on my right hand had grown slightly larger, and its color deepened from orange to red.

"Our task is done," the alpha said as he began to back away. "We will take our leave. If you ever have need of us in this area again, Druid Zekiel, howl for us, and we will come."

"Thank you, alpha." I nodded to him with respect, and the wolves turned in unison and bolted away.

"Level 11!" Muu looked confused. "Levels go up one hundred in experience, right? So, it'll take roughly one thousand one hundred experience to get to the next?"

"That's how it was for us." I smiled.

While there seemed to be a lull in any action. We took the time to allocate our points. I put two into strength and constitution and one into dexterity. Kayda had leveled up, so I fixed her up with two points to wisdom and one to strength.

Name: Zekiel Erebos
Race: Celestial Kitsune
Level: 21
Strength: 47
Dexterity: 36
Constitution: 32
Intelligence: 50
Wisdom: 35
Charisma: 17
Unspent Attribute Points: 0

"Thanks for the experience, broski." Bokaj bumped my shoulder.

"Yeah, no shit." Yohsuke smiled. The others nodded their appreciation. Even Zhavron had leveled up, though his level was hidden for some reason.

"I've been meaning to ask, Zhavron—Why can't we see your level?" I asked bluntly.

He looked at me in surprise. "Well, I wear an item to obscure it. It gives me an advantage in battle."

Huh. That was a neat idea. *Maybe we could do that and lure people into being stupid with us.* I grinned at the thought.

Or maybe not be stupid ourselves.

"Well, that's all for this quest, guys." I shrugged. "What now? We can teleport back to anywhere we've been, or we could try and go to the High Elves and see what that symbol we were shown means."

"We could do that." James nodded. "Yeah, I'm kind of curious about this whole "High Elf magic" thing. If they were strong enough to beat ass on the human Wizards and Sorcerers—I'd love to see what they're capable of."

"I heard they're pretty much dicks," Yohsuke said. He was picking through the dead casters' pockets. "Got some gold here, no items on them. Must have been purists or something. Not even the robes appear to be enchanted."

"Yeah, they don't like other kinds of people, especially the Drow and Orcs," James said, "or anyone, really. If you aren't a High Elf—they hate you."

Zhavron grinned sardonically. "So you were listening to that little history lesson I was giving Muu while I was beating sense into him, then!"

"Sounds like a good time to me," Muu grunted. "Do we know where to find any Dragons?"

The question caught us by surprise, and we all glanced his way.

"What?" I tried to wrap my head around the question. "Why would you want to find a Dragon?!"

"Well, not any old Dragon, a green one, like me," Muu explained. "I was thinking if Zeke has the blessing of an elemental king or whatever and Mother Nature herself—Jaken is a Paladin for a Goddess, and Kayda is a flying myth—why not try to get some other serious magic on our side?"

After a moment of stunned silence, none of us had a real answer.

Finally, Jaken spoke, "Yeah, that's not a bad idea, actually. We have two of their kind among us. Maybe we can find out where one lives and then go seek their help?"

"Yeah, but how likely are they to want to give it willingly?" I asked. "You all know something of Dragons. Winterheart was an ancient Dragon. Old as *fuck* and highly intelligent. We can't guarantee that the next Dragon we find would be as amenable to our cause as he was. If it hadn't been for Maebe sticking up for us, he wouldn't have done shit."

"What other option do we have?" James threw his hands up. "We either go as we are to see a bunch of dickheads and *maybe* get some help—or we go see if we can find some powerful creatures who may be interested in giving us some juice. At least with the second option, we have to go somewhere with a lot more likelihood of quests, EXP, and loot."

"If you all are going hunting for Dragons," Zhavron stood and arched his back in a stretch, "I'll take my leave. I want nothing to do with that venture."

"Okay, how about this then?" I offered. "We teleport back to Lindyburg, drop off Zhavron, then figure out our next move. But if we're going to look for some Dragons and shit that could *really* fuck our shit up—we need to make sure that we are properly outfitted. That means a trip to Djurn Forge."

"Well, then we are definitely parting ways." Zhavron laughed. "Dwarves hate Orcs something fierce. Can't say as I like them much either. Jaken seems comfortable with it though, so to each his own, I guess."

I grinned at him. "It's an acquired taste, Dwarves." I looked at him for another moment. "Hey, can I take Norla's form?"

"How do you mean?" The Fighter asked after giving me an odd look.

"I would just have her bite me, then take her animal form for use in a fight. She would be completely safe."

The dire wolf, who had been standing at the side after the confrontation, trotted over to Zhavron and butted her head against his shoulder. "I suppose so."

I offered my hand, and Norla gingerly craned her head forward to just barely break the skin. It stung, but I could feel the wolf being added to my assortment of animal forms.

"Thank you," I grunted before healing myself. "Now, there was talk of trying to recruit Dragons to the cause?"

"Sounds good to me." James shrugged.

Yohsuke came over and clapped me on the shoulder. "Think we could see about talking to Shellica about another kind of adaptor? Now that I think about it, we never asked her."

"We could always try." I frowned. Had we really forgotten to ask her about that?

I shifted into my human form for safety and looked at the others. "You guys ready to go?"

The group nodded and grasped hands. I put Kayda back into my collar. Then I felt a bump at my leg and saw Coal look up at me.

"Shit, sorry, bud." I reached down and touched his head like I had before and watched as the flame that made his body siphoned into me. "That's going to take getting used to."

Chapter Nine

We arrived in the alleyway next to the Marching Mercenaries Inn. The ground was covered in snow and so were we. We pulled off our snow-covered cloaks and walked casually inside.

The place was starting to get busy. It was mid-afternoon, so people were ordering food and drinks for their work day.

Giledt looked up at us and grinned. "Welcome back, boys! Need a room? If you like, I can have some food ready too."

"Thanks, Giledt, the food sounds amazing!" Yohsuke smiled at the bartender and sat down. "What's on the menu, man?"

"We're having mutton glazed with a rare fruit that a gentleman brought us from the southern portion of the continent. It is very sweet but has a bit of heat to it." Giledt rolled his eyes as if in the throws of pleasure. "We pair that with a rice, steamed vegetables, and a warm bread with butter. I hear good things."

"Shit, I hear good things." I smiled. "I'll take some of that. Zhavron, you wanna eat with us, bud?"

"I think I will." The old Orc smiled at us. "The idea of fine alcohol is attractive too! Giledt, my friend. I've missed your mugs."

"They missed you too, Zhavron." Giledt poured the Orc three mugs of alcohol, one a pale brown, one medium and another heavy and frothy. "The usual for a brave man."

"Bless you." Zhavron looked at us. "Let me drink these before we eat." He then all but bounced back to the table we had first found him at and sat down to his drinks.

Alright, you weird ass.

"And Zeke, I could send for Vrawn if you like?" Giledt leaned over to try and say it quietly, but almost every one of my friends had sensitive hearing.

So of course, catcalls and cheering erupted, forcing me to shake my head to be understood.

"We aren't staying long, Giledt, thanks." I blushed and tried to wave his attention away.

"Nonsense!" Giledt laughed. "Even if it's only for a night, she would *love* to spend some time with you." He looked at me closely and winked before whispering, "She wouldn't even charge you, if you catch my drift."

I blushed even more and let my head fall a bit. My friends clapped each other on the back and watched as I suffered a little more.

"It's not that I don't want to see her or say hi, but we are leaving as soon as we finish our business." He looked confused. "Today. We have something we need to do, and it could be very dangerous. The last time we saw each other was... nice. I don't want to ruin that, you know?"

Giledt's lips pursed in thought, then his left hand snaked out and grasped my face, pulling me closer. "You're trying to spare my friend or yourself?"

His intense, glaring eyes burned into mine. Without blinking, I answered honestly, "Both of us."

"You aren't embarrassed of her? By her?" he pressed. I heard chairs scrape and my friends gathered behind me. More chairs scrapped the ground and mercenaries stood in my peripheral vision.

"Why would I be?" I asked softly. "She's beautiful in her own way, and she seems to like me. I don't want to upset her or lead her on."

Giledt held my face away at arm's distance and waved the people behind him off. He let me go, then the smile returned to his face.

"I'm glad to know that you have her best interests at heart rather than some foolish pride or other such ignorance." He poured me a glass of the medium alcohol. "On the house. Forgive me, but I get a little protective of my friends, and Vrawn has been a very good friend to me indeed. If you would like, I can pass her your regards?"

"I would like that. Just let her know that I appreciate her forwardness and that I hope she is well. If she ever needs aid, she can send word to Sunrise Village." Giledt looked confused again. "It's a small village south of the Lightning Mountains. It's where my friends and I are from."

"I see, thank you. I will let her know." Giledt picked up a mug to begin cleaning. "Do you know if they have need of mercenaries there?"

The question caught me off guard. Did they? They had the bears, but were they enough if the Children of Brindolla came back en masse?

"They might have need of some for a village guard, if you had some people—*good* people—who might want to settle down and take up root. The folk there are good people, and I don't want to send anyone there who would try and take advantage. The smith is a personal friend of mine. And there's a Paladin there that I also call friend. Know what? Everyone there is a good friend. We would be *very* upset to know they had been taken advantage of."

"I'll pick a few of the mercenaries I know who are looking to get out of the life and head that way then," Zhavron spoke from next to me. I hadn't seen him walk over because I'd been too preoccupied by Giledt. "I know a few of them would even be happy to help train the locals to pick up blade and bow if needed."

"You giving up on being a merc?" Bokaj asked.

"After traveling with all of you, I needed a stiff drink, and now my old bones need to rest." The Orc smiled at us and patted me on the shoulder. "If you'd like to discuss payment, we can take a last meal together and do so."

I nodded, and all of us went to sit with Zhavron at his table. Muu made the motion with his hand, pointing two fingers at his eyes, then back at the other man, meaning that he was watching Giledt, who simply smiled. Likely after our little misunderstanding.

After we were seated, Zhavron began speaking, "I wanted to let you all know that I appreciated your company. In all my years as a mercenary, I've not traveled with a funnier, more protective bunch. Thank you for having me."

We thumped the table and made our own affection for him known.

"Even if the lot of you were impetuous, slightly entitled, and complacent, self-absorbed and stubborn."

"Sure, just toss that shit out there, old man."

"About payment," he began. "My typical fee for hire as a retainer is twenty-five gold a week. We were gone just about one. Then for things such as training, fighting, council and guard duty—one hundred. Deductions for my spirited and apt student, as well as the discomfort I caused you all—that leaves us at one hundred gold pieces." With a grin that showed his tusks, he added, "And a pint!"

I smiled at the others and sent a telepathic message, *You guys want to sweeten the deal for him?*

How so? James asked.

Listening, Yohsuke responded.

The others just glanced my way. *There are six of us, including Muu. How about we all pitch in fifty? That'll be three hundred.*

I heard a low whistle, and Bokaj looked at me. *That's a lot of scratch to give a guy.*

Zhavron leaned toward Muu. "They do this a lot."

"You have no idea," he responded knowingly.

A lot or not, he treated us as best he could and dealt with our shit. Not to mention, he did knock Zeke's zombie ass out so he couldn't do more damage, James retorted.

I nodded and caught Muu looking our way, curiously.

I'm in, Jaken said finally.

"Muu, give him fifty gold," I ordered, "and nothing more. We will cover the rest."

Muu looked like he was about to question my judgment, but I gave him a placating glance. He shrugged and reached into his inventory obediently and pulled out the necessary amount to pass to Zhavron.

I reached into my own inventory, and the others mirrored my movements almost eerily, then deposited fifty gold on to the table. The others placed their money next to my pile and Muu's.

"That's too much," Zhavron growled at us. "The allotted price is what I earned, by my word."

"And we thought your time was worth more," Yohsuke shot back. "Fucker."

"If you want to earn it, pick fifteen of the people you had in mind and leave town as quick as you can," Jaken said. "Go directly to Sunrise and tell them that we sent you to begin guarding the village. Here," he pulled out what looked like a handkerchief and rubbed his head and pits with it, "show this to the bears guarding the area, and they should grant you passage."

"Bears?" Zhavron snorted. "I'd sooner show them a sword, not some stinking rag. And what the Hells will that do other than get me eaten?"

"You touch any of those bears, and you'll pay," I warned. "Those are the Bear Queen's personal guards for her allies and our friends."

"You'd better explain the state of things there if you want me to take over." Zhavron clapped his hands and ordered another drink as the server sat our food down. It smelled delicious.

We explained as much as we could without giving our original mission away. We could let Willem decide if these guys could be trusted enough to know about that. Zhavron listened closely, the alcohol having little to no effect on him yet.

"So, bears, a Dwarven smith, a Paladin, and Children of Brindolla?" He chuckled. "Sounds like a good time to me. I'll do my rounds and leave in a couple days. Gives me long enough to collect the right people and get things squared away on my end." He lifted his new mug in a toast. "Be safe out there, boys."

A chorus of, "You too," rang out around the table.

We finished our food and waved goodbye to Zhavron, and as we were leaving, an idea struck me. I walked over to the bar and got Giledt's attention.

"Yes, Zeke?" His eyebrows raised a bit.

"I was wondering if you had heard any rumors about any of your mercenaries meeting Dragons?" I asked in a low tone. "Specifically green or black."

He frowned, then began to think. He called over the other bartenders and barmaids and began asking them each if they had heard anything.

He turned back to me with a frown and a shake of his head. "Closest thing anyone has heard in a while is about some dungeon down south in the jungles near Mizmaori having some kind of giant snake the locals worship as a god."

"Any kind of myths?" It was a stretch, but the things I had thought mythic before were *literally* in me at that moment. So, there was that.

"I haven't paid attention to fairy tales since I was a kid." He frowned. "Sorry."

"Hey, don't worry about it." I shook his hand. "Don't forget to give my regards to Vrawn. Let her know I hope she's okay?"

"Oh, I'll let her know." He grinned. "Don't *you* worry."

I smiled back and shook my head. I walked outside to the others and joined them in the alleyway. "Djurn Forge?"

The others nodded, but as I was about to use the spell, Yohsuke stopped me, "Hey, you gonna be okay going underground like that?"

"I mean, the spell doesn't have any restrictions other than places I've been within the certain amount of miles," I shrugged, "and the number of passengers. Other than that, it should theoretically work."

"Oh shit!" Jaken put his hand out at me. "Remember the huge doors to get into the city? With all the runes? I think someone said something about that preventing people from teleporting directly in."

"Oooooh," I whispered. "Okay, so we adjust trajectory to the gate to the city. No big deal."

We joined hands again, and I focused on the location I wanted to go. It was well within range of the spell to take us. I triggered the spell, the necessary mana drained from my reserves, and it felt like we were being sucked through a straw for a moment before we landed where we wanted to be.

We stood in front of a fifteen-foot tall door of silvery-blue metal with large runes carved into it. I had no idea what they did, but I was inclined to believe Jaken.

Jaken bellowed, "Hail, clan Ironnose, may your mothers never claim you, and your beer be stronger than your noodle arms!"

The small door on the right side of the large ones flew open and three Dwarves with red beards and hair barreled out.

"Who said that about me arm?!" the one in the lead roared. He looked around and saw Jaken smiling. "You!"

"ME!" Jaken smiled back. "You aren't any better looking than last time, Ironnose."

"Aye, and ye never were," the Dwarf spat but smiled. "Back to visit yer kin?"

"Here to visit kin and forge," Jaken spoke for us. He pointed to Muu. "We need to get this one up to snuff and armed for some dealings with Dragons. Y'all know any?"

The three Dwarves burst into laughter. Finally, the leader spoke up, "Aye, do nae let them know ye plan ta fight. Or see yer fancy items. They like to take things."

"Don't worry guys," I said with a friendly smile. "We'll be careful."

"Come on in then, lads." They ushered us forward and closed the door behind us. "Ye remember where yer compound is?"

"We can manage," I informed them.

We stepped off to the side of the entry where I cast Mental Message to Brawnwynn that we were in the city.

"Yer here?!" he responded excitedly in my head. "I'll be right there to the gate. Same one ye used last time we came here?"

I sent an affirmative, then a message to Granda, "Hey, Granda. It's Zeke—You wanna come to the Mugfist compound in the morning? We have a few orders for weapons and armor from you. Custom things, I think."

"I'd be more'n happy to come and accept an order from ye and yer friends, Zekiel," the elder Dwarf responded happily. "Me son and I shall come on the morrow after the morning meal."

I looked to my friends. "Granda will be there in the morning."

They smiled, and Muu looked confused. So Jaken leaned over to explain things to him. While he did that, the others kept an eye out for Brawnwynn.

I sent one last Mental Message. This one was to the old crone.

"Hey!" I shouted loudly in the message. "Shitty bat. We're in the city to get more stuff done. You want to train? Maybe enchant some more of our gear?"

Her cackle rang through my head in a chilling way, my fur stood on end, and she finally said, "Tomorrow."

"It's settled," I told the others. "Shellica will also take any orders we have as well. So if anything you think would be useful, make a list to give her."

After another ten minutes of waiting, Brawnwynn separated himself from the crowd of people in the walkway and walked forward with arms wide open.

"Lads!" Brawnwynn shouted. His tan skin, ruddy cheeks were stretched in a smile partially hidden by his long, black beard. His black hair was up in a top knot with his customary double-headed battle axe strapped to his back. His black eyes sparkled with mirth as he approached us.

He swept Jaken up in a massive bear hug and then moved over to me.

"Gihgurg," I grunted as the air was crushed from my lungs. "Hi-guh-Brawny."

"Ho there, lad." He looked to the others. "Welcome back! Oh? Who is this with ye?"

"This is Muu," James introduced him. "He joined our party a little while ago, and we figured we would come back and get him properly equipped."

"Welcome then, Muu." Brawnwynn stepped forward and shook his hand. "Ye lads always did keep strange comp'ny. Seems a strong one. And yer armor looks fine there, lookin' to upgrade to better materials?"

"I sure am!" Muu grinned.

"Well, ye came to the right place for it." Brawnwynn slapped his shoulder. "Come! The clan is lookin' forward to seein' ye again."

Brawnwynn led us through the crowds and haggling customers. People stared at the motley crew that we were, but that was to be expected in a Dwarven settlement.

We arrived at the Mugfist compound with squat buildings made of stone and Dwarves outside training in the grounds.

"Look, a gaggle of shite has come crawlin' back to the clan!" One of the Dwarves in the yard greeted us. Several others chuckled as we entered the gates.

"Oh? Look at that wee axe in yer hands," I shouted back, mimicking his accent. "Bet yer wife has a bigger one, eh?"

Brawnwynn howled in delight, "He got ye good, Sethral!"

The other Dwarves laughed and the one who had spoken first, Sethral, smiled at the joke.

"I don't have a clue what the fuck is going on," Muu whispered to me.

"It's a common Dwarven custom to insult people, especially family or clan members, when you see them," I explained in a low voice. "It's a sign of affection and regard. I'm not sure if there's a custom for nobles though."

We hadn't made it far when Farnik, Brawnwynn's father burst out of the center building of the compound.

"Who said that shite had come crawlin' back to the clan?!" Sethral raised his hand. "Ye should know that at least shite has a use, lad!"

The whole yard, Jaken, me, and the others burst with laughter.

"Welcome back, lads and new friend," Farnik greeted us.

Farnik looked very much like his son, a little broader in the chest and shoulder, sure. His beard was plaited and had metal beads keeping it orderly over his mithral plate mail. His stern gaze almost distracted from the milky left eye bisected by a scar running down the center of his brow and cheek.

He shook hands with all of us until he stood in front of Muu.

"I am Farnik, current leader of Clan Mugfist, and I extend our hospitality to ye as a friend of the clan." The older Dwarf offered his hand to Muu in friendship.

Before Muu moved, I cleared my throat and asked for a moment with him. We stepped back as the leader dropped his arm and nodded.

"Before you clasp his forearm, you need to be sure you meet his gaze. And don't insult him right away." Muu nodded at me and returned his attention to Farnik.

Farnik offered his hand again, and Muu clasped his forearm with a clap of metal on metal.

"I appreciate your hospitality and hope that I can bring you honor as your guest." Muu bowed a bit at his waist. He fixed his gaze on Farnik's left eye and said seriously, "That's quite an intense scar—you must have really pissed the missus off."

I gasped, Yohsuke spat some water out of his mouth, and Brawnwynn stilled. Not one eye in the grounds strayed from the two figures.

"Baha—bwahahaha!" Farnik doubled over, his good eye streaming tears. After his laughing fit subsided, he looked Muu in the face and wiped a hand across his cheek. "Oh, lad. Would that me wife were here ta hear that one. Would've made her smile an' feed ye like her own, it would've."

He looked at the rest of the Dwarves in the area, still silent and watching. "What're the lot of ye gawkin' at? How could he have know'd?"

I hadn't even known, but I figured she must have been busy when we first came to Djurn Forge. It was going to come up now, though.

The other Dwarves nodded and made placating gestures and went back to their sparring and training.

I swear, if they didn't kill him, I very damned well could have at that moment.

Brawnwynn came over to us and motioned that we all come inside. Farnik clapped Muu on the shoulder good-naturedly, and we all stepped forward to follow.

After we cleared the doorway, Brawnwynn turned and looked at his father. "Don't fret, da. I'll let them know what happened. Ye should go and see to the others. Let them know that no disrespect was meant."

"Well look at ye, orderin' about the head o' the clan?" Farnik teased, and the younger Dwarf paled. "Relax, boy. I'm not so weak as I'd let the tale go untold. Go fix the others, ye let me do the tellin' o' me wife's honor."

Brawnwynn nodded and stepped through all of us and outside the door.

"Come, let's go to the mess and have a chat." Farnik turned and walked off down the hallway toward a door at the end of the hall.

"What the fuck, man?!" I whispered harshly.

"I didn't know!" Muu whispered back. "How was I supposed to? Did you?"

Jaken prodded us both. "None of us did. He said he would explain and that it was okay. Relax."

We followed Farnik through the door into the large dining hall that lay beyond. This was where we had shared many a meal with the rest of the clan. And many a laugh. But it seemed from the somber mood of the Dwarf leading us that today would be a little different.

We sat down as Farnik poured all of us a tall mug of mead, then water for Yohsuke, and finally a mug of mead for himself. He took a long draft from his mug, filled it again then wandered back over to us.

"When first we met, ye remember Brawny tellin' ye bout the time we had been invaded by a large number of Drow forces?" he asked us. All of us but Muu nodded, so he continued, "Largest invasion we had ever see'd. Scores of the dirty Elves and their slaves—Driders, Drow Elves twisted by their dark deity and given the lower half a large spider and all other manner of ill begotten creatures."

There were stories of the Dark Elves in our own world as well, tales of their cunning and cruelty to anyone, their own, other races—fuck, if you weren't them they hated you and you fucking knew it. They usually boasted highly powerful Mages and martial prowess. Not to mention they enslaved hundreds of Goblinoids and other creatures to fight with.

He lifted his mug in contemplation of how to continue, took a sip, and sighed. "They dug straight up beneath us, center o' the city. They were crazy. Driven mad by some fell power. Never see'd anything like it. The Mugfist, as ye know, act as the standing army. Warriors, we be. Weren't none finer than me wife, Gerty. She led our forces, along another score o' warriors from some of the other clans tha' could spare the men straigh' away. I led the second wave o' defenders, with the masons who could close tha' bloody hole the damned Dark Elves had made."

Fell power? I peeked up a bit. *That could be a minion. Or fuck, even a general? Maybe. Let him finish man.*

Farnik shook his head with a smile. "It were a bloodbath. See'd a beautiful savagery from me wife like I had never see'd before. She moved and wove her battle axes through more'n a dozen Kobold slaves, slew a Drider, an' squared off against a half dozen Drow warriors. Only a couple o' her most trusted warriors at her back. She worked quick, even as we got to her, she were almost finished with 'em when the worst happened."

A tear slid down his right cheek, but his words never quavered.

"As she were preparin' to strike at the last two, a bubble o' darkness burst where she had been and this horrible sucking sound. Then the screams of me wife and her captains. Then nothin'."

His lips contorted in rage and his gaze was faraway in that moment. "Then I saw her, this she devil in black robes and a spider in white tattooed over her features—priestess of Lolth with her hand outstretched and this cock-sure grin."

"I could nae control meself!" He slammed his mug so hard the hard clay object shattered, and we all jumped. His formerly more cultured tone and vocabulary falling into more common Dwarven verbiage. "Me wife, her mithral plate as fine as ever forged had been there but a wee moment before in full glory to the Mountain. I screamed me rage at the world and went at her. I remember naught of the proceedin's but that I ended the fight with me bare hands round the dirty Elf's throat, her eyes rolled back, and foam from me own mouth on her cheek."

He sighed as if the memory of his rage had sapped his energy now in this moment. Looking at him, he appeared older. Shaken. He blinked, clearing away some of that age and a little of the hurt faded, but it wasn't completely gone.

"Couldn't find a body after." Another tear strayed into the line of his beard. "Could nae give'r a proper burial." He looked at Muu. "Ye didn't know, lad, and that were a good one—it were. But a lot o' the lads remember losing their general and one o' the greatest Fighters they ever know'd. Hell, she taught a good deal o'em how ta hold an axe. It's a sore spot, be ye sure."

"Farnik, I'm so sorry," Muu tried to apologize.

"Do nae apologize, lad." He took a moment to compose himself. His barrel chest expanded and his back straightened. "I will nae have a guest be hated for their ignorance, not in me home. Not with me clan. Zeke, if ye would be so kind as to send a message to my son? Have him bring the clan here in a few hours. We will hold a feast tonight to celebrate yer return."

I complied with his request, and Brawnwynn replied that he would see it done.

"Now, tell me—where is Balmur?" Farnik asked curiously.

We looked at each other, and Bokaj cleared his throat. "It's kind of a long story after we left you. So, if you'll get yourself another mug—I'll fill you in."

It took a while, with some of us filling gaps and differing perspectives at times, but when we finished our tale, Farnik's grave expression left me a little troubled.

"This is bad, lads." Farnik growled. "Cousin Balmur needs whatever aid the clan can give. Ye said ye had planned to look for Dragons?"

"Specifically green or black," James put in. "We aren't sure how the others would treat us."

"Quite right." Farnik stood and began to pace. After a moment, he stopped. "You'll be properly equipped. I'll have a runner sent to Granda and the witch right away."

"Already taken care of." I tapped my head. "I sent them both messages when we arrived. They'll be here in the morning."

"Good work, lad." He nodded. "And yer funds? That clan can front ye whatever the cost ye'll need for better gear, do nae fret."

"We're good on money, Farnik," Jaken stood and walked over to the Dwarf, "but it means a lot that you're so willing to help us."

"He's clan!" Farnik shouted. "All of ye! What good be the clan if we can't get our cousin out of the Hells?"

"Here here!" Muu stood and shouted.

"I like him, ugly shite that he is." Farnik smiled despite the gravity of the situation.

"I have that effect on people." Muu preened.

"What be ye lad?" Farnik asked.

"I'm a Dragon Beast-kin," Muu said but continued when Farnik shook his head. "My class is Fighter."

"Have ye an interest in the axe?!" the Mugfist leader asked excitedly.

"That's more Zeke's territory," Muu advised. "I'm more a spear and shield guy myself. Though I do have ideas about a lance."

"Bah," Farnik swatted the words away. "Anyone who's anyone knows that the axe is what kills, but ye know what ye need. We can help train ye to fight if ye like?"

"Yeah, I'd like that. Thanks, Farnik." Muu smiled.

"Aye, lad." The Dwarf smiled menacingly. "We'll train ye up right proper."

"Oh no," Muu whimpered. "What did I do?"

Chapter Ten

After a couple hours, the food had been prepared, mead brought to the hall, and Dwarves filled benches with us at the front of the hall with Farnik and his kids. Before the feast began properly, Farnik stood and motioned for us to join him.

"Brothers and sisters of the clan," he bellowed. "For too long, we have suffered from the loss of our general, my beloved. Too long have our heads hung low out of hurt and sorrow. Let us raise our mugs to our lost, drink, and sing of their glories."

We all raised our mugs and shouted, "Mugfist!" before drinking.

Farnik addressed the clan once more, "Brothers and sisters of the clan, I have learned this day tha' our cousin, Balmur, has been banished to the Hells by a fallen foe.". There was a cry of outrage and for war. "Aye! And we shall have it!" Farnik pointed at us. "They seek power, better items, and in the coming time, Dragons so that they might take the fight to the Hells and WIN. HIM. BACK!"

The Dwarves in the hall shouted and roared so loudly I thought I would go deaf. There wasn't a single member seated.

"We, Clan Mugfist, warriors, fighters, soldiers, and devout as stone, will assist this group as well as we can," Farnik shouted. "Be there any among ye who wishes to withhold his support or deem it a waste o' the clan's power—let them speak their piece now."

One Dwarf, his beard neatly kept with streaks of gray and white, stood with his axe in hand, and he stared at Farnik hard. "Ye ask ol' Liltorq what he thinks? I thinks we should be with these boys when they invade the Hells. I thinks we should go NOW!"

The Dwarves around him stood and chorused his sentiment with robust yeahs and ayes.

"Ye know we can nae leave the city unprotected," Brawnwynn reasoned. "I trust Jaken, Zeke, and all the others to see to it that Balmur comes back. And we will give them the aid they need."

"Aye, well said, Brawny." Farnik patted his son's shoulder. "The Dragon Beast-kin, Muu, is a Fighter who fancies the spear and shield." A bout of laughter and good-natured teasing erupted in the hall. "That's what I said, but he seems adamant. We will see to it he's as hard to kill as the others before his time here is up. On the morrow, Granda and the witch will come to see about their gear and arms. And we will see the arms holding those arms are stronger still. Are ye with me?!"

"AYE!" the clan roared.

"Tonight, we mourn and grieve—celebrate our fallen in true holding with the Way," Farnik hefted his mug once more, "and tomorrow, we prepare our folk for war! Let the feasting begin!"

Dwarves of all ages and ranks tucked into the food before them, eating boisterously, bellowing insults back and forth, while a small band of clansmen struck up a lively tune in the back corner of the hall.

After the food was demolished, barrel upon barrel of mead, beer, and ale were carted into the room and tapped for consumption in an almost-double-fisted fashion.

We watched as the Dwarves began to pound their mugs and sing a song to their maker. A song about their fallen comrade and general.

One Dwarf, a stout and chiseled figure with tan skin, no shirt on, and chest hair about as thick as his beard stood on a long table and shouted a tune.

"The Drow, they thought her line was weak, to enslave us all they did seek.

The odds looked rough, but she was tough, and her line held them all.

Her plate of mithral covered in gore, her axes takin' sev'ral more.

They piled on and fell the same, and all Dwarves will know her name—"

As chills crept over my flesh I watched as more than two hundred mugs, frothing alcohol swung into the air in a toast, and every voice shouted, "GERTY THE MUGFIST MAIDEN!"

"She swept them off and went for broke, fell enemy did start to choke.

Until that bitch of a witch had come to claim our Geeeeerty."

The tune of the song fell somber, and the Dwarf picked up the tune again with tears in his eyes and his chin held high.

"The darkness came and claimed her life, her final act created strife, for the enemy knew naught of thee,"

Every eye in the room turned and watched as Farnik stood with his head held high and thrust his own mug into the air.

The music began to grow at a steady pace as the muscular, shirtless Dwarf began to chant again.

"He lost his eye in the fray, to take the lives of all in the way and get to his Gerty.

He took his axe, chopped and slashed, and down a drider crashed.

Another fell and another still, his lust for blood never to fill—until he took the priestess by her neck and shook'r violent to her death.

Their leader gone, the lines did fall, and in the hole, they crawled—the winner of the day—"

The Dwarves drank deep of their mugs, some wept even as they drank, and only a somber, single voice rang out, *"Farnik the bold. Farnik the final. Farnik the savior without his Gerty."*

Farnik's daughter, Roslyn, her cheeks mottled red and her eyes moist sniffled, then raised her voice.

"Her strength be missed, since last she kissed this cheek of mine," she motioned toward her brother, *"And thine. Her time was short as we all might know, but ne'er did she fail to show her love in all the clan to grow. And should ye fret about her loss, go to the yard with axe to toss—our loss, our grief be free and gone. All for the memory of Gerty."*

Farnik took a drought from his own mug as the final word left the singer's lips. Another Dwarf stepped over and poured more alcohol into his leader's mug.

"To Gerty," Farnik said simply.

The whole of the clan lifted their mugs solemnly, drank after Farnik and kept drinking until there was nothing left to drink.

A bleary-eyed Farnik looked over to us, refilled his mug and beckoned for every mug to be filled. Once everyone was topped off, he turned to us.

"I offer this next toast in oath to you all and to the clan for Balmur." He turned to the clan. "I swear, here and now with all of ye as witness—Clan Mugfist will do all in its power to assist in Balmur's rescue. We will stop at nothing until he is safe with us. And Gods have mercy for any poor bastard who gets in our way!"

The clan roared and thrust their mugs into the air.

I wiped a tear from my eye; the clan's song about their former general and beloved Gerry had sent chills through my body but had touched my soul. Fuck, I hoped someone sang songs about me like that someday.

Muu was smiling and dancing with some tiny Dwarven lady off in a corner with clan members banging a beat for them to step to. He was surprisingly nimble.

Jaken and Bokaj sat speaking quietly to one another, and Yohsuke was looking over the food.

James was knee-deep in Dwarves who wanted to wrestle and even though he had a few drinks in him the same as I, he looked better prepared than I was.

After so many toasts, obligatory drinking and booze with the food—my vision blurred too far, and the darkness at the edge of my vision stepped forward into victory as slumber took me.

I woke up at some point with a terrible headache, cottonmouth, and a mug of water next to my face. A wool blanket rested over my shoulders, and a small pillow was under my face.

I sat up and smacked my lips a little too loudly for my taste as the sound caused my head to throb a little more. I drank the water as quickly as I could while surveying my surroundings.

The majority of the Dwarves were gone. A few rested on the benches of the tables, and the chanter from the previous night was passed out on the table where he had been.

My friends had left me where I fell it seemed, since they were gone. I stood and stretched slowly. I snuck out of the room as quietly as possible, wishing I had some of the root the Willem had given me after the party at his tavern. Christ.

I walked down the hallway slowly, stepping over the prone and passed-out form of several Dwarves.

Gotta hand it to these guys, man. They know how to fucking drink, I thought to myself. There was no telling what time it was, but I made my way to the reception room and stood by there. I fell back to sleep after a bit on one of the comfortable couches and used the blanket still over my shoulders to cover myself.

"Zeke." Hands shook my shoulder. I growled low, then turned over. More hands. "Zeeeeke."

"Step aside," I heard a somewhat familiar voice. "WAKE UP, YOU USELESS FOX!"

I'm not proud of it, but I swung at her full force and received a soul-crushing cackle and thin air for my efforts.

Shellica, thin for a Dwarf with gray, plaited hair and bright green eyes stood in a dark colored robe, staring at me. She flashed me a mischievous grin. "Welcome back, lazy ass."

"Gods, how I wish a rock had crushed you," I groaned, only seventy percent serious.

Despite the fact that Shellica and I acted like we despised each other—she had taught me a lot. She was like the mean ol' grandma you liked because she was shady as fuck and taught you the cool shit. Though there were times you wished she would just shut the hell up and make cookies.

"The fuck do you want?" I yawned. She stuck a finger into my open mouth, and I bit down as hard as I could only to miss. "Leave me be, shitty granny."

"No," she replied with a sweet grin. "You are going to be coming with me for more training while the others wait on their orders." She thumped my leg. "You may even see what it's like to be a real enchanter. By the way, the fuck had its way with your fur, boy? They left a real mess!"

I blinked twice and looked to my friends who stood aghast behind her.

"She just make a splooge joke about my fur?" I asked them.

Yohsuke nodded, and Muu grinned before replying, "I think so. I like her."

"Don't get used to her. She's going to die." I stood up and cracked my neck menacingly.

I summoned Storm Caller, then acted like I was about to take a swing at her and all she did was cackle.

"She's not afraid of Zeke?" Muu leaned over to Jaken and asked.

"I fear no one, little Dragon," Shellica shot over her shoulder.

She turned to face him fully. "Show me the items you wear and tell me what you are thinking about enchantment-wise. We will see what can be done for you."

Muu obeyed. He summoned his spear and laid it on the table. Then his boots, bracelet, and rings. Finally, he put his armor on the table. Shellica started with the boots.

"These are interesting and well done." She put them down. "Why do you wish to be able to jump farther and higher?"

Muu responded with, "It's part of my fighting style. If I want to fight an enemy, I want to get to them quickly. And if I do it with a spear, I need to be able to stab and pierce quickly. Plus, attacking from above would be cool."

"Clever." She nodded. "I will make an improvement. Zekiel? Attend me." She motioned toward the items before her. "The boots were a good touch. The metal you used to attach the enchantment was well done, and they were attached well. Good work. Your engraving was slightly shallow on one side. It could have been stronger. The rings were good. I am impressed. If you had better materials to work with, the enchantments would have been much better."

She pointed to the ring of Regrowth. "This was a true work of art, I am highly excited to see you thinking outside the box as it were."

"Thank you," I said wearily.

"Now, this armor," she touched it, "show me the engraving." I pointed to where the symbols I had engraved were. "Very clever to hide them. You could have done more than just make them lighter, though. See the leather that the armor is on? You could have enchanted that to make everything attached to it lighter, then enchanted the plate itself to be stronger, therefore increasing the defense."

"Ah, I didn't think about that."

"Obviously." Shellica grinned. "That's why you still need me."

"Rot in hell, old hag." I sighed.

"I will join the Mountain when I die, thank you," she cooed. "Now, the shield. Why is it not enchanted? Did you grow lazy?"

"Actually, no." I motioned Muu toward the weapon. "Once he squeezes the lever there," Muu demonstrated the way the blade popped out, "the blade thrusts out and stays in that position until put back. With there being that kind of mechanism, I wasn't certain how to go about enchanting it. If I enchanted one portion—say the shield—to negate the impact taken by weapons on the user, would that harm the mechanism inside and make the weapon thrusting out not work right?" I then pointed to the blade. "And vice versa, if I were to enchant the blade itself to increase piercing damage, would that make it easier to pierce the shield? With so many different scenarios and 'what-ifs', I didn't feel it safe for me to enchant it without ruining it."

Shellica's eyebrows raised slightly in surprise and appreciation. "There's hope for you yet, lad." She patted my arm, and I felt my cheeks burn a little in pride.

"For a complicated device like this, I would enchant the two individually—the blade before it was attached and the shield before the blade was inserted." She motioned to the blade. "If the weapon portion was enchanted beforehand and given a special treatment—which I will proudly show you—the two enchantments would not negate or harm each other. Tell me, what level is your enchanting as of now?"

"Level 29, ma'am," I answered.

"Excellent." She clapped. "Almost to craftsman. Good—at that level, you can begin adding other materials to augment and improve your enchantments."

"Ooooooh!" I whispered in wonder.

"Indeed." She smiled. "Young Muu, you will compile a list of enchantments you would like on your armor. I will prepare for what I can, and I will perform the enchantments myself. All of you, think about it and if you would like one more item apiece, make a list."

The others began to discuss, and Shellica interrupted, "*One* each. And it will cost you—albeit at a discount due to past transgressions."

She rounded on me. "Do not think I do not see how bereft of enchanted gear they are—you have fallen dangerously close to neglect, lad." I opened my mouth and closed it. She was right. "Ah, the beginnings of wisdom set in. Leave a Fighter with poorly enchanted gear? Feh!"

"Thank you," Muu said with a smile as she smacked me again.

"Another one with manners." Shellica grinned. "Tell me, lad. Have you any interest in enchanting?"

Muu shook his head. "I don't have the mana for it. Though, picking up a craft would be nice."

"What are your highest stats?" she asked curiously. "And what of the rest of you? What do you all do as a craft?"

"Constitution, strength, and dexterity," he answered simply.

"Cook," Yohsuke said proudly.

"Smith, and Balmur worked with accessories like y'all," Jaken said.

Bokaj raised a hand. "Woodworking or carpentry."

"I don't have anything yet, but I don't use mana," James said. "I don't really want to craft if I'm being honest. Not my style."

"A young one who knows his mind?" Shellica stood in front of James a moment. He didn't budge. "I like you too."

She looked back at Muu. "If you are amenable to it, I could put you into contact with a tanner who will happily take you on and show you the basics. She owes me a favor."

"So, I would be making leather?" Muu asked uncertainly.

"You would—if my memory serves—learn proper ways to skin animals, treat the pelts for various things, and maybe even make your own clothing." She thought a moment. "At the very least, you would be able to provide leather strips for Jaken's weapons and other simple gear if you don't take to crafting simple armor. Not everyone has that level of skill."

"That sounds pretty cool!" Muu agreed. "Thank you, I really appreciate that."

"Oh, I really *do* like you, lad." Shellica cackled. "Zekiel. Attend me. We go to my workshop for training."

I groaned audibly, and she cackled again as we left my throbbing skull aching more deeply than before. Farnik looked like he had seen a ghost as we walked by him. He nodded in respect to me, and he mouthed the words, *Be strong*.

I had a feeling I would need that strength if my last dealings with her were anything to go by.

We wound our way through the crowds, more than one Dwarf seeing Shellica and taking care not to cross her path. The Light Hand Clan leader took it in stride, her steps never faltering once.

As we walked through the crafting section of the city, a simple affair with stalls outside shops run by apprentices showing off their masters' skills. We stopped at one stall, a small Dwarven child who looked to be the human equivalent of an eleven-year-old with round checks and not a whisker yet to be seen took one look at the Dwarf with me and bolted into the back, shouting in Dwarven.

Though she was smiling, I could see something else.

"It hurts you," I began thickly. "The way the others run from you."

"If only you paid this much attention to your crafting," Shellica responded sourly. "They fear magic—don't understand it—because it is a thing worthy of their fear."

"But it was a gift from your God," I reasoned, my still-booze-addled mind refusing to heed social etiquette. "Shouldn't that be something worthy of their respect? And admiration?"

She looked at me then—really looked—and for once, there was no mania. There was a depth of understanding and hurt that I could never imagine peeking out from my own eyes as she told me, "What use have we, the chosen of our creator, for respect and admiration that only He deserves? We create, we bless, we enchant. But we do so in order that His work can continue to live on in the works of our people. People fear what they do not know—this is especially true of my kin as they are a thick-headed people—and magic is something that most clans have lost touch with over the ages. We are the last here in Djurn Forge to hold to his teachings in magery. We are not the folk to run to our pa when people treat us mean. We do not blame Fainne for the others, for He has blessed us more than we could ever hope to have imagined. Leave us to bare the weight, lad. We do so gladly."

The depth of her sadness and her faith in her people and Fainne were beyond touching. I reached out and touched her shoulder lightly. "Later."

I knew there was more to this, and it just wasn't in me to leave it alone when I saw someone suffering. I wanted—needed—to help. To show I could be there for her somehow. I might still be burping up booze fumes from the night before, but I'd be damned if I wasn't going to try my best to help her deal.

She seemed to understand what I meant, and I let my hand fall away. As my hand fell, a thickly muscled Dwarven woman stepped out from the shop behind the stall we stood in front of. Her brown hair was shorn close to her scalp on the sides, and the top was braided long, wrapped tightly around the top of her head.

"Shellica, why'd ye scare me boy?" she asked in a deep voice. "Yer gob be bad, but nae tha' bad I don' think."

"It's only as bad as yours is manly. You're big as an ogre, you lumpy shite with legs." Shellica crossed her arms and grinned at the other woman. "Hello, Natholdi. Been a while, old friend."

The two of them rushed forward and hugged one another for a long moment.

Natholdi spoke first as she pushed my trainer out to arm's length, "Ye ne'er come 'round fer tea, Shelly—Hells look'it ye!—skin. And. Bone." She emphasized each word with a prod at

Shellica's physique. "Ye bet'er come 'round and have a *proper* meal ta fatten ye up right! Look'it me boy, thick like his ma, he is."

"He's a handsome one too." Shellica smiled. "Chubby cheeks and all. Has himself a good ma."

"Aye." She nodded, then her sight fell on me. "Ye were always one fer strange comp'ny Shelly, lass, but a sylph?" She sniffed and observed me. "One tha' smells like he could nae hold a mug if we gives one, ta boot?"

The thought of alcohol made me have to choke back a dry heave.

"Careful, Natholdi," Shellica scolded. "He's recognized and claimed by Mugfist. Farnik himself greets him like a son. He and a Fae-Orc along with several other odd ones. They're good folk with a good mission." She looked around to be sure no one was close enough to hear then whispered. "The Mountain Himself has seen fit to bless this one with my same gift."

Natholdi's sucked air through her teeth. "Aye?" She looked me over once more. "Be tha' why yer here? If'n he has yer blessin' true, ye donae need me ta teach him—wha' can I do fer ye?"

"I'm here about that favor," Shellica said simply. "He has a friend—a Dragon Beast-kin named Muu—with Clan Mugfist. Good head on his shoulders, Fighter type. You would like him. In the mornings, when you're busiest, he will be training to fight with the clan. In the afternoon's though, I want you to teach him the basics of your trade. Skinning, tanning—the works. Quick as you can, but the right way."

"How long?" Natholdi grinned.

"Four to five days," I said. "He's got weapons and armor being made by Granda. Then the enchantment time—which won't be long with Shellica."

"Oh," the thicker Dwarf sounded disappointed. "I though' ye were gonna gimme a challenge. I'll train him up, donae worry, Shelly. I will nae le' ye down."

She placed her thick thumb and index finger in her lips, and a shrill whistle ripped through my ears. "Gah!" I held my hands over my ears and looked at her angrily.

She smiled back, and her son came careening out of the shop. He hid behind his mother's legs.

"Get ye out here, boy." The boy's ma hefted him by his brown shirt and lifted him around so he stood facing her. He kept stealing not-so-subtle glances at Shellica. "Oi, look'it me boy."

His attention snapped to his mother, and he squirmed at the intense look she gave him.

"Ye be disrespectin' a dear friend o' yer ma's, boy," Natholdi scolded. "Yer nae tha' type o' lad, righ'?" He shook his head hard enough I thought he'd be dizzy. "Good lad. Get ye to the Mugfist compound and ask fer a Dragon Beast-kin called 'Muu.' Tell the clan he's ta follow ye ta me, so's I can train him proper."

He nodded quickly. She shook her head and put a hand on her hip before asking, "What'd I say ta do?"

The boy frowned in concentration and then spoke, his little Dwarven voice light and child-like in tone, "Ye said ta go and fetch a dragon called Moo, and bring him ta the clan. Ouch!" His ma had flicked him in the forehead. "Ta ye! He's ta follow me ta ye, and ye'd train'm up proper."

"Which clan did I say?" she asked with a slight growl.

"Mugfist!" He held his fists up in front of him like an old-timey boxer. "They's the ones what fight fer us!"

"Get ye gone, and be light-footed 'bout it too, or I'll box yer ears boy!" She swiped at him, but he ducked under her meaty hands and took off without so much as a glance behind him.

"What a good lad you've got there," Shellica said wistfully, a small, sad smile on her face.

"Aye, he's clever ta boot." Natholdi smiled back. "Has a memory on 'im donae doubt. Boy can skin a buck as large hisself quicker'n a drunken Dwarven Fighter can finish his fourth mead too. He'll be bet'er than his ma some day."

"Aye. Thank you old friend." Shellica hugged her friend fiercely.

"Bah." Natholdi swatted at her playfully. "We're even, Shelly. Now, ye be comin' 'round fer tea and a proper meal, or I'll come ta ye. And nae a single door be stoppin' me, lass."

"I swear it, I will." Shellica smiled at Natholdi, and we were off again.

After we were a good couple dozen feet away, I had to ask, "What kind of favor did she owe you?"

"That is not a proper question to ask anyone, lad," Shellica replied gruffly, "but if you must know—I saved her life once when we were younger. I would never have collected on it, especially since she is my friend—but if it will make her stop bringing it up—so be it. I can have a proper time with her now."

After another ten minutes of silent walking, we were in her clan's home. It was a compound similar to the Mugfist Clan's in size and structure layout, but the buildings were made of metal the likes of which I hadn't seen anywhere else.

We entered the gates with a wave of her hand that set them to opening. We walked unimpeded into the central building, and I watched as Dwarves worked with their tools with freshly heated precious metals. Etching devices, chisels, and other sophisticated tools carved symbols and engravings into gems and completed trinkets. No one seemed to really care that the head of their clan had come through leading a Kitsune like myself.

We stepped into a cell that I was intimately familiar with. The walls and décor were spartan. There was a furnace, enchanted to never grow cool and be at a constant perfect temperature. The bed was austere with simple linens, and the workbench was tidy with a few items placed at the rear.

I waited until the door was shut completely before I stepped over to Shellica and gave her a hug. She was so shocked by it that she didn't move for a moment. I felt her arms wrap loosely around my waist for a moment before they dropped.

"What was that for?" She asked curiously.

"For not being as much of the crazy, hard-headed witch that everyone makes you out to be," I explained. "It has to be easier for you to be scorned by everyone if they do so for a reason, right?"

"That's a brave thing to say to the woman who has your ass for the next few days, lad." She smiled, her green eyes sparkling in amusement. "Don't think that will earn you any leniency."

"I know it won't." I grinned back, all of my canines flashing. "I expect nothing less from the devil herself."

Shellica began to cackle, chilling me to the bone. I hadn't heard this depth of mania before. Her head was thrown back, and I saw her teeth shining in the fair light of the room.

"Is it too late to run?" I asked skeptically partially teasing but mostly actually scared.

"Aye," Shellica growled and advanced on me, pulling accessories out of her pocket. "Much too late."

"NO!" I shrieked.

Those of you who remember her way of teaching involves a lot of me making things, quality stuff, and her *tossing it into a furnace*.

Fucking hell. Not this again!

Chapter Eleven

The first thing she did was have me create items of greater strength until I was dizzy with it. This took the majority of the first day, and each item I made was somehow flawed enough that the evil bitch threw them into her furnace.

"Tell me, the spear that I saw this Muu with," she said as she tossed another small ring into the fire and a part of my resistance to violence with it, "you enchanted that, correct?"

"Yes," I growled. I stared into the furnace and watched the metal accessory melt.

"Where did you get such a sophisticated idea?" she inquired. "You should not have been able to do this at your level, at least not that enchantment specifically."

"I don't know," I replied honestly with a sigh. "I had been thinking about what you did to my axe. About the weapon returning to the owner faster than a comet. I think with my newly obtained racial changes, I was able to give the idea more juice than even I was aware of. I didn't even set a distance limit with it—I was just consumed by the stars and let my mana go until I felt it was right. It took everything I had."

She scowled in thought. "I see. That bottoming out your mana reserves would lend to it, I think as well. It is a damned good enchantment. One to be proud of, lad."

"Thank you." My chest had puffed out a little, that was for sure.

"But everything else is shite," she howled at me. "Here! Make something of this. Make it do something with fire!"

She tossed me a set of what looked like brass knuckles, but they had four sharp spikes half an inch long protruding from the knuckles. The base the spikes were on was wide and swept back over the fist and back of the hand close to the wrist where it ended. The grip was grooved to allow the fingers to sit in it comfortably.

I turned them over in my hands, getting a good feel for the weight. I put it over my fingers and felt how it would move and react to motion. It left room for the wrist to move freely and even covered the side of the hand on the outer side opposite the thumb.

I sat it on the workbench before me and closed my eyes. What could I possibly give it to make it suitable to fire damage. It was one that I had the most trouble with when I was beginning, but then again, I was considerably weaker and didn't know everything.

I felt a stirring in my core; heat pressed against my ribcage from the inside. I could feel Coal looking outward at the item. I could metaphysically *see* or envision this taking place inside my body. Like the place he was in inside my being was this cool little room that he laid in and waited for me to call to him.

I picked the weapon up and held in the palm of my left hand before I began to focus on the engraving I wanted to use. I drew my mana out and formed the shape around the outside before drawing it close to the surface. I pressed my mana evenly across the surface and scored it a little deeper than usual.

The engraving was a larger, more intricate one, so it took a little more mana than I might normally spend—about 300 MP total—but it covered the front plate from the bottom of the spikes to the top near the back of it by the wrist portion. The engraving was the top view of a wolf's head with the side portion a side view and the front, the open mouth.

I was vaguely aware of Shellica watching out of the corner of my left eye.

"What I'm about to do is something I haven't been able to try yet, so I'm not sure what will happen," I mumbled. I saw her step back a bit. Then I refocused on my efforts.

As I waited a minute needing to recoup my mana, I focused my will and intent on what I wanted. I wanted this weapon to become the embodiment of fire. I envisioned it becoming the inferno but the owner being able to wield it without it harming them. I saw the wolf I had seared into it biting, burning, and rending flesh from bone with the wicked spikes as the fangs.

As I was beginning to concentrate on adding mana to the item, the soul of flame touched my mind and added a newer, fresher perspective of the element. Not just heat but intensity. Burning purpose. Destructive power personified. I saw Coal, his mouth roiling with flames, baying into my mind as my focus and intent sharpened with his aid.

I began to pull the mana from the center of my being and rather than the cool pressure I had felt before—this was like trying to handle a flame, but it didn't burn the way I felt it should've. Like a bath that is *just* this side of comfortable. I brought the mana—red now rather than blue with a feeling of fire itself—under control and began to pour it into the engraving.

As the mana drained from me into the item, I watched as some of the red, flaming mana began to evaporate, and my mana drained at an alarming rate. I continued to focus, but as I poured my mana, I imagined it leaving my body in a funnel and spiraling into the engraving.

It helped a little, as it wasn't draining quite as quickly—but it was far from my normal control. I managed to get 350 MP into it before I ran completely dry. I sat the item on the workbench and nursed my head as a headache began to take over. A groan escaped my lips.

"Quit your bellyaching." Shellica snorted.

I took a quick assessment of my body, in and out. My mana pathways felt like they were charred. I ached all over, and Coal seemed content as he yipped at me from inside my body.

I heard a gasp of surprise and looked over to see my trainer staring at the item in her hands.

"What?" I groaned. My body was recovering as my mana began to refill.

She tossed the item to me, and I caught it easily enough. The first thing I noticed was that it was warm to the touch. I looked it over, the engraving a deep orange and red depending on the lighting that shined on it.

Fire Fang
+ 10 flame damage, + 5 piercing damage
Wearer's fist becomes wreathed in flames that only affect the object of their dissatisfaction.
Knuckle Buster crafted by Master Smith Milgarth and Enchanted by Craftsman Enchanter Zekiel Erebos.

I whistled low. "Damn."

"I agree." She snatched it out of my hands before I could think to protect it. I reached for it, and she smacked my hand. "Ah-ah. You have attained craftsmen level, what is it actually?"

I checked and saw that—on top of reaching level 31 enchanting—I saw a notification that said I could now use other components to augment the strength of my enchantments.

"Thirty-one," I said dazedly. My mind felt a little fuzzy, but was that from the shock of leaping two levels in my craft, or the fact that Coal was excitedly trying to tear my insides apart.

I thrust my right hand away from myself and summoned the Flame Wolf with a flex of will and the familiar burn of the soul leaving my body. His corporeal form materialized, and I instantly felt better.

"So *that* is where you learned that?" Shellica said. She stepped closer to my familiar and began to look him over. "I thought you said you had a bird for a pet?"

"I do," I explained. Coal pranced next to me happily as she observed him. "This is Coal. I'm looking after him for the Primordial Flame Elemental until he's strong enough to return. He was trying to eat my insides after that, and it really hurt."

Coal yapped at me.

"Why would you do that, Coal?" I scolded.

Warmth blossomed across my being as he sent emotions to me. They all seemed to indicate that he was happy.

"It's not nice to chew on me when you're happy!" I tried to be serious about it, but the more I looked at him, the more I realized he was seriously just a puppy. It didn't matter that he was almost as large as a full-grown wolf.

"You will not scold him like that, lad," Shellica reprimanded me. She stood between us with her back to him and winked. "I doubt he will do it again." She turned to face him. "Isn't that right, wee doggy?"

Coal hopped in place and began to playfully lunge toward her and scamper back. I didn't know if I could take that as an affirmation, but he seemed happy.

"Suppose we could take a break, lad." Shellica smiled at the wolf. "This next bit will mainly be theoretical knowledge and learning what components will aid you in certain kinds of enchantments. Bring out the bird. Let me meet her properly."

I looked around the smallish room and smiled. "We may want to go outside."

She led Coal and me to the courtyard behind the building we were currently in. As soon as we were outside, I let

Kayda out of the collar around my throat. The black smoke that was her body solidified on the ground in front of me, and Coal began to bark wildly at it.

Kayda's wings burst open in a stretch as she finished forming. She looked at Coal curiously; as he was much smaller than she was, she didn't see him as an immediate threat. She did ask though, *Food?*

"Hahaha, no baby—he's not food." I stepped forward to her and affectionately patted her neck. "He's my other familiar—at least until he's strong enough to go home."

Kayda buffeted me with questions, images, and thoughts so quickly that I was forced a step back.

"Hey, easy." I motioned for her to stop. "One thing at a time!"

Brother? Nest-mate? she inquired. I saw an image that she had pulled from my memories of her nest. The cracked and broken shells of her siblings. A weight settled on my chest at the sight of them. I stepped closer again and pulled her into a hug.

"Yes, love," I whispered to her. "He's a brother. So we have to protect him. Okay?"

She spread her wings to the full breadth they would reach and screeched to the heavens, *BROTHER!*

I heard Shellica gasp and watched her shrink back a step.

"Sorry, she's just excited to meet Coal for the first time." I put my arms out wide to try and hush her and soothe her a bit.

"Quite alright. She's magnificent."

Coal crouched in fear, his tail tucked between his legs and his ears flat against his skull. Kayda regraded him; her head twitched to the side curiously before hopping over toward him. She was completely engrossed in him and had no interest in her surroundings.

Brother? Kayda tried to get his attention, but Coal was still afraid and backed away a little further.

"Coal," I called. He looked at me. "She's okay. She's family. Like you. She's a familiar of mine, like you."

I sent a series of commands to Kayda through our connection, and she agreed to settle and sit as low as she was able. She laid down, settled as comfortably as the stone beneath her could afford, and waited patiently.

I stepped over to Coal and tried to reassure him. I sent loving and kind thoughts to him. I sent him memories of Kayda when she was only a chick and how I felt about her. How I loved her as if she were my daughter. How she would never hurt him. Or eat him.

He warmed up after a moment of petting and comforting. He stood with me, and we began to close with the giant bird slowly. When he was close enough to start trying to smell her, Kayda slowly offered a wing to him. He sniffed it, then sent me a feeling of cold. I laughed.

"She can be cold at times," I agreed, "but she doesn't always do it on purpose. Only if we have to fight, but you don't have to worry about that."

Coal, heartened by my humor, stepped toward Kayda. He began to snuff and snort at her body to gain her scent. She leaned forward and watched him curiously again. As the wolf looked up, he came face to face with her, yelped, and bolted away.

A chorus of laughter and catcalls rang out from behind me, and I looked back to see dozens of the Light Hand Clan Dwarves outside seeing what the commotion was safely by their homes and shops.

Kayda took umbrage with their jeering and stood to her full height. She spread her wings wide and hopped in front of both of us protectively then gave a cry that sounded like a thunderclap.

More than a few of them stopped laughing and began to go about their feigned business as if they had to be outside earlier and had become sidetracked.

"BWAHAHAHAHA!" Shellica fell on to her back, she was laughing so hard. When she could finally breathe enough to speak, she called, "Cowards! The lot of you!"

They ignored her and shuffled off to do Gods knew what. Coal stood behind me, eyeing the still chuckling Dwarf, and Kayda side-eyed the hell out of the Dwarves as they left.

"Kayda, chill," I warned softly. Then I chuckled at the unintended pun. The best kind.

"Shellica, this is Kayda, my familiar and companion," I introduced them belatedly.

"Aye, I can tell, lad." Shellica stepped in front of the bird and smiled wide. "You're a pretty lass, aren't you. May I touch you?"

Smooth. I snorted. *Better to ask her than me.*

Kayda shook herself a bit and let her head down far enough to allow Shellica a pat on top of her skull. She was gentle, and Kayda appreciated the light hand.

Damn, another one. Was I on a roll today or what?

"So soft—cool to the touch, too," Shellica observed to no one in particular. "You're sure you want to stay with this one? I'd have you safe and fattened up in no time."

Kayda looked at me with a slight bit of snark. *Oh, you little shit!* I laughed aloud at her.

"Hey, she gets fed plenty, and she's already spoiled as hell," I let Shellica know. "Yohsuke would be pissed if you took his favorite eater."

"The dark one?" Shellica's confused features crinkled up. "He cooks? How odd."

"I mean. I have a living elemental creature that lives inside the core of my being until I summon him, so... which is weirder?" I snickered with my hands motioning to the still-growling Coal.

"That's fair." She shrugged.

After that, we went back into the building with Coal and Kayda put back into their respective domiciles. I promised to let them out more though. They were living beings after all.

As Shellica took me through the list she had of components that I could add to my workings. I began to note that she was a little less tense. Not as harsh in this moment. It was nice.

"Now, the reagents and components that you will work with will be simple." She pulled some objects from her pocket. "Diamonds, topaz, obsidian, quartz, sapphire, and emeralds—as well as most other precious stones—are what you may end up using. Typically, this is in powdered form. If you have these items, it would be a good practice to learn how to create powder yourself as they can be expensive to procure."

She opened one of the objects, a small container of what looked like lead with a fine powder that refracted the light a little inside and sat it on the bench. "Powdered diamond."

She also set a whole ruby and pearl next to the container. "Raw ingredients such as these can be crushed, ground, and applied at a whim if you have the necessary tools."

"Next, we have filings." She produced a drawstring bag the size of my fist and opened it to show me light-blue metal shavings. "This is a little more advanced but still within your realm. What I have here are mithral filings gathered before they hit the ground at the forge. You can use these to give a weapon a tougher quality enchantment. Say you wanted the item to be more durable? This would be a good component to use for that enchantment."

She stepped back to allow me the opportunity to look over each of them. The filings were interesting, but the method confused me.

"If you wanted to use shavings or filings like these," I pulled one out; it was the size of a pencil lead, "how would you get these to fit into the engraving? Would you have to make it larger to specifically fit it?"

"I had hoped you might ask!" Shellica grinned and produced a bracer made of iron. "Now, this will be for demonstration purposes and not for any kind of actual use. Attend closely."

She closed her eyes and ran her fingers over the metal top portion of the bracer, meant to help protect the appendage beneath. Where her fingers touched, grooves were left behind. After she was finished, they connected to make a shield. The engraving was no thicker than what I might normally do on my own. Definitely too small for the filings to fit without trying to place them in with tweezers.

"Now, as I focus my intent and harvest my mana for the enchantment, I take a pinch of the filings. A generous amount never hurts, but too much—like mana—can be harmful to the overall product. As I siphon my mana into the engraving, I wait a moment, then," she sprinkled the filings over the engraving, "finish pouring my mana into the engraving until it's done and you're finished. Now—tell me what you notice that is different without touching it."

As I looked over the item, I saw what I was looking for immediately. "The filings are gone, but the engraving is no longer just an outline filled with invisible mana; it looks like filigree made of mithral. Almost ornamental."

She clapped me on the shoulder. "Yes!" She tossed the item into her furnace before continuing. "The component 'disappears' but what is left mingles with the mana you are using to change the properties of the item. Now, the filings I added were to do what, do you think?"

"Well, the item you had was something that would be worn by a low-level Fighter—who wears iron at a higher level?" I shrugged, thought a little more then began to try and relate my thoughts. "With the shield engraving, I imagine that your intent was on defense, rather than simply durability. Right? You wanted to increase the defense of the item and not change the overall look too much."

Shellica frowned slightly. "Half right." She stepped over to her bed and took a seat.

"I did have defense in mind, but I also wanted the item to take on the durable and light-weight properties of the mithral component." She wagged her finger at me. "'Who wears iron at a higher level?'—indeed. Some of the most intelligent Fighters lure their opponents into a false sense of security exactly like that and come out on top every time. Because they are smarter. You are one such warrior, no?"

I had used some tricks and events to my advantage before in a fight. She was right.

"My apologies," I replied humbly.

"Do not apologize!" Shellica stood upright and stomped over to stand before me and hiss, "*Be better!*"

I nodded dumbly, and she eyed me a moment longer before gently smacking the back of my right ear and continuing with the lesson.

"Now, the component lent those extra properties while I focused on the one because those are properties that already exist within that specific component. Now, this is meant more for filings and shavings of metals that will typically produce these results." She motioned to the gems. "Gemstones and other precious stones or metals will give other properties. Some gemstones will give elemental properties a boost, while poorly matched components will cause other effects or even degenerative effects. Can you think of such a case? An example maybe?"

"If I were to use pearl, made in the ocean, with a fire enchantment?" I hoped I was right.

"Quite so." She pulled a small stone that I didn't recognize out. "This red stone is called an elemental crystal. They are found primarily in the elemental planes of existence. If you were to find them, take them, and you will be a wealthy man. Now, that is all for today's lessons. You grow tiresome, lad, and I have a little work to do. Tomorrow, you will bring the requests your friends have. And take that weapon with you. I am sure that craft-less monk will appreciate it."

"Thank you for teaching me." I nodded my head, then all but bounced out the door.

On my way back to the compound, I paid attention to the people around me. The Dwarves tended to throw cautious looks my way, but I just minded my own and walked proudly.

After a while, I reached the Mugfist Clan's compound and walked in unmolested. Some of the Dwarves called out to me in passing. One asked if Shellica had been gentle, and I just laughed.

Two Dwarves practicing throwing axes at a target ribbed each other on my way by, "Ye know, *I* ne'r came back to me clan alone after so much time with a lady."

He threw his axe, and it hit the outer ring. His friend threw his, and it landed a little closer to the inside, it clearly not a bullseye.

"Reckon he weren't tha' good at it?" He waggled his eyebrows before continuing. "Mayhap she were embarrassed she chose such an ugly sod?"

The audacity of these little—I summoned Storm Caller from my inventory and whipped the great axe between the two of them and split the target straight down the middle.

One them whistled. "Good thing he has a good throwin' arm—no' good for shite else! BAHAHAHAHA!"

Both of them roared with laughter, and I couldn't hide my anger and embarrassment—but mostly it had actually been really funny. Assholes.

As I was walking past a more secluded section of the buildings, I noted James was sitting alone in a meditative position. I heard a low rumble from his chest, and he was floating a little bit.

"Hey, Zeke," he mumbled without opening his eyes.

"Hi, bud," I replied. "Brought you a present."

He sighed and sank until he was back on the ground. I offered him a hand to stand up, and he took it. I pulled Flame Fang from my inventory and held it out to him.

"Dude!" He slid it on to his hand and jabbed with it. "This is amazing! How the hell did you manage this?!"

"Coal helped some, but mainly it was that new ability I got from the quest rewards."

"Dude, you could make some badass fire weapons!" James punched me lightly. "This is so fucking cool! Thank you!"

"No problem, man." I smiled at him. "Hey, you wanna spar a little bit?"

He looked at me incredulously. "You want to fight with me?"

"Yeah, no big deal. Just a little sparring." I shrugged and added, "Not to mention, Zhavron was right—we need to keep each other sharp. We need to train. It hasn't been all that long since he told us to dig our heads out of our asses."

"Yeah, man. Let's go have some fun." James grinned wolfishly.

We walked back to the training grounds in time to see four warriors pile on to Jaken as he fought to keep a hold on his shield. He growled and threw his shield arm out and away from himself, kicking one of the Dwarves in the stomach and launching him into his friend.

One of them had the brilliant idea to bring his axe in close and use it as a club to whack Jaken across the ribs. The others moved in to assist their clever friend.

"En garde!" Jaken shouted and let go of his sword.

For the first time I had ever seen it in person, though we had known it could do it, the sword began to move as if wielded by a spectral Fighter. It weaved, slashed, and stabbed at the Dwarf on the right-hand side. The others began cursing and calling it cursed and trying to get away.

Jaken seized the opening for the Dwarf that had hit him and socked him across the jaw with a back-handed shield slap. He fell to the ground unconscious, and the others continued to back away.

"Do you yield?" The Paladin panted with a bloody lip. I could see from where I stood that he was favoring the impact site on his ribs.

"Aye, call off the cursed sword!" One of the Dwarves all but shivered.

"Fin," Jaken barked at the sword. It zipped to his open hand, he caught it, and returned it fluidly in a single motion.

"Since when the *fuck* did you decide to start using that?!" I cried in disbelief. "You know these guys don't like magic."

"That's the enchantment I asked for, man." Jaken shrugged. He cast an AoE heal on himself and the Dwarves with him. "I just haven't needed to use it. It's a multiple enemies kind of thing. My shield too."

"Fuck," I spat vehemently. "I wish I had thought of that."

"You gonna order a new weapon, man?" Jaken asked. "If we're going to be taking on Dragons, it may not be a bad idea."

I thought about it for a moment. He wasn't wrong, but I did love Storm Caller.

"We didn't bring any materials with us, though," I reasoned.

"You could ask Granda if he will look into a special order," James supplied.

"Yeah!" Jaken slapped him on the arm. "Not to mention, you know he's always got things being brought to him. Let him work for you and he will, I'm sure of it."

"Let me let him know." I closed my eyes, cast Mental Message, and began speaking to Granda. "Granda! It's Zeke. I know it's last minute, but could we talk about a weapon for me as well?"

A long second later, I heard the elderly Dwarf's reply, "Aye, lad, have Jaken bring ye to the forge after a bit. He knows the way. We can discuss it over a bite."

I looked over at Jaken. "He wants us to come over in a while. Wanna keep James and me alive while we beat the shit out of each other?"

"Hell yeah!" Jaken grinned and rounded up his sparring partners to watch with him.

I took my shirt off and my boots, feeling a little lighter in just my padded breeches. The fungus grass and stone felt weird beneath my feet, but it wasn't unbearable. James stood at the other side of the yard and stretched himself a little vigorously.

"Putting on a show?" I called over to him.

"Oh, you know it, sister." He smiled back and pulled his arm in front of his chest, stretching it parallel to the ground, then switching arms.

"You guys using magic?" Jaken called the question to us.

"Good question!" James said as we walked forward. "I'm good without it. You need the handicap?"

"I'll get mine without it." I tried to appear aloof, but I was a little nervous. "Besides, magic wasn't all that helpful against Rowan. We need to be ready to fight by hand if the situation arises again with the next general we fight. Or even the next minion. It would be better to try and prepare now, right?"

The others nodded in agreement, both their eyes unfocusing as if to recall our battle with the general. Sure, we got the drop on him, but we might not get the drop on the next one. We needed to be ready.

It had been a long time since I had sparred an opponent I knew was more suited to that style of fighting than I was. Sure, I had taken martial arts when I was a teen; five years of that and then the Marine Corps Martial Arts Program had ensured I wasn't insanely rusty, but hand-to-hand combat was quite literally the only way James handled shit. This was his money maker.

"Yo, Jaken—you gonna ref this shit?" I asked.

"I can do that," he replied happily enough. "So, no magic. No Ki. Just good, old fashioned ass whoopings for all."

"Sounds good to me," I cracked my neck and rolled my shoulders a bit to loosen them. Despite my trepidation, I was still excited to see what I could do.

"Alright then, ladies." Jaken held his hand up, then dropped it. "Start!"

One second, James was six feet away. I blinked once, and his fist was connecting with my stomach in a way that left me breathless and angry.

"You gonna make it?" he teased.

I put my left hand toward his voice and flipped him the bird. He chuckled, but I didn't see his feet move. I shot my hand forward and lunged into the grasp. I missed by a country mile. James was already behind me.

"Gonna have to be quicker than that." He laughed again as he began to move his feet in a rope-a-dope fashion.

I took a second to clear myself of the mounting frustration I felt, the Werewolf's haze beginning to set in around the field of my vision. I shook my head and beat it back a little as I settled into a stance I hadn't taken in a while but still felt natural. My legs were a smidge wider than shoulder length apart, knees slightly bent, and my fists waist level in front of me.

James took this as an invitation to attack, and he swept closer to me. As he crossed the twelve feet between us, I tried to gauge where he was going to try and hit me. I went with my gut feeling and shifted to the right as soon as he was close.

I raised my fist at the same time as I pivoted and connected with his shoulder, but it was hardly a tap to the practiced monk. He used the momentum of my shift to fling his knee up and into my ribs. A light enough hit, but it was where it hit that hurt the most.

It seemed like his hits were crazy fast and accurate, but that was all that was behind them. The strength at my disposal was going to be what helped me. I would just need to hit him hard enough to negate his speed.

I felt his knee coming back for a now-third strike, bent like I was hurt, and grabbed his other leg. I yanked it as hard as I could and shoved with my shoulder. He fell to the ground, and I got one solid hit to his chest before he pushed me away with his foot and rolled into a low stance.

"Got ya," I grunted with a smile. I felt the beast in me reveling at the idea of me winning, and the red haze deepened.

Time for me to go to him, I thought. *No reason in letting him be the aggressor the whole time. We are the predator.*

My mind snapped back into my own thoughts with a colossal mental yank. I wasn't about to shift and kill my fucking friend.

I relaxed my body and paced toward him slowly with my hands slightly flexed and near chest level. This way I could grab, smack, punch, or slash with my claws if needed.

James stood and walked toward me. Gone was the teasing look, replaced by one of determination.

I stepped into range, and the real beatings began. James's fists and feet beat into me with a rhythm all his own. It was so hard to figure out, and he hit the same places almost every time. But I gave as good as I could. I slammed an elbow into his right shoulder. Caught his left bicep with a clawed hand and slapped him in the face once with the back of my fist.

James just shrugged it off, and push kicked me away from him. I was strong enough to stay on my feet, but I still slid a good six feet away. Then he began to move as if I weren't there.

James flowed seamlessly from punch to kick, block to punch, double block. His limbs worked in unison to fend off imaginary attackers and savage them after a successful defense.

As he moved, his body began to glow with pale, white light that flowed from the center of his back to surround him in a shell. His breathing was steady—quiet even—as he peppered the air with a flurry of blows that made a whiffing sound as his fists picked up speed. The light began to collect at his fists and legs, specifically his shins and feet, where it left a trail behind as he moved.

In a final furious movement, he leaped into the air with a kick that tossed him into a backflip and then he landed with his right fist punching into the ground and his left knee stabilizing him. Where his fist connected with the ground, the earth was obliterated. There was a crater slightly larger than the size of his fist.

Jaken and I both gasped, and the monk used our awes to move in.

James used the space between us to bolt forward and leap at me. At the last second, he twisted his body, and I saw his foot careening toward my face—then I remembered nothing.

"...ke..." I heard a ringing voice, then a little louder, "Zeke!"

I opened my eyes to see Jaken and Yohsuke kneeling over me.

"You got knocked the *fuck* out!" Yohsuke teased, and Jaken just laid a golden-glowing hand on my chest. I felt better immediately.

"Damn." I groaned. "Anyone see the bus that kicked me?"

"I'm so fucking sorry, man." I heard James's voice from above my position.

I craned my head back and caught a glimpse of his worried expression. His pale skin with black scales along his cheeks like freckles.

"Why?" I sat up slowly. "It was a good fucking kick, man. Shit. I appreciated it until I went night night."

The Dwarves with Jaken chuckled heartily, and I smiled at them with fake menace. "You boys want some of this? Let me get my axe..."

They all coughed and stuttered about needing to go eat or some such, and they scurried off.

"What the hell was that glow though?" I groaned as I stood.

I rubbed my jaw and opened it as a test. It felt fine.

I had recognized the start of the show as the beginnings of forms. Forms, sometimes referred to as katas in karate, were things that young martial artists learned to help practice and perfect movements and skills needed for defending themselves. But that other stuff? No clue. I motioned to his hand with concern.

James held his hand up in front of him—it was slightly dirty but otherwise completely unharmed.

"That was new," he said simply. I watched as his hand flicked up, and his face looked like he had begun reading something. "Martial Trance—allows the user to take on a meditative stance in combat to collect and concentrate ki. The ki can then be stored or used to devastating effect by the user. Two uses daily. Trance is broken if the user takes direct damage."

"That is fucking amazing." I clapped him on the shoulder. "You just unlocked that?"

"Yeah." He looked confused. "I haven't even heard of the other monks getting this. Why now? Why me?"

"Gift horse, mouth." Jaken grinned his typical grin. "It's been a while. Let's get to the forge. And hey, maybe we can see if maybe Granda can make you a similar weapon to that one, James."

"Sounds good to me." James smiled and must have dismissed his status screen because he began to follow Jaken.

Sure, I could try to be like James and beat him, but he was better than me. And I would have to be okay with that and fight in my own way. I would use the experience though, and I would sure as fuck keep training with my friends.

The three of us walked through the streets, taking a route that I hadn't seen before. It was a different section of the city. There were more compounds similar to the others that we would see. Some had large statues of Dwarves holding weapons at their gates in positions of honor.

One such statue we passed had a nose that looked suspiciously like it was forged of iron. I smiled at the vision of the few members of that clan that I had interacted with, and I could see that being an idol of theirs.

As we continued walking, Jaken finally said something through our earrings, *I'm going to let you guys know now—where we are going is one hundred percent safe. Even if it's hot as fuck. Just, mind the lava—*

"Lava?!" James stopped in his tracks.

Ssh! shut up, man, Jaken hushed him and stepped toward him.

He looked around and continued in our heads through our earrings as we started forward once more. *While people know that there are lava pools in the area, they don't know how close they are to this portion of the city. It's a well-kept secret and for good reason.*

And what reason is that? I had to admit, I was a little worried about it.

Granda will be able to explain it better than I can. Come on. Jaken continued walking forward at a quicker pace, and we followed once more.

We came to a larger gated compound with three large buildings in the front and another even larger building in the back that dwarfed the others. They were all made of a combination of stone, mithral, and a blackened material I had never seen before.

"What's that black stuff?" James beat me to the question.

"They call it stone heart," Jaken explained. As we walked by, he stopped to touch it. "The Dwarves say that it's a creation made by their god to keep the magma away from the surface world. They can only mine so much of it because to mine more would mean putting the surface in danger. What I've found, though, is that this is a composite material that has mixed lava with ore veins for a stronger material that cools after a long time. Touch it."

We obliged him. The material felt warm to the touch—not uncomfortably so but warmer than stone should've been.

"This stuff is *hundreds* of years old," he whispered. "I'm pretty sure that the mixture is mithral as well because it melds well with the metal and the stuff is damned near impossible to break without the right tools and methods for mining. And that's a family secret."

"What're ye doin', lad?" A Dwarven woman with thick muscles, a rosy complexion, and brown braids eyed us. "That be Jaken? Who are these 'uns?"

"Granda asked us to come by and have something to eat with him," Jaken explained.

"Oh, aye?" Her eyebrows raised. "Well, follow me then, lads. I'll take ye ta Granda."

"Thanks!" I smiled at her.

"Ah, yer the fox, then?" She came closer to observe me. She looked over to James. "Aye, an' a Dragon Elf? Wow, ye keep strange company Jaken, lad."

"I do." Jaken grinned at her. "How have you been, Deltrif?"

"Been good," the Dwarf grunted. She turned and began to walk off. "Been working on tryin' to level me smithin' and minin' up as best as I can. Be at around levels thirty-one and fifty-three respectively."

"Congratulations!" Jaken slapped her on the back. She barely moved. "Remind me, and I'll buy you a pint."

She smiled and winked at him. "Oh, I will."

We walked after that in amicable silence. There was no sound of hammers against metal. There was no forge-like ambiance this evening. There were the sounds of singing, drinking, and eating in the building we walked by, but otherwise, it was quiet.

We walked into the larger building. The inside was filled with row after row of anvils with no furnaces to heat the metal anywhere in sight, but it was sweltering inside. If I hadn't had Coal inside me and the benefits he brought me, I would have been cooking. I could only imagine how Jaken felt in his armor.

James looked perfectly fine, comfortable even, the rat bastard.

We climbed a set of stairs to a room that appeared to look out over the floor below. This must be Granda's office.

Deltrif knocked on the door, and we heard shuffling a second before it opened. Granda stood behind the solid oak planks with a soft smile. "Welcome, lads, welcome. Come in. Deltrif, if ye would be so kind, have the servers bring a fine meal of whatever they be having downstairs."

"Aye, granda, I'll see to it." She gave the older Dwarf a peck on the cheek and waved bye to us. As she walked away, Granda smiled wistfully. "Beautiful lass. Strong, like her ma.

Forges like her gran da." He added that last bit with a sly wink and a flex of his arm.

"It's good to see you again, Granda." I walked over and shook his hand. The old Dwarf pulled me into a hug and patted my arm before squeezing it.

"Reckon ye could swing a mean hammer," Granda observed with a look of appreciation. "Yer at, what, forty-six strength now? Sure you don't want ta pick up smithin'?"

My eyebrows raised in shock, "Forty-seven—how did you know? And I'll stick with enchanting; can't beat Jaken at everything, can I?"

Granda slapped his knee and pointed at Jaken as they both laughed. "Got ye good, lad. That was a good one. Aye, Jaken be learnin' quick. Took ta the forge quick."

He walked over to the other side of the room. This wall was made of glass panes, and it did look out over the workshop floor. There was a medium-sized cot for him to lay in and a desk with several different designs of weapons or armor on them. It was hard to see from the entrance.

The rest of the room itself was—surprisingly—covered in small trinkets and forged knickknacks. Hundreds of them. Each had a spot on shelves at the back of the room of varying sizes and complexity.

One I saw looked like a tin soldier. Another was a wickedly curved dagger with a hilt that had a beard as a pommel. Another was a cup that reminded me of a canteen cup.

"Admirin' me collection, Zeke?" Granda had produced a long-necked pipe. As he packed it, he glanced over the shelves. "Every generation since I took me place as clan head, every would-be smith makes me an item. They let the metal speak to them, as they should, and bring me the product. Then I decide on if it be worthy—if they be worthy." He lit his pipe and took a few small puffs before walking over to a particular piece. It was a small disc with a portion missing—a crescent moon.

"This piece here was from yer friend, Jaken." He showed it to us with a grin on his face. "Took to hammerin' it right away. Took his time though, right proud I was. He molded the metal with his heart. He calls this 'un Luna. One of me favorite pieces. It'll be with me even when I rejoin the Mountain."

I looked over at my friend and saw there were tears forming in his eyes. I knew why too—his little girl at home. He had to miss her fiercely. Same as I missed my little boy. I wonder what he was doing. Probably sleeping right at that second. It had been night when I had gone to sleep on earth. Radiance, in her wisdom, said that there was a severe time dilation that meant that my physical body, all our physical bodies, were still technically asleep.

I offered him a small nod in recognition, and he looked away. A moment later, we were accosted by the smell of delicious steak, ribs, and a mountain of steamed and sautéed veggies.

"Help yerselfs, lads." Granda piled food on to his plate with a thanks to the servers. "Eat yerselfs a hearty meal. We'll have no' one rumbly belly here."

The servers laughed at his hospitality joke, and we all tucked into various plates of food with the alcohol that customarily came with it. After the food was devoured and Granda belched with gusto, we sat back and stared at each other blearily as he re-lit his pipe. After a couple puffs, a long pull, and a cloud of surprisingly sweet smoke rippled from his nostrils, he addressed us again.

"Thank ye fer abiding the Dwarven custom of no business with food in yer fat gobs, lads." He took another draw of the pipe and observed us a moment longer. "Ye wish fer another axe then?"

"Aye," I replied. "Something different. I was wondering if you had any of that spell steel? What was it called?"

"That's the name, man," Jaken corrected me. He produced a similar pipe of his own, and I looked at him oddly. "What? I smoke back home too. Besides, this stuff is nowhere *near* as bad."

I shook my head and looked back to Granda.

"A weapon the size ye would need be a tall order, lad." Granda puffed in thought. "Be mighty expensive—even with yer discount 'cause I like ye."

"Could you maybe do a plating? Or an alloy?" I asked hopefully.

Granda looked at me strangely. Closed his eyes a moment. Another moment passed. He took a long, hefty draw on his pipe, then shook his head. My heart fell. This was going to either be prohibitively expensive or just not happen.

I looked back up at him, and he had a sad look on his face.

But I had just told likely one of the smarter and best smiths in the whole of the Dwarven city that I had doubted his abilities. Even unknowingly.

"I'm sorry, Granda—I had no idea..." I trailed off as his cheeks drew up into a sly grin.

"Knew ye would'a been a fine smith, lad." He took his pipe and smacked it on his boot before he stood. "Wait ye here. I'll be right back."

He all but flew out of the door to his room and down the stairs yelling unintelligibly in Dwarven. Five minutes later, Granda and two other Dwarves, twins, charged back into the room with sacks over their shoulders. The two other Dwarves, bald-headed with greying beards and wolfish grins nodded to us as they began to upend their loot on to the desk.

"Stop, ye silly lads!" Granda cried. "Me designs!"

James was there in a blink to grab the precious papers and set them aside as metal pieces clanked on to the desk unceremoniously.

"Thank ye, James—good lad." Granda patted his shoulder and began to sift through some of the metals they had brought to him. "Now, these be metals that take a spell with little resistance. We took into account that it would be for an axe, so I had the lads grab metals we had a goodly supply of. Now, we will check to see which of 'em will work well with this."

He produced an ingot of the pure white metal that he would be working.

"Lads, sing to the metal." Granda thumped the ingot on to the desk and looked expectantly at the two Dwarves with him.

"Aye, clan head," they said in unison.

They turned to the metals before them and began to hum. One of them, the one behind the desk, began to sing a deep song.

At first, I was confused, but Granda stepped over to translate for us in a hushed tone.

It was about the beginning of the world from what I could understand. Of how Fainne gave the Dwarves metal to search for and use to create the way he had created them.

The second Dwarf, the one in front of the desk, picked up the ingot, held it before his lips, and began to sing to it in a much deeper tone than his brother Dwarf. Before my eyes, the metal in his hand began to vibrate slightly, and as it did so, he nodded to his brother.

After that exchange, the Dwarf behind the desk began to sing lower than he had before. This verse he sang was about the finding. The finding of the first vein of ore and how the Dwarves had celebrated and sang the praises of their find to Fainne for days. That he had returned that love with more ore and different kinds. That each ore had a brother and an opposite. That every ore was valuable in its own way.

As they continued to sing, some of the ore began to vibrate in return. Each one that did, they picked it up carefully and held it to the ingot. Once they came close, they tapped them together, and a single peal of sound rang out. The first one, both Dwarves shook their heads and the Dwarf holding it sat it down, picked up another and held it up. Another no. They repeated the process six times until, finally, a beautiful ringing echoed around us.

As they sat the ingot on the desk and handed the ore to Granda, they finished their song together.

"Our thanks to the mountain for giving us this ore, our love to our father for favoring us with more," they sang.

Their voices died down, and they smiled together at all of us. They began gathering the other ores into their bags once more and finally stood in front of Granda.

"Thank ye, lads." They shook Granda's hand as he thanked them. "Ye get ye downstairs and tell me Deltrif that ye earned a sip o' her gran da's," he lowered his voice to a whisper, "secret stash of ale. She'll know ye has. But just this once, lads. Honor."

"Honor," they spoke back with a slight bow of their heads.

Granda turned back to us and lifted the two metals. "Well, this will be interesting. I've never know'd ta have this metal—call it Mage bane—make any kind of alloy with another, let alone with Spell Steel. It's much easier to work with though.

The key will be getting it to the proper temperature. We don't have the proper things we would need to do so."

"Could we make something for you?" I offered. "Between Shellica and I, we could possibly make a bucket that would be able to withstand the lava."

Granda froze and looked to Jaken, who immediately held his hands up in his defense. "I only told them and swore them to secrecy. They understand what's at stake."

Granda eyed the two of us and nodded after a moment. "Good judgment call, lad. I wish ye would have let me know first, but ye weren't reckless with it. And what did ye have in mind, Zekiel?"

"Well, walk me through your process. You need to make ingots first, right?" I asked.

"For a sophisticated weapon as I'd be makin'? Aye."

"How do you do that?" I began to try and put together ideas in my head.

"We have a smelter that we've built over a pool o' lava that helps melt the ore down, and then we take the melt and pour it into a mold. Then they cool," Granda explained, "but the heat necessary for us to smelt this would need to be even hotter than the smelter can manage. Mage bane be needin' a large sum o' heat ta work, much *much* more'n spell steel. Ta marry the two? We'd need more than the heat above the lava flows."

That gave me hope. "So if we were to make a bucket that could withstand the heat of the lava itself and the tools to handle it safely?"

He thought about it for a moment, so I decided to sweeten the deal a bit. "I will pay you for the tools, and I will pay for the enchanting. After, you can keep them."

Granda thumped the desk. "I'll give ye the tools, let ye pay for the magery, then I'll take that price out o' the weapon for letting me keep the Mage tools."

"I can see that being agreeable." I smiled. That had honestly been the best case scenario for me. "But what else?"

"Come, let's get ye the tools." He began down the stairs, then stopped with a serious look on his face. "I trust ye'll let me do the designing?"

"I will." I smiled, then pointed to James. "James wanted something similar to this as well." He showed him Flame Fang. "Can you help?"

Granda looked the weapon over. "Design is by one of my kin. Ye want another of the same, or something different?"

"Either way." James shrugged happily. "I just want to be able to do extra damage with my fists."

"I'll put word out ta me smiths and see who wants it. They'll fight over it like wolves, 'ey will, and the best design will win out. Ye trust me ta choose for ye?"

James nodded, and we continued down the stairs. Granda took us across the building to the far wall that had what looked like open nooks that reminded me of open-faced lockers. Each one had a nameplate and several tools inside. Down the row, closest to the rear wall, Granda opened a door, went into it, and grabbed a large, thick metal bucket with a lid, a long pair of tongs, and a pair of thick gloves.

"Here," he passed them over to me, and I put them into my inventory. He dusted his hands off, then looked at us. "Ye have any specifications on what yer weapons be like? O' course, other than having the spell steel added to yer weapon, Zekiel."

"Yeah, could the counterbalance on the head of the axe be a hammer's head?" I asked.

Granda nodded and looked over to James. "All I want is to be able to punch people. These ones have spikes, and that's cool. But maybe a little something that can pierce a bit more?"

"Aye, we can take it inta account," Granda said with a wink. "Anything else, lads? Ye want ta stay for a pint?"

"We need to get back and be ready for tomorrow, Granda, but thanks for the invitation," Jaken said. "I'll see you for more training in the morning?"

"Ye'd bet'er!" Granda growled. "Working on some good items, hear?"

"I hear ya." He pushed his fist forward, and Granda rapped it with his own.

Our walk back was quiet enough as I began plotting what kind of enchantments I would need to possibly do. I'd better use some components too. I'd have to see about maybe having Shellica go with me to get some in the morning.

Chapter Twelve

That night, I was visited by Maebe in her shadow form.

"Hello, my champion," she greeted me quietly.

I damned near jumped out of my skin and tried to hide it, but she was already giggling.

"Hi, Mae." I sat up.

My shirt was off, and I had let Coal come out. He had to sleep away from the walls, and on a sheet of metal the Dwarves had furnished me with to protect the floors.

"I see you have collected another pet," she observed. It was strange that the Flame Wolf had no idea she was there, but given that the spell seemed to be for people of Celestial blood, maybe he couldn't hear her at all.

"I have." I smiled. "His name is Coal. I'm keeping an eye on him, helping him get stronger until he can go home to the Primordial Flame Elemental."

"Ah, so you are a protector now?" She stepped clear of the shadows and moved toward me in her shadow form. She sat next to me on the bed. "I come bearing news."

I looked at her. "Have you finally heard from Samir?"

"I have." She folded her hands in front of her on her lap and spoke. "He says that you are not to come back to his lands unless it is in pursuit of a creature like the one he took care of."

My stomach sank a bit, and my heart felt heavy. I knew it was a long shot, but I wanted to be able to see her again.

"He did, however, give me leave to come to you," I could see a small smile on the shadow's face, "and he has shown me a way to cross over to you and return."

"This is great news!" I almost shouted. "But wait," I looked at her, "what's the cost?"

Her shadowed gaze fell, "I see you did not forget your time among us, but the cost verse the reward was minor to me. I am free to come to this side of the veil whenever I please so long as the Seelie Fae are allowed to do the same as I in this realm. Not come here, but that they can send representatives."

"Okay, so they have some people here trying to—what?—make themselves out to be the better of the two representatives from the Fae realm?" I smirked. "They're monsters. Their beauty is a lie. No one will be able to believe them over you guys because your people have already begun doing good works in your name."

One of which was taking over as leadership for Maven Rock. Nurturing the people.

"Like I said—it was a small price to pay." She smiled.

I tried to hug her shadow, but my arms passed through. "Soon." She nodded. "I will go so that you can sleep, but when you are ready, I will come. I will not be able to control where the tear is, but I will send a shadow to you so that we can find each other."

I smiled reassuringly. "I can't wait."

She nodded once, then the shadows dissipated where they were.

I laid down and tried to fall asleep, but I was too excited. It took a while, but I got there, eventually.

I woke up the next morning to Coal scratching at the door and barking. "Wassat, boy?" I groaned. My mouth was dry, and my tongue felt thick. "Lil' Timmy fall down the well?"

The Flame Wolf looked at me oddly and sent me the impression of food.

"Fair. Let's go get some then." I scratched my chest, then stood to get dressed. I grabbed some fresh clothes and changed before stepping out the door with Coal in tow.

We walked into the mess hall, and I grabbed a plate of food from one of the kind Dwarves running the line. I also grabbed a large plate of meats, then another. The Dwarf behind the table looked at me oddly, but I gave him a wink and walked off.

I strolled outside with Coal nipping at my heels. "Quit that shit!"

He growled and barked at me again. "Look, man. If I spill this food, I put you back without eating."

He seemed to understand the threat because he slunk sullenly behind me.

Once we were in the courtyard, I called Kayda from the collar and sat Coal's food down. He tucked in immediately and took huge chomps of bacon and ham into his jaws.

Kayda watched him eat, fascinated at his voracious manner. He finished the food quickly, then began to look for more. He looked up at her plate and began drooling. Kayda reached down with her beak and scrapped off a large piece of ham. Coal caught it on the way down.

Brother funny, she spoke to me. She eyed him, then repeated the action.

"Sweetheart, you need to eat too," I reprimanded her gently. She eyed me for a moment, took half the food from the plate and ate it herself in a show of her size. Then she shoved her head at Coal. Getting the idea, I sat that plate on the ground, and Coal snatched up the remainder happily.

"You know, you share really well," I observed out loud to her. Through our connection, I said more, *You would've made a great sister. I know you'll take good care of Coal. Thank you.*

Kayda bumped my shoulder with her head affectionately and then ducked her head down next to her brother. Coal's tail wagged wildly and began to lick the side of her beak in gratitude.

"Time to go home, guys." I called Coal back into my body in a burst of heat. Then I touched Kayda and willed her into the collar.

I reached out to Shellica via Mental Message, "Wake up, shit granny. Could you meet me in the markets? I need to find some components for an enchantment that I'll need for Granda to make a weapon for me."

A pause, then, "He wants you to enchant something for him?! When will you be there? I'm on my way now."

I laughed and left the compound to head toward the market. The city was bustling. Merchants called out their wares, and I watched as several different sales took place. I spotted Shellica waiting for me near a stall and walked over to her.

"About time, lad," she muttered sullenly. "What are you enchanting?"

"A thick, lidded bucket, a pair of long tongs, and a set of gloves," I told her bluntly. "I need to enchant the bucket for heat resistance and transference. The tongs to resist heat, a lot of heat, and the gloves for the same."

She narrowed her eyes at me. "What is he doing?"

"Just has to superheat a couple kinds of metal to make an alloy. Nothing he can't handle." I shrugged and continued to play it off. "Just needs specialized tools is all."

"I see," she grunted. "Well, it sounds as though you will need powdered ruby and a lot of it. Follow."

She led me to a stall three down from the one we were at. The sign said the name in Dwarven, but the jewels and precious stones on the counter gave me an idea of what was sold here.

After a respectful exchange with the Dwarf running the stall, I had three medium sized rubies, a large pearl and a frightfully large diamond. The price was two hundred and twenty-five gold pieces for that, and I was loathe to think about how much she was going to gouge my coffers.

Steeply priced, but the components would last me a while from what Shellica said. "That diamond will last you some time. As you level up and gain a little more experience with them—component quantities used in enchanting lower."

"That's good." I sighed. "I'd hate to have to spend that much every time I run out."

Shellica grinned at me. "That was with my clan's discount, lad."

I groaned loudly, and she cackled at my distress.

After we had returned to her place and worked on some more of the fundamentals with components and enchanting form, she decided to let me watch her enchant the tools.

"I will not have a craftsman work on the tools to be used by a legendary smith such as Granda Stone Hammer," Shellica scolded me when I argued about doing it. "The Dwarf is damned near pushing past grandmaster rank."

"Is that possible?" I cocked my head to the side.

"If anyone can manage to find out, it's him," she whispered. "Now, watch me."

She began to run her hands over the outside of the bucket, her mana coursing into it and leaving behind complicated trails of thin, scale-like grooves. They made the gray bucket look like a Dragon's egg. She took the item, laid it on her desk, and pulled out a diamond tool that looked like a kind of mallet, then a small chisel head with a head attached to tap.

She began to expertly tap in certain places along the first ruby's surface, and I watched as pieces began to chip and fall off.

She took her time and finished that one, then gathered the bits into a solid stone bowl that looked to be made of stone heart. She grabbed a diamond pestle and began grinding the flakes and chips into powder slowly.

When she was finally satisfied, she shook out her shoulders and began to focus with a single hand on the bucket. Shellica began funneling her mana into the tool before sprinkling a small amount of powdered ruby over it. The item glowed a dull red for a moment—throbbed as if alive—then stopped. The scales all around it had taken on a reddish hue.

She observed it for a moment, smiled, and set it aside. She did much the same for the other two with the exact same kind of design.

Once they were properly enchanted, she looked at me and asked, "Can you tell me what enchantments I could have possibly used?"

I thought for a moment before responding, "The Dragon egg design is something I wouldn't have expected to use because it seems too cool of an idea for me to get away with. But much like a Dragon egg, I imagine it meant to be protective while allowing heat to transfer and heat whatever is inside the 'egg'. The gloves and tongs are similar in design only. They are meant only to protect and serve as a barrier against extreme heat."

"Very good!" She clapped. "I also gave them a boost in strength—or durability—in cases of long heating."

She walked over to her doorway and shouted, "Vilmas!" then left the door standing open to allow a small Dwarven woman in.

"Yes?" she asked. Her hair was a stark white against her darker skin.

"You will take these three items *directly* to Granda at his forge." Shellica pointed to the items. "Do not say anything other than that you have a delivery for Granda. He will know that you are coming. Go."

The Dwarf scurried over and gasped as she took the items.

"Yes, yes." Shellica rolled her eyes. "*Go.*"

"Yes, m'lady." Vilmas careened from the room at top speed, and I heard a loud bang and a crash accompanied by an impish, "Sorry!" and Dwarven cursing.

"She seems like a timid one," I observed.

"She is, but she's a damned good enchanter, almost at grandmaster herself," Shellica said with a slight smile. "Sending her on these kinds of errands forces her to leave the compound and interact with others. Poor lass doesn't like leaving her room much."

"Ah, and here I thought it was just you being abusive." I laughed at her flat stare.

"Message Granda, lad," she ordered.

I obeyed with a huge grin, "Granda, it's Zeke. Vilmas from the Light Hand Clan will be bringing you the tools you need. I hope they are what you need. She's been ordered to give them only to you."

After a slight pause, "Thank ye lad. This will add a few days to yer time here, I'm afraid. My apologies."

I sent him another Mental Message, "That's fine. You take your time, and I'm sure the wait will be worth it." I thought about the time we would already be spending here and gulped, swiftly adding, "Just, uh, don't take too long?"

"Aye, I be hopin', lad," he responded, and we left it at that. "Fret no'."

"Now, you will begin enchanting more items today," Shellica informed me. "Begin with these."

I turned and saw that there were more than forty-five rings on the workbench that hadn't been there before. I groaned, and Shellica cackled wildly.

"Think of this as payment for my services just now." She then cackled even more. "Those ones you used before? Shite. These? These ones we keep."

"Gods, I hate you," I snarled.

"I love you too, lad," she informed me sweetly, "but you're not my type. Now, get to work!"

I took a few deep breaths to assist my resistance to the strangle Shellica effect and then got to work. Her snappy orders on which enchantments to use and which components to add came before each new item was even touched. Her remarks and corrections saw me through the morning, but she didn't toss one ring into the furnace, so there was that.

Odd as it was, I would think she wouldn't throw them away because she wanted to be paid for her services. That, or she didn't mind me slaving away for her. The evil witch.

I felt her hand cross the back of my head and focused on my work.

That much enchanting of a high level did increase my level in enchanting by another two though, putting my enchanting to level 33.

"Why did I just level up with all of that?" I asked Shellica during a break. "Normally, it takes longer."

"The more complicated the enchantment along with the addition of components allows for more experience to be earned," Shellica explained, then took a bite of a sandwich someone had brought her. She passed one to me as well, and I tucked in before she went on. "You've also been increasing the range of your enchantments. The more you do of one specific kind, the more powerful it may become—certainly—but the less experience you earn, the less you grow as an enchanter. That's why you had such a leap in levels after adding the component to your enchantment."

That made sense. "So, the broader my spectrum of enchantments and component use—the more potential growth I could experience?"

"Put lamely like that?" She shot me a sly grin. "Aye."

"You can be a real pain in the ass, you know that?" I shot her the finger.

"I can be?" she replied, feigning being hurt. "Well, I suppose I can spare a few more hours to heal your wounded ass. There are another twenty items for you to enchant, and these will be *far* more complicated. Let's have some fun."

I groaned again. "This is also payback and punishment for not bringing me the list of item enchantments your friends wanted like you were told to!"

"Fuck!" I facepalmed and then remembered—I know, how often does that actually happen? "We will need to replicate the telepathy earring for Muu. I know that one for certain. I also know that most of the enchantments he's going to want are going to be for jumping high and far. He may also want his weapons enchanted. I'll ask them all tonight."

"Good lad." She grabbed a quill, ink bottle, and some sand and began to write what I had said. "Anything else off the top of your head?"

"Yeah, do you know how to make an astral adaptor?"

She shook her head. "That's an art for the High Elves. It takes a highly condensed, specially treated crystal with grandmaster-level enchanting techniques that I cannot even hope to know as they are so heavily guarded. I'm sorry, lad."

The look on her face was resigned, but she also looked ashamed.

"Hey, don't worry about it," I said. "Yohsuke will be alright, and I'm sure there are things you can do that those asshats could never even dream of."

"You're a sweet lad, Zekiel," she walked over closer to put a hand on my furred cheek, "but you won't get out of this. Enchant—now." She patted my face and pointed to a pair of gloves.

"Well forgive the hell out of me for trying to be kind. Old biddy."

We worked until I finished these items. I didn't screw any of them up "too terribly" as my disgruntled taskmaster had put it. No levels gained from it, but I couldn't be too greedy, could I? But I felt I should be closer to it. Unfortunately, there was no way to really know until it happened.

I went to each of my friends and asked them what they would like as an enchanted item. I started with Yohsuke, who was up to his elbows in pork, pulling the tender rump apart for dinner later.

"Well, since she can't make me a weapon—how about a bracelet with a shield?" He shrugged. "I'm not strong enough to make a physical one worthwhile, but if she can make me one that will just activate in a certain direction for a small amount of time or until I drop it, that would be cool. And thank her for me, for at least letting me know where I have to go for a new adaptor."

"Yeah, brother. No problem," I said as I wrote the item description down. "With my added weapon, Granda is gonna be a few more days, but it should be worth it."

"Right on, shitty, but I guess it would be better to be prepared." He smiled and added some spices to a bowl over the fire in the hearth. "Hey, sorry for bailing so fast on you the other night after your sparring match with James. I had to get back to the kitchens to work on dinner."

"I understand, man." I patted his shoulder. "No worries. How you holding up?"

"Great, man." He grinned as he clapped his hands and began to knead a loaf of bread. "Leveled up my cooking a bit before you came in. Level 35."

"Nice! What can you do now?" I wondered. The scent coming from the food around me set my stomach to growling.

"Well, food cooks slightly faster, and I get prompts telling me if food is bad or ripe." He picked up a vegetable. "See this? This shit is bad, but I can cut the bad part out and use the rest. Makes it a little more economical to actually make food. Also, I'm a lot better with spices. The umami of this stew is gonna be out of control, man."

"Yoh, what?" I couldn't hide the confusion. "Umami? You for real?"

"Hell yeah." He tossed his head at me and acted like he was going to lunge at me with a smile. "We gettin' technical up in this bitch. Bitch! By the way, that's the savory or meaty taste sensation produced by amino acids and shit. Not real shit, though. I don't cook with that."

"That's wild, man. I had no idea."

"Shut up, puto. I know it." He grinned at me and picked up a large knife. "Now get out and let me focus before I cut you."

I laughed as I fled the room and let him do his thing. He seemed to be more serious about cooking than I had ever seen, though there was that one time he made some breakfast burritos that time I went to visit him a few states away. That shit had put us both into a food coma. So good.

Then again, he was a sibling. How many times had I made my little sister food, and she had enjoyed it. Never. Haha, she was a picky eater at times, but he had siblings of all ranges and liked to cook, so I took it that he had grown his love of cooking when he was younger.

As I was walking outside, I saw James in the training grounds with Jaken. The two of them were discussing something as I walked over to them.

"Hey guys, what up?" I asked.

"We were just talking about the enchantments we want." Jaken held his fist out for me to bump as a greeting. "James was also filling me in on some of the stuff he's been trying to learn."

"So, I've been trying to do some research–" James began, but I stopped him.

"You?" I asked incredulously. "Stop the *fucking presses!* Holy shit! You?"

"You want me to beat your ass again?" James raised his eyebrows.

I closed my mouth. "Nope. Continue."

"Researching legends on Dragons," James continued as he shot me a glare. I made a fake whistling gesture with my lips and looked around. "Now, unsurprisingly, books aren't all that popular here, but I found a couple on smithing with Dragon scales and Dragon parts. It also gave locations where we might find different kinds of Dragons too. If we're going to the south, into the jungles, that's where we are most likely going to find some green Dragons. The black Dragons are a little harder to nail down. There hasn't been a recorded sighting of one for more than three centuries according to the Dwarves' historian. And she said that it was last seen in the east somewhere by the dead lands."

"Yo, dead lands?" Jaken whispered to me excitedly. "You know what that means, bro? Undead. My time to truly shine."

"Good man." I patted James affectionately despite the near-dirty look he threw my way. "Good shit. What were you guys thinking enchantment wise for your shit?" I scratched my chin. "Also, hasn't it been a little weird that we've been everywhere lately and haven't run into so much as a minion of War?"

"I would like my new sword to have an enchantment that will make it weigh less, be sharper, and more durable," Jaken said. "It doesn't have to move on its own like my other one. This one is for when I let that one play on its own. And yeah, it has been, but you can't expect them to be too close together, right?"

I looked over to James, and he shrugged. "I don't know what I'm going to get yet. It'll be a few more days, like Granda told you for your weapon. Jaken told me. So, when I know, I'll let you know." He thumped his book. "I can also check and see if there's any kind of rumors here among the tunnel patrols that might suggest there being minions underground. See if they found anything strange."

"Okay, so to be decided." I wrote that down. "Y'all know where Bokaj or Muu are?"

"Muu went to go do his crafting training," James informed me.

"And Bokaj went to go buy some better tools, as well as light metal strings for his instrument," Jaken said. "He said he would be back soon."

"Who said they would be back soon?" Bokaj said from behind me, making me damned near shit myself.

Tmont purred loudly at the sight of me and butted her head against my knuckles. "Hey, T. Why didn't you warn me he was there?"

She just looked at me steadily and walked away.

"What's up?" Bokaj asked his visage grim.

"Well, my weapon is going to set us back a few more days, and I was going to see what you wanted to have enchanted while we wait." I took out my quill and got ready.

"I mean, there's really nothing I need that can be done here." He half shrugged. "They can't make me a bow, and I'm almost done with my guitar. Maybe some rings or something? A helm. I don't fucking know. I'm almost done with my instrument."

"What if that gets enchanted?" James put forth.

"What?" Bokaj looked confused.

"Yeah, what she said," I looked at the Dragon Elf, and he just grinned and motioned to all around us.

"This is a fucking fantasy-type world, man." He threw his hands up. "Why the fuck *not* have an enchanted guitar?"

I looked over in time to see Bokaj smile. "Yeah, okay. We can do that. I'll finish it tonight and leave it in my room for you to get enchanted."

"Okay then." I wrote down *enchanted guitar*. "Where the fuck are you going?"

"I'm going out with a patrol to do something, man." Bokaj shook his head. "I can't sit here and just fucking train and do nothing—Balmur is still in the Hells. I'll be back. The patrols don't last more than a day or two." He looked at the others. "I know you guys care. I know that you worry, but I'm losing my fucking mind here, man. I'll be back, and if I'm close, I'll let you know via earring. Later."

He stalked off into the compound and left us there in silence for a moment before I sighed. He was right to be upset, and he was allowed to do what he wanted. But fuck, man.

"Off to find Muu, then." I nodded to the others. "Be back in a bit."

"Later!" Jaken waved. James just nodded toward me back and walked off as well.

I made my way down the now-familiar route to the traders' alley in the city and walked until I found the stall I was looking for. The same little Dwarf was outside minding the stall, putting things up for the day as I walked over. He froze when he saw me.

"Do you remember me?" I asked softly. He nodded. "I'm here to see my friend, Muu. Can I come in?"

He looked around to make sure no one was watching, then spoke to me as he walked over. "Are ye a real fox, mister?"

"I am." I knelt down beside him. He seemed like a good kid.

"Yer tails be real?" he asked in wonder, to which I nodded. "Could I see 'em?"

I shifted slightly where I knelt and showed him my three tails as they wagged back and forth slowly. He watched, fascinated.

"Wow," I heard him whisper, just barely audible. "Ye enchant things as well?"

"I sure do." I smiled.

"Could you teach me?" he asked, suddenly very close to me.

"Um, I think that would be up to your ma." His face fell. "Tell you what, though." I made a great show of looking around at the other vendors and merchants. Some eyed me. Others looked at both of us in open curiosity. "If you'll promise me two things, I'll enchant something for you in return. Okay?"

"Wassat?" He bounced.

"One, always listen to your ma. She seems a nice lady and loves you dearly." He continued to listen. "And the next time you see Shellica, you tell her thank you for doing the things she does for the glory of the Mountain. I know you don't understand, but she will. And she may even let you learn to enchant a little if you impress her."

"Aye, I can do tha'!" He nodded.

"Do you swear?" I asked him in a grave tone.

"Aye, mister." He stood stock still and put a fist over his little heart. "I swears on me Way and for the glory o' me beard that I will do as ye ask o' me."

I narrowed my eyes at him, then smiled. "Go get your skinning knife." I watched as he bolted away while motioning for me to follow.

On my way in, I grabbed what I could and placed it in the box I had seen him loading and brought it with me. It was light for me, but for as young as he was, it would've been a decent load. Good kid. I smiled to myself and sat the box on a table inside.

The shop we were in was clean and smelled slightly of oils and chemical treatment as well as leather. I heard a stern voice in the rear of the place and went to see what was going on.

This room was brighter than the previous one, and I soon saw why. The room in the back had a low, stone table in the center with grated drains beneath it. There were racks and frames on the left side of the room with an enchanted wall that glowed slightly. On the other side of the room, there were shelves with various instruments, tools, and vials of chemicals and powders that lined the wall.

"A'right, lad, now—gently pull the hide back an' allow the blade ta do the work," Natholdi coached.

I watched as Muu bent over some kind of carcass that was on the table I had seen, slid his fingers under the flesh, and slid a blade down the chalked line on the flesh.

"Good." Natholdi repositioned herself next to him and pointed out of my sight. "Now, make a clean slice under each side of the legs—mind the anus—aye, an' then under the tail to connect the cut."

Muu shifted his shoulders and slowly did as he was told. I heard what sounded like meaty fabric tearing. As gruesome as it sounded, I had to admit that he seemed good at it.

"Excel'ent work, lad." Natholdi patted him on the back. "Yer friend is here. Take a mo', but hurry back."

"He can come over here and talk while I work," I heard Muu mumble.

I had to smile. How many times had I stood in the doorway of his room and harassed him during a boss fight and not blown his concentration?

I nodded at Natholdi, and she smiled back. "Gived me ano'er brigh' apprentice ye did. Quick wit has this 'un."

"Thanks, Natholdi." I took her aside for a moment. "Look, I made an oath with your boy that he swore he would follow, so I'm going to enchant his skinning knife for him."

"Tha' old thing?" She tapped my shoulder. "Was gonna wai' fer his name day, but he can have it now, I s'pose." She looked toward the entrance to the room, backed up three paces, and reached up on top of a shelf for a box that she pulled down.

As she stepped forward with it, her son walked slowly into the room.

"Get ye here, boy," Natholdi told her son sternly. He shuffled over to his mother, looking from her to me with clear worry. "What'd ye do?"

"I dinae do anythin', ma," he said with worry.

She narrowed her eyes. "I hear'd different. Do nae lie ta me, lad. Speak."

"I dinae do anythin' bad," he amended. "I made a dwarves' oath wi' mister fox. He gived me the terms, I found 'em agr'able, an' I gived him me word. Just like ye would've."

"Oh, aye?" She observed him with a little haughtier of a gaze. "Be ye thinkin' yer Dwarf enough to keep yer word gived to a stranger? What were the terms ye speak of, boy. An' how do ye 'spect to keep 'em?"

He looked to me, closed his eyes, and spoke, "I swore on me Way and me beard tha' I will always listen ta me ma 'cause she loves me dear. And tha' the next time I sees Lady Shelly ta thank her fer her service ta the glory of the Mountain. Even though I donae know what it means righ' now—she will. And tha's the importan' part. Aye, mister?"

I nodded. "That's absolutely true."

I looked over to see the look of pure, unadulterated pride on Natholdi's face. With tears in her eyes, she knelt before the boy and held the box in front of him.

"If yer ta have a proper gift from an exchanged oath, ye need a proper skinnin' knife. Here ye are, me boy."

He gingerly handed me his old knife, then slowly lifted the lid of the box. Inside, in a sheath of finely made leather beneath it, was a skinning knife. The design itself was simple—the mithral blade had a wicked-looking hook at the base of the blade opposite the true cutting edge. This gave way to a slightly serrated edge that stopped and led to a smooth edge that led to the pointed tip of the knife. The bladed cutting edge was finely honed with a kind of bell shape to the bottom. The handle also had a simple design of sturdy-looking wood that would fit his hand for years to come. It was oddly shaped for me, but he loved it.

"This fer me, ma?" he asked in wonder. His hand was poised over it, but he was afraid to touch it.

"Aye, pick it up, me boy," Natholdi encouraged him. "This was ta be fer yer name day, but ye earned yer name today."

He picked it up reverently. He admired it in the light of the room and smiled brightly.

"Can I see it?" I asked. "I need to hold it to enchant it."

He nodded and handed it gingerly to me. I looked it over again as I decided on a design that would help him remember his oath to me.

"You're going to see me do magic now," I informed him and Natholdi. "There's no need to be afraid. You are both safe. I swear it by the Mountain."

They nodded, but Natholdi still took her son's shoulder and pulled him to her. Despite that, I smiled and focused on the design, then brought my mana to my fingertip. The mana began to take shape. Once it was fully formed, I pressed it into the blade so that it passed all the way through to the other side. Both Dwarves gasped slightly. The boy looked like he was about to cry.

"I need you to trust me."

He bit his lip and nodded once.

I had accidentally done this earlier, but it had worked out well, so here went nothing. I brought out some of my diamond powder, a generous pinch, and focused my will and intent. As I funneled my mana into the item, I sprinkled the powder over the blade and continued pouring my mana in until

I felt it was enough. All told, I had spent 300 MP on the little item.

I looked it over and smiled—it had turned out better than I had hoped. The engraved hole was in the shape of a three-tailed fox, but rather than being a hole, it was sealed with pure diamond. The cutting edge was now diamond and wickedly sharp.

Fox's Promise

So long as the owner of this item upholds the tenants of the oath made to the Kitsune Zekiel Erebos, this blade will cut true, never dull, never rust, and never stain or chip.

Skinning knife made by Master Smith Sandier Stone Hammer, enchanted by Craftsman Enchanter Zekiel Erebos.

I handed it to his mother, so she could see that it wasn't cursed. She held the item to her chest, and I watched as her lip quivered slightly before she nodded her head at me once.

"Ye take care o' this tool, lad," she advised her son, "and it'll take care of you. Aye?"

"Aye, ma," he said as he held his hands level in front of him. "Does this mean I earned me name?"

"Aye, lad," Natholdi said as she handed him the tool. "But we shall wait fer yer da ta come home afore I tell ye. We thought long an' hard on it, aye? Ye want yer da ta be here?"

The boy's eyes lit up, and his smile split his face. "Aye!"

He looked over to me, Fox's Promise in his hand and his thick thumb tracing the image I had imbued it with, "Thank ye, mister. This is a real nice thing, I swears I'll keep me word ta ye."

"I know you will." I ruffled his downy hair playfully. I kneeled down next to him and beckoned to come closer. "You know, I met the Mountain once? Me and Shellica? Did you know he made you special?" He looked at me skeptically. "He did. And you know what he told me to do?"

"Wassat, mister?" he asked.

"He said to work hard, fight well, and drink with friends." I pointed to his new knife. "I need you to make some quality items for your people. I need you to make sure that the weak around you—those who can't protect themselves—are protected. And I need you to make lasting friendships that you can share a pint over. If you can do that for me, I think the Mountain would be happy with you too. What do you think?"

As I spoke those words to him, I prayed silently, deeply, that I would one day be able to say something similar to my own son. To help push him to always be his best self and to think of others over himself.

"That sounds a lot like him," I heard Shellica's voice behind me.

I watched the fear and uncertainty pass over the little Dwarven boy's face in waves. He held his knife up in front of his face by the hilt, gripped it tightly, and closed his eyes. When he opened them, there was a determined look on his face.

He marched right up to Shellica, his back rigid and his steps as measured as a child's could be. He stood in front of her and showed her the knife in his hand. She looked at him curiously but remained quiet.

"I was wrong afore, Lady Shelly," he began. His voice wavered, but he nodded to himself and pressed on, "I was wrong ta treat ye like I did. Me ma holds ye in high 'steem, and I knows why now. Ye do a lot fer the glory o' the Mountain. I wanna say, thank ye. Thank ye fer all tha' ye do. An' fer doin' it, though we other Dwarves donae know what ye always do."

Shellica looked from the boy, shocked at his words. Then she tapped the knife before her. She gasped and held her hand out for it with a small, "Please, lad?" He handed it over to her without complaint, and she gasped again.

"This is a very, *very* nice tool, young one," she said as she handed it to him hilt first. "Guard it well."

He smiled at her from ear to ear—and while he was feeling brave—he wrapped his arms around Shellica's waist. "I 'preciate what ye do, though I donae understand."

Shellica smiled, her features softening and hugged the boy back. Her hand on the top of his head, she leaned down and whispered as dwarvenly as I've ever heard her speak, "Yer welcome. Get ye ta yer ma, sweet boy."

He nodded once and skipped over to his momma.

"Master Erebos." Shellica stood and turned her back to me. "A word?" She swept into the next room swiftly.

I looked at Natholdi holding her son. I nodded once to her, then looked to Muu who was still absorbed in his work.

I walked into the next room, ready for hell to find my trainer with her arms crossed. "Yes?" I raised my eyebrows.

"What. In the Nine Hells. Do you think you are doing?" She tried to keep her voice calm. Though I could hear the anger in her tone, there was something else too. Her shoulders shook slightly. Her typically stoic, manic-looking face was a little less composed.

"I gave a gift to a child I felt deserved it," I answered truthfully. "So far as I have seen, he has upheld the tenants of his oath to me and so long as he does—his blade will work better than anything like it."

"I saw the enchantment, lad," she growled. "You foolishly gave him a tool that could break at the slightest displeasure of his ma."

"From what I could see, she's so proud of him that as long as he remains true to himself—he should be fine," I retorted.

"Natholdi seems to love her son greatly. Not to mention the fact that the tool will only do those things so long as he's *not* listening to her."

"And what if we're attacked again, and he's tryin'," she took a moment to compose herself before continuing, "and he's trying to defend her? What if she tells him to flee and he refuses? That tool that he has would likely be his only defense and you've given it to him. You make this right!"

I thought about it for a moment, then nodded. "You're right. You're absolutely right. I wasn't thinking. You're sure it's not because he thanked you."

"Don't you start that with me, child." She growled. "I told ye ta leave it alone. We bear this responsibility with honor."

"Yeah, but there's no reason that you need to suffer for it," I shot back. "The Mountain may have made all of you tough, but you aren't stone yet. You feel. You are capable of falling—and you all walk the same path. The same Way. Your path is no less perilous and fraught with decisions and loneliness as his would be in the same position you are in. And guess what—even though he doesn't know *exactly* what you do, he understands that it's for the glory of your god."

She stood there and glowered at me silently, so I added in low, pleading tone, "He's not afraid anymore, Shellica—he even asked if I would teach him enchanting! You may not take him, but he understands that it isn't evil anymore. Think of a whole generation of Dwarves who understand what your clan gave up in order to be able to help protect them with magical means."

Her eyebrows raised slightly, and finally, she asked, "What is it you think we gave up?"

"Kinship with your fellow Dwarf," I persisted. "Nights in the taverns and pubs with your people celebrating a hard day at work. The ability to walk down the street without someone spitting in your direction to ward off evil. People thinking you're somehow less of a Dwarf than they are."

Shellica frowned, her eyes lowered toward the ground. Finally, she looked back up and nodded once. "Yer not wrong, lad. Forgive me. I was not myself. It's been some time since a young one approached me so. I thought it some sort of trick until I saw the knife."

"I love the things you've taught me." I put a hand on her shoulder. "I'm grateful. And this is my way of accidentally showing that gratitude."

"Accidentally?" She looked at me oddly, then began to cackle. "Never mind it, lad. Come on."

Before she walked back into the room, I stopped her with a click of my tongue. She looked back. "What?"

"What's a name day?" Heat flooded my cheeks at my ignorance.

She smiled and stepped closer to me, "That is the day that a young Dwarf earns his or her name, typically on their twelfth year, though there are cases where it happens sooner if the parents get a good feel for the child."

"It's not a clan decision?" I wondered.

"If the Dwarves are a part of a clan, the clan head could help with the decision. Also if they're fortunate enough to apprentice outside a familial trade, their master would be able to give input," Shellica explained. "But Natholdi and her husband are clanless, and her boy is apprenticed only to her. So the ultimate decision is their's."

"There are clanless Dwarves?" I whispered harshly. "How?!"

"Their lot was taken and destroyed when the Drow came in their largest invasion." Shellica looked toward the doorway to the shop and a large Dwarf, easily the tallest I had seen stepped inside. He wore simple clothes, a pair of black breeches tucked into brown boots, and a brown and white shirt. The brown portion around his stomach looked to made of sturdy leather that the cloth on top was sewn on to.

"And we have nae decided ta join another for lack of their interest," he added. "Hello, Shelly. Come 'round for a proper meal? Who's our guest?"

"Granite, hello." Shellica walked over and gave the large figure a hug. "This is my apprentice, Zekiel. He's a member of the Mugfist Clan."

"Mugfist, eh?" He stepped in. The Dwarf's beard was blond and long with beads and other decorations braided in. His eyes were a sharp brown, and he had an easy smile that put me at ease right away. His muscled form loomed closer, muscles rippling with each easy step forward. He was a big dude.

Reminded me of someone really strong who looked like they had a stomach, but they just had abs that were thick as hell. Like powerlifters. They looked fat but could toss around hundreds of pounds with ease.

"Hello, Zekiel of Clan Mugfist." The Dwarf offered a meaty hand for me to shake. I clasped it and he introduced himself, "Me name's Granite."

"Nice to meet you, Granite." I smiled at him and hoped he wouldn't crush my hand in his. His grip was firm but not overbearing. Good man.

"Tha' me husband?" I heard Natholdi called.

Their son burst through the door with his knife held out in front of him, and Granite acted before any of us knew what was going on.

He grabbed the boy by the wrist, flicked the knife down and round while still in the wielder's grasp, and had him on his rump with the blade pointed away from his son but the handle in his chest. Granite had his knee behind the boy to support him and patted his head affectionately.

"Remember, son," Granite spoke calmly despite the flurry of motion, "always take care ta practice safety wit' yer blades, aye? Could get hurt, or more importantly, hurt someone else. An' how do we feel about tha'?"

"Only ta defend, only ta protect, always ta do right an' ne'er neglect—the oath of we who follow the Way," the boy spoke the words passionately as his father and mother mouthed them along. "Ta watch fer our brothers and sisters, an' help 'em live another day."

"Aye, good lad." Granite bent down a bit and placed a kiss on the top of his son's head. "Wha's this, now? A new skinnin' knife? Let's have a wee look."

He held the blade up to the light and whistled low. "Tha's some right proper craftsmanship, there." He poked his son gently and pointed to the diamond fox. "Whassat, lad?"

"I made an oath, da!" he said. He turned around and knelt so he could talk to his dad closer. "I swore on me Way an' me beard tha' I would listen ta ma, cause she loves me, and thank Lady Shelly 'cause of the work she does fer the glory o' the Mountain!"

"Yer first oath?" Granite spun the knife deftly around his fingers, then offered the hilt to his wife. "An' I take it ye made it to mister Zekiel?"

"Aye!" The boy turned to me. "Sorry, fer not learnin' yer name afore, sir."

"Think nothing of it." I chuckled. "You remind me of my son, though you're a lot older than he is."

"Ye have a boy of yer own then?" Granite asked. Natholdi seemed to take interest as well.

"I do," I said simply. "He's far away right now, but he's with his mom, and I can't wait until I can see him again."

"Well, I donae know what I would do without me boy, friend." Granite stood and patted his son. "Yer welcome among me an' mine. As his first oath, ye be an important part of who he be now. We'd be honored if ye would be with us on his name day. And ye, o' course Shelly. Yer next ta kin."

"Thank you, Granite. I would appreciate that," I offered. "When are the festivities?"

"Tonight?" Natholdi asked.

"No," Shellica growled. "Ye'll not take away my opportunity to spoil the lot of you. We will have it at the Light Hand Clan compound, and I will hear nothing otherwise. Hear?!"

Granite laughed, and Natholdi just shook her head before saying, "Yer too good ta us, lass. Ye treat us better than clan."

A strange look passed over Shellica's face. "Ye are better than clan. Yer kin. I saved yer life, girl. And ye've been me best friend since then." She looked over to me and collected her thoughts before continuing, "Until now, I've been afraid to ask due to the social repercussions, but it seems to me that times are changing here."

She stepped over to the couple, Granite towering over her and Natholdi much broader. Both of them seemed confused.

"I, Shellica Light Hand, leader of the clan of my name, do hereby formally invite you, Granite and Natholdi, to become kin, not just clan, but blood of my blood. Should you accept, I will take you and yours and all of your line into my care, so long as I may live and so long as my name is among those carved in the memory halls of the Mountain. Should you refuse, know that you will remain my staunchest friends and that I will continue to love and support you as I have. Friends, what say you."

Warmth crawled through my body, and I felt my fur stand on end. I watched Natholdi gasp and look to her friend, then her husband. Granite didn't seem surprised, but he did look to his wife. They seemed to share more in that one look than I have seen others pass in full conversations.

Granite looked over at Shellica then took a knee before her. "If ye will take me kin as yer own, I will accept ye as me clan leader, and I will support ye in any endeavor I am able. I swear it as speaker of this home by my beard under the Mountain."

"Rise, Granite Light Hand, and take your place with the rest of my family," Shellica said with a smile and tears in her eyes. "If you would like, you can be accommodated in the compound, though I do know your business here is important. If you would like to stay here, you can."

"Thank ye, Shelly." Natholdi rushed over to Shellica and gave her a big hug.

"Whassat mean then?" The little boy's eyes were huge at all that was going on.

"Means you're gonna have quite the party, kid," Muu joked as he walked through the door from the other room. "Oh, hey Granite. Eat anyone today?"

Granite laughed as he looked over at Muu. "Oh aye, Natholdi, yer right, he should o' been born a Dwarf!"

Chapter Thirteen

We spent some time that day after working on things that would be appropriate for the party the next evening. Shellica released me to my own devices once more, and I left to go back to the Mugfist compound.

I began to think about the name day celebration. Were the Dwarves' traditions that similar to our own? Natholdi had said that the knife was a gift for his name day. There was so much I didn't know. I needed to ask someone some questions.

I couldn't seem to find anyone, and Brawnwynn wouldn't answer my question because he was busy training some new warriors off somewhere when I tried to find him, so I went elsewhere.

"Hey, Farnik, I had a quick question," I said after casting Mental Message. "What is an appropriate gift to get a Dwarven child on their name day?"

"Name days be mighty important in Dwarven culture, lad," Farnik responded readily. "Meet me outside the compound, and we can discuss it more. I had things to do anyway."

I smiled to myself and began to walk a little faster. As I wove through the people around me, I noticed that fewer of the Dwarves openly stared, and a few even nodded respectfully my way. I returned nods in the same manner they were given, and I made it over to the compound.

"Ho there, lad," Farnik greeted me. He wore chainmail with the Mugfist crest on it—I swear if you can't see the mug in a Dwarven fist... never mind—and he had a wicked looking battle axe attached to hooks on his back.

"Hey, Farnik," I greeted him and slowed down. "You, uh, expecting a fight?"

"Always." He bared his teeth for a moment. "Forgive me, Zeke. I don't take ta the city without bein' prepared anymore, though the clan thinks I should have a guard. Feh! Me? Hardly. Ye had questions for me about name days?"

"Yeah," I stood next to him, and we began to walk in no particular direction. "So, his mother gave him a skinning knife that I enchanted for him, but it was pointed out that if he ever needed to defend himself, it would be a poor weapon because of the enchantment I used."

"Aye?" Farnik encouraged me to go on.

"So, I was thinking, what if I got him an axe or something?" I continued.

Farnik stopped and shook his head and hands at me. "Nooo, lad. No. A Dwarf's pride is to give his child their first axe. Who's the lad's da?"

"His name is Granite. His mother is Natholdi," I explained.

Farnik whistled. "Oh lad. Granite be a right good one to have on yer side—donae get the boy an axe."

"You know Granite?" We were in the merchant section of the city now.

"Aye," Farnik said. He patted a Dwarf on the back in a friendly manner. Like he seemed to know everyone. "Granite be a damned skilled warrior. A berserker—real barbarian kind of Fighter who loses themselves to their emotions. How ye doing, Gwently?"

A Dwarf who ran the stall with assorted weapons and various other metal workings waved at Farnik. His beard was red and short, probably due to age. His hair was pulled back into a ponytail, and he wore chainmail as well.

"Ho there, Farnik!" the Dwarf greeted. "What ken a do ye fer?"

"Need a name day gift for Granite's boy," Farnik informed the merchant. He looked at me. "These are weapons from the Stone Hammer clan, so Granda's kids and kin made these. Ye'll be hard pressed to find better in the city. Though there is a stall for other clans' wares down the way."

I looked over some of the items on display. There were axes, which were out of the question—I'd rather not piss off the Dwarven bear. I looked over some of the knives. There were some quality weapons I did feel he could learn to train with in the meantime. There were several short daggers. A knife. I even saw a bandolier of throwing knives. All of them looked good.

I grabbed two of the short daggers and the bandolier of throwing knives. That last one was more for me than anything. If I could give someone a kickass gift—no matter how impractical— I'd do it. I mean, who doesn't want to throw knives, right?

Farnik nodded at my choices and pulled out a sack of coin.

"Woah, hey, woah." I put a hand on his shoulder to stop him. "I got this, Farnik. These are my gifts. I'll take care of them."

The older Dwarf snorted and loosed a good-natured chuckle. "Ye can use yer coin for yer gifts, Zeke. This be the clan's contribution to a Dwarf whose name ought strike fear inta the hearts o' many. While I was killin' me wife's murderer in that Drow raid, Granite took on an entire swarm o' their minions, several Drow, and a drider on his own. He stopped at least three other clans from experiencing the loss that he did. The Dwarf is a legend. We took a collection the day I heard his boy was born."

"Shit," I grunted. And here I had been basically smoking and joking with a fucking legend. Yeah, leave it to me to find the most important person in a room and make an ass of myself.

"So wait, if he's so important—why was he clanless?"

Gwently spoke up, "Granite were the kin' a Dwarf to no' let others know his pain. He works the mines day long, no one bothers him. Mines the ore hisself most days. Weren't neglect the clans had fer makin' him a home—were out o' respect tha' he an' his was left ta their own fer fear o' upsettin' him."

"If I got that right," I said slowly as I turned to Farnik, "he whooped some serious ass in that fight, and all of his clan fell but him. And instead of having him choose a clan to join, you left him to his own devices so that he could recover. Out of respect for him and his loss?"

"Aye," Gwently put in. "Smart one here, Farnik."

Farnik chuckled, and I looked over to see a mischievous glint in the merchant's eyes.

"So what's the money for?" I asked.

"It's fer his first set o' armor." Farnik tapped it and slid it over to the merchant who took it, pulled ink and quill from a shelf below the counter, and began to scribble the order down. "Every member of the clan put in two silver. To be honest, it'll be more than enough to cover most of his armor into adulthood. But they won't know that until it's needed, will they Gwently?"

"Who the fuck are ye again?" Gwently joked, and they clasped hands. "That'll be two gold, lad."

I passed him the money, and he nodded at me.

"Will ye be treatin' these weapons, lad?" Farnik asked curiously.

"Treating...?" I mouthed. Then it dawned on me. "You mean enchanting?"

He looked uncomfortable but nodded and cleared his throat.

"I mean, yeah I can." I tapped my temple in thought. "I hadn't thought of it, to be honest."

Farnik cleared his throat again, seeming a little worried as he cast his eyes about. "Hem, uh, well, every lad deserves a good present fer his name day. An' I seed Granite's boy in passin'. Seems like a good lad, big like his ma and da with a good head."

"Yeah, he's a pretty good kid," I agreed.

"Well, good. I'm glad I could help ye," Farnik scratched his head. "Be there anything that they need?"

"Well, they officially joined the Light Hand Clan this morning," we began to walk back toward the Mugfist compound slowly, "and Shellica told them that they would be having their name day tomorrow at their compound."

Farnik stopped and looked shocked. "Granite and Natholdi joined that clan?!"

Before I could control myself, a sigh escaped my body.

"Look, lad," Farnik held his hands up in a placating motion in front of him. "I know ye work with her, but ye don't have to force yerself to defend her."

"I'm not forcing myself, Farnik." I checked around us for listeners. People saw Farnik, but they also saw me, and I kept them at bay for a bit longer. "She and her clan do a lot for your people with their magics that you don't know about."

"Magic ain't right, lad," Farnik explained as if it were the most natural thing. "It be fine for ye using magic 'cause you're not a Dwarf by blood, but their magic ain't natural."

And he really believed that. "Do you not know about their blessings from Fainne?"

"The Mountain has never been known to give his people magic powers," Farnik explained indulgently.

"Farnik, I've met him," I explained. "He gave me a deeper mana pool and the ability to engrave things with mana. He didn't give them magic powers. He allowed them the ability to enchant weapons and items with magic for his glory."

"Ye met him?" His eyebrows were raised in surprise. "What was he like?"

"He was really nice." I shrugged. "He was made of metals, and he seemed to be really cool. He didn't seem the type to baby people, but he was supportive of my trying to master my craft. You haven't been visited by him?"

"Aye, that sounds like the Mountain from our teachins." Farnik smiled at the idea. "And ye say he supported yer enchanting? No, lad. I be a warrior. The way I feel close to the Mountain is by fighting. I feel his touch at times but never see him."

"He gave me the ability to form my mana into shapes so that I can engrave better."

Farnik nodded but frowned. "Why would Shellica's people not pass on their support from the Mountain?"

"Because they take their duties to the Mountain seriously," I explained with hope. "They do it for Him and Him alone. If they can keep doing their thing and enchanting some of the weapons and items you all make, then they're fine."

"But the others scorn them." He seemed confused, then began to rub his forehead with the butt of his hand. "How much they suffer from other's fears and not knowin'? It ain't Dwarven. Come on, lad, we got work to do."

He waved me forward, and he marched forward with purpose that he hadn't had before. "What do you mean by that?"

"We got a party to prepare for!" He grinned at me. A few minutes later and his obstinate refusal to answer my questions saw us inside the grounds of the clan's home. Farnik called out, "Clan meeting! Get yer arses to the back courtyard in five minutes! Pass the word."

Dwarves scattered to spread the word and then fell into line behind us as we began walking toward the rear of the complex. It took a little longer than five minutes for everyone to gather, but once they were together, Farnik addressed the whole clan.

"Mugfist!" he shouted, threw a fist into the air, and his people did the same. "Lads and lasses of the clan, I have grave news for ye. We of the Mugfist and all o' this city have come dangerously close to losing our Way."

There was a collective gasp, and the Dwarves in the yard began to shout questions. Some looked horrified and damned near began to riot.

"We and all the other Dwarves in this city have made a rather large slight against the Mountain and his people," Farnik continued as he threw a hand into the air for quiet. "Every time ye crossed the street, spat in the direction of, or acted odd to a member of the Light Hand Clan, ye spat in the face o' the Mountain."

"How?!" one Dwarf shouted incredulously. Another bellowed, "Magic in Dwarves ain't right!"

"I felt the same," Farnik growled and slapped his hand to his armor. "I swears I did, but the truth be laid out afore me, and I come with a chance to make things right. Listen well."

He then began to speak to them about our conversation, about the things that I had observed in my time working with Shellica, and then me meeting their god. People balked at that, but then they remembered I was clan and they took it as a sign of favor. Farnik explained things that he had noticed as well—how Shellica and all of her clan had treated the other Dwarves with professionalism and courtesy despite being treated as pariahs.

"Clan Mugfist," Farnik finally said, tears of horror flowing down his cheeks, "a time has come where we can begin to restore our honor with the Light Hand, but it's only the beginning. Tomorrow, their newest members, Granite, his wife, and boy are having the lad's name day celebration. We already committed to getting him armor, but we can do more. What say ye?!"

The gathered Dwarves roared with approval. Some in the crowd wept openly as they shouted. Others pulled items out of their beards, the hair attached to them, which if I recalled correctly, was an attempt at penance for a wrong done against another. Those who did so brought the items and locks to the front and piled them before Farnik.

"Aye, we all didn't know—but ignorance nae be an excuse," Farnik shouted gravely. "I say we offer 'em fifty barrels. With a promise of another fifty to come. They will not drink their own stock tomorrow. Aye?!"

"AYE!" the others shouted.

"I will go to Shellica as a representative of the clan, and I will pay for our lack of honor and our unknowing hindrance of their Way. Stand with me, brothers and sisters. What say ye?"

"'Tis only right, 'tis only just," the group chanted together. "A Dwarf in debt does as he must."

"Truth." Farnik nodded solemnly, but there was a look of understanding calm to him that I hadn't seen. "I treated them unfair, we all did. Let us hope that our example leads others to correct their Way. Go! We prepare."

A flurry of motion, Dwarves beat feet in all manner of directions. More than one Dwarf came to me to ask about Fainne. They wanted to know if he was healthy with all that was going on—the fighting against War and his invaders. I tried to pass what precious little I knew, and they seemed satisfied with it.

"Thank ye, lad." Farnik clapped me on the shoulder. "Ye gived us a chance to restore our honor and right a dire wrong. Ye be damned near as good as any natural born Dwarf, aye?"

"If you say so, Farnik. I'm just happy I could help. Also, don't tell Shellica I told you all that."

"Why not?" he asked with true concern on his face.

"I'm worried she'll kick my ass," I groaned.

"Bwahahahah!" Farnik burst with laughter. "Oh, aye. That she will likely do. She were stoic about it a long while, likely bore it with pride. But yer clan, lad. Ye has to tell me what ye know'd. Ye would've been in the wrong not to."

"Thank you for that out, man." I smiled at him in relief.

"Don't mean she won't flay ye regardless, but ye did the right thing." Farnik grinned wolfishly, and I began muttering about him being an asshole. He took it in stride.

Chapter Fourteen

The whole next day, I spent helping the rest of my clan prepare barrels of mead, ale, and beer to be taken to the Light Hand Compound. Between wagons, I prepared the items that I had bought as presents.

The two daggers I enchanted to stay sharp, pierce armor better, and to be more durable with a little bit of my diamond powder. The throwing knives I enchanted for accuracy without any components. Not too powerful, but they were for a kid, so that was okay.

I placed them into a box that Farnik gave me, then dressed in my padded armor that I had gotten from Maebe, and prepared to go to the party. Another tradition was for Dwarves to attend name day celebrations in their armor, bearing their clan crests proudly. This was to show the young Dwarf who had earned their name what they could aspire to be—the level of honor and respect they could attain through dedication to themselves, their respective crafts, and their Way.

"Get ye goin', lad," Farnik shooed me off. "Ye go an' be there fer Shellica an' the boy. I will personally bring the offering to the party meself. If ye can make 'em keep their stock out of the way, it'd be appreciated, but donae lead 'em to what I be doin'. Aye?"

"Okay, buddy." I patted his shoulder and hooked my axe to a harness I now wore that had hooks on the back. The dyed-black leather had been oiled and smelled like pine. Storm Caller only shifted slightly as I walked toward the Light Hand Compound. Inside, I saw lanterns shining brightly with golden light hung from hooks along the fencing, then silvered lights from the lanterns on hooks inside the compound scattered here and there.

There were Light Hand Dwarves all over, stringing light and streamers—prepping the grounds for the evening's festivities.

"Ho there!" I called to one of them. She turned and nodded to me. "Do you know where I can find Shellica?"

"She'll be 'round back sortin' the tables and benches round" She pointed toward the same area I had let my familiars out before.

"Thanks!" I called as I bustled off, dodging Dwarves and counted at least thirty barrels of something stacked neatly beside the tables with mounds of food on them.

"What're you doing standing there like a lump?" Shellica called to me from a large stage with another table on it.

She wore a suit of armor with white metal scales down it. The chest piece was six pieces of the same material that had been weaved together—almost as if sewn—by silver threads of metal. Two plates sat against the top of her chest, two more beneath near her ribs, and the other two beneath her arms going around her back. The scales beneath were small and moved as she did. She wore a leather and metal plate skirt of matching material and carried a staff with her like a walking stick.

She clapped her hands and growled. "Get up here and help me!"

I jogged over and up a small set of stairs to stand beside her. "What's up?"

"Me, and I don't like it," she harrumphed. "Look at the tables and see that they are aligned.

I did as I was asked. There were six rows of tables arranged in a huge crescent shape that fanned out centered on the stage with the shortest row in the front and the longest in the rear.

"Looks good to me," I informed her. "Do we really need so much alcohol?"

"Do you really doubt our guests will not go through all of that and more?" Shellica raised a brow sarcastically.

I laughed to myself and nodded. "That's fair."

"I know." Her eyebrows furrowed. "I think we have done what we can. The guests will be here in an hour or so. Let the others do their jobs with all of this. Come, let us go over some more of the knowledge you have as an enchanter."

We spent that hour going back over some of the things I had been learning. Shellica had me adding several different components to items I was working with. Never at once, but as I worked, I became more and more adjusted to the prospect of this kind of exchange working well. Though, one thing bothered me.

"If there are so many kinds of components that I can add, why not some of my blood?" I asked between two items.

"Adding blood to an item through enchanting is a *much* more advanced skill as an enchanter," Shellica spoke gravely, "but using blood with any kind of magic runs dangerously close of turning the user—no matter how experienced or strong—toward the path of necromancy. Toward the eldritch magics. Vile and detestable they are."

She spat on the ground three times then crushed the third globule of spit under her heel.

"That's some powerful hate for that kind of power," I observed cautiously.

"Is nae power, lad." Shellica wagged her finger, and her normally cultured speech slipped. "It be poison."

"That's true." Vilmas poked her head into the room. "Forgive me, my lady, but I couldn't help overhearing. The eldritch magics offer 'power and control' but they never truly deliver. They constantly encourage the Mage who partakes to do more and more vile things in search of power."

Shellica pointed and nodded at the other Dwarf. "That's correct. What can I do for you, lass?"

"The guests have arrived, my lady." She bowed her head and disappeared from sight.

"Come along, lad, you're a guest of honor." Shellica waved for me to follow her as she began to get up.

"Because of the oath?" That was a little ludicrous, right?

"A Dwarf's first oath is very important in our society," Shellica explained as we made our way into the hall. She closed her door and tapped it three times—the lock shot into place—and we continued on. "Even if the oath be something so simple as your own was—it is Dwarven Way to honor them."

"I can respect that." I shrugged. "Far be it from me to begrudge a Dwarf's Way."

Shellica snorted, and we were outside a second later. There were Dwarves everywhere. No different from any other day, but they were all in shining suits of armor, plate mail, chain mail, and all of these gleaming weapons dazzlingly reflecting the silver and gold light around us.

We made our way to the table on stage slowly. Many in the clan wished to talk to Shellica, and there were representatives from the different clans and Dwarven council that I hadn't known existed.

Once we took our places at the table on stage—mine was next to Shellica but toward the outside of the table—the crowd quieted and waited for Shellica to speak.

"Light Hand!" She held her hand aloft, and a shroud of light began to cover it. A majority of the Dwarves returned the gesture, and it left more than a few of the guests looking uncomfortable.

"Long awaited is the day a young one has when they claim their title under the Mountain," she addressed them. "Long awaited is the day they prove to all who matter who they are and what they stand for. I had the extreme honor of witnessing the proving of such a young one yesterday morn. Who swore his first oath to someone outside his kin."

The gathered crowd began to hoot and holler boisterously, pounding tables and clapping their gauntlet-covered fists against their armored chests. Shellica nodded with a smile until they quieted.

"In that same morning I welcomed three more into my kin." She motioned toward a shadowed area of the compound grounds off to our right. "Please, all of you welcome Granite, Natholdi, and their son—the newest members of the Light Hand Clan!"

The three Dwarves walked forward proudly as the crowd roared their approval. For the second time in my life, I saw the Dwarves lift their legs and stomp in unison. Their thudding legs imitating the heartbeat of their god, Fainne, and his approval. I looked out into the crowd and saw fierce approval and glints of mirth and pride in the eyes of those gathered. The hairs on my body stood on end and shivered in a chill of nerves.

Granite wore a simple set of trousers, his chest was bare but for the scars and tattoos he had of Dwarven faces and runes. He wore a single shoulder pauldron of obsidian carved into wicked-looking, pointed mountains. Covering his fists were gloves that sported large spikes. Natholdi wore a set of leather armor dyed red with runes and capped with obsidian. She wore a set of battle axes on her hips, and their son wore a simple tunic and trousers with his skinning knife belted to his waist. They climbed the stairs and stood in front of the table opposite where their chairs were. The boy next to Shellica in the center, his father next to him, and Natholdi at the end. Shellica walked out from behind the table and motioned for me to follow with her hand hidden from sight.

"All of you, be seated as we hear the name of this child and assist him in his first steps along the Way as an adult proper."

The crowd sat silently and watched raptly as Granite and Natholdi stepped forward.

"I, Natholdi Light Hand, watched as me son embraced a simple life o' masterin' a trade, knowin' tha t'is nae as glamorous as smithin' but nae less important ta his people. I have judged him ready o' his name." Natholdi held her head high as she spoke. Despite her stoic and proud demeanor, tears dripped to the boards next to her feet. "As a show o' support an' dedication ta his commitment, I've honored him with a finely crafted skinning knife, that he may master hiself as he masters his craft."

Granite stepped forward, his bearing much the same as his wife's.

"I, Granite Light Hand, bare witness to the strength of my son's character. I been proud to see him stand tall against others his age who would seek to shame him for his lack of clan an' think they were his better. I been even more proud to see him wear his wounds with pride and defend others from the same treatment. I have judged him worthy of his name." Granite reached behind his back and lifted an axe, double headed and made of black steel sized for a child larger than his son, into the air for all to see. "This axe is a show of potential. Given to my son so that he may defend himself along his Way and keep the tenants of the Mountain until he finds himself one with the stone once more."

Granite looked to his child, faced him, and knelt to one knee in front of him, still towering over the boy easily. He took his right hand and reached out to cup his son's face with it lovingly. He dropped that hand and used it to lift the weapon up so that the boy could take it. Granite's son lifted the axe with surprising ease and rested the head of it lightly on the ground before bowing his head slightly to his father. From this angle, I couldn't see the boy's face, but I saw Granite offer his son a small smile before he stood and took a step back.

"Clan representatives and those among my own, I introduce my latest apprentice and claimed member of the Mugfist Clan—Zekiel Erebos." There was a whisper through the crowd that stopped almost as soon as it began. "He is the bearer of the child's first oath." Shellica motioned me forward and nodded. "He will speak of the encounter."

Nervously, I stepped forward, then spoke. "I, Zekiel Erebos of Clan Mugfist, had the privilege of sharing an oath with the boy. The tenants of the oath were that he listen to his mother, as I found that she was a good person and she loved him dearly." I glanced at Shellica, but she simply stared ahead. "And that the next time he saw the Light Hand Clan head, he thank her for what she and her clan do for the glory of the Mountain—despite his lack of understanding. True to his word to the Mountain and against his beard, I watched as he suppressed his fear and thanked Shellica Light Hand properly. As a reward for this oath, I have enchanted his skinning knife to the best of my abilities as a craftsman enchanter. I find that any name he is given will be appropriate in reflecting his courage and sense of duty to his word. I am honored to walk along the Way with him."

I hoped that my rambling had done something to honor the boy and his parents as I stepped back. I would kick Shellica's ass for not telling me I had to speak in this. She probably knew I would've told her to buzz off if she had. Jerk. As I found my place, Shellica stepped forward.

"I, Shellica Light Hand—along with the clan of my name—have brought this child into my family as blood and kin," Shellica addressed the gathered crowd. "In a show of loyalty to kin and to the growth of my clan, I have given this boy a home. A home where he will be able to wear his name with pride. A home where he and those of his line will be safe. A home where he can grow and bring further honor and glory to the Mountain. But most importantly—I bring him the love of Fainne, the Mountain."

She knelt next to the boy, and all the Dwarves of her clan stood and began to raise their voices in song. As they sang wordlessly, the ground began to shake visibly. Rubble from the roof of the cavern where the city was built in the bones of the world fell and landed directly in front of the boy. A small glint of reflected light from within the rubble caught my attention, and the singing stopped abruptly.

Shellica reached into the rubble and pulled out a large, round orb of stone larger than her hand. She offered it to the boy who took it with confusion and wonder plain on his face. Those gathered were shocked, and I had to admit I was too.

"When you learn your name, set this on the ground and smack it with your axe," Shellica instructed the boy quietly.

She stood and looked to the crowd before addressing them, "Be there any among those present here this day who would deny the evidence given to this young Dwarf's merit to walk among us along our path to the Mountain? Be there any among you who wish to right a wrong against this family?"

The crowd was quiet for a moment, several Dwarves standing, representatives from other clans that Shellica had spoken about earlier in her introduction for me. They brought their gifts and cut braidings of beard hair to show their sorrow and recognition of a slight done against them. I heard a few mumble about not giving them enough in the wake of their loss. Another older Dwarf said that he regretted not offering them a home after what happened.

Finally, after the other Dwarves had shuffled away, Shellica, stoic as she had been before, as if this portion were expected, raised her arms to address the crowd once more—or would have if it wasn't for a commotion from the side of the building that had the barrels of mead.

I watched as fifty Dwarves baring the Mugfist crest on their polished armor marched stoically into the courtyard followed by five carts that had barrels of mead. The marching Dwarves split into two ranks and divided themselves so that they framed the carts that stopped flush with the front row, but the most surprising thing about this procession was Muu, in slightly-spiked armor so dark it seemed to eat the light, standing next to Farnik. The Mugfist Clan head wore a humble tunic of white, a black belt, and knife with matching white trousers. He wore no boots and nothing on his feet. His beard was washed, clean, and without any adornments. It flowed almost to his waist with the braids and items in it normally, but now, it dragged almost on the floor. His fists were closed, and I could see he held something.

Together, they approached the stage.

"Farnik, this is highly irregular, lad." Shellica stepped in front of the child and the rest of her new kin.

"Aye," Farnik agreed sadly. "Aye it is, but it be truth. I come to ye now as head of me clan to make right a vile wrong to yers and to ye. I come on behalf of me clan. I pray ye will hear me apologies."

Shellica nodded and stepped aside so that the others were able to see the Dwarf before them.

"Granite, Natholdi, lad," Farnik stepped forward and set several clippings and braids of his beard on to the pile of the others. "I wronged ye in ways I cannae begin to tell, but the most important being that I did nae offer home and love to the Dwarf an' his kin what helped defend this city as I took me vengeance fer me wife's murder. I will ne'er be able to make that right. I hope that ye will take these as a token of my penance and honesty in this."

Granite began to step forward but stopped at a hand from Farnik.

"I appreciate ye, but me words ain't done." He looked to Shellica. "Shellica Light Hand, I fear I have wronged ye and yer clan worst of all. We, this entire city and all our kind here, treat ye as outsiders. As wrong. We who are supposed to support all as they walk the Way. We who are tasked by the Mountain to defend his children. We have made yer lives harder. We have made it much harder to follow the Way, the gravest sin a Dwarf can commit against another."

He reached across his body with his right hand and drew the knife there. It was wickedly sharp and flashed once. Twice. Three times in the silver and gold light as Farnik took it and sliced into his beard. He cut it raggedly, sometimes sawing through the locks of it before he stood with the majority of his once glorious facial hair in his fist. Tears streamed down his slightly barren cheeks. Portions of longer hairs stuck out here and there. It looked as if a child had taken a pair of clippers to their hair out of curiosity and now this was the mess left.

He held the shorn hair out to Shellica first, then turned to the crowd and shouted, "Be there no others among ye who see the wrongness of yer ways?! We scorned good, Mountain fearing folk doin' what they could fer Fainne's glory! We were wrong!"

The twin ranks of Mugfist Dwarves had tears streaming down their faces into their own beards after bearing witness to their leader's shame. One after another, they knelt where they stood with their heads low.

Several other Dwarves joined Farnik. They borrowed his blade, put their forehead to his as they wept, and did the same themselves. They cut their beards to the quick as swiftly as they could and offered the result to Shellica. After the first five, others joined the procession, and finally, a strangled cry came from the stage next to me.

Shellica, shaking with tears streaming down her face, had fallen to her knees. She screamed in agony at what she saw before us, and the Dwarves stopped what they were doing.

"Shellica, are you okay?" I asked as I bent down beside her.

She shoved me aside. "What're ye lot doin'?!" she shouted hoarsely. "Me clan nae once told any of ye that we was hurtin'! We beared our honor and yer contempt stoic in humility ta the Mountain. We needed no pride. No support save fer his blessing. I'll nae have ye shornin' yer honor fer mine! Stop this!" She looked to the Dwarves of her clan who held each other for support at the sight of so many other important figures offering penance for a deep wrong. "If yer of me clan an' ye forgive 'em, shout 'aye!'"

There was a roar of "ayes" so loud that the cavern above us shook and more rubble fell. This time, it was not the feet of the Dwarves that caused the heartbeat of the Mountain to be heard but the massive diamond—larger than the compound itself—that was unearthed above us. No rubble hit the ground.

Not so much as a mote of dust. There in the heart of the diamond for all to see was the face of Fainne.

His mithral face covered in a golden beard and eyes cut from emerald. The top of his bald head shone in the light below. His smile, warm and loving, graced all.

Motion caught my eye, and I looked as I saw dozens of Dwarves fall to their knees, clutching their weapons—not in order to fight but because they were solid. They provided an anchor.

None of them had met their god. None of them had seen him. Spoken to him. Not the way that I had. And not like Shellica, who passed his blessing on to her clan for him.

As I looked around, I saw others had frozen entirely. Mugs held to mouths floundering for words. Ale, mead, and other alcohol spilling down armored chests. Cups knocked over.

A bass rumble shook us, and I realized that he had opened his mouth. I looked back up. I understood him. We all did.

"Children, I can sense your sadness." His eyes took all in. "This day was meant to be a special day, Farnik, me boy. And Shelly-lass. All of you, you are forgiven. Shellica, the Light Hand Clan no longer need suffer in silence, and ye lot who thought ye slighted them—didn't. Ye made their faith in me that much more worthwhile. But times are changing, and as the facets of a gem change when ye shift yer hand, so too must our people. All of ye are witnessing the dawn of a new age as we defend ourselves from War and his forces. The birth of Dwarven magic users is nigh."

He shifted his gaze to those on stage. "Granite, berserker and father—bestow upon yer boy his name, that I may bless him."

Granite, mouth moving in silence, slapped himself and looked at his son. "Lad, yer name as ye have earned it. Ye, as witnessed by all here, shall forevermore be known as Fainnir. He who walks with the Mountain. Bring glory to yerself, the Mountain, and Dwarven kind."

Fainne's face nodded, and he spoke now to the newly-named Dwarf, "Fainnir, set that stone down and break it with yer axe, lad."

The shocked lad sat the black stone down, brought the too-large axe down on it, and a burst of light took the stage.

"I, Fainne—Craftsman, Mountain, Metal Bringer, and Harbinger of your kind—bless this child named after me with the gift to bring about a new age to Dwarves. May he bring honor to himself and his kin." To the rest of the crowd, he said simply, "Love each other, and know that I love you though I am not always here. Work hard, my children."

The light faded a moment then returned, and the diamond was still there—a reminder of His presence above the city. A reminder of the new facets his people would soon see.

I looked over to see Fainnir shocked, looking at something. "What is it, Fainnir?"

"Me status screen." He looked at me, then his parents. "It says me class is Stone Mage!"

"The hell is a Stone Mage?" Muu asked from off to my right. He was standing next to Farnik once more. "And who the hell was that?"

Chapter Fifteen

Mead and ale flowed in abundance. Half of that was joy at having been forgiven. The other?

The other was at having met the embodiment of everything a Dwarf could hope to be. Their God. The Mountain.

As we walked around and made sure everything was fine, I overheard conversations about what they had seen. I heard snippets like, "Can ye believe the Mountain blessed this child hisself?" or "So the Mountain's beard looked like tha'? Tha's the goal then, aye?" My favorite was what one Dwarf said to his friends after downing four consecutive mugs of alcohol, "We go'a tell *ever'ody.*"

The most pleased by all of this was Fainnir. He was tickled to have an all-new class to his kind, and his parents couldn't be more proud.

"I cannae believe tha' the Mountain came to me boy's name day!" Natholdi bragged before taking a large gulp of ale.

"Aye!" Granite smiled. He took a large drink of his mug, then looked at his son. "Yer the first of a kind, I thinks, lad. Drink yer ale, Fainnir. It's fer the glory o' the Mountain."

"Yes, da." The young Dwarf tipped his small mug up into his mouth and lowered it to show his rosy cheeks and a happy grin. "Tha's right good, tha' is. Muu! Drink yer ale, lad. S'fer the glory o' the Mountain."

"Don't you tell me what to do, you half-sauced half pint," Muu teased, but he took a drink as well. "You like what I brought you?"

"Oh, aye!" Fainnir tapped the shield with the head of a Dragon on it. "Thank ye. An' thank ye Zekiel fer me daggers an' the thowin' knives."

Oh, man. The kid was sauced already? "You're welcome, bud." I patted his head and took a drink from my own mug. "So, what does it say that you can do with your class?"

"I dunno." He shrugged happily.

I do. I heard the rumbling of stone grinding against stone in my head, and I felt the pressure of something in my right palm, the diamond wall around the flame pulsed as the Primordial Earth Elemental spoke to me, *Hello again, tiny Druid. I have seen you using the strength you borrowed from me. I have witnessed you be good to the dwellers of my domain and the children of my friend. Have the child call out to me from my back, and he will have another friend. Do this for me, and I will bless you further, as you have blessed him.*

QUEST ALERT!

***Earth's little buddy** – The Primordial Earth Elemental has asked you to encourage Fainnir to stand on the earth and call to him.*

Reward – Earth's strengthened blessing.

"Fainnir!" I called to the boy and stood. The alcohol in my system made me a little warm, but it was nowhere close to me being drunk. "Fainnir, come here, let's do something. I got some magic you can do."

The small Dwarf hopped from his chair and promptly pitched over on to his rump. A resounding cheer erupted from everyone in attendance. Hell, some of the Dwarves even clapped. Farnik hooted from a table that had been brought out that he and his clansmen sat at drinking merrily despite the earlier sadness. When Fainne forgives—his people take that shit to heart.

Fainnir stood up, raised his arms into the sky, and a louder cheer burst forth. He waddled unsteadily toward me, and Muu offered him an arm. Between the two of us, he finally stood in the center of the courtyard between the stage and the people here in support.

"What I want you to do is close your eyes, hold out your hand, and call out to the Primordial Earth Elemental," I explained.

"Ye wan' me ta do wha'?" he responded blearily.

"Hold your arm out, like this." I held my right hand up with my fingers spread slightly. He mimicked me unsteadily. "Now, say 'Primordial Earth, I ask of you, show me what I can do. Please'."

He looked at me oddly but closed his eyes, "Primo'dial Earth, I ask ye, what can ah do? Please."

Nothin' happened. "Try again, Fainnir! You got this!" I gave him nod with a grin I hoped looked supportive.

He hiccuped, looked around in consternation, then knelt on the ground, "Oi! Were ye nae listenin', lad? Could ye help me learn me powers 'ere, or no'?" Unsatisfied, he smacked the ground a couple times with his palm.

A rumbling began beneath him, and a pile of rubble and stone formed where he had smacked the ground. When it was almost as tall as Fainnir it stopped growing and began to take shape. The center—core, whatever—was thick and oddly shaped with thick legs and arms protruding from it. There was a mouth and two diamonds for eyes.

"Woooow," I whispered. I had notifications, but I ignored them.

Fainnir stood in front of it with wonder in his eyes. He no longer seemed intoxicated. "What's yer name then?"

The little figure looked at his summoner and clacked his jaws together, then spoke in a surprisingly deep voice, "You summoned me, master, and father saw that you were worthy of the title you bear. I came to serve and to teach you."

All the Dwarves in attendance were quiet. Some looked a bit apprehensive until Granite called, "Aye, that's all well and good, lad. But—do ye drink?!"

The other Dwarves toasted, bellowed laughter, and a chorus of "C'mere little stone" sounded throughout the place.

"I do not require sustenance," the creature said. "I can consume things, but I do not need it for survival."

"Why did your father send you?" I asked the little creature. "What are you? What do we call you?"

"He sent me to teach the little Mage," it looked at me, and I swore the thin little mouth of stones turned up into a smile. "Hello, friend of nature. Father wishes to let you know that your assistance was crucial in this meeting, and you will be rewarded appropriately. My name is hard to pronounce in this tongue, so the little Mage may name me. I am a lesser earth elemental. The smallest of my kind."

"I'll call ye..." Fainnir tapped his foot for a moment in thought. "Rocky? No. Stone? Ach, no. Oh, how about Earthbreaker? Nope, you're of the earth."

"How about Pebbles?" Muu offered.

I looked at him. "You sure that's not copyrighted? Or trademarked?"

"The fuck does that matter?" he threw his hands up and shouted at me.

"No reason." I looked anywhere else while smiling.

"Pebble is suitable," the elemental decided.

"I know this is probably going to be one of those times that someone says 'duh,' but what exactly does a Stone Mage do?" Muu asked.

"A Stone Mage's focus lies solely in the use of the element of earth and the union of that element with mana," Pebble explained. "After that union, their will becomes the will of the ground around them. This is not a new concept, as far as those who use elemental magic, but master will have a *much* stronger affinity for my element. He will have access to a stronger tier of earth magic than that of any normal Mage."

Muu and I both whistled. We looked over at Fainnir. He was staring at his hands now. Whispering something.

"You okay, bud?" Muu asked, concern passing over his features.

"Ye cannae hear tha' voice?" he whispered to us urgently. "It's like a cave in in me noggin. A rumble in me heart."

I smiled comfortingly, and Pebble stepped closer to him and patted his arm stiffly. "That is father. He speaks through the earth to you. It is not something that happens often. It means he likes you."

"Must mean he likes me too." I smiled and put a hand on Fainnir's shoulder. "He speaks to me as well."

"Father likes you greatly, Druid." Pebble looked at me oddly. "You have not accepted his reward yet, have you?"

"No, I haven't," I shook my head. The little elemental smiled his weird smile and patted my leg.

"Father says that you should." And he tottered back over to stand next to his master.

I looked at him a moment longer and opened the blinking notification.

QUEST COMPLETED!

Earth's little buddy – The Primordial Earth Elemental has asked you to encourage Fainnir to stand on the earth and call to him.

Reward – Earth's strengthened blessing.

About time, tiny Druid. You've been instrumental in a good deal since you have come to this realm. I sense that you have strengthened your bond with Flame and carry his pet. Allow me to gift you this. I like you, tiny Druid. Continue to be a diamond to others, and good luck on your endeavors.

"Wait," I blurted. I felt the immense pressure on my mind stop as it had begun to pull away. "Do you know where we may be able to find Dragons?"

I have no such beings in my realm, and my influence on the Prime is... limited. Perhaps you should find time to speak with your Mother. Good luck, tiny Druid.

Did he just... I swear, if an elemental equivalent to a god just "your mom-ed" me, I'm going to put my axe through something, I grumbled my thoughts as I tilted my head back to relax a bit.

Abilities unlocked!

Stone Weapon – Caster creates a weapon made completely of stone. Cost: 100 MP. Duration: Until dismissed or out of caster's hand for more than 1 minute. Cooldown: 10 seconds.

"Hot damn!" I clapped my hands.

"What's up?" Muu asked. "Get a new ability?"

"Yup!" I smiled at him. "But enough about me, what about you? I meant to ask you about what enchantments you wanted for your new weapons and gear when I saw you the other day, but then things happened while you were busy."

"It's cool, bud." Muu waved it all away. "Uh, if I'm being honest and not at all holding back, I'm going to need to be able to jump a lot better than what your boots could give me—no offense."

"None taken." I pulled a quill out. This one I had enchanted to never run out of ink while I had been training with Shellica. The design had been similar to the water basin I had made in the Fae Realm. I began to take down what he had said. "Continue."

"The jumping thing," He thought a moment. "Lighter armor—this stuff is badass, but it should be lighter and more durable. My short lance is fine. I'd like to keep it, but I did put an order in for one made similarly with a stronger metal. The enchantment on this new one, I'm thinking lightning. Anything it touches should get fried to a crisp." His face began to take on an almost-childlike expression. "And for the great lance that Granda is making me, I want to have it do ice damage, but I also want it to pierce things really really well. The piercing should be priority, though. Ah, boots—jumping because duh—and they will have spikes that will help me gr–"

"Woah!" I tapped him on the forehead with my finger to break him out of the rant. "You're like a kid making a Christmas list. Jeez. What about your shield? The blade and the shield need to be separate, so what do you want?"

"Sorry about that." He thought a moment then said, "The shield should be impact absorbing, and the blade... The blade should be poison damage."

"Okay." I finished writing. "I'll talk to Shellica and see what can be done."

"Thanks, man." Muu smiled, then grabbed my arm and sheepishly continued, "I do want to let you know, I appreciate you all taking such good care of me."

I smiled back at him. "Dude, you don't even have to say anything. Ever. You saved me from myself—you and Yoh—and I will never forget that. So, when I got you—I got you because I know that you will do the same."

He pulled me into a firm hug, then gave me a big kiss on the cheek, the cheeky fucker, and I watched him walk over to

Farnik's table, lift a mug, and shout, "To Fainne!" The Dwarves roared in delight and drinking ensued.

"He's a good lad," Shellica said from behind me. I didn't jump—I'd heard her walking toward me. "He gave you a list then?"

"He did." I handed it to her and she looked over it. "I'm certain those are all doable?"

She snorted. "I could do them hungover and half asleep."

"Keep drinking the way you have been, and that's what you'll do," I observed lightly. Her cheeks were rosy tinted, and her speech was getting a little slurred. "The rest of our items should be done tomorrow or the day after."

"Aye, and I'll do them all," she smiled sweetly, "or I won't, and I'll let Vilmas work on a few of the ones I think will help her gain some experience."

"I trust your judgment," I replied simply.

"Something wrong, lad?" Shellica walked over to stand beside me. Her steady gaze looked up at me.

"I caused a lot of unnecessary guilt in a lot of your people today." I closed my eyes and the scenes of Dwarves cutting their beards—their physical badge of pride and honor—off and putting it at Shellica's feet. "If I had kept my mouth shut... If I had kept my fucking mouth shut, none of this would have happened. I put everything at risk for Fainne to come here because of the turmoil I caused."

"You aren't wrong." She patted my arm. "I told ye to leave it be. Ye didn't."

I nodded, and I felt her strong grip on my elbow and looked down at her. Tears streamed from her cheeks.

"I'm glad ye didn't listen, ye thick-headed child." She pulled me close to her and hugged my waist. "If ye hadn't been clan to Mugfist already, I'd adopt ye as me own."

"That would send your son into a rage," I snorted.

"He wouldn't know." A look of longing and a frown crossed her face. "He left us shortly after you did. I reprimanded him too hard, but he had to learn. I awoke one morning to find that he had gone, claiming to know how best to walk his own Way."

"I'm sorry to hear that, Shellica," I tried to offer her what comfort I could.

I know that a mother's love is a crazy thing, and she was pretty fucking crazy already, but that she had torn into him for how he treated me for trying to learn my craft and then being an asshole about it was nice. It showed that she cared, not about just me but him, the racist piece of shit I thought him to be.

"I am too. Come. Let's enjoy the festivities."

After that, we drank and made merry. Everyone continued to drink and sing loudly.

At one point, Farnik—piss drunk and teetering dangerously—shouted, "Granite! Where are ye, ye legen'ary bashard? Come hel' me clean me face!"

Granite, also piss drunk, stood and walked from the table on stage, stopped at the edge, and looked down at the ground. He gave a little, "hep," as he fell down and promptly landed face first on the stone.

Bellows of laughter ensued as he dragged himself slowly to his feet and began to trudge toward Farnik. Farnik had climbed slowly up on the bench he'd sat on, and Granite held his hand out for something to use as a razor. Someone handed him an axe, and he began slowly shaving the leader of the Mugfist Clan.

They used the head of beer in a mug next to them as a cream and made a working shave of it.

I winced more than once as the axe drifted dangerously close to Farnik's nose.

When he was done, Granite handed the axe back, lifted Farnik by his hips up over his head, and shouted, "Look'it the wee baby!"

Farnik howled with laughter, and the entire place just unloaded whatever was in their mouths. Food. Alcohol. Vomit. A combination. It was a great time.

At some point that night, fifty-one Dwarves, a drunk Dragon Beast-kin, and a drunk as shit Kitsune stumbled into the Mugfist compound as quietly as bears trying to mimic loud-ass raccoons in a garbage can.

All I remember is making it to my bed, then passing out while trying not to vomit.

After a few hours—I hoped—I woke up to clanging and shouting.

I didn't need to dress, as I still wore my clothes, so I rushed toward the sound of a familiar voice.

"–THEN YOU WAKE ME UP AFTER I HAD BEEN UP DRINKING ALL GODDAMNED NIGHT WITH YOU. AND YOU." Muu advanced rapidly on a Dwarf with a shield and hand ax. "YOU DRANK MORE THAN ME, AND YOU EXPECT ME TO BELIEVE THAT YOU'RE READY FOR THIS SHIT?!"

I watched as Muu parried a chop at his chest with ease and jabbed forward with his spear. The Dwarf skirted the blow, then tried to back further away.

"OH, no you don't." Muu lunged forward, still shouting, "*YOU* wanted this, sister—I'm just here for a good fucking time!"

"Dude!" I roared, then winced at the volume. "Shut the fuck up!"

Both of them turned to see me standing there with my axe at the ready.

"Fuck you too!" Muu shrugged nonchalantly and brought his spear back into a ready position. "Besides, I just got a new ability that I can't WAIT to use."

"Can you at least wait to start shouting like that, you stupid bitch?" Yohsuke grumbled beside me. He was dressed in chef's attire already and was blearily looked around. "May as well go check on the food I put in to stew overnight. If you need help beating his ass, let me know."

"No help needed." I growled and stepped forward menacingly. My head felt thick, like my tongue. I needed to pee. And my head—oh fuck, my head. I didn't need this shit. "Back off, bud." I shooed the Dwarf away. "I think I'll have a go."

"See?" Muu motioned brightly. "It's working already!"

I stopped, clearly confused. "What is?"

"My ability—it's called 'Rant', and it lets me just rant at people and so long as I do, it makes people want to attack me. Pretty cool, huh?" Muu grinned. "There's a duration of ninety seconds, but the cooldown is two minutes, so it seems like I won't be able to use it too much."

"The fuck are you talking about?" I growled again. "I just wanna beat your ass for waking me up!"

"See, still in effect." His smug-looking face looked real punchable in that moment, and I lunged forward.

I ran headlong into a wall of Dwarves that I hadn't seen because I was so focused on Muu.

"Let it go, lad," one of them ordered. "He's go' the right of it. Yer brain is mead-addled and his Rant ability was more effective than he thought'."

"The hell are ye doin', lad?" I heard Farnik's voice, but I saw a shaved Dwarf with a few bits of gauze here and there dried to blood. "Why're ye tryin'ta beat yer friend?"

"Because he pissed me off and he doesn't understand that people are trying to sleep!" Then I felt the anger ebb from me and grinned. "So it was an ability. You asshole."

"Shut up, boy." Shellica yawned as she walked through the gates with Granda beside her. "Not his fault ye can't hold yer mead."

"I'll beat your ass too," I spat, my anger returning slightly. "What do you want?"

"Do ye nae want yer weapon, lad?" Granda asked with a small smile on his face.

That stopped me cold, and my anger fled. "Nope, I want that." I turned to the Dwarves holding me. "I'm cool guys. Lemme go."

They released me from their collective grasp and stepped aside quickly.

"So it were true," Granda spoke quietly as he stepped closer to Farnik. He put a hand on the shaven clan leader's face and closed his eyes. "Ye did a brave thing, lad. Yer a good Dwarf. I be honored to walk the Way with ye."

"Thank ye, Granda." Farnik clasped hands with the elder Dwarf, and they began to walk inside.

Those of us relevant to what happened next began to file after. The Dwarf who had been sparring with Muu had left with the ones that had tried to hold me back.

"Should someone go and wake the others?" Muu asked.

"I'll let them know," I said and used my telepathy earring to relay my message, *Hey guys, Granda and Shellica are here. Come to the meeting room.*

Five more minutes, dad, James grumbled into my mind.

I'll be there in a couple minutes, Jaken said. *I'll grab James too. I can still hear him snoring.*

"Thanks, bud. You coming, Bokaj?" I asked.

Tmont wouldn't give me my fucking bed last night after I came back from patrolling, so I'm there already. Bokaj yawned into all our heads.

I smiled at the thought of the great cat hogging his bed and not biting my tail.

What a dickbag. Yohsuke chuckled. *I'll bring you guys all some food here in a few. Start without me, and I'll catch up.*

We walked through the doors to the meeting room we usually used to find Bokaj sitting on the small couch wrapped in a blanket, and a pillow tossed to one side.

"Morning all," he greeted us blearily. "What's up?"

"We be letting ye pay fer yer toys, lad." Granda smiled and walked over to greet him kindly with a shake of the hand. "And ye can have 'em, I s'pose."

"Good enough for me, Granda. Good enough for me." Bokaj grinned and stretched as he stood up.

"Well, we not be standin' on ceremony," Granda looked at Jaken first. "Yer sword were a treat ta make, Jaken. Keeped it a wee secret. I gived it to Shelly-lass fer enchanting as ye asked, an' here be the result."

He pulled the sword from his inventory and sat it on the table. The blade was long and straight, easily a foot wide at the base by the hilt that led to a boxy tip. The blade was made of mithral, same as his other items, but this one's engravings were large and grand. They spanned the length of the entire item.

"The core was treated special to keep it from bein' too stiff. The cuttin' edges be sharper than a berserker' blade, bet yer life." Granda pointed to the hilt of the weapon. It was long—nearly two-feet long. "This was me grandchild's thinkin' an' I liked it. Yer gonna be able ta have more control with it bein' so long. Yer strong enough ta handle it."

"Thanks, Granda," Jaken whispered softly as he touched the weapon reverently.

"As per your request, the weapon has been made lighter, sharper, and is more durable than typical mithral," Shellica explained. "Take good care of it, lad."

"How much do I owe you both?" Jaken opened his inventory.

"Bah, ye put your coin purse away, boy," Granda ordered. "Ye can sort that after all is given."

He pulled the next items out of his inventory. A large sack of something metallic clanked on to the table. Then a sack that he sat down gingerly.

"Bokaj, I felt so bad the last time I saw ye here and nothin' fer ye that I had me kin makin' arrowheads fer ye." Granda pulled one out to show it to him. The metal was black with red veins throughout it. "These be Mage killers. Made from metal called Mage bane. It ignores a good amount of magical defenses. It were a good thing fer me people ta work on, as we don't get the call fer arrows as Dwarves—aye?"

Bokaj nodded to the elder Dwarf in appreciation and picked up an arrowhead to examine as Granda moved on.

"This was a joy ta make as it were quite the tinkerin' challenge for me ol' self." Granda grinned ear to ear as he pulled out a fist weapon that mimicked the one I had enchanted for James. The wrist portion was a little longer over the wrist and thicker as well.

"There be a mech'nism like the one in Muu-boy's shield." He nodded to Muu. "'Preciate tha', lad. Now, ye have yer standard punch plate, here. Then when ye squeeze this here lever, the blade appears."

He handed it to James to put on and try out. The lever was inside a gloved portion of the weapon that responded to the pressure of a closed fist, then a flick of the wrist.

"Call it Dragon's Tooth," Granda said proudly, but James and I snorted a bit. "Wha'?"

"That's similar to the weapon I enchanted for him." I offered.

"Well, that's the name!" Granda growled. We held our hands up to appease him. "Movin' on. Shelly-lass?"

"Aye, Granda." Shellica moved over to James. "This item is enchanted to assist you in beating through Mage defenses, specifically the bladed portion."

"Ooooh," James and I both whispered.

"Next, we have Zeke's weapon, right proud o' this'un, I am." Granda pulled a weapon from his inventory and sat it on the table with a grin.

It was a bo staff. Granted, it was a *metal* one. The metal had deep grooves that looked to be some kind of rune work that I wasn't familiar with. There was also a black leather grip wrapped around it and grafted under the metal somehow.

"This looks great, Granda—but are you sure this wasn't meant for James?" I asked skeptically.

Shellica and Granda howled in delight, and the old Dwarf began to dance.

"The hell is going on?" I picked the weapon up.

Magus Bane

+13 damage against magic, +10 damage to casters

Weapon has a one in five chance to drain mana from an injured caster to give to the wielder. A one in three chance to take mana from destroyed spells.

Engraved with the names of the Dwarves whose sorrows abounded, this weapon cuts through magic the same way the wielder cut through centuries of misunderstanding. Good job, lad.

Great Axe crafted by Grandmaster Smith Granda Stone Hammer, enchanted by Grandmaster Enchanter Shellica Light Hand.

"Just like I said, lass, I said 'nae even he can see the blade'." Granda continued his little dance.

"That you did, Granda." Shellica grinned. "That you did. I'll let Granda explain, lad. You can imagine why I gave this weapon to you enchanted as I did."

I nodded and looked to the elder Dwarf who had stopped dancing and looked around curiously.

"Farnik, lad—Could you get me a mug o' celebratory mead?" he asked.

"Aye, breakfast'll be here in a moment. I'll run and get the drink now." Farnik smiled.

As soon as Farnik had left the room, Granda's demeaner changed, and he began speaking in low tones, "I trust the lad, but this cannae leave this room, aye?" All of us nodded, and he continued, "The items Shelly-lass enchanted fer me worked so well that I could make this alloy for the first time. The lava did the trick. While I be beating on it, the metal were gray, but once I finished it and sharpened it—it turned invisible. Luckily, I were finished with it."

"There is that, thank you, Granda." I looked the weapon over again. "It's perfectly balanced, so how do I know which side is which?"

Granda leaned over me and pointed to a glyph that looked like the head of an axe with the blade on one side, and the other had a hammerhead.

"This is amazing." I pulled Granda close to my body and hugged him. "You too, Shellica, come here."

"I'll have ye enchanting things day and night if ye touch me, lad," she growled in warning.

"Well, I'll just go fuck myself then," I said pleasantly.

She eyed me oddly. "No! Not like that! Oh my Gods, ew."

"Just shut up, dude!" James grunted.

Muu was all but bouncing now. "My turn?"

"Aye, yer turn, lad." Granda smiled and began to pull three items from his inventory. One was fourteen feet long, slightly blue-ish but looked like crystal and looked like one of the lances old-timey knights would use. The second item was an almost exact replica of his original short spear

"This be yer lance that ye asked about," Granda explained. "Has ice elemental damage and is made out of pure crystal. The hand wrap is attuned to yer touch. Shelley?"

"If anyone touches it, they will likely lose their hand, as would anyone you might attack." Shellica then motioned to the next items. "I also enchanted these for you. The short spear is enchanted to do lightning damage and has a chance to paralyze your foe. The shield has poison damage and impact reduction."

She reached into her inventory and pulled out the same mildly-spiked armor that Muu had worn the night before and sat it on the table.

"Your armor has been lightened considerably, the defense is higher, and it is more resistant to magical damage," Shellica's explanation ended abruptly as Muu shrieked in joy. Then she continued, "The same for the leg armor. Your boots were harder. I had to choose between a set of jumping boots and sticky foot. So I chose the jumping enchantment, and I am giving you a ring that will allow you to stick to things for a short time at a small mana cost to you."

"That's fair." Muu nodded. "I really appreciate it, Shellica."

"I told you I liked you, lad." Shellica patted his cheek. "I also have two gifts for you. I heard from Granda that, like an idiot, you didn't request a helm be made for the armor you will wear. So, I commissioned one for you. I enchanted it to be lightweight, increase your accuracy, and protect you from blunt damage."

She pulled the item from her inventory and pressed it to his body. He equipped all of the armor and cut quite the intimidating sight. The helmet conformed to his draconic head and had a set of horns that came out from a little above and behind his visor that curved back like a Dragon's horns might.

"Very nicely done, Granda," Shellica nodded to the smith, and he smiled, "but if he is to gain the favor of a Dragon of his brood, wearing black scales could be offensive. This is my second gift."

She pulled a strange liquid from her pocket and sprinkled some on each piece of armor before muttering a phrase in dwarvish. There was a muted "pop" and Muu's armor was as green as his scales except for the horns and the shield.

"Woooooah," he whispered as he looked himself over. "Thank you, Shellica!"

"You're welcome, lad," She patted his cheek again. "I discussed the price with Granda, and after your discounts with each of the clans, we decided on a flat rate of one thousand gold pieces."

Muu whistled low, the rest of us nodded. That was a damned steep price. "Let's all put in one hundred and eighty. That makes it an even thousand and a forty gold tip for these two to give to anyone else who did good work for them," Bokaj explained.

All of us nodded and began to withdraw the funds. Granda and Shellica didn't try to argue—they knew better by now how stubborn we were about paying for quality work. I ponied up Yoh's share so he could pay me back later or not—the dude fed us all.

We all sat our coinage on the table in front of them and let them sort the division of it out.

"This item is also for Yohsuke." Shellica handed me a bracelet with a round shield engraved in it.

I put it on the table to give to him later, then she turned to look back at Muu.

"I have one last set of things to give you, Muu," Shellica said. She passed him an earring that looked similar to our telepathy earrings, but his was simply a stud. And also a small bundle. "That bundle is from Natholdi, Granite, and Fainnir. They asked that I tell you, 'If ye donnae come back alive, they'll kill ye. And that ye have to visit to tell Fainnir stories.'"

"Oh, for sure." Muu reached down and took Shellica into a hug that she returned. "Hell, I'll write it all down from the beginning while we're on the road. I'm sure he will have a lot of fun reading it. And if not? Well, I'll beat the hell out of him. With love."

Shellica laughed at that, and she turned her gaze to me. She walked over and wrapped her arms around me.

This doesn't feel too bad at all. All of my party members turned to look at Muu. On the ridge just above his ear hole was the stud. *I bet I look so fucking good in this shit.*

He turned and noticed everyone staring at him oddly. *What are they looking at me like that for?*

Out loud, "What?"

"You silly bastard," Yohsuke almost fell over from laughing so hard after he set our food down. "You're projecting your thoughts with the earring. We just heard all of that."

"Nope," Muu refused. He shook his head and waved his arms in front of him in denial. "Not possible."

"You thought, and I quote, 'I bet I look so fucking good in this shit.' Then you wondered why we were looking at you." Jaken grinned so wide the smile could've swallowed his face.

What the fuck? How did he know that? Muu thought quickly.

"Dude, stop using the earring!" James smacked Muu's shoulder. "It takes an act of will to use it."

"I'm not trying to!" He looked genuinely distressed. "I mean, I can feel it in my ear. Maybe, focusing on it being there is it?"

"Yeah, a new piercing will do that," Bokaj agreed. "You just have to learn to ignore it."

Ignore it, got it. Muu nodded his head as if he understood.

The rest of us either groaned or rolled our eyes. This was going to be an interesting time.

Chapter Sixteen

We spent the rest of the morning with the Mugfist Clan, eating and planning. So far as we were aware, we were going to be traveling south to try and find this giant snake, serpent—whatever it was—to see if we could find us a green Dragon or something akin to it that might be able to help.

Who knows, maybe we would find a minion of War! But still, I was hoping it was some kind of Dragon so we could get into the Hells.

Farnik and the rest of the clan walked us to the large gate to the city and wished us well on our travels.

"Get yerselves back here, lads," Farnik ordered. "Ye get strong and get our cousin outta the Hells."

We nodded, and then I felt a chill pass through me. I looked over to the shadowed area just outside line of sight of the door and saw a familiar figure. It was Maebe's shadow.

I walked over and greeted her, "Hey, Mae, how are things on your end?"

"They are as to be expected," she replied. "I am ready. Are you available to come to me when I arrive? If I recall, I may well come to the city that we transported you to."

"You guys care if we go get Maebe?" I asked the others. I got random stares of confusion and then remembered—I hadn't told them what I knew. I spent a few minutes filling them in so that they knew what was up.

"You should've told us you were in contact with her man," Bokaj glared at me. "Maybe she knows how to get into the Hells!"

"I told her what happened and she didn't say anything about it." I shrugged. "She may, but it's a stretch."

"So, she could potentially help us out?" Muu spoke before the others.

"Yeah, she's ridiculously powerful," Jaken explained for me. "I'm cool with it. It's not like we're going to fight a general right now, so we don't need the element of surprise, and having her with us could be a good thing."

"Secret weapon type shit." Bokaj nodded. "I'm down."

James gave a thumbs up.

"She lets us do the fighting," Yohsuke said. "We can't get stronger if she's doing any of the work."

"I'm sure she could agree to that," I said.

"I find that agreeable," Maebe said from beside me. "The dark one has his priorities right. I truly do like him."

"Yeah, he's a good dude." I smiled at my friend. "So, you think you'll be in Maven's Rock?"

"Yes, I have been in contact with my emissary there, and they have reported the city thinks well of me. That and the last tear in the veil went there from my throne room, so that should serve."

"Okay," I smiled at her. I could see that she was wearing something meant to be worn for travel, but the details here were a little fuzzy. "I can't wait to see you."

"Nor I you," she responded sweetly. "As soon as I drop this spell, I will pierce the veil and be there. I am uncertain as to how long it will take, but I will send to you when I arrive."

"See you soon." I waved as her shadow dissipated. Then seconds later as we were trying to decide what the best route would be to take, I saw the shadows burst into life in a way I hadn't seen before. Maebe's shadowed form was much more detailed now. I could make out more detail in the clothes she was wearing. A loose blouse, a skirt that fell to her mid-thigh and led to boots that looked painted on.

"Eroan assures me that I await you in Maven's Rock," Maebe purred, "but when you arrive here, be careful. The High Elves have sent delegates to meet me. We are just outside the tower. I am told you know of it."

"Okay, we'll be there in a minute." I turned to my friends and passed the message on. "Y'all ready?"

The others nodded and joined hands with me before I cast Teleport. After the unpleasant squeeze and the thud of landing feet, we opened our eyes at the gated entrance to Maven's Rock. Luckily, no one was paying attention to us as a procession of people made their way into the city. Farmers, merchants, and other travelers entered with no one to stop them. It was a nice change.

The city was much the same as we had left it, though the healing rain had definitely stopped. The people seemed more at ease now. They spoke to each other about current events. The news was as Maebe had said—the High Elves had come.

It took us about fifteen minutes to get from the gate to the square nearest the tower in the center of the city. The crowd there was huge. People of all shapes and sizes were interested in seeing the two biggest things that there were to be seen: their mysterious new benefactor and the Elves who had come to meet her.

We began to try and push our way through, but we didn't want to hurt anyone, so Muu made a suggestion.

How about we take the high road? Muu pointed up at the rooftops above us. It looked like it would be about fifteen feet from the ground to the top.

Without even giving us time to think, he jumped up—way up—and landed on top of the roof with a firm thud. No one seemed to give a shit at the moment, so he bent over the side and stuck his short spear down. Jaken gave Yohsuke a running boost up the side of the wall to grab the weapon above the spearhead, and Muu pulled him up.

Bokaj was quick enough to leap up off of Jaken's shoulders before Yohsuke was all the way up and pulled himself up. I stepped over to Jaken, clasped my fingers, and heaved him up the side of the wall so that Muu could help him up.

I cast Mental Message and sent it to Maebe, "Mae, we're here by the tower. If you look on top of a roof, you'll see the rest of the party. I haven't gone up yet. You okay?"

"A small show of power would be appreciated. I am slightly weakened by the spell I cast," she said back.

Hey, Maebe's weak from the crossing. She's asking that we put on a show. No casualties and only engage if someone starts some shit. Those last two were from me. I looked up to see Muu and Bokaj give me a thumbs up. *We don't want the citizens to think she's a monster or ruin her position here.*

I shapeshifted into my owl form and flapped my wings to gain altitude. As I breached the skies above the crowd, I saw Maebe standing next to Eroan, the Elf that had remained behind to govern this place and prepare it. In front of them was a group of five robed figures with three archers in the rear and a pair of what looked like some kind of Elven Fighters over to the right and partially in front of the robed ones. There didn't seem to be any open hostilities.

I flew lower, then dropped from the sky to land on Maebe's shoulder gently. Eroan twitched, but otherwise, his expression was unreadable.

"So the queen of the Unseelie has a pet owl with strange feathers?" one of the robed figures said as if to be teasing. His features were hidden beneath a hood, but his voice was cultured and what I could see of his clothing was that it was high quality.

"She has a champion," Eroan corrected in a clipped but courteous tone. "Master Erebos?"

I hopped off Maebe's shoulder and landed beside her on her right and assumed my true form. "Glad I could make the party," I bowed to Maebe at the waist slightly. "Forgive my tardiness, my Queen."

"Thank you, Zekiel." She smiled at me pleasantly and then looked to the High Elves before her. "You have come to speak—speak, or leave my city."

"We merely came to try and meet the savior that your 'emissaries' claim you to be, though imagine our surprise when this queen from the Fae is here with mere mortals," the lead figure spoke again. I still couldn't shake the feeling he was being demeaning. "I see a beautiful woman, for certain, but how can we be so sure that you are who you claim?"

"Do not feign needing to test the abilities of a queen, peasant," Eroan growled. "Can you not see the majesty that stands before you? Have you failed to note Her Majesty's Celestial body? The living incarnation of night and winter? I give you my word that she is who she claims. Do you swear that you are here under the guise you claim?"

"I find her body *very* Celestial," his smug voice slimed its way to us, "and I swear nothing to rabble."

Game on, boys. It's showtime, I growled to the others.

I whipped Magus Bane off the rack on my back and threw it forward, flying at the front figure who put a hand up almost lazily. A large opaque-blue dome appeared around all of them, and my new great axe smashed into the shield with a sickening crack. The shield cracked, and the caster's body went rigid.

"You *dare* attack me, dog?" he spat vehemently. "It seems that the Fae Realm has let their pets run rampant far too long."

The two who looked like Fighters brought out astral adaptors, and the other robed figures took up a casting stance, like they were about to start fencing. The archers had arrows nocked and trained on me instantly.

"One guy versus all of you?" I feigned fear. "How could I *ever* hope to win?"

"You shouldn't, dog," one of the robes in the middle boasted. "We are the guard of a lord. We would never fall to some disgusting creature such as yourself."

"Well, that's unfortunate," James said behind them. He thrust the blade of his newest weapon into the barrier, and it cracked more.

I brought my axe back and activated Cleave as I swung it forward again. A single arrow pierced the top and landed between the leader's legs, shattering the barrier completely.

"Probably not smart," Bokaj called. I risked a glance toward the rooftop. Yohsuke was there beside Bokaj, but Jaken was gone, and so was Muu. "You move again, and the next one goes through your head.

I heard metal armor behind me and, "Hello, Jaken," from Maebe, letting me know who was there.

I heard a whistle and looked up in time to see a blur of green falling from the sky toward the leader of the High Elves.

"Fuck," I cursed as I tossed my axe back over my shoulder and tackled the fucker to the ground.

A second later, a cacophonous *boom* and a shower of dirt, gravel, and stone pelted us. As I shoved the person away from me, his hood fell, and I could see fair Elven features, blonde hair, and blue eyes. His narrow features went from shocked to furious as he realized what had happened.

I stood and saw Muu standing in a crater about a foot and a half deep and three feet wide with a big, shit-eating grin on his face.

"You're an asshole," I commented.

"Not as big a one as he is." Muu pointed at the exposed Elf. "Ugly bastard too. Wish you would have let me land on him."

"You would do well to mind your tongue, *experiment*," one of the Fighters hissed as he helped the other stand again. "Your betters will never forget the debt you owe us for freeing your kind. Why you weren't slaughtered instead, I will never understand."

"Can I kill him?" Muu asked lightly.

"Hold your hand, vassal," Maebe said as she walked by him slowly. She looked at the guests. "You have seen the people I have chosen to ally myself with. I am fine here, and I will not bear your insults again. Leave here, or I shall vent my displeasure to your ruler. Believe me when I say that she is *well acquainted* with what I am capable of."

The lead Elf's eyes bulged a bit before he held a hand up to the others. They turned and began to walk away. As they were leaving, one of the Fighters made a point to bump into Bokaj as he was walking toward us.

When they collided, Bokaj grunted, "Oh shit! I am so sorry." His hands were all over the guy as if he were looking for injury. "Are you okay? You're alright? Okay? Man, I am such a schmuck. Sorry again, man. I hope you have a nice day. Sorry about the whole almost having to kill you thing. You work out?"

By the last question and the bicep fondling, the other man shoved my friend away rudely. "Get away from me."

"Bye!" I watched as my friend waved at them all until they were gone, then Bokaj turned around with a huge grin on his face.

Sensing that bloodshed had been avoided, the crowd began to lose interest and started to disperse. Some of them eyed us curiously, attempting to be stealthy about it, but when we didn't seem to return their interest, they left too.

When we were in the clear, Eroan had us follow him into a squat home opposite the square of the tower. The outside was bright yellow and inside the walls were a simple blue. The place was scarcely decorated but functional.

"Hardly fit for a queen, your Majesty, but this is all I have unless you wish to have use of the tower." Eroan spoke from a bow.

"Neither," Maebe spoke dismissively. "I will be leaving soon. Zekiel, tell me, who is the green one?"

"This is Muu, he's like a brother to me." I brought him over and introduced them properly. "Muu Ankiman, this is Queen Maebe, ruler of the Unseelie Fae and heir to the darkness and winter."

"Oh, that last one was a new title." Maebe smiled as she stepped forward. "Thank you, I shall have to use that." She looked Muu over slowly. "Tell me, second brother of my only friend, where have you been?"

"I got here after they had come back to Sunrise," Muu explained simply. He looked back at her and smiled. "Zeke has told me about you. You seem really cool. It's nice to meet you. Uh, my lady."

Maebe quirked her lip up a bit and turned to the others. "I heard of your... set back. I will endeavor to help you how best I can. Thank you for agreeing to allow me to accompany you."

"No problem!" Bokaj forced a smile at her, then looked at Yohsuke. "Hey, man, I got you a present."

"What's up, man?" Yohsuke walked over to Bokaj, and the Ranger grinned wildly.

"I kind of stole this for you." He held out an item to Yohsuke, who took it with uncertainty on his face. As soon as he touched it, he pulled Bokaj into a fierce hug, his new shield bracelet tinkling as his hand moved.

Y'all thought I forgot, huh? Yeah, I see you. I can learn. Sometimes.

"You sly motherfucker!" I looked as Yohsuke held the item out for us to see, and it was an item similar to one he used every time we fought—an astral adapter. This one was pure white with no embellishments or trinkets. A warrior's weapon if anything. Possibly part of their uniform.

"What can it do?" Muu asked curiously.

"It's just a basic one, but it's so much stronger than the basic one I have now," Yohsuke explained. "This one is a plus nine where the other one is a plus three."

"Awesome, man." I clapped Bokaj on the shoulder. "That was some smooth distraction work there."

He grinned at me then nodded to Maebe and used his earring to speak to me, *Maybe you should go and speak to her alone for a minute? She's been eyeing you something fierce. Ask about the Hells.*

I will. Thanks, brother. And again, good shit. I patted his shoulder again.

I stepped over to Maebe and gently took her hand and nodded toward a door. She nodded back, and we walked through it together. The door led to what could have been the dining room at one point in time. I could see the entryway to the kitchen and the room was large enough to hold a full-size table with at least eight chairs.

As soon as we were alone, she pulled me toward her and hugged me tightly. Her embrace was a little cool against my skin, but it felt so nice. Her long, pointed ear tickled my cheek slightly. I held her out from me to get a better look at her.

Her build was as it had been last time I saw her, curvaceous even in her black travel clothes. The skirt was tight, and the blouse was loose. Her skin, dark as the night sky with thousands of white pinpricks that looked like the stars in the heavens. Her long, thin fingers against my arm squeezed gently, and I looked up to see her smile radiantly. Her perfect white teeth flashed, and her dainty nose crinkled a little. But her eyes were so captivating. They were a green so deep that it could've been a sea of four-leaf clovers for all I knew.

She brushed her black hair with multi-colored highlights back behind her right ear and looked at me funny. "You are staring so intently, Zeke. You never looked at me like this before."

"I missed you," I offered with a small smile in return. Her long ears came away from her face at an angle tilted only slightly back toward the rear of her head. It made holding her hair easy, and the gold, silver, and platinum earrings that she wore in them looked so good against her skin tone.

"I feel the same of you." She pulled herself back into me, and I hugged her back. I let my head rest on top of hers and took in her scent. She smelled of lilac and like a cold winter morning after a snowfall. I felt her hands against my back, and it was comforting. I kissed the top of her head and felt her tense a bit.

"I'm sorry, Mae," I said and let go. "I was a little overwhelmed."

She smiled as she looked up at me, our faces only four or five inches apart. "It was not unpleasant. Just new. No one has done that to me before."

"I'll run new things by you before I do them." I took my hand and cupped her cheek. Her jaw fit in my palm perfectly as she gazed up at me.

"Thank you for coming so quickly." She rubbed her cheek against my hand before stepping away. "I will be back to my full strength soon. If you want to leave now, we can."

"Do you have a mount?" I wondered, then remembered, "Also, you wouldn't happen to know of a way into the Hells would you?"

"I have something I can summon for transport, yes," Maebe answered, then frowned. "No. I used the one favor I had to summon that demon for Yohsuke. I am sorry."

I couldn't hide the disappointment I felt stirring in my heart. So the Dragon it was. Or a serpent. Whichever it truly fucking was. Damn it.

"And Zeke?"

I looked over at her. She began to levitate until she was slightly taller than me. She put a delicately shaped hand on each side of my face and then kissed the top of my head. It felt odd but nice. I laughed a little bit, and she grasped my hand as we walked out together.

The others watched us rejoin them in the large room they were in.

Are they dating? Muu asked to no one in particular.

Nah, he's her friend, Jaken supplied. *Though, that could change soon if he keeps playing his cards right.*

You guys, I don't even know if she's interested in that. I rolled my eyes.

It was Yohsuke who came across with the heavy hitter, *You, me, Jaken, James—all of us—could die here, man. If you think having this time with her would make it just a little more bearable? I say go for it. I know where my heart is, and I'm fighting to get back to her. And I know you have your boy to think about, so I'm not worried.*

I looked at him stunned; the others nodded in agreement, and Jaken even threw me a sly wink and a thumb up.

Y'all are crazy, man. Bokaj shook his head. *I'm team Vrawn. She's the girl he needs. Big, burly, and takes what she wants. Bubba Vrawn. Any luck on the Hells?*

"Oh, that's fucked up, man," I laughed so hard that I had to let Maebe's hand go, "and no. No luck."

"What is it that is 'fucked up'?" Maebe asked curiously.

Muu eyed me for a moment, then spoke up, "Not too much. Just trying to give Zeke some encouragement to pursue a... new interest."

I'm going to murder you, you little bastard. I glared at him, and it only made him laugh.

"What is this new interest?" Maebe's hand found mine again, and my anger abated slightly.

"We can talk about it later." She looked uncertain. "I give you my word."

I felt that all too familiar weight settle on my chest.

WARNING!

You have given your word to a denizen of the Fae Realm. While you are not within the realm, the beings of that plane of existence carry with them a true power to hold others to their oaths. If you break your word, the consequences could be dire.

I hadn't planned on breaking my word, but *fuck*.

"Very well then." She smiled reassuringly at me. "Eroan, we are leaving now. You know what you must do—do it. Everyone? Are we ready? Do we need anything?"

"Nope, I'm good," I said. "What is he supposed to do?"

Maebe blinked and answered, "He is to ensure that the people here are taken care of as well as to ensure that the High Elves do not return without my knowledge."

Cool. That was a good idea.

Muu shook his head, and James said, "Let's get it."

The others agreed, and we were on our way. Maebe used her glamour to hide, make herself look like a normal woman to others, but with my True Sight, I saw right through it. The entire time we walked through the city, she was watching those we passed. Her curiosity of the Prime Realm was so cute and mildly terrifying due to the fact that she could easily lay waste to this entire place.

"Wait, what is that?" she asked at one point as we passed a bakery. I saw her point to a small tray with what looked like a cookie.

"It's a cookie, I think," Yohsuke answered before I could. "Seems kind of plain, but the people here did just get shit under control."

"What is a cookie?" Maebe looked at it more closely. The baker eyed us suspiciously.

I tossed the man a silver coin, and he held up five fingers. I took the hint and grabbed five of them from the plate. I handed one to Maebe, tossed one to Yoh and asked if anyone else wanted one. Jaken nodded, and so did Muu.

I popped the item into my mouth and began chewing. It was sweet and tasted a little nutty, but I couldn't place the flavor entirely. As I ate mine, I watched Maebe's face light up. This regal woman, whose very word could begin a war that would shake an entire world, was finding such pure joy in a cookie.

"I could make a better one," Yohsuke grunted, "but it's okay."

"You can make these?!" Maebe asked in delight. Yoh nodded and smirked at her reaction.

After another twenty minutes of walking through crowds and crowded areas of the city, we exited the southern gate and summoned our mounts.

Thor was happy to see me, and the others seemed to be in good spirits.

Maebe closed her eyes for a moment and flexed her hand in front of her. "Reymire, come to me."

The shadow beneath her grew larger and larger until it was the size of Thor. Then it stood and began to crawl out of the ground. The beast who came looked like a pitch black lion. The mane shook out easily, and it observed its surroundings before lovingly headbutting Maebe on the shoulder.

Maebe mounted the lion with ease, and we set out on our way. We rode for a few hours before the light began to fade and we decided to set up camp. We all did our part, and even Maebe walked the campground in a wide arc, a trail of shadow falling behind her on the ground. Once the circle was complete, a dome of shadows closed around us, and I had to admit—it felt weird.

"What was that you just did?" I asked as she sat next to me.

"That is a barrier spell," Maebe explained. "It will keep creatures and anything weaker than me from spotting us and attacking us in our sleep. There will be no need for a watch."

"Won't people see it?" Muu asked. "Forgive me, I don't know much about magic."

"That is alright." Her genuine smile seemed to put Muu at ease. "The spell is simple. Anything or anyone that looks at the barrier directly will simply gloss over it. If something plans to walk through it, they will experience a sense of dread twenty-five feet away from it and will avoid the area. As we were inside the spell area when it was cast, we can come and go as necessary for unpleasant business. Just be aware that once you leave the area—you are exposed."

"Good to know," Jaken said as he prepared to go outside of the circle.

"Hey, Muu, you gonna open that bundle or what?" Bokaj asked loudly. "Come on over here and show us what you got!"

He stood up and walked over to the others, and as I stood to do the same, Bokaj gave me a thumb up and another wink with an exaggerated eyebrow waggle.

These nosey motherfuckers, I thought to myself. *I kind of preferred the surly Ranger to this one.*

"While we have a moment, you had something you were going to talk to me about earlier?" Maebe sealed my fate.

"Yeah," I said slowly. Partially trying to rid myself of the sudden dread I felt and partially to try and find the right words to convey how I was feeling.

"You can speak plainly with me," Maebe reassured me. She put a hand on my knee to comfort me, and I put my hand on hers.

"I told you I missed you," I began. She nodded, and I continued, "Well, in that time that we had together in your realm, I began to develop feelings that I hadn't expected. Feelings that, as time went on here, began to develop into an interest. There is a saying where I'm from, 'absence makes the heart grow fonder'. That was the case for me."

She seemed slightly confused but tried to comprehend the idea. "So, you are saying that while you and I were separated, your thoughts and emotions toward me deepened?"

"Yes." I nodded, probably a little too enthusiastically. "That's right! And seeing you again, being here with you now, it's even more on the forefront of my mind of how much I like you."

"I like you too." She smiled. "That is a new thought for me. I am familiar, in an academic sense, to this feeling, and I am capable of feeling attraction to things. I find the way I feel with you pleasing, and something I would like more of, I think."

"I understand." I pointed toward my friends. "I've been exceptionally lucky to be surrounded by people I can trust. Friends. Brothers. Men willing to fight and die for me because they have no doubts I would do the same. I sometimes forget that I'm your first friend."

"I am glad of that, though," Maebe commented. I looked at her a moment so that she might elaborate. "You have been very understanding of my role to my people. The part that I play. You have made no plays at power. You ask for nothing but my company and that I be myself. Whoever that may be. Your presence has given me things to ponder, things to learn of myself and those around me. It has given me you."

"I'm happy I can do that for you." I was short on words otherwise, but I had to be honest with her. "I'm worried that with how I feel, that I might hurt our friendship—and that's not something I want to do."

"How would you being fonder of me jeopardize our friendship?" She cocked her head slightly to the left. "That seems like a fruitless thing to concern yourself with."

I bit my lip and nodded—she wasn't wrong.

"I guess I should be a little more courageous and just come out with it, huh?" I observed aloud. I looked at Maebe. "I want more. More than just your friendship." I held my hands out to allay her reaction. "I don't want more power. I don't want to use you. Hell, I really only want to grow closer with you."

"So you wish that we become closer." Her demeanor changed slightly. Her back was a little more rigid, her shoulders square, and her chin a little higher. "You do not wish for power. You do not wish to use me? You do not seek my throne or to allay my foothold in this realm?"

"I won't stop you unless you or your people harm the innocent," I told her truthfully.

"I would expect nothing less." Maebe smiled slightly. She relaxed a little. "What is it that you would have of me?"

"Honestly?" She nodded quietly. "Just you."

"I do not understand."

"Do your people date each other?" I asked softly.

"We predate many generations of sentient beings in this realm," she informed me. "I fail to see how my age has anything to do with this conversation."

"No, no," I laughed, "do your people court each other? Take on relationships with another of a more... relationship minded focus?"

"He wants to ask you to be his girlfriend!" Muu shouted.

"I'm going to *murder you*," I roared and stood.

"Zeke," I felt a hand on my arm, but the grip was ridiculously strong for the small hand grabbing me. One thing about the Fae—Maebe in particular—is that they are inhumanely strong. I looked back, and she pulled me down next to her. "Are you asking for me to be your lover?"

I blushed fiercely, and for the third time that day, I seriously thought about testing if the Gods could bring us back with Muu as my test dummy.

"It's a lot deeper than that for me, but in a sense—yes," I admitted. "I would like that deeper relationship with you."

She thought for a moment quietly. Not looking at me or anyone else in particular then said softly, "I must think on this."

She rose from her seated position and left the safety of the shadow dome and walked out of sight.

I... wasn't sure what I had expected. Nothing? I hadn't even pictured this conversation happening in the first place, but now that it had, I felt drained.

"That wasn't a no," James offered with an attempted reassuring smile.

"Let's just eat and get some rest," I said tiredly. "I don't much feel like sparring suddenly."

The others seemed to understand, and I did my best to ignore the sympathetic looks they slid my way occasionally as I ate my dinner of fire roasted chicken and potatoes in silence.

I let Kayda out of the collar and summoned Coal so the two could spend time in the fresh air. I stipulated very sternly that Coal was not to leave the safety of the shadow dome unless I was with him. He seemed to understand. Kayda went off to hunt for the two of them after promising to stay close. He dug himself a hole in the coarse ground so that nothing would catch fire and then curled up.

I curled up a bit later in my sleeping bag with Coal at my back a foot away but carefully not touching me and tried to put the thoughts of my bumbling earlier out of my mind.

I must have dozed off after a while because I felt motion next to me. I came to quickly with my claws ready to gouge the hell out of some eyes when I felt a cool touch on my face and saw Maebe.

"Come with me," she whispered quietly.

I checked the others over as I got up. Everyone was in a state of their individual rest. Coal raised his head and blinked at me bleary-eyed then laid back down. Kayda watched us leave and then settled beside her adopted brother.

We walked through the dark plains for ten minutes and mounted a hill to sit beside each other. We sat there for some time before I had to break the silence.

"Mae..." She reached out and took my hand.

"Do not apologize," she said softly. "It has been some time since I took a lover. Even longer since I allowed myself to believe it was for anything other than political gain or power."

She leaned into me, and I wrapped my arm around her on instinct. She tilted her head up and looked at me, the stars above us reflecting in her eyes.

As I looked down at her, she smiled. "I choose to trust you."

She raised her chin slightly to me, and I leaned down until just before my muzzle met her lips—I quickly shifted shape into my human form—and kissed her softly. Her lips were soft and cool, like a pillow freshly turned. I loved it.

Her hand touched my chin as she explored my lips with her own. When we came out of it breathless and giddy, she sighed.

"I trust you too," I whispered into the top of her head. We laid back against the side of the hill and watched the stars. Both the ones in the sky and the ones on each other. We stayed there for some time simply enjoying each other's company.

Chapter Seventeen

Mae and I walked back to camp hand in hand. The night was still relatively young, and I was starting to get tired. Everyone was still asleep when we walked through the dome. Kayda slumbered closer to my sleeping gear and Coal.

I ducked into my sleeping bag and undid the toggles that kept it closed and opened it for Maebe to slide in next to me. As she did so, she looked at me differently.

"Yes?" I asked.

"This is my first time seeing this human form," she explained. "The features are about the same, but there are differences. That, and before, I didn't take stock of you as a potential match." She must have seen my face fall or something because she added, "Not that you are not attractive to me."

I leaned down and pulled her into my arms easily. "Thank you." I kissed her once more on the top of the head. Then we settled in for the night.

I fell asleep with Mae's hands around me and slept probably the best I've slept since I had come to this world.

... Eke's sleeping with her. Is this common? Did they make up? What's going on? I heard Muu project. He hadn't mastered leaving anyone out of messages yet.

I didn't see them come in, but it seems new to me, Jaken answered.

I smiled and felt Mae brush her hand over my hip. She knew I was awake.

"She and I are fine," I said aloud. "This isn't the first time that we have shared a bed, but it is as an item."

"Congratulations, you two." Yohsuke stepped over to us. "Yo, you dressed?"

I looked down, and my shirt was off somehow, "Yeah man, I have my pants on."

"Cool. Breakfast is on, be done in a bit." He smiled.

"Anyone wanna spar?" James asked.

Muu stood. "I'm game."

The two of them went out of the dome to get a morning workout in, and I stayed where I was. Maebe was warm against me, and I dreaded having to lose that so soon.

"I must ask you, Zeke," Maebe spoke after a moment. I looked down at her expectantly. "Have you had any other lovers while here? Any of these 'girlfriends'?"

"No." I shook my head. "The remotely closest I have come is to a woman named Vrawn, and she came on to me."

"How so?" She frowned in thought.

"She kissed me on the cheek, then kissed me fully," I explained. "She works in a bathhouse as a worker? Uhm... fuck it. She helps wash patrons, and if they are interested, she will sleep with them."

"And you didn't partake?" She looked at me oddly when I shook my head no. "Are you uninterested in women? Is there a lack of ability? Are you shy?"

I had one of the "excuse me" moments—you know—where you blink a moment and look at the person.

"Most healthy men would not refuse a woman who is willing to alleviate their stresses for coin." She frowned deeper. "I do not mean to be rude, but this is a common practice even in my culture."

"Where I'm from, it's frowned upon, but I realize that as long as everyone is a willing participant of age—it's their choice." I shrugged. I suddenly felt the urge to not be laying there, but I continued, "While I found Vrawn attractive in her own right, I didn't want that. But I made sure that she was well compensated for her time, and she was grateful. We're even friends now. The fact that I understood what she did and still treated her with dignity was something that I think she liked."

"You paid her for her time but didn't take the service?" Her eyebrows raised slightly. "Okay. I believe you."

I nodded once, and as I was beginning to try and sit up, I felt a hand on my thigh and stiffened.

"Are you alarmed?" She tilted her head to the side with a smile. "I have to make sure what I now claim as mine works."

"It works," I said softly. I knew my friends could probably hear our soft speaking, but the embarrassment of the questions and the curiosity was a little too much. "I cannot believe this is happening, but believe me, it works."

"Ah." Mae nodded. "You are shy, then. This is okay. I will tend to you, Zeke."

Ooooooookay. Time to get up. Oh god. I kissed her forehead, and her smile deepened.

She grabbed my thigh again. "Wait." She looked toward my friends. "I do not do this often, so I will make this as painless as possible."

I saw her eyes flare pitch black and a dark sphere burst around us.

"What did you just do?!" I asked.

"This is a seclusion spell that will not last long," she explained. "I wanted to offer you an apology. I did not mean to cause you distress, nor did I mean to imply that you were broken. You are so strange to me. Your ways are so different. I wanted to let you know that I will take care of you."

I laughed a little. "It's okay. I forgive you, and I mean it, things work down there." I blushed a bit more.

"I cannot wait to see," she pulled me closer to her and held my cheek before kissing me deeply.

The spell dissipated and my friends were around us ready for a brawl.

"You didn't answer our telepathic calls, and now, here you are again." Jaken blinked. "You okay?"

"Don't worry, guys." I waved them away. "We're fine. Thank you."

They looked us over for a moment longer before going back about their business.

"Have you learned any of the Celestial language while you have been here?" Maebe asked me.

"I've tried to look over it, but it's a little harder for me to understand," I admitted.

"If you are amenable, I will be happy to teach you," she suggested. "We can study it in the morning and at night after your sparring sessions."

"Mandated sparring?" I teased. "Cool."

She blinked at me once. "Yes. I can summon beasts of shadow and ice that you and your friends can kill with little consequence."

"Our friends," I corrected.

"Do you think they will so readily accept me?" she wondered.

"I think so," I answered honestly. "Truthfully? They kind of already have."

"I see." She nodded. "We will study now."

We spent until breakfast reading through the book that I had. She taught me the proper syllables for different characters and how to pronounce them correctly.

"There is a pause before the next portion, here—if you run it together it becomes incorrect and highly rude," Maebe explained. "You're essentially calling them a heifer."

I groaned, and we continued. I pulled out the coal etching of the symbol that had been drawn by the Celestial in Sunrise.

"Do you know what this says?" I asked, and she took it.

"It is not so much a word as it is a phrase." She blinked, then turned it upside down. "'The way is barred to the unworthy.' I believe it would also count as a familial crest to certain people. Who, I don't know."

Did that mean that we were unworthy? Or that anyone who wasn't them was. I told the others, and it gave them a little to think on.

Breakfast of eggs, toast, and some lightly fried tomato was served, and we all ate heartily. Watching Maebe devour her food and request more was hilarious to me for some reason. She always came off as so sophisticated at times, but she was so surprised that Yohsuke was such a good cook that she wolfed down twice what we ate.

So not the picture of royalty that I had colored with purple crayons as a kid.

Once we had eaten, we cleaned up the camp and continued on our way.

Over the next few days, we rode through small villages and more plain lands. We saw some strange looking birds that reminded me of emus with red and green feathers. They kept their distance, even after I tried calling to them. My guess was that they weren't social to humans—even Druids.

Finally, we entered a town with an inn that seemed nice enough for us to stay in for the night. Before we had entered and well outside visual range for them, I shifted into my human form. Couldn't freak them out too bad, and I didn't need someone gunning for my tails, right? The others took rooms together, Jaken and Muu, James and Yohsuke, and Bokaj was the odd man out. He sighed and began to mutter about missing his best friend, and I understood.

We had dinner there and set up a meeting with local merchants in the morning to resupply. Well—less a meeting and more let us buy your shit in bulk. We mainly just wanted fresh produce like veggies and whatever fruits they had, but they were cool with it.

The food was pleasant enough, and the alcohol was appreciated as the soft beds would be. As we all retired for the evening, the others before us, I noted some strange stares from the people who saw us. Some were curious, like the children who played around us. The adults were wary of us, but that we had a Paladin of Radiance among us went a long way toward them being cool with us. Other than that, I didn't think much of it.

The room we were staying in had a larger, full-size bed. The mattress was stuffed to the brim with straw, and it was very soft.

As Mae and I prepared for bed, I had to ask, "So, what is courtship or this type of relationship like for you? In your culture? What kind of relationships have you had before? What do you like or prefer?"

She looked at me curiously before answering, "As I touched on earlier, many relationships among the Fae are for power and rarely genuine feeling, but it does happen. That is with most of my kind. I, as a monarch, am expected to play the political games and maneuvering necessary to strengthen my hold over my realm and secure my power and position. I have played those games before, but they never lasted long. I always found the plotting and the betrayal—attempts at betrayal—to be boring. I have taken some lovers out of boredom or to try something different, but no more than would be casual. I prefer to be a little more aggressive than I have been, and I like you. Do those answers suffice?"

"More aggressive?" I looked at her uncertainly.

Look, I'm not clueless—I know that there are people out there capable of being more aggressive and that this includes women, but this whole conversation took place with a Fae Queen who predates me by *hundreds* of years. Her idea of aggressive could mean a knock-down-drag-out brawl where the winner got their way for all I knew. All that mattered at that moment to me was that I liked her, and I was trying to get to know her. Got the idea? Cool.

"Yes, I also told you that I was unfamiliar with your culture and how you would react to some of my ways." She thought for a moment before continuing, "I suppose this means that you and I should discuss what we are comfortable with. I must admit, this is my first relationship in this manner."

"Okay, how about this," I stood and began to pace slowly. "If either one of us is uncomfortable with something, we can just say, 'butterscotch'."

"Why would we say this word? Is it special?" She sat on the bed where I had been. "Is it an activation word for a spell?"

I shook my head with a smile. "No, dear. It's a safe word. It's a word that only you and I know, and when one of us says it, the other stops what they are doing."

"This word, what significance does it have to your people?" she asked curiously.

"None." I grinned stupidly. "It's just a type of pudding and a word that no one might expect to hear in bed unless they need something to stop. Pudding is a sweet snack where I'm from."

She nodded, and the way she came at me was regal, beautiful, and feral all at once. I had no need of a safe word then.

* * *

I woke in the morning—sore—but refreshed. It was nice.

Maebe lay next to me. "Good morning, pudding," she purred.

I did not tell her to call me that. She did that, and I was as pleasantly surprised as you are. Let me enjoy my life, thank *you*.

"Good morning." I pressed my lips to her forehead. "Do you know what time it is?"

"The sun has not breached the horizon yet," she informed me.

"How do you know that?"

"I am the heir of winter and darkness," she teased me. "The night is my domain."

I trusted her judgment in this. She moved her hips just enough to get my attention. "Yes?"

"I know that we must resupply," her eyes hooded slightly, "but there are things we must discuss."

"What is that?"

"How is it that these 'girlfriends' of your world are treated?" She rubbed her index finger along the back of my hand.

"It depends on the relationship and the people involved," I admitted. "I've had relationships in the past that were great. I've had some that weren't. I've been the bad guy in a few as well. I've made stupid, stupid mistakes that no one should make, but they happen. I can continue beating myself up for them, or I can move on and try to do better."

"And this redemption you seek, it is with me?"

"If you would like it to be," I spoke honestly. I hadn't thought about it that way. "I don't think I see this as a need to redeem myself. I'm not perfect. I've learned things as I've grown older. I don't want to be redeemed—I want to move on."

"That was very wisely put," Maebe observed.

Suddenly, a notification popped into my vision.

CONGRATULATIONS!

You have proven that you aren't just a rolling ball of death with an axe by stating—and believing—something truly wise!

Reward: +1 wisdom.

"I guess the universe thought so too." That was super nice of them. Of course, the rolling ball comment had been a low blow, man. Shit. "Think we should go and check on the others?"

Her ears twitched for a second. "They still slumber. We have time. What is it you expect of me?"

I blinked. I hadn't expected that question, though to be honest, I hadn't even thought we would be here.

"All I want is for you to be yourself with me," I touched her shoulder lightly, "to truly be who you are and to do what you like with me. I want you to be happy, to enjoy yourself. But most of all, I want you to be honest. If you don't want this—at any time—tell me. Don't suffer because you worry about losing my friendship. It would take some serious shit to do that."

She thought a moment that seemed to stretch forever. Her angular features were lost in the introspection, and thoughtful expressions covered on her face. Finally, she nodded silently.

"Mae, I need your word on that," I spoke softly.

She looked at me sadly. "This means that much to you?"

I nodded back, and she sighed. "I, Maebe, do hereby swear to you that I will strive to enjoy myself in this relationship with you, be myself so long as we both are comfortable, and if ever I should not want this, I will tell you."

I glanced at the notification solidifying her word to me and dismissed it.

"Thank you," I whispered against her hair.

We got up after that, dressed and prowled downstairs in hopes of food. The breakfast they served us was fresh. It wasn't long before we were joined by our friends, and then we resupplied. The townsfolk still stared at us as we left, but I like to think it was maybe because even as she tried to be a normal-looking woman—Maebe was still beautiful.

We traveled with light conversation that day. Muu spoke to Jaken about different fighting maneuvers they could try. And then Bokaj. Finally, he turned his sights on Maebe.

"Forgive me, your Majesty," he began. "I heard you have a pet Dragon?"

"He is more an... odd and nosey uncle than a pet, but what about Winterheart?" She turned to look at him gracefully. "By the way, in social settings such as this, you may refer to me as Maebe. I implore you to use your best judgment should the social scenery change."

"As you say." He nodded. "I was wondering if you might be able to tell us what to expect? Maybe he had told you stories of his kind when you were with him?"

"Winterheart was more a show than tell kind of Dragon." Maebe's lips quirked into a small grin. "I remember him telling me stories of great battles he had read about in the swirling snows of his magic. Unfortunately, he was basically raised by my mother until she had me. He has almost reached the age of becoming a great wyrm."

"What's that?" James asked.

"The pinnacle of Dragon society," Maebe explained as she stretched in her saddle. "As Dragons age, their power compounds. Great Wyrms are within the last century or two of their life cycles and have amassed a great deal of their strength, cunning, and they often horde a great many things."

"So, if we find a Dragon with a huge-ass horde, we need to beat feet," Jaken proposed.

"If by that you mean to run? That is correct," Maebe affirmed.

We rode on, stopping every evening for some sparring, food, and rest. As the days ran on, the scenery changed. The plains and hills gave way to forests and valleys. As we walked toward one such valley, I had Kayda scout ahead after we were a few miles out of the last village and summoned Coal, so he could travel with us. Poor guy was so sick of being cooped up.

"I know we're in a hurry, but let's slow down," Jaken ordered.

"Why?" Bokaj asked.

"Potential ambush sites." Yohsuke pointed to rocky outcroppings along our path and higher above us.

Kayda wasn't seeing anything, but that didn't mean something didn't have a home field advantage. There were plenty of creatures out there that were at home in mountains like this. Let's just hope that our numbers where enough to discourage anyone from trying some shit.

We made it for another day traveling at a more reasonable pace and having someone watch different angles.

It was the third day within the crags and canyons that trouble finally showed its ugly, lumpy head. We stumbled on to a camp of sleeping... somethings. Giants? Let's say they were giants. They looked like them what with being all massive and having clubs the size of small trees near each sleeping form.

We stopped well away from them, their prone forms still breathing easily as we began to plot their demise with our earrings. It took a couple minutes to flesh out a plan.

First, I would have Kayda take Bokaj up the side of the canyon to a small landing a little ways up. Once he was there, he would release a volley of arrows straight down into the sleeping giants. Then while they were confused and hurt, Muu would be dropping in on them like a meteor. He would only be able to go for one of them, so that left the rest of us with mopping up the leftovers. Coal would try to do what he could, but with him so low a level, we didn't want him in the fray until the last of them were close to falling.

Kayda picked Bokaj up and lifted him to his spot for the beginning of it. Before he started the attack, he signaled Muu to leap into the air. He did so, but we had misjudged the distance he would be able to cover in a single leap. As it looked like he wouldn't make it far enough, Kayda rocketed to him, and I watched—stunned—as the Fighter used the back of my familiar as a springboard to leap even higher and farther.

Bokaj drew his bow and unleashed a torrent of arrows that multiplied in a cone as they sped toward their targets. The volley did as we had thought it would. The giant forms were up and screaming in pain and confusion. We began to close in slowly with Jaken and me in the lead, while Yohsuke and James brought up the rear. Maebe had decided to distance herself from the fight so she could resist the urge to fight along.

I heard the tell-tale whistle of a falling Dragon Beast-kin and watched as Muu connected with one of the creatures furthest from us. I saw the creature fall and watched as the other two looked toward him.

"Go!" Jaken barked. Wind split next to me, and I watched a dark blur speed toward the other two giants from my right. I took Magus Bane and activated Cleave, then Wind Scythe, before throwing it at the creature who looked ready to try and grab Muu.

I cast my newest spell, Stone Weapon. A large hammer grew out of the ground, and I snatched it up in both hands. I whipped it into the kneecap of the other giant. The sickening crack and roar of outraged pain made me grin manically. I let the hammer fall as I bounced back out of reach before grabbing my axe and jerking it out of the skin of the other giant. The blood made the blade visible, and as soon as I touched it, I watched my mana pop up by twenty-five. So it worked on every enemy. Oh, this was going to be a blast.

I felt a rough tug on my axe as the giant I had tried to fell like a dead tree tried to snatch it from my grasp. Instead, I hung on, and as he shook me violently, I watched Muu's lance drive through his chest, the icy weapon now covered in crimson.

Closer now, I could see their levels.

Giant level 25

"Take that!" he gloated. The beast turned, and his grip slipped; the weapon left his grasp. "Shit!"

As the impaled giant tried to relieve me of my axe once more, Jaken's longsword began to slash at its arm. I looked over to see his shield floating behind him as a guard. Jaken had his greatsword out and slashed at the one Muu had stunned with his surprise attack. The Paladin had ordered his main weapons to fight and defend as he focused on trying to end the stunned enemy.

Yohsuke and James were beating the hell out of the other creature, his once flabby, pink skin bruised and bloodied as the two dexterous Fighters weaved in and out of his melee range. It roared wordlessly and charged at them, running straight into me and taking my axe with him.

"He's got my axe!" I shouted. "I'm going for a fire spell. Buy me some time while I get it ready, and don't let him hit you!"

"No shit!" Yohsuke shot back. The giant in front of him whipped his arm out and snatched Yohsuke into his grasp. "Fu–" He gasped as the air left his lungs rapidly. His arms were pinned, and his weapons were next to useless at his sides.

I watched as six arrows burst from the arm, and a huge cat slammed into the creature's chest, knocking him off balance. Tmont had almost doubled in size, but she shrunk after I had blinked once. Kayda dropped on to the creature's head and began to buffet him with her wings. As the giant opened his mouth to try and bite her, his yellowed and chipped teeth dripping with spittle—she screeched, and a ball of lightning flashed into his throat.

In his hurry to get his hands to the source of his pain, the giant threw Yohsuke against the wall of the canyon. A few large stones and rocks fell down and completely obstructed our view of him. And more fell on top after that—he'd been buried.

"YOHSUKE!" I roared. "Jaken, get there!"

I lunged forward, my axe forgotten, to try and get the rubble out of the way. The giant flailed wildly as I leaped between his legs into a forward shoulder roll. A glancing blow caught me and shaved off ten percent of my HP, but I didn't care. I pushed one stone aside and caught a giant fist to my left rib cage that sent me careening away. My health plummeted to thirty percent, and Coal was standing over me, protectively growling. I saw Jaken start my way, but I shouted as best I could, "Get Yoh!"

Jaken, pissed off and visibly shaken, started throwing rocks faster, his sword and shield working overtime to drop the fucker swinging near him. I looked at the other one and saw that the lance sticking through him was beginning to put a layer of frost around the wound. Muu was gone, and Kayda was keeping it distracted the best she could.

"Coal, help me kneel, buddy." He put his muzzle beneath my ribs and began to try and lift me up.

Once I was in a kneeling position, I cast Heal on myself, and my health was back up by one hundred points. I took a moment to collect my will and began to draw my mana into a ball in my hands. I used the tinkering ability I had to make the mana burn, then rotate until it was a small ball the size of a tennis ball that was spinning like a basketball on a Globe Trotter's finger.

"Coal, go get that giant's attention, the one by Jaken, and bring him toward me, but don't get too close," I ordered quietly.

I have the flailing one, guys. Stay away from him. I spoke to the others through our earrings. The others didn't acknowledge it, but I had a feeling it didn't matter.

The Flame Wolf dashed toward the flailing creature and began to bark rabidly at it. As he did so, I began to compress the spell in my hand but kept it rotating. Coal bit the creature's leg, and it reared toward him and began to stumble along after it, Kayda thrashing even more furiously. The spell she had cast was running out, and the giant's health was a little over thirty percent.

As soon as he was close enough, I ordered my familiars to back off and flock to me like they were trying to defend me via mental command. It worked like a charm. Bokaj and James began fighting the axe thief giant, so there were no other distractions.

He stomped up to me, shouting in a guttural language that I didn't understand. His drooling, dumb face and beady eyes went from a look of rage to one of victory when he saw me breathing heavily. My mana was close to bottoming out, but he was close enough now that I could do what I had planned. As he bent down to try and bite at me, I tossed the now golf ball-sized flame ball into his mouth and leaped as far from him as I could.

Coal dove forward to keep the creature from following me, and a concussive boom shook me hard enough to knock me from my feet. The creature was gone, and Coal stood behind, slightly larger and stronger looking.

I turned in time to see Muu throw his short spear through the last creature's head. It roared and fell, twitching and shuddering. James, slightly beaten up and with a bloody lip, did a front flip and used the momentum to kick the creature in its throat. The last little bit of red drained from its HP bar and we all received some EXP.

I limped over to where the pile of rocks was beginning to thin and began to toss some aside. It was hard work, but with all of us pitching in, we were able to move the worst of the rocks out of the way.

"Yoh?" I called into the rocks as we sifted through them. "Yohsuke. Come on man, answer me."

Light filtered into the rubble, and we finally found him. His eyes were open, his face a grimace of determination.

He was still warm. He was bleeding a little bit, sure, but he was still whole that I could see.

"Hey, come on, bud." I pulled him out of the rubble easily. He still didn't move. "Hey, this isn't funny, man. Come on. Snap out of it."

"Zeke, let Jaken have him," James said. Muu started to pull on me too. I couldn't understand why they were trying to take my friend.

"He's fine, guys—he's just playing." I grunted as I tried to pull away. Bokaj was skidding down the side of the canyon toward us with a worried look on his face. "We got him, man, don't worry."

Maebe was there suddenly. "Dear Zekiel, let the Paladin have him." She took me by my hand, and I struggled to pull away, but her iron-like grip was set.

I watched as Jaken poured a mana potion into his mouth and swallowed and began to mutter and make broad motions with his hands. His fingers moved in complex formations and symbols that confused me too.

"What are they doing?" I asked the woman holding me. "Why isn't he snapping out of it?"

"Zeke," she opened her mouth. Closed it. Frowned and then looked me in the eyes. I saw a flash of light behind her, and through the muted burst of magical energy, I heard her say, "Zeke, your friend didn't make it."

Chapter Eighteen

"My name is ..." I heard my voice say as if in a feedback loop. It echoed around me. "And I'm a puto."

That memory. That day had been crazy. He and I had to do some stupid shoot for a command hike, and we had been goofing around. I could clearly see him sitting in the duty van with me, the sun beating down on the California base around us, and me with his tiny-ass cover on my head being stupid with him.

The next thing I saw was the first time we had met. My buddy, another Lance named Mike, had taken me to the Com-Cam shop to meet a friend of his from the schoolhouse. We walked in and this short, skinny Mexican man with what looked like almost-permanent five o' clock shadow around his mouth and jawline greeted both of us. I found out he loved video games, and shortly after that, the three of us had been thick as thieves.

I saw the nights we had spent cooped up in his room, beating video games and shooting the breeze. Then the night that he had saved my life. When I'd had possibly the worst day I had ever had at work, and my thoughts and heart had turned against me. And he was just there—asking me if I wanted to come over and play some video games for a bit.

He was in every sense of the word—my brother. Every facet of his being had been so crucial into my being "me" that what was happening now was impossible.

For the first time in a long time—I prayed. I prayed to whoever would listen, and I felt a warm presence brush against my consciousness. I opened my eyes, and I saw Kayda leaning over me, her normally blue irises had gone a shade of deep violet and radiant gold. I knew those eyes, or at least, I thought I did.

"It has been some time, young Druid." The voice I recognized—Mother Nature.

"Can you help my brother?" I skipped the preamble.

"Death is as much a part of my will as life is, little one," she chided softly. "Why should I intervene in the natural order of things?"

"Because I serve you." I began to panic. "Because of our mission to help save this world. Because of the things we are doing."

"Do you serve me?" Kayda's head tilted oddly. "I have seen little evidence of this. You have helped a few dryads. You have even helped strengthen two of my allies. But nature still suffers at the hands of those around you. The jungle you go to now is slowly being consumed by some form of disease. Find the source, and cleanse it for me."

"If I agree to do this, will you help ensure my brother comes back?" I asked with more hope than I should have.

"I have already," she replied, "and so, as a portion of my fee, I require you do this. If you should fail to stop the disease in time, his life is forfeit. Please me, and I shall reward you all. I can give, and I can take. I have given already, and I happily will do so again. So long as you do your part. Remember, little one—Druid is not a mantle to be discarded when it does not suit your purpose."

I blinked, Kayda's eyes were their usual blue, and she looked over me with concern.

"Yoh!" I sat bolt upright and began to look for my friend. He was still on the ground, and Jaken looked distraught.

The still body that was Yohsuke opened its mouth, sucked in a huge amount of air, and began to cough and hack until a thick, viscous black liquid erupted from his mouth. As it hit the ground at Jaken's feet, it screamed—loudly and shrill—and began to try and crawl toward any shadow that it could, but it swiftly stopped and died.

I fought my way to my feet and cast Heal on Yohsuke just before I got to him. I pulled him off the ground, still coughing a little, into a fierce hug.

"What the fuck happened?" he croaked. His voice was hoarse from the coughing and hacking.

"We lost you, man," I said gently. "That thing threw you into the canyon wall. Then we had to fight to get to you. Do you remember anything?"

He looked confused and shook his head quietly. The others came over to pull him into individual hugs and pats on the back. Maebe walked close to him and looked him over.

"I am glad that you have returned, friend Yohsuke." She nodded at him, then took my hand.

I pulled her close to me for comfort. Then I had to share what happened and what needed to happen.

"So, thanks to Jaken and the Mother—yes, Mother Nature—Yoh is back," I began. Everyone's eyes were on me. "She's pissed because I haven't been very Druid-like in my dealings with this world. So, she's given me a mission. Where we're going, the jungle is dying of a disease. I don't know what kind, but I do know that if we don't stop it, she's gonna be pissed. And that will be deadly."

"She's gonna take me back if we don't do it, isn't she?" Yohsuke asked quietly. His eyes looked haunted, but he blinked that away just as quickly as I had recognized it. "Well, looks like we just have to play ball."

"You okay?" James asked Yohsuke.

"You know me, man." Yoh tried to sound confident and just barely eked by with it. "Nothing can stop the overlord."

We nodded quietly and began to search for loot. The giant creatures—Hill Giants, Maebe had called them after the fact—didn't leave too much behind. We were able to collect the weapons that we had ended up losing to them by accident and then found a couple leather scraps that Muu said were trash. The camp was clean as well except for bones of unfortunate travelers, bison, and other strange animals. Muu had gone from level 11 to level 13, though.

None of us were in a talkative enough mood to see how he had spent his points.

We only traveled for another few more hours that day, opting to find the safest place we could and having wards in place thanks to Maebe. Everyone slept pretty roughly that night. I took a watch, not because I didn't think we wouldn't need one but because I knew if we were going to proceed, we had to do so smarter. And not being able to sleep helped too.

I thought about some of the abilities I had and decided on a craftier way to respond to threats in this place.

As I sat thinking, Maebe sat next to me. "Please, do not be offended, but that fight went poorly. You all spend so much time together. Why did you not use that unity to fight those hill giants?"

I blinked at her question, and I had no answer. By her thinking, we should have planned better. Should have known things may not go the way we thought they would.

We needed to work better as a team. We were pretty damn strong, but we needed to grow more. Together. Using our different abilities to our advantage.

"You're right. We need to improve. I guess focusing on being sure Muu was good and getting Balmur back has driven our efficiency down."

She seemed satisfied that I was thinking on it and left it at that.

I took a moment to decide on Coal's stats. He had gotten to level 5 after that last fight. A huge gain.

Name: Coal
Race: Flame Wolf
Level: 5
Strength: 5
Dexterity: 7
Constitution: 6
Intelligence: 2
Wisdom: 2
Charisma: 6
Unspent Attribute Points: 12

Awesome. So his intelligence and wisdom had gone up one point, and his charisma by two when he had leveled up to this point! Okay. That left me twelve to use, so I bumped strength, dexterity, and constitution up by four apiece.

Looking at him, Coal seemed much healthier and more robust now. Good. Cuter too. He nosed my foot and thumped his tail happily. He didn't get a spell though like Kayda had, but that was okay.

In the morning, we were on our way. Everyone was still a little groggy when we came upon an enemy I didn't want to see—an Ettin.

The lumbering monstrosity was easily forty-feet tall with two heads that bickered back and forth in a guttural and foul language. He wore a simple loincloth and had a spiked club that looked like it had been made using spears.

We ducked back behind a large rock before it could spot us, and I filled the others in on my idea.

"Ettins are smarter than the others we fought," I began.

"Fucking duh, it has two heads!" Muu whispered harshly. I glared at him before he looked away. "It does."

"This thing could end up having some kind of magic," I continued. "We have to hit it and hit as hard as possible. As quickly as possible. Unload on this guy because the guys we fought earlier may have been his lackeys."

"How are we going to do that?" James asked. "That portion of the canyon is huge, at least eighty to a hundred feet wide. With all that room, he can do whatever he wants."

"I'm going to see if I can't trap him and cause a cave in that will lock his ass up. At least for a bit." I thought for a moment, then added, "No promises, though."

I focused on the element of earth and shifted into my earth elemental form. I looked like a larger, stronger version of Pebble except that I was made of diamond. Wholly of diamond. I focused and pushed myself into the ground. As I melded with the earth, my vision vanished completely, and I felt a *oneness* with the stone that I had become. I knew where my friends were, and as I moved toward the Ettin, I could sense it too.

I also got the sense that I wasn't going to be able to move the earth because I no longer had a physical form. I could potentially cast a different spell, though. Yeah, that would have to work. It was all I had left at this moment. I moved beneath the creature, feeling the weight of its mass, then got an idea. I decided to explore the rock face of the canyon walls and see how they felt. If we could trigger another rock slide, we might be able to do some serious damage to this guy. I found a couple faults and made a note of them in relative position to where I felt the Ettin.

I popped out of the ground behind the creature and inwardly began cursing.

Ettin level 37

I briefly refocused on the faults, then touched the Ettin while casting Iron Maiden. The stone beneath the Ettin turned liquid and rose around the creature, his level 37 health taking small bits of damage from the spikes that formed inside. Soon, he was completely encased in stone that solidified into an iron-like shell. I threw four Stone Spikes, spear-like projectiles of diamond, into the areas I had felt the faults to weaken them slightly. The spikes held there, and I shifted back into my Kitsune form.

I looked at the timer for the spell and saw that it had been cut in half when I shifted out of elemental form. Fuck.

"Get out here, guys," I shouted. The others joined me, and I pointed to the faults, "Those are going to be how we do this. We hit him with our heaviest spells and attacks first, then topple that on to him. If he survives? Well, we beat the shit out of him."

"Solid enough of a plan," Bokaj observed. "I still have some of the arrows you enchanted, so don't get too close."

"And I'll take care of the canyon wall," Muu stated. He pulled his original short spear from his inventory and rolled his shoulder. "Then I'll go for him."

I felt a strain internally and summoned Coal. He was ready to fight by our side.

"Yoh," My friend looked even more determined, "you good for this one? You need to sit it out?"

"Fuck no, this bitch is mine." He spat and began to mumble and press his hands together in a series of motions I hadn't seen him do before. Heat and a vile stench of rotten eggs began to emanate from his hands in waves. "Soon as that spell of yours ends, step aside."

"You got it, boss." I shrugged and stepped aside and began casting my own spells.

I brought my flame tinkering to the forefront of my mind, added it to my Stone Weapon spell, and formed a great axe with it. The total cost was 250 MP—half my mana.

I felt the Iron Maiden start to dissolve and shouted, "In three... two... *NOW!*"

I activated my two piece combo of Cleave and Wind Scythe, then sent the spelled weapon careening into the upper body of the Ettin.

I saw Yohsuke snarl and heard the word, "Fallemeara!" As his hands shot forward, a roiling bolt of flame four feet long shot forth and spiraled toward the creature. Then another that Yohsuke cast using his ring.

I saw two arrows fly at the Ettin and detonate, and an arm went flying into the sky. A rumble sounded, and I watched as the canyon wall between the two faults I had found began to crumble and pitch forward in a roar of falling debris and stone. The stone hit the somehow-still-standing Ettin and knocked it on to its side. His health bar was low, but he was still alive.

"Watch out." Muu pushed me aside. He brought his spear up, and I spent the mana to imbue the weapon with my buff, Star Blade, for some added damage. An aura of black, like the night sky with stars sprinkled throughout, burst from it as he prepared to launch it.

Muu must have activated his bracelet because the weapon damned near warped from his hand and sprouted from the creature's eye, then back to his hand for another throw. By this time, Yohsuke had cast his Black Snow spell that caused a flurry of inky, dark pellets to eat the final dregs of the Ettin's life away.

Once it was completely eaten by the snow, we did find a rather sizable bag of coins—three hundred gold, seventy-four silver, and two hundred fifty copper that we gave to Muu. There was a toe left behind that said it was an alchemical ingredient, but I didn't want anything to do with that.

Muu tucked it into his own inventory with a smile that ended up turning into a gag as he got blood on his hand.

We skirted the rubble, then mounted up to move on. Jaken led the way, and I hung back to try and pick Yohsuke's mind.

"Hey man, how are you doing?" As I looked him over, he looked tired. Really tired. And angry.

"I'll be alright," he grunted.

"I didn't ask how you'll be—I asked how you are," I pressed as we looked about for more enemies.

Kayda was scouting again, and Coal was back inside me. He had leveled up three times this time and Kayda once. I'd already bumped everything into constitution for her. His were to strength and dexterity.

Yohsuke was quiet for a few minutes, pensively watching before finally saying, "I saw her," quietly.

"Who?"

"My wife." His lips twitched. "I was right there. I could feel her there next to me. I heard her say goodnight to me, and like a stupid asshole, I went back to sleep. And when I did, I was staring at you guys. I was there. I was home."

Fuck, I thought to myself. Out loud, "I'm sorry, man."

"Don't be." He sighed. "It's not your fault. Hell, it's not anyone here's fault. It's that shitstain War and his posse. If we don't try to stop them, my wife, your kid, Jaken's kid—everybody back home would be fucked. So, I'm here to whoop some ass and chew bubble gum, and I don't have any fucking bubble gum."

I nodded, a grin on my face from his reference to an old movie lightening the mood a bit.

"And, hey—thank you for going to bat for me with Mother Nature." Yohsuke reached out and offered me his fist.

"Don't thank me, brother," I said back. I had to lean over a little bit to bump his knuckles as his bone griffin freaked Thor out a little. "It would be the truth no matter how lame it sounds—you would do the same."

He nodded quietly, and we let it go after that. No sense dwelling on it anymore. I trusted that over time, he would be able to work through this, and he knew I was there to help.

That night, Maebe and I discussed what would have happened if I had lost him and that I didn't know confused her.

"You would be that distraught?" she asked curiously.

"I would," I explained. "He's been my best friend—like a brother to me—for years. He and I have helped each other through so many hard times. Losing him would break something in me. Make me less... me."

"So, your experiences with him helped make you who you are." Maebe's head tilted to the side. "They have helped shape you, and if he were not there, you would lose your edge? Like a sword without a whetstone?"

I tried to think of a more suitable explanation. "More like a random spell cast into a tavern brawl. It could be okay. The effect could be small, or it could be disastrous and deadly. Having my friends makes me less likely to start killing people without reason." An idea came to me, and I added, "Like if your mother or Winterheart were to be hurt. Or your people. How would that make you feel?"

"My people?" Her eyebrows raised in surprise. "I would be outraged that anyone thought themselves powerful enough to weather my wrath. My mother? She is stronger than I am, though my title lends me the strength I need to defend myself and others. If something were to harm her, I would be afraid. Winterheart." She closed her eyes in confusion. "If someone were to take Winterheart from me, I would run through their line like a wraith, causing no end of death and destruction excruciatingly slowly."

I patted her hand. "Exactly. I would lose my mind just like that. I would turn into a monster if any of my friends were to get hurt like that."

"I see." Her lips pursed slightly. "Thank you for bringing these thoughts to my attention. If you will excuse me, I must contact my people. It has been several days, and I would like to check in on them."

She left the camp quietly. She returned an hour later, and we ate quietly. So far as I could gather, everyone was still hit hard about almost losing someone. Bokaj was taking it rough too, probably more so because he ate so little and hadn't been as talkative since then.

"So, once we get stronger, we're gonna be on our way to the Hells," Muu stood and stretched a bit as he spoke. "We have to cleanse a forest, talk to a couple Dragons, then find a way to get into the Hells and get Balmur, then defeat the General there."

"Yeah," Jaken confirmed.

"Well, that's not too bad." Muu shrugged. "That's only four things. Five if you count the Dragons individually."

We all looked at him like he was crazy.

"It's true," he explained. "Look, we can sit here and think this is some huge quest that's taking forever, and we can let it kill us slowly, or, and I'm leaning this way, we break it up into more manageable chunks. Give ourselves some small goals to reach and keep hauling ass."

"Them's pretty words, man," James motioned to all of us, "but they don't do anything to alleviate the fact that we almost got our asses handed to us. Yoh died! That's pretty fucking rough no matter how you cut it. And Balmur is still in the Hells."

"Yeah, he is," Bokaj punched his fist, "and he doesn't get anything from us moping. Yohsuke looks pretty fucking determined too, so let's get our heads out of our asses and get this shit done. Muu, good thinking."

"Thanks, man." He blinked in surprise. "Oh hey, I got a point in wisdom."

Chapter Nineteen

It took us the whole next day to get out of the canyons that we had entered and began to see the outline of the jungle in the distance. A day later, we could make out the individual trees.

Each night, we made more of a point to work together and plan tactics with each other—different group fighting movements and "special team moves" as Muu had dubbed them.

Some of them were obvious, given our abilities meshed well in open settings like this. In a canopy like the jungle? There was no telling how much room we would have to fight. We were excited about a few of them, even naming them ridiculous names so no one could guess what they might be.

Daily life resumed a little quicker as time moved on. Hell, I'd even started to try and communicate more with Mother Nature. She was quiet at first, probably thought I was just trying to talk my way out of things, but eventually, as I began to ask her questions and wonder how I could help the world around me, she answered.

Her answers were never words, though. Not really. As our time on the trail wore on, I began picking up on subtle things here and there. After a while, we came across a lake that was in sore need of water, if not the whole area around it. There were clouds in the sky, but nothing that looked like it would even remotely provide any kind of precipitation.

After thinking while we had lunch and seeing several animals come over to the place to get what water they could, I decided to try something. The same kind of enchantment I had used in the Fae realm was out of the question. The amount of mana to keep this whole thing filled would be insane. So I took my water elemental form and cast the spell Gentle Rain.

***Gentle Rain (Water Elemental)** – Caster calls a small cloud that relinquishes water for one minute that will replenish a small amount of health to allies and harm foes in a sixty-foot radius. Range: 60 feet. Cost: 200 MP. Cooldown: 3 minutes.*

The small amount of rain that fell as a result of my casting wasn't enough to fill the water to the brim of the lake by any means. Kayda who stood nearby understood what I was trying to do and flew into the sky. She began to fly in a tight circle that slowly opened. As it did, clouds began to come closer and closer to where she was. She began to hum in her mind, and I could feel the melody build as the clouds closed closer on us.

The once-plain looking clouds began to swell, and I could feel the wind being swept up as a storm brewed. Droplets began to speckle the ground as all of us watched in awe of what we were witnessing. Soon, a fully-fledged downpour fell in that spot. The water level rose steadily until it breached the sides of the lake and began to run aground.

I tried to let Kayda know to stop, but from what I felt when I touched her mind—she was lost to this new ability.

I shifted back and called to her, "Kayda! That's enough!"

Still nothing. She was lower now but still well out of a normal person's reach.

"I'll get her attention," Muu spoke over the din of the growing storm. "You just be sure to heal me if shit hits the fan."

I nodded and watched as he shook himself out before crouching low and leaping into the air at Kayda, yelling as loudly as he could to get her attention, "TWEEEEEEEEEEEETYYYYYYYYYY!"

A flash of azure light and a screech of metal being hit filled the air. Muu was flung from her violently by a lightning bolt that had careened out of the clouds closest to him between the two of them.

"Jaken!" I grunted at the Paladin, and he was in motion before I could even blink.

I thought of the spell I wanted to cast and sent it at her in hopes it would garner her attention. The Winter Blade, a large shard of ice in the shape of a long sword flew at her, followed by one of Yohsuke's Astral Bolts. His spell struck mine ten feet from her, and the blade erupted, as it normally would in a large burst of ice and pain. The burst spell sprinkled on to my familiar, but she continued to ignore it.

Mother Nature, if you're listening—now's the time to help us out, I prayed silently.

If she wasn't bothered by pain, and she didn't care if a friend was hit—maybe she would respond to fear. I stepped closer to her, closing the gap between us by another ten feet. The wind and rain whipped at my clothes relentlessly.

I took a couple of breaths to prepare myself, then one last deep one before activating Predator's Call. I bellowed a roar for all I was worth. It echoed over the wind and carried much farther than I thought it would have.

Kayda's head whipped around, and she looked at me in confusion before diving away from the clouds toward us.

"What the hell was that?" Muu groaned as he limped toward us. There was a blackened scorch mark along the front of his armor that traveled down to his waist. I had to admit, though—it was dope as shit.

I looked over Kayda's status screen and didn't note anything out of the ordinary, but that didn't mean something wasn't up.

"She must go, child," I heard Mother Nature's voice and looked up to see Tmont with the tell-tale lavender and gold eyes.

"What do you mean?" Uncertainty crept into my heart.

"You cannot care for her in the way that she needs right now," the Mother explained patiently. "I know that you try your hardest, but she was a rare beast before the Fae Realm tampered and offered her more power. She needs training. There is one such being who can offer her the sort that she needs, and he lives with the Kirin—far to the north of here."

"Will she be okay?" Muu asked. Yohsuke was suddenly very close to me as well.

"I will see to it personally that she survives her time in transit." Tmont's head turned toward my familiar. "Little one, you must fly and find the one I speak of. I will be with you along the way. Take a moment, then go."

I watched as the color bled from the great cat's eyes. Then the cat looked around in confusion.

I looked over to find Yohsuke and Muu standing next to Kayda. Muu was hugging her and whispering, "I'm gonna miss you, you big, feathery asshole."

Yohsuke reached into his inventory and whipped out a large piece of meat that looked to be seared to perfection.

"I was gonna save this for dinner, but you can't fly that far on an empty stomach, bird." He tossed it up to her, and she snapped it, bone and all, down her gullet. "Stay safe, and come back strong as fuck."

She reached down and butted her head against each of them lovingly before turning her sights on me. She sent a flash of sadness and longing.

I smiled and summoned Coal. He bounded around all of us, and Kayda chirruped to him. He stopped and loped over to her slowly, then stopped and sniffed at her. She reached down and nuzzled his side with her cheek. Her goodbyes to her little brother said, she turned to me.

I tried to smile at her reassuringly, to let her know I had faith in her, but I couldn't do it. I had already almost lost my brother. And now my familiar? Fuck, man.

I stepped closer to her and gave her a good hug, careful not to crush her wings. Then I smiled at her sadly. "You better come back to me, love. Go learn fast. Be safe. I love you."

She looked at Maebe, her eyes narrowing slightly. Then she did the strangest thing I think I'd ever seen her do in our time together. She looked from Maebe, to me, then back and brought her wings around in front of her as if to hold something. Maebe nodded once, and it was over.

Love. She looked at me, then the others and repeated the thought. I passed the sentiment on to the others, and we waved her off into the first leg of her journey.

"Thank you, Mother Nature, for watching over my baby girl," I whispered to no one in particular. Radiant warmth blossomed all over my back, and I turned to find that the clouds had broken over the lake, and the sun was staring brightly at us.

We decided to move on then. Nothing to really keep us there other than depression. Coal ran along with us for a little while before he got tired, then I took him back into myself, so he could rest.

It felt weird not having Kayda here. Granted, she had been able to get out a lot more lately because we weren't in a confined space anymore. It was just a comfort to know that she was there, you know?

"She asked that I protect you," Maebe said from my left. I looked over to her and found her sitting completely facing me on her mount.

"And you agreed." I nodded.

"I did," she began, "and that means that I need to tell you that your way of fighting is odd."

"I'm aware that my skills would be better suited either focusing on spells or up close fighting," I sighed, "but my abilities are more suited for a jack-of-all-trades kind of deal. That's how my role works best with the party."

"Not that." She looked over at the others. "Jaken uses the spells and tools he has to great effect, taking the brunt of the damage and somehow managing to keep you all alive when he can. Bokaj allows his kitten to hunt for him, and he uses ensorcelled arrows to devastating effect. I'm sure when he begins using his bardic abilities, he will be a force to be feared."

"Okay," I narrowed my eyes at her, "I know my friends are good at what they do. Hell, James beat the shit out of me the other day when we were sparring."

"Exactly, he uses his mobility to great effect." She motioned to Yohsuke next. "The little shadow, he makes certain that while he is using his sword, he is casting several other spells and using his items with deadly accuracy. He is largely the reason that second giantling died as fast as it did. And Muu, he is a special one. I have never heard of his style of fighting, but I have seen that he is passionate about it, and it has worked well for him."

"I'll bite—how can I improve myself?"

"You are a Kitsune." She motioned to me. "You have three tails. You have the ability—naturally—to shapeshift faster than any other Druid, and you can do so into any form you want. You can shapeshift several times in a moment, and it costs you *nothing*."

"So you think I should shapeshift more?" I had to admit, the thought had occurred to me, but I didn't think that was all that was coming my way.

"I think you should shapeshift more intuitively." She pointed to herself. "If I know that an enemy has a certain reach that can go so far, what would I do?"

"You would stay out of their reach." I shrugged. She made a go-on motion with her hand. "Or get in so close that their attacks can do nothing."

"Exactly!" She clapped, and her radiant smile dazzled me. "You can go from fox-man, to bear, to fox, to any other number of creatures. You could have taken fox form, run, and turned into an owl, then attacked from any angle afar or dropped on him like the Dragon-kin."

"Is that a shortened term for Dragon Beast-kin?" I was pissed I hadn't thought of that before.

"Do not change the subject, my pet," she purred. "You know this to be true. You need to be thinking of these things."

"I do, don't I?" And that did give me a thought. "Hey Muu!" The Dragon-kin looked over at me. "I got a thing I want to try later, just remind me!"

"'Kay!" he hollered back.

Maebe's victorious chin raise and regal demeanor at that moment were both annoying and super adorable.

"I'll deal with you later, miss know-it-all," I growled playfully.

She looked me dead in the eyes and asked, "Do you know what we call that in my culture?" I shook my head, interested in learning. "Queen."

And her shadow lion mount put on an extra burst of speed. I watched her hold her hand up to her mouth as she laughed. I heard Bokaj, Jaken, and James start laughing as well.

"She fuckin' punked you, boy," Yohsuke teased.

"Great, isn't it?" I grinned back. It was nice to be able to laugh again.

* * *

That night, Muu and I were set to spar, so we decided to have some fun. Well—*I* decided to have some fun.

He pulled out his short spear and adopted a good fighting stance. I walked up to him, sat Magus Bane aside and cracked my knuckles.

"That's hardly the smart thing to do," Muu observed as we began to circle each other.

"Don't worry about me, princess." I loosened my limbs and relaxed a little.

"Fine by me." He stilled, and for a moment, I didn't think he would move until I felt the spear sliding against my right side.

I looked down and saw that, if he had been trying to stab me—he could've.

"Illusory Thrust," Muu offered as an explanation.

"Very fucking well," I grunted. "Kid gloves are off now. I'm gonna beat your ass with my bear hands."

"I'd like to see you do that." He smiled.

I promptly shifted into my Ursolon form and smacked him across his helmeted head, sending him sprawling. I growled a laugh at him and deftly dodged a slice at my chest. I bear danced to the right, then shifted into my fox form and danced beneath his legs.

"Hold still you piece o' shit!" he spat at me as he tried to stab me. I beat feet away from him a little way, then took my owl form. I lifted into the air and looked down to see that he was right there with an arm outstretched.

Inwardly, I was cursing up a storm because that meant I would need a swifter take off time to make this a viable tactic.

So, instead of trying to get away, I gave him what he wanted. I dropped the panther on him.

"Ah!" he shouted as my six-hundred-pound bulk dropped on top of him. "Fuck. YOU!"

He tried to stab at me, but I batted at him with both paws and foiled his worst attempts. I took a good slice on the forearm and hissed at him angrily. I took my powerful back legs and shot them into the core of his body to rocket him away from me. Then I shifted into my owl form once more to help slow my descent.

Muu landed on his back with a grunt and a gasp. I touched down next to him and shifted to fox, then once more into my Ursolon form. I pressed my forepaw against his throat and growled threateningly.

"Cool, man." Muu sighed. "That was fucking cool."

"It was how you, as a Druid, should address an enemy when you can," Maebe added. "Your magics are powerful, and you're strong as well. Very strong. Your strength is what makes you more attuned to the animalistic side of your powers. It is what will give you an edge. Not to mention that you have the blessings of two of the Primordial elementals. This makes you the only one I know of."

"It's that rare?" Muu asked after I stepped away from him.

"The elementals have been wary of mankind and spellcasters in general since before the Reckoning." We stared at her blankly, and she continued, "It was the year-long destruction of human Mages, Wizards, and Sorcerers who brought their magics to bare on their peers and nature. They were responsible for the creation of those like Muu and many of your other friends."

I had shifted back during her explanation and shook myself out. "So, that's what the High Elves were talking about."

"Yes." She threw her hands out to the side gesturing to our surroundings. "When they did this, they had been at the height of their powers. They sought to subjugate all of humanity, Elves, other manners of creatures, and even the elementals. So, they—the Primordials—sought to separate themselves from that side, and they have. You are the first I have seen them give power to directly."

"Well, what about spellcasters who use elemental spells, like fireballs?" Bokaj asked from the far side of the cooking fire.

"That is use of mana. That summons the flame and gives it structure." I racked my brain and thought of the Fireball spell. "It was the mana that opened a channel—insignificant in size really—to the elemental planes and allowed the caster to borrow magic of the appropriate type."

"So what, they give Zeke is a larger channel?" Jaken asked.

"Possibly." Maebe shrugged. "That is between them and Zeke."

"That's pretty much what they did," I offered. "They gave me a permanent channel in the form of these tattoos on my hands. They allow me to take on a form of their type. Though, two of the primordials like me a bit more than the others. As I'm sure you can guess. Hell, the flame Primordial likes me so much, I can tinker with fire spells and add flames to others."

"Yeah, yeah—you're special," Muu teased as he elbowed me. "Big whoop, you wanna fight about it?"

"Didn't I just beat you down with my bear hands?" He looked confused, then closed his eyes and silently flipped me the bird. "Love you too, buddy. But yeah, I'll be better about how I fight from now on."

"You wanted to show me something?" Muu asked finally.

"You know about the fastball special, yeah?" His eyes lit up, and he nodded at me. "I was wondering what would happen if you were to use the bracelet and throw me."

"Oooooh, toys with the boys!" Muu clapped his hands together and prepared himself.

"Mae, could you give us a target, please?" She took my hand in her own and lifted the other out toward an open piece of ground sixty feet away from us.

The creature that burst forth was a large variation on a person but seven feet tall, and it resembled the small shadow Goblins that she used in her room.

"It will suffice?" Maebe looked at me with curiosity.

"It will." I kissed her cheek. "Thank you. Muu, toss me with the bracelet—hard as you can."

I shifted into my fox form and hopped into Muu's outstretched right hand. I laid my body as flat as I could and prepared for what came next.

Muu raised his arm, hiked me back like an Olympian, and hurled me forward impossibly fast. The wind shear from the force exerted on me made it so hard to see and get any kind of reading, but I heard someone yell, "Shift!"

I shifted into my Ursolon form and hit the shadow creature so hard that it split in half. The shadows slid back into the ground, and it faded completely.

I stumbled to a stop and fell to the ground in a dizzy heap, grumbling, "Last resort. Ooooooh, last resort."

"*That was amazing!*" I heard Muu shriek in amazement. His maniacal laughter and cackling would have given Shellica a run for her money.

"Yes, I must admit that hit quite well, but you might want to consider a distraction in order to get the most effect from that," Maebe advised.

I trundled back to the group, and we had some dinner. A nice bit of stew to put our hungry stomachs in proper order. That night, we laid down, Maebe and I together—and just watched the stars.

I wondered if Kayda had made it to her destination okay. I hadn't been able to feel her since after she left. Maebe must have felt the tension in my body because she turned to me with a knowing look.

"You are worried about her?" She asked, though I gathered she knew the answer was yes. "She is a strong creature, Zeke. She will learn as she can, and then she will return."

I brushed her multicolored hair from her face and gave her an appreciative peck on the forehead before saying simply, "Thank you."

As we laid together quietly, the looming jungles south of us, I got the feeling that there was more that we weren't seeing. That the place itself was wrong. Not in the same way that creatures affected by the influence of War's minions and generals—but perhaps more alive than that. Changing, growing. I could almost taste discontent and anger in the air. Was this the disease that was eating the forest?

I cast my thoughts toward home. My own culture, already so war-like and quick to corruption, would never stand a chance. And we didn't have magic to save us. We had guns. Explosives. Nuclear warheads. We could end ourselves in a matter of hours.

Before I could control myself, I growled low in my chest and felt my lover stir. "You feel that as well?"

"I can describe it, I can feel it—but I can't place it," I spoke softly.

"This is malice," she whispered. "What lies in that area has been tainted by it, and it has seeped into the land and poisoned it. The source will likely be what you seek."

"We have company," James said softly.

I looked out toward the forest, and there was a great cat, much larger than Tmont or me in my panther form. His mane was matted and stringy; his muscles stood in stark relief against his bones. The lion looked deadly, for certain, but malnourished. His tan hide was injured, and I could smell death in the air. It looked around sadly, and I cast a spell I hadn't used as much as I probably should have—Nature's Voice.

I waved to Yohsuke and made a motion with my hands for food. He pulled a half haunch of meat out of his inventory as he had given to Kayda before she left and tossed it to me as quietly as he could.

I stepped through the dome with Maebe following closely and Jaken with his shield as well on my right-hand side.

"Hello, friend," I started. The lion drooled at the sight of the meat in my hand.

"So hungry," he growled. "Druid? You are a Druid. The Mother said you might come. I did not believe her."

"Eat now, save your strength," I said and brought the food closer to him.

He took it gratefully, and I set to work on him. First, I cast Heal on him, then Regrowth. I watched as his wounds knit back together and the blood sloughed from his skin to the ground. So it hadn't been his.

Sickening tears, the cracking of bone, and tearing of sinew was all that we heard as the beast feasted.

After he was done and all that remained was a small nub of the bone that he chewed and sucked on as he eyed us, Muu and the others stepped out to join us.

I indicated myself and my friends. "I'm Zeke, this is Maebe, Jaken is the one in metal, Bokaj is the pale Elf, Yohsuke is the dark one, James is the Dragon Elf, and the Dragon-kin is Muu."

He regarded each of them as I said their names, but he bowed to Maebe.

"I recognize all of you as the Mother's chosen," he spoke. "I am Laongal. I will be your guide. Has the Mother taught you her cleansing magics yet, Druid?"

"Healing spells?" I couldn't keep the confusion from my voice, and he looked slightly alarmed.

"You know not how to cleanse the land?" Laongal gasped. "How does the Mother expect you to succeed?"

"We have our ways," I offered lamely. Honestly, I was betting she wanted us to take the problem out at the source, and she would heal the jungle. "You want to sleep with us tonight?"

"If you would have me, I would be happy for the reprieve," the lion replied tiredly, "and also, if you have any more meat, I would appreciate it as well."

We stepped into the shadow dome, and Maebe snapped her fingers. Her tiny shadow Goblins crawled into existence and with them pulled a huge haunch of meat from an inky pool between them. The meat, bloody and thick, went a long way toward feeding the beastly lion. He left half of it alone after a while and went about cleaning himself.

Maebe and I laid in our shared bedroll once more, and Laongal wandered over to us. "A mated pair? You have done well for yourself, Druid. This one seems powerful. She will hunt well."

I looked down at Maebe who was smiling, and she added, "I am quite adept at hunting. Mate."

A rumbling purr that sounded suspiciously like laughter came from the lion where he laid down. He eyed our surroundings a little more before closing his eyes. From what I saw, he didn't sleep easily, but I guessed it was better than sleeping out in the open, and the equivalent to his god had told him we were cool.

Sleeping that night was odd. I had a dream of the trees around me in the jungle we were going to being rotten to the core. Brittle and the wildlife having to flee—only to die without necessary shelter and food. The death toll was in the hundreds of thousands. I watched as a large shadow loomed over the jungle, and the trees came to life, attacking anything near them. Blood everywhere. So much blood.

My breathing, small frantic puffs of air began to show as if the humidity of the jungle surrounding me no longer mattered. My upper arms began to tingle, then burn slightly. I looked down, and delicate handprints were seared into my skin.

Maebe.

I was dreaming, and she was trying to wake me. I came up out of the dream to find that my biceps were covered in frost the shape of her hands, and she looked at me with concern.

"Are you well?" Her eyes darted over my physical being. "You began to shake and growl, and you kept repeating "no" over and over."

"It was a nightmare, but it felt... different." I looked over at all of my friends. The Elves were awake and watching me intently. Muu snored peacefully. "I don't know what the hell is going on in there, but I think we need to be careful in the jungle. I can't shake what I felt about it."

"We'll be cautious, man." Jaken walked over to us and looked me over. "You, uh, think that could've been a vision from the Mother?"

"It was," Laongal spoke up with his head on his paws. "When the Mother is pleased with her people, she sends them visions. A vision of your coming was sent to me from her, and I fought my way here."

"Fought your way here?" James looked toward the jungle as he spoke.

"Yes, there are creatures in the jungle that had once hidden in the shadows of the cliffs beyond that are emboldened by the disease spreading among the wildlife, trees, and brush inside. I did not fight many, but the ones who thought I would be easy prey were proven wrong."

Jaken began to look him over once more. "So your malnourished looks made them attack? Is the food dying too?"

"The disease spreads mysteriously from plant to prey." The lion yawned. "We do not eat the sick. Otherwise, we risk being poisoned ourselves. Food is becoming more scarce, yes."

"What are these creatures?" I asked.

"Spiders," Laongal spat. "They don't even have the decency to be food when they die—just disgusting."

"Fucking spiders," Bokaj groaned. "It had to fucking be spiders."

"I know the feeling, man." I watched as some of the others shivered. "Fuck spiders."

"Among other creatures of the dark," the lion muttered. "Nasty things, soul-crushing despair is what they breathe, but those only come out at night, the light of day being too potent and harmful to them."

"Vampires?" Yohsuke perked up a bit.

"No, beings of shadow and hatred."

"Oh." He shrugged and laid back down. "No use discussing it all right now. May as well rest while we can."

We did our best to rest that night, not knowing what the next day would bring.

Chapter Twenty

"I do *not* like the way this place smells," Muu whispered.

My fur—that had been on end since we breached the tree line—swayed in the slight breeze coming through the trees around us, and the scent of decay was all I could gather.

"Be on guard, all of you," Laongal ordered. His tail swayed back and forth as we followed him. "The jungle is alive, and it may bite."

"Well, they better have fuckin' pancakes, baby, 'cause Daddy's a hungry lumberjack," I spat.

"What?" Jaken put a hand on my shoulder. "What the hell was that supposed to mean?"

"Lumberjacks eat panca... I've got a bigass axe, man. Leave me 'lone," I spat angrily and walked ahead as the others began to chuckle.

The greenery around us was still lush and healthy. The air here was humid and thick, but these plants seemed to be doing well. We walked for a while, strange bird calls and the cries of what sounded like monkeys in the distance all around us.

The sky began to darken as the trees began to grow closer to each other. The canopy above us thickened considerably. While it wasn't too dark to see by, it was thick shadows and deafening sound from then on.

As we worked our way deeper, the jungle began to turn. Some of the trees became bleached and white in spots. Fungus grew in some places, large mushrooms with huge, spongy tops.

"The sickness has spread further," Laongal growled deeply. "We should stop here. Druid, speak to the Mother."

My eyebrows raised slightly, but he wasn't wrong.

I did something that I hadn't done since I first pleaded with her to allow me to take her strength. To make me a Druid. I began to speak to her in her tongue, the tongue of the wild—Druidic.

Through a series of bird calls, growls, snarls, and other animal sounds, I pleaded, "Mother, Lady of the Wilds, I beseech you—grant me strength. Help me know how to heal these lands. Help me breathe life back into these trees and the earth here, please."

The world around me fell away, and not in the traditional sense. I didn't fade to black. I wasn't taken anywhere. No animal came to me. Just silence. Pure silence. Then a small, light sound of laughter.

I turned to see a human-looking woman in her mid-forties. She wore a toga, oddly enough, of creamy white and a band of leaves wrapped around her head. Her face was only mildly wrinkled, but there were smile lines beside her purple and gold eyes. Her middling-length hair was a deep gray with streaks of white near her temples.

I was face to face with the Mother. I looked left, and I saw Tmont and Bokaj standing beside us as well. Just as stunned as I was.

Out of instinct, I knelt where I was and grabbed Bokaj's arm to pull him down beside me.

"We finally meet, little one." Her voice was much lighter than I thought it would be, but it definitely had that motherly undertone.

"Mother," Bokaj and I said in unison. Tmont growled and dipped her head.

"Come to me, Tmont." The panther stood and padded toward the physical—or was it metaphysical—manifestation of the planet and all living life on it. She leaned down and scratched the panther on the chin lovingly. "Good kitty."

She regarded us after a moment, "Stand. I will not have you kneel as if I was a god, and I am not as displeased with you as I once had been."

She walked over to us and put her hand on my cheek. "You have not yet earned my favor back—but you are well along your way. Maintain this course, my child."

I nodded, suddenly unable to find the words to express myself.

She stepped in front of Bokaj. "Our dealings have been minimal, Ranger—but I have seen the way you care for your companion and found it endearing. I shall bless you as well."

She stepped between us and pressed her palms to our heads, and a searing pain burst through my skull. A thousand needles jabbed behind my eyes, and I lost my footing. On my knees, my head on the floor, I received a notification.

Blessing received!
New abilities unlocked!
Purify – Caster uses concentrated bursts of mana in order to purify the target of the spell of disease, poison, or other maladies. Cost: Dependent (minimum of 100MP). Range: 25 feet. Cooldown: N.A. Number of Targets: Mana total divided by 10 (total potential targets: 5).

"Thank you," Bokaj groaned.

I held my fist up and gave her a thumb up to indicate I felt the same.

"The pain will fade, little ones." Mother Nature's voice sounded distant now. "Be well, and good luck. Remember our deal, and watch out for yourselves."

I looked up, the dull light still too bright for my eyes and noted that our friends were still gathered around us.

"You saw her, did you not, Druid?" Laongal was suddenly next to me.

"We both did," Bokaj mumbled. He was holding his head, same as I was.

"Bokaj, you wanna help me clear this place out?" I grumbled.

"Yup." He stepped over to a pile of fungus on a tree, and I approached the tree closest to me. "Watch our backs."

Once I was close enough, inside the range of the spell, I cast the spell on the tree and watched in wonder as time seemed to reverse and the spots of fungus and sickly white began to recede. Once they were cleared from the surface, the mana traveled deeper and deeper. Another hundred mana burned clear. The roots were now purified. I watched as fungus on the ground began to shrink, shrivel, and die once it was cut away from the root system.

I looked over and watched as the same thing occurred with Bokaj.

That had been about 200 MP for me and Bokaj's full 250 MP, since his tree had been slightly larger and the roots further. So this could take a while. That had been all of his mana. So this was going to be rough going if we were to try and clear the whole damned jungle while we looked for the problem.

"This is going to take forever," Bokaj groaned aloud. "There's got to be another way."

"Could you enchant something that makes it easier?" Jaken asked after a moment. "Maybe some arrows? A ring? Anything that might give us the ability to use the spell?"

Can I do that? I wondered to myself. I mean, I had given Muu the ability to use a modified version of my Regrowth spell with a ring. Maybe I could do the same with another ring?

But the one I had was shitty; it may not hold this kind of enchantment at such a low quality.

There had to be another way.

"Hey, Jaken—think the Celestials can help cleanse this place?" I asked our Paladin.

He thought it over for a moment, "I don't see why they couldn't. Though I would suggest that you do it. Just in case."

I nodded. It was a good idea. I could shift without any mana expenditure.

I reached for the magic in me and cast Summon Celestial. The normal rent in the air opened before me. The tearing sound filled the air as the veil between the Celestial realm and our own opened wide for a figure to step through.

Instead of the angel warrior Samu, there was a woman, roughly nine feet tall, in radiant armor that made Jaken and Muu's armor look like shit.

"Hello summoner," she spoke, her tone commanding and breathy all at once. "How can I assist you?"

"Hello, I'm Zeke." I motioned to the forest around us. "There's some kind of disease here that it will take us forever to purify as we look for the source. I was hoping you might be able to help us somehow?"

"An open-ended request?" Her golden eyebrows arched. "Highly unusual. Samu was right about you."

She began to walk about the area with her eyes wandering the scene. She stopped in front of Maebe with a curious expression. "Queen of Ice and Darkness."

"Lady of the Rank and File," Maebe returned mildly. "A pleasure to make your acquaintance. Can you assist?"

"I cannot do anything about this disease itself, no. It seems to be highly resistant to radiant energies." The angel turned her gaze on me. "I can tell you, however, that what you seek is further south and west. You will know it when you come to it, but be prepared for a fight. Good luck to you all."

She stepped back through the rent in the veil and was gone.

"Well, that gives us a heading." James shrugged. "Laongal, do you know what is that far down?"

"Cultists, all manner of ill that have been quietly living in the jungle for decades." The lion bared his teeth. "The denizens of the area usually stay away from them and their experimentation. They've left us well enough alone. I had thought to take you directly to where the spiders call home, as I was under the impression that they were responsible."

"We may be able to take care of them once we solve this issue. We'll be here for a bit trying to find something." Yohsuke glanced at the sky above us. "Bokaj, you know where we're headed from here?"

"Yep." He pointed toward a trail that diverged from our current course and nodded. "That's the best way to go, though Laongal should still lead us since he knows the environment best."

"I will agree with that," Laongal rumbled at us, I translated. "If we are to try and see what is going on, then we should travel as far as we can today. One more night and we shall have you at your quarry."

A thought occurred to me, and I approached our guide. "Laongal, would you mind if I took your shape?"

"I would be honored, Druid Zeke." The lion sat for me, then bit my hand so I could take his lion form.

"Thank you. Let's head out, bud." I shrugged my shoulder to relieve a little tension from the bite and began to eye my surroundings.

Here and there, I would cast Purify on the worst of the diseased plants around us as we moved along. There was one animal I saw that was sick, a large, vaguely toucan-looking bird, but the beak was razor sharp, and the wings were longer than the body when folded closed. The vibrant colors of its feathers had begun to gray, its blue head feathers sprouting mushrooms and some moss.

I cast Purify on it and watched as the color and life returned to the bird, and it flew off as soon as it could. I saw as it left that the same fungal coloring it had was on the branch as well and cast the spell again. The life returned, and it was a whopping 400 MP after that. The disease had been deeper than I had expected. Fuck.

For the next few minutes, the mana headache kicked my ass. Thankfully, I regenerated at a good rate.

Other than the events of the day previously and trying to rid our surroundings of the worst disease as we went, nothing happened.

That night, we had the shadow dome around us once more, and we watched as creatures of fungus—not just covered in fungus, but *made* of it—loped through the areas of shadow around the trees just outside camp. They looked like mushrooms with lichen and other decaying things growing on them with sharp teeth and dead, gray eyes, but they seemed to sense that something was nearby. I watched as they sniffed and snorted around the area.

As they drifted closer, they growled at the field around the dome but didn't venture too close. As they gathered, I tried to get a reading on their levels. They all seemed to be around our level. The highest ones being level 25, and those ones looked like wolves.

They eventually left us alone after a while. The Elves took turns meditating, while Muu and I tried to get what sleep we could with their noisy asses snooping around.

I was a little grouchy when I woke up but otherwise rested and ready to take off. Where those creatures had been, let's just call them Shroomies—No? Okay, how about Fungal Beasts? Better? Cool—had snooped, the disease had returned, their close proximity bringing it back.

One of the smaller trees looked particularly gnarled and eaten away. As I stepped into range to try and clean it up, I damned near shit myself as it pulled itself from the ground and drudged forward with a jack-o-lantern-like face. It swung at me with a newly made, branch-like arm, and I had to drop to get under it in time. I stood and got a read on it.

Fungal Beast (Tree) level 27

"Fuck me!" I shouted as I backed away. "Kick the shit out of it. It's gotta be too far gone for me to try and purify."

"On it," Jaken grunted as he stepped between me and a wooden spear with razor-sharp leaves on it. "I know I don't even need to suggest what it might be weak to."

Yohsuke and I grinned at each other and shouted, "Fire!"

I cast Filgus' Flaming Blade, then began to funnel more mana into it to make the blade into a great axe. I just *knew* it could be done.

NEW SPELL CREATED!

Filgus' Flaming Great Axe – Caster summons a great axe made of pure flame to fight with. Cost: 80 MP. Duration: 10 minutes. Cooldown: 30 seconds.

"Oh, daddy loves new toys!" I growled triumphantly. I leaped over Jaken's head and activated Cleave before striking at the Fungal Beast in the upper boughs of its body. It shrieked as a few of the limbs fell away and burned. I used the trunk as a stepping stone and kicked myself away from it, barely getting out in time to avoid Yohsuke's Hellfire Arrow as it beamed straight into its face.

It shrieked again and its health was falling slowly but surely. I danced around Jaken, then James who was using his Elemental Fists and his Flame Fang weapons to beat the hell from the creature, and I slashed horizontally with my flaming great axe. It charred the bark, and the creature began shrieking again.

I watched as its roots began to try and wiggle their way into the ground on my side. That couldn't be good.

"Go for the roots!" I barked at the others. "Bokaj, take the trunk. Where the fuck is Muu?"

Deciding I didn't have time to babysit the Dragon-kin at that moment, I started slashing at the roots near me. I would slice through a few of them, and then the tree would turn on me. Yohsuke sawed through a couple, then the same occurred.

At least until I heard the sound of wood splintering, the crackle of electricity, and the telltale whistle and shrieking laughter of an airborne dragoon reached our ears. I shoved James away from the tree and dove out of the way as Muu crashed into the top of the Fungal Beast.

SLAM!

The crystalline lance under his legs like a pogo stick, I watched as a good majority of the wood at the top of the tree turned to ice and shattered at the force. A great chunk of health was sheared from the HP bar after that, and the rest of us were able to fell the tree in seconds.

"Solid work, dragoon," I grunted, then pulled him close. "How about a little fucking communication next time you do something like that?"

"I tried to use the earring, but for some reason, it wasn't going through. I figured it would be best to just attack and do what I know I should be doing," Muu explained. "Try it. Try using your earrings, all of you."

I willed my thoughts to project to my friends, the same as I had dozens of times before and got blank stares in return.

"I think there is something here fucking with any kind of mental signal or communication magic," Muu said as the rest of us stared at him. "Try your other communication spells."

I used Mental Message and tried to speak to Muu with my back turned, "Testing. Testing." I turned and looked at him, and he shrugged.

"I cannot use Shadow Speak," Maebe spoke and sealed it.

"Okay, so something nearby stops communication," Bokaj said. "We go by mouth from now on."

"Your mom goes by mouth," Jaken teased. We shot him half-hearted dirty looks, and he laughed anyway.

"I would wager that it would be the cultists," Laongal said. I had made it a habit to cast Nature's voice so much that I didn't even think about it anymore.

So, at least that worked. I would have bet that it had something to do with it being more about talking in person than over distances.

"Probably right," Yohsuke offered. "Anyone else level up? That just pushed me over the edge."

I looked and found a level up notification. Everyone else raised their hands. Muu held up two fingers.

Christ, man. What I wouldn't give to be making those gains again, I thought as I slipped the little green monster in my heart another knockout punch. Jealousy has no place among friends. That bitch stays in the dungeons.

I bumped my strength up to fifty even with three points, then added a point each to dexterity and constitution, taking them to thirty-seven and thirty-three respectively. Then I mentally berated myself for not thinking to summon Coal so that he could level up a little bit.

Then again, against a monster that size, what could he have done? Pee on him?

I felt a distinct sense of anger in the core of my being and felt Coal lift his leg. *Don't you fucking dare, Fido.* He lowered it slowly as a threat, and I got the idea. Little bastard.

We were much more cautious moving forward, and everyone's idea of preparation was to ensure we knew to use flame magic.

As we walked through the jungle, eyeing trees carefully and treating the worst of the infected wildlife, we caught the scent of decay and heavy death.

"Think we're close?" Muu whispered to us. We just kept moving, but it sure seemed that way.

Within ten minutes of dedicatedly sneaking forward—we caught sight of a village.

The layout was circular, the houses and buildings well-built and maintained, but there were no signs of life.

"You guys cover me again. Hopefully, we see something," I looked once more, and nothing had changed. "You see anything that even remotely looks hostile—light it up."

I walked back a little ways and took my owl form, then took off. I weaved my ways through branches and boughs, minding my distances between things and surveyed our surroundings first. This place was surprisingly untouched by the disease that was spreading through the jungle.

It made no sense. If this was where we were supposed to go, how was this place as normal as this looked?

I tried to get closer to the village itself, but I saw something that really set some alarms off for me—a barrier.

I dipped low toward the ground, being careful not to touch the barrier and noted that where the barrier touched the ground, there was blood. I looked and tried to find any signs of bodies, but nothing was immediately visible.

I turned to find a lumbering figure that looked like a zombie with mushrooms in its human-looking face reaching toward me with one of its arms. I clawed at the air as I whirled midair and dropped to the ground to shift into my fox form. I heard the thud of arrows peppering the figure and the ground and a distinct squelching that made me pause. I turned and saw Muu's older spear disappear from the body of the creature and another few arrows sprout from it. I shifted and planted my Ursolon paw into its chest and shoved it into the barrier.

It turned to dust.

I quickly turned and saw no more of the fungal creatures, then waved to my friends. I kept a lookout while they crossed the distance toward me and the barrier.

"Thanks for that, guys," I said after shifting back into my fox-man form. "If this barrier does what I think it does, then we're in trouble."

"Well, I saw it turn that thing into dust, so that means that it's keeping something in there, right?" Yohsuke checked. He looked at the ground under the barrier at the blood. "Blood magic. Think it was a cultist?"

"No doubt," James grunted, and Muu nodded agreement.

Bokaj walked over, careful not to touch the translucent energy and eyed it. "So, how do we get in there?"

"We could break through it." James held his fist up with the blade out.

"No." Yohsuke touched his shoulder. "That would give whatever is inside an escape route, and we might never find it."

"The barrier will hold whatever is in it, but tonight, I can get you inside." Maebe stepped over to the barrier and eyed it before turning to the rest of us. "Until then, we must rest. Get what sleep you can, and prepare."

We fell back to the tree line where the thickets were the heaviest and closest and set to work.

Once we had our meeting place and best vantage points, I nodded to the others and turned to gather some essentials from around us. If whatever was inside could cause and spread this disease from inside a barrier, we were in shit creek and our paddle was in a crocodile with a taste for flesh.

Looking at the area around us, the trees had grown much larger than that of the ones on the outer rim of the jungle. I touched the bark of one of them and tried something I hadn't before. I spoke to the tree in Druidic.

"Hello, friend," I began, honestly not knowing if it would even understand me. "I was wondering if you could help me. My friends and I need to go in there, and we need something to help us keep the disease away from us. You're the strongest tree I can find here. Can I trouble you for something—anything—that could help us?"

I waited for the tree to respond somehow, with no overt results. I heard the wind blow through its limbs. I looked up in time to see a limb dip low for a moment, impossibly low for the height it was up there. I heard a crack and thud as the tip of the limb snapped. Another. Then another. Two more. Finally, one last limb tip landed at my feet. Each was a foot long, the widths varying slightly from each other but just barely.

"Thank you, friend." I felt a leaf drop on my head in return and returned to the group to get busy.

I took a moment to think of the designs I wanted to etch into the wands. I decided on a simple, swirling design of a tree, much like the one that had given me the pieces. It was a simple process and only took a moment for each of the wands to be etched the same way.

"Anyone have an emerald?" I asked the others. They began checking their inventories, and finally, Jaken raised his hand.

"It's uncut. That okay?" I smiled at him, and he tossed it to me.

It was roughly three inches wide, thick and long, but it was rounded in a lot of areas. Very rough. It was perfect.

"I'll buy you a new one, man," I told Jaken, but he waved it away. "Fuck you, I'll get you a new one."

He grinned, and I turned back to my work. I took about twenty minutes or so to scrape the hell out of the precious stone with my claws. As the scrapings and powder began to fall on to the leaf that I was using to collect it, I said a little prayer to the Mother in my mind. Hoping like hell this would work, I took a moment to pull some of the larger chunks out of the powder, then prepared for the enchanting portion.

I focused on keeping the person that has this item on their person or in their inventory free of the disease that was plaguing the area. Of constantly purifying the owner. As I funneled my mana into the design, I took a good-sized pinch of powdered emerald and sprinkled it over the item.

I repeated the same process for each, though halfway through, I needed to stop and file off more powder. Each wand took my full amount of mana to prepare, but the end results were *worth it*. Not to mention, I had leveled up my enchanting again. I was level 34 in my craft.

Nualo Wand of Purity

Owner of this wand is granted a measure of protection against the disease spreading through the Nualo Jungle. Restriction: The item must be on the owner's person.

Wand given of Dregnortillo's free will and enchanted by Craftsman Enchanter Zekiel Erebos.

"Muu, when you were working with Natholdi, did you happen to keep any leather?" Muu looked over at me, curiosity in his features. "I could use some pieces to tie these to us so our hands are free."

Muu reached into his inventory and pulled out a large roll of leather, tanned properly and thin. "How many cords do you need?"

"Well, possibly only one each for you and Jaken." I thought about it some more. "I'll need a few to tie them directly to the rest of us. Around the neck and possibly around the waist or under the arms? FUCK!"

Bokaj and Jaken both jumped out of the corner of my eye and looked at me for clarification. "I forgot to make one for Tmont, man. Shit."

I felt a small thud on my head and looked up in time to see the limbs of the same tree shaking slightly. A perfect replica of the original wands was between my feet.

"Thank you, Dregnortillo!" I called to the tree. I went through the familiar process of enchanting it, and after a few test cuts on the leather, we were all able to secure the wands to our bodies.

After that, it was time to rest and prepare for the coming excursion into the cultist village.

Chapter Twenty-One

"You must awaken. It is time." Maebe gently shook me awake. I had fallen asleep using her legs as pillows while she gently ran her nails over the top of my head between my ears.

"Thank you." I smiled up at her sleepily.

I sat up and stretched out a bit. The light was gone completely, but somehow, there were lights on in the village. Must have been enchantments. The moon was high above us, half full and beautiful to behold.

"I know I don't have to ask, but will you be alright out here, Maebe?" Muu wandered over.

The queen of the Unseelie Fae regarded him for a moment that seemed to make him squirm before answering, "I will be well, friend Muu. Your concern is... appreciated."

He nodded to her and walked away again with a mildly worried look.

"He means well, I know," Maebe watched him steadily as he left, "but he is the only one who actively engages with me other than you usually, and I enjoy seeing him squirm."

"You are one sick individual," I teased her. Her confused look made me chuckle. "Sick as in there's something wrong with you mentally. It's meant to be teasingly unless someone really *is* sick. You'll get it eventually. Hey, I'm gonna miss having you watching my back. Also, don't worry—the guys will open up to you eventually."

"Do not worry," she replied coolly. "If I do not believe that you are safe, I am coming in after all of you. Experience be damned."

"Glad to know the cavalry has our back." Jaken smiled at her and offered her his fist.

Maebe, who had seen the gesture thrown around dozens of times, clenched her fist and rapped her knuckles against Jaken's. He grunted and shook his fist, and Maebe stepped forward to check and see if he was okay before Jaken's telltale shit-eating grin was visible.

"Got ya." Maebe was confused but actually returned his grin.

"You will not 'get' me again, little Paladin." Her grin had sudden feral implications.

"Fuck, she's scary as shit," Jaken muttered with a shiver as he walked away.

I kissed her cheek and shook my head while I walked over to stand next to the others at our agreed upon entry point. We watched together as Maebe's hands began to move surely in gathering motions. Shadows began to pull from the tops of the trees, beneath them, and even our own shadows began to move toward her.

After a few heartbeats, she sent the shadows along the ground toward us, and we scrambled out of the way. The darkness crawled up the side of the barrier, causing a burning scent and a crackling sound. Maebe pressed her hands together with her palms out and pushed them forward toward the barrier. Then she pulled her hands apart with a small hiss of effort, and the shadows gripped the barrier and pushed a hole large enough for us to walk through.

As soon as we moved through, the opening was gone, and Maebe was just on the other side of the barrier.

"Be safe, and remember—if you take too long, I am coming."

I nodded and turned back toward the village. The sense of death and decay was stronger here than it had been with those creatures the other night. I felt a warmth on my chest where the wand was strapped to my body. It made moving a little odd, but the emerald and wood were both sturdy, so it was alright. From the looks on my friends' faces—they felt it too.

As we moved through the village, the simple buildings of unpainted wood were untouched. There was nothing of real note inside any of them except a pile of mushrooms here and there. If you ignored the fact that they looked vaguely person-shaped and sized, it was a cake walk.

But there were dozens of those same fungal grave sites indoors. Then there was the building furthest from our entry point, a large one with paintings and runes that I recognized as Celestial from my book, but I didn't dare pull it out to research them right then and there.

"I don't like the way that place looks," James said flatly.

"What do you wanna bet that's where these assholes worship?" Yohsuke crouched slightly and started forward. Jaken was in front of him in an instant.

"Let me." He put a hand on Yoh's shoulder and then began to cautiously move toward the building.

The dark wooden doors were wide open and bolted that way, as if to encourage the members of the community to come in and worship at all hours.

The ramp that led to the doors wasn't a steep one, but it was worn and clear except for the smallest mound of mushrooms we had seen. I frowned as I tried to ignore the fact that it had most likely been a child. Hopefully, they hadn't suffered.

"I say we blow the bitch from the outside," Muu mumbled behind me. I turned to look at him. "Place feels wrong."

"There could be people inside," Jaken reasoned before he shook his head. "No. We're going in."

"You gotta have spells in rings, do 'em now," James said. "Zeke, I think it should be Purify. Pump it all in there."

I raised my eyebrows but couldn't find any fault in that idea. Yohsuke offered me his empty ring, and I filled it with a fully-powered Purify spell before handing it back. I still had a spell stored in my ring of storage—Mass Regrowth. I'd be keeping that. No telling what was going to happen, but I'd rather have that.

We waited a few minutes for my mana to fully recharge before we trudged up the small slope into the building.

There were more mushroom mounds inside as we entered and our eyes adjusted to the dim light. There were torches along the walls that lit the room well. I counted at least two dozen mounds at a glance, but what truly caught my attention was a hooded figure seated on an altar as if he were seated on a wall.

"Ah," the figure's tone sounded odd. As if there was no genuine surprise in it, and he was trying too hard. Like seriously bad voice acting. "A fresh round of potential hosts."

"We aren't anything like that," Yohsuke spouted angrily.

The scent of decay was strongest here, and the more I looked at the figure, the more my skin began to crawl.

"Of course," he slowly held a hand out to his side, like he was cautiously patting a dog. "You must be here to worship me in your own ways. These other people did. They were the ones who summoned me, you know?"

I was going to tell him to shove it, but Bokaj touched my hand softly, I looked, and he shook his head and mouthed, *Wait*.

"They were tired of those uppity Gods above constantly having their way. Foiling plans. Stopping their adding to their numbers. So, I offered them the means to achieve their end."

"But you aren't a god," James accused.

"Of course not." The creature chuckled. It pulled the hood from its head. Beneath was an average-looking man with a balding pate and smooth, sallow skin. His eyes were gray, but where the whites should have been, there was blood—not running but an angry red. "The Gods are weak, imperfect things clinging to tenants set forth to subjugate the weak so that their worshipers' blind faith will fuel them."

He stood slowly. Almost cautiously, like he was afraid of moving too much or too quickly.

"I, on the other hand, am strong enough to take the strength from many in a more direct route. I am all, and all eventually are me." Slowly, a benevolent look passed over his face, the creepy smile mechanical and puppet-like. "Once this barrier fades, as I am already corroding the blood magic that seals me here, I will be free to grow and become the god I am meant to be. What they cannot be. So much more than the mere minion that I once had been."

"So, then what are you right now?" Jaken asked. His shield and weapon had been out from the start, but he had begun raising them a little as the thing had begun speaking.

"I am Decay." The man's neck popped audibly as his head tilted a little too far. The question marks above his head and HP bar changed to reflect the name. "I can feel the Radiance about you, Paladin. Come, let me cleanse you of that abominable lie that your 'beloved' goddess has fooled you with. Allow me to show you the truth."

Decay level 32

"Sure." Jaken shuffled forward, and the fight was on. We couldn't let this thing do whatever the hell it wanted.

Jaken's longsword slashed, shining in the light slightly and stopped as Decay flicked his hand out.

"Foolish, but I do not blame you—I blame the lies." It hissed and stepped forward slowly.

Even though its movements were clunky and stilted, it hit Jaken hard enough to throw him through the wall behind us and into the yard. *Shit.*

I brought my axe to the ready and watched as James was just suddenly there in front of Decay, his Dragon's Tooth blade slicing toward the figure. Then I watched Yohsuke step forward and slash with his Astral Blade. Decay's right arm fell, and the scent of rotting produce became overpowering. Yohsuke shot back off his feet as James fell and flattened himself with a shout of pain.

His health bar plummeted by fifty percent, and the issue made itself known. A black arm with a dark, fluctuating cloud of noxious looking gas around it, flexed. The muscles of it were insanely perfect, and it was a little clearer why it had seemed so weird for the creature to move. I looked, and his display changed.

Decay level 38

"I had so hoped to keep this body intact a little while longer." Decay sighed, attempting to adopt a saddened look. "That just means one of you will have to remain intact. Oh well, necessary sacrifice for a better world, eh?"

"You talk too fucking much," Muu spat vehemently, then launched his older short spear at Decay from twenty feet away.

The spear's flight stopped in Decay's monstrous stank hand and immediately split in half. The clatter of metal on the rough wooden floor was a wake-up call.

"Get out!" I roared. I shoved Muu toward the hole in the wall. Bokaj was already moving with his bow working overtime. I created a stone hammer with Stone Weapon and smacked

Decay in the chest while he was distracted by the arrows that peppered his chest and still-human arm. Where each hit, more of the gas filtered out of the wounds, and the arrows turned to rust and disintegrated. The hammer hit forced him back ten feet, but he kept his footing.

I grabbed James and threw him toward the hole in the wall as he flashed with Ki, his health pulsing back up to full.

Decay began to walk forward toward us, and I abandoned the hammer toward his face with extreme prejudice. It was highly unlikely that it would hurt him, but if I committed to an attack over running, I was more vulnerable than I could risk at that moment. Better to be rid of the now-useless spell and join my friends outside.

The night sky was a little lighter as the moon rose above us, but the creepy sight of Decay stood in the doorway. He snapped his fingers, and the mounds of mushrooms began to stand. They were vaguely humanoid, but they were crooked and crumbly in places. One of them grabbed me around the chest from behind, its arms touching the wand touched to my chest through the cloth. I felt the wand heat against my fur, and the arms loosened a bit.

Enough for me to dive backward and on top of it before rolling out of the grip. Once I was upright, I slashed at it with Magus Bane. The axe sliced cleanly through.

I caught sight of my friends making short work of the horde of decomposing dead and then caught movement toward the building. Decay walked among them, and each one he touched brought his barely depleted HP bar closer to full. Even as he touched them and they turned to dust, his focus was on us. He stepped within range of Yohsuke and the Spell Blade punched forward with his ring.

Six of the creatures dropped in clouds of dust, and Decay snarled savagely as a portion of his face was hewn away by the spell. His true expression of rage peaked out, and the blood red of the human eyes was mirrored by a glowing, red orb staring out at us. The mouth that the flesh didn't cover was too large and had too many teeth. Once more, his level went up, the more his true form was exposed.

Decay level 55

More arrows peppered the body, and a concussive blast of force and fumes shook me from my feet. I slid on my back longer than I might have thought. My health dropped steadily, and I coughed. Eighty, seventy-five, seventy, sixty-five percent. Shit.

I stood and limped toward the majority of my friends. James managed to get away from the blast, and I didn't see Muu, so I figured he was skyward.

I used the ring of storage I had and cast Mass Regrowth on myself, Bokaj, Yohsuke, and James.

I looked at my friends, banged up and hurting despite the healing and regeneration that they had received. I looked at the angry Decay and noted that he was still above three-quarters health.

He stood and surged forward, slamming into Jaken's shield with the one human fist it had left, knocking the floating thing aside. Jaken's sword danced, attempting to slice at him with a glowing golden light surrounding it. It was doing a little damage but not enough.

Yohsuke threw a Star Burst at him, and the creature batted it aside and into James. He punched it and flew back on to his back. The monk flashed with Ki, and he began to sit up.

Muu brought out his lance and attempted to help Jaken keep Decay's attention. The blackened hand snatched an arrow out of the air and plunged it into Jaken's shoulder, his health decreasing to sixty-five percent.

I shifted into my owl form, took to the air above them, and saw our opponent kick Jaken away from him, and Muu backed away slightly.

I picked that time to shift to fox form, then to Ursolon and plummeted toward Decay's head. I thought I was going to land on him and smiled, but he stepped out of the way and kicked me so hard I flew twenty feet to his left into a smaller building.

I dropped to sixty percent health and tried to drag myself back to my feet. It hurt so badly. This was going shitty, and yelling ideas to each other was out of the question because he would know.

I came out of the hole in the smaller building and watched Yohsuke land a single cut on Decay before the adaptor was slapped from his hand, and then the creature backhanded Yoh away from him.

I came back out and took stock. James was trying to dodge the asshole as he swung at him, taking damage from being too close. There was no way. The more we hurt him, the stronger he got, and he had more mushroom creatures joining the fight from inside the chapel area.

"Mushrooms!" I called, and the others began trying to kill them, Tmont crashing out of the house beneath Bokaj's position to slice into a few of them.

They fell, but they were coming still, and Decay had begun using them to heal again.

Fuck it, there's no way we can beat this thing on our own, not if his level keeps going up so much and he can heal like that.

I bared my teeth. "Butterscotch!" I shouted loudly over my shoulder.

To their credit, my friends didn't look at me half as oddly as Decay did, and he had thrown his arms in front of himself defensively.

The night around us stilled, and I watched as a wave of shadows depleted from the area that we had left Maebe outside the barrier. A slight whiffing noise reached my ears and a grunt, then quiet.

I watched as Maebe, Ruler of the Unseelie levitated regally into the opened grounds of the village.

"You are truly beginning to show wisdom." Maebe smiled sweetly at me. She looked at the others, then Decay and frowned. "Why is a Greater Fiend here? Why does it feel so wrong? Is it that it could be a minion of War?"

"I am Decay. I come to cleanse this world and take my place as the rightful ruler of all. War holds no sway over me anymore. I am above him."

"I am Queen here," Maebe shot back simply. She held her hand out, and I stepped closer to her.

"Don't touch him. He can cause serious damage that way." She acknowledged my advice with a nod and clenched her fist.

A snap of cold flash froze the ground in a straight line and ice burst from the ground, smacking into the creature. He shot from his position into one of the buildings behind him.

Maebe's other fist radiated pure midnight energy, and she pressed the palm to herself. She ran the hand down her form, and the shadows coalesced into a dress, long enough to touch the ground as she floated there.

The creature stepped from the rubble, and I watched as Muu rocketed toward him from above. A good majority of the human meat suit was gone now, and as Muu closed with Decay's position, a handful of energy slammed into Muu and threw him into a building behind us. As soon as the front wall burst, Bokaj was there and casting his own Heal spell on the Dragon-kin.

Oooooouuuuch, fuck that hurt. Muu's thoughts projected to me.

I looked at my friends, and they had heard it too.

"Mae, keep him still. I have an idea." I touched her shoulder softly before I moved toward my friends.

Get your wands out, guys. We need to stab him with them while Maebe has him distracted.

Jaken, Yohsuke, and I collectively pulled our wands from our bodies and handed them to James. I touched him and gave him Shadow Blessing to help him sneak and dodge a bit better.

I'll wait until he's really distracted, but as soon as I'm done—I'm hauling ass away. James walked away from our huddle, trying to psych himself up and get to Bokaj and Muu.

Maebe and Decay were trading blows. Decay sent shockwaves of disgusting energy at her, and she countered with shadow and ice. He sent one such shockwave at us, and Maebe deflected it with a wall of ice. Another building fell, and the barrier began to crackle a little. Like watching the fuzzy channel on cable, it was kind of there, but the fuzz was distracting.

Decay began to make a gathering motion with his hands and focused his sights on Maebe completely. As he prepared to loose his foul spell, James materialized behind him and stabbed down with all his might. Decay shrieked inhumanly and dropped to a knee, the spell forgotten momentarily as he clawed at the wands sticking into him.

Decay level 26 (55)

I nodded at Muu, who had since joined us and shifted to my fox form before leaping up into his arm. For the second time since he had come to this world, my former roommate pulled back his arm and used his bracelet to hurl me forward. I strobed with my eyes, blinking rapidly until I was just close enough to shift to my fox-man form. I didn't dare touch him; he was truly losing his human shell now. It melted swiftly.

If I add a flame element to my Purify spell, could that do a lot of damage? It was worth a shot. This shit dragging on could be disastrous.

No, what I did was stupid. I felt a warmth around me that felt close to how Coal felt, then reached into my mana reserves and cast equal parts Purify with my flame tinkering ability. I spent all my mana and shoved the concoction toward Decay's kneeling form as I flew over.

"*Raaayyaarrrrrrrhggg!*" Decay screamed. My body hit a large beam of some kind in the temple or whatever it was, and I tried to shift myself so that I could see.

I looked at my health bar, and it was low, about thirty-five percent. I had a broken bone icon and another unfamiliar one that looked like shaking symbols under the health bar that said I was paralyzed.

"Fuck," I grumbled. I had to trust my friends.

I heard motion, shouting, and a loud crash that shook the ground hard enough to rattle me a bit more. A purring sound from behind startled me, but I couldn't even flinch. I realized that it was Tmont when her tufted ear swayed into view.

My mana had recovered enough by then that I cast Nature's Voice and asked, "What happened?"

"The cold one crushed the smelly one after you and the others injured him gravely. Once he was hurt like that, the one in metal with the shield cut him with his glowing sword." She searched for the next words as she sat beside me. "As did the dark one who feeds us all. The lizard who does not care for me tried to help but was tossed away, and the scaled one hit him a few times. Master's performance was the most interesting. His arrows made the smelly one look like a porcupine."

"That seems a biased position." I couldn't help laughing at her descriptions of my friends. I'd have to tell them later.

"Yes, well, your tails are very unprotected as of right now," Tmont observed pointedly.

"Sure thing, Puss," I retorted. "Did anyone get hurt?"

"Other than the cat hater, the smelly one hurt your mate a little bit, but she seems to have taken care of the worst of it." She purred louder. "She is a fine one to aspire to. You would do well to heed her, master's friend. They come."

"Yo, Zeke, you gonna just lay there and milk that shit or what, motherfucker?" Yohsuke stomped into the building.

"I'm paralyzed, you asshat." I tried to sound angry, but honestly, I was happier to know that aside from possibly a bruised ego, my friends were okay.

"Hey, Jaken, you got anything that will heal being a little bitch?" Muu called. "I think Zeke needs two."

"Oh, you're all catching hands for this shit," I growled. Kind of hard to be menacing when you can't move—but I tried.

"Think we should shave him?" Bokaj quipped. "We all have very sharp tools."

"I swear, I will sick Coal on all of you," I grunted.

Jaken must have come in because I was being picked up and moved outside. I looked down, the only way I could look in my ragdoll state. I saw Jaken's leg armor and then Maebe's shadow dress. Jaken handed me to her, and she carried my limp body for a moment. We were inside a building before I realized it and I was on a bed.

"What about the disease?" I asked after seeing some of the dust on the floor in here from those mushroom person mounds.

"The majority of it inside the barrier was sucked back to the abyss with the fiend," Maebe explained. "You will be fine here. The others went to clear some of the disease as best they could. You may do your work, Paladin."

Maebe's face backed out of view, and I felt radiant energy surround my body and move inward. I could feel my broken bones returning to their former positions. I felt a small pinch in my upper back and then immediate relief. Without even looking at my statuses, I could tell I'd be able to move now.

"Thanks, man." I held my fist up for Jaken to tap.

"You got it, bud." He looked me over a bit more, then sighed. "Gonna need you to stop doing crazy shit like that, man. You scared the hell out of me. All of us. I'm gonna go check on the others and keep Bokaj company as he tries to stem the spread of the disease. Rest. At least half an hour. Spend your stat points however, but you need to rest."

I frowned and checked my notifications.

CONGRATULATIONS!
Level Up!

Name: Zekiel Erebos
Level: 25
Strength: 50
Dexterity: 37
Constitution: 33
Intelligence: 50
Wisdom: 36
Charisma: 17

Unspent Attribute Points: 15

"Three levels!" I sat in stunned silence after that. "How big of a boss was he?"

"He would have probably been as hard to kill as I would have," Maebe explained. "He even gave me enough experience to level up once. That was very nice."

"Congratulations." I smiled at her.

"You did a brave—and stupid—thing, Zekiel Erebos." Her eyes narrowed dangerously, and I honestly thought I might have to use my safe word again. "What were you thinking?"

"I was thinking that if we didn't kill him, this place was doomed. This place, my friends, and you—everybody in Brindolla—was in danger. I had to do what I could, and that was the best way I could think of to do a lot of damage in a short amount of time."

"It wasn't a bad idea, but the execution lacked foresight." She huffed. "If you had told me what you had been planning, I could have cushioned your landing. I could have helped you."

"Communication is key, got it." I looked at her, taking in the features that I had grown ever so slightly more accustomed to. Her features were drawn, and she looked tired. Worried. "Are you okay?"

"That was a good fight, but it is the first time in quite some time that I had to think of others as more than a numerical advantage on the field of battle." Her tired eyes closed, and she sighed deeply. "Do not do something so reckless like that again without at least telling me. Do we need a stupid word too?"

I snorted and held my hand over my mouth. "Beg pardon?"

"Like a safe word, but something you say before doing something stupid so that I may help you," she leaned closer, her breath mingling with mine, "or so that I might dissuade you."

"Ooh, I like that idea. What word do you have in mind?" I spoke in a lowered tone. I leaned a little further up, my body rising from the waist.

"I think there was another kind of dessert you have told me of in passing conversation that you enjoy. I think you called it 'pie?'"

I didn't mean to, but I laughed so hard I almost headbutted her chin, and she looked at me in surprise before joining me. We just sat there, close to each other, laughing hysterically at the fact that a Fae Queen, one of the strongest beings I knew personally had just said the word "pie" to signal when I was about to do something stupid.

It was wild how innocent she could be at times. Her beautiful green eyes sparkled with obvious mirth, and I couldn't fight the urge to just keep smiling there with her.

"Allocate your points, Zeke." She kissed my forehead and brought her own status screen to her attention.

I sighed, wishing for more, but that could come later. Points to play with, man—focus.

I bumped my dexterity by three points, constitution by two, and the final ten I dropped into intelligence. My mana bar deepened in blue a little more, and I felt myself grow a little lighter. I felt healthier.

I watched as Mae allocated her points, however many the Fae had to use. I couldn't see the information, but I saw her motioning and thinking. It looked similar to the way my friends and I did it.

"Did the asshole at least have the courtesy to leave any loot behind?" I asked her after she stopped touching her screen.

"The fiend minion did, yes." She dismissed her status screen completely and addressed me, "He left behind a large sum of platinum, a mask of some kind, and a sword, surprisingly."

"Oooh." I nodded my head. That did sound like some reasonable loot. "Any ideas on who wanted what?"

"Muu has decided to take both the sword and the mask, though he has agreed that it can change hands at any time as needed." Maebe thought some more. "Yohsuke claimed the money to be split as best as possible once things had calmed down."

Yeah, that was fair—dude was really good with money, and he was honest, so we could all trust him as the treasurer indefinitely if needed. Though it could be his decision if he wanted the responsibility.

I stood from the bed and stretched carefully to ensure that everything worked correctly. I felt a hand grasp my butt teasingly, and I turned to find Maebe's radiant smile.

"Hello there," I greeted her as if she hadn't been there.

"Indeed." She stood. She kissed my cheek and added slyly, "Later."

"I'm taking that as a promise." I waggled my eyebrows provocatively.

"Do." She walked outside.

Play later, there's work to be done, devil. I shook my shoulders out and left to look for things to purify and earn my favor with Mother Nature back.

It took the majority of the night for us cleanse the area closest to the cultist—formerly cultist—village. I wound up falling asleep earlier in the morning, eventually crashing out. We stayed in one of the buildings that had been left untouched by our fight with the fiend. We all had our own rooms, and it was nice to actually sleep in a bed once more, despite the fact that the owner had likely been turned into dust by either the asshole we had fought or us. Maebe's company that night was reassuring and needed after the ass whooping we got.

I woke well rested, ready to take on the world. And honestly? It felt like I had by the end of the day. We traveled toward where we had come into the jungle with Laongal as our guide and began to systematically cull the disease that was left behind. Luckily, with the reason for its entire existence gone, the rate it spread had become more easily manageable, and it was easier to clear from the local fauna.

Still not a peep from Mother Nature, but we checked everywhere we could for the sickness. After a day of searching with the village as the epicenter and finding nothing—we suspected it was completely cleared, but Laongal did have news.

"The spiders," he hissed. "Next, you must rid us of the spiders."

It was dark now, and all of us sat together, enjoying a savory meal of poultry marinated in a thick concoction of Yohsuke's preparation days before that had thickened enough to be used as a light gravy over rice. It was terribly good.

"What can you tell us about them?" I said after swallowing a large bite.

"They do not taste good, and I hate them." He growled. "Also, they are things meant to remain beneath the land. There is a crater just before the cliffs that opens into their realm, but they had never ventured beyond it because of the land around it. The creatures were too strong."

"Then how did they survive?" James asked.

"They have an ability that draws prey into their domain, where they have the advantage in numbers and terrain." Laongal bit into the haunch, a different one this time that Maebe's minions had brought for him. "Outside of their hole, they have to explore and take control slowly, but picking off the sick and starving was not an issue for them. They have taken control of the land there, draining the resources and killing the creatures, trees, and the very land itself with their mere presence."

"Okay, so do they have any weaknesses we might be able to exploit?" Yohsuke passed a small loaf of sweet bread to us that would contrast the savory taste of the gravy. Bless him.

"They are weak individually, but they always travel in groups. I was lucky in that there were already other animals resisting them actively as I was passing through on my way to you."

I snapped up the sweet bread covered in the gravy and some rice from my bowl and swallowed, then added, "So all we have to do is lure some away and take them apart systematically. What are the places they hold like?"

"It is difficult for me to describe, but know that I will lead you there and that you will surely know the place when you see it," Laongal replied darkly. The blood and gore on his jowls lent him a much more terrifying visage than normal.

So we prepared for the next day how we could— enchanted arrows, stored spells, and a lot of hope that we weren't the flies beckoned into the web.

Chapter Twenty-Two

"Okay, you were right—these spiders are assholes," Jaken grunted as we came into a *much* darker and desolate portion of the jungle.

The greenery had been eaten away, replaced by thick strands of dark gray webbing, and corpses littered the ground. The best part was there seemed to be no unnatural decay here that we could see.

The corpses, shells, and husks of life had been surrounded and obscured by webbing. Some were intact, perfectly molded to the bodies inside with a couple of holes to signify they had been turned into milkshakes already—or would those have been protein shakes? Yummy.

We tread carefully while avoiding the worst of the webbing, our feet shuffling at times. Other times we had to jump a little to clear some.

"Someone had better be watching our six. And three. Nine. Fucking high noon and shit too," I grumbled. I really didn't fucking like spiders, man. "Should we burn some of this webbing?"

"You run the risk of harming more jungle than freeing it from their influence," Laongal growled. His nose began to twitch, and he sneezed. "We are close."

I pulled Storm Caller from my inventory and prepared myself as best I could. I was exceptionally happy I had my favorite bug zapper with me right now. I wished Kayda was here; she would beat the shit out of some spiders. Sure, I could use Magus Bane, but I could call Storm Caller back to me, and I couldn't do that with my newest weapon.

I also kept Coal in for this one, just to be safe. We should be fine, but there was no reason to risk him so soon. Right?

The burning could still happen. Easily. I had a pretty nice tinkered with Fireball spell stored in my ring right now.

Webs consumed the boughs of the trees above us. There was nowhere to go or see that didn't have an abundance of the gray, silken material. Then I heard an eerie noise that sent a thrill through my body. The distinct chirruping of cicadas that usually announced the summer months began to fill the air, and dozens of large spiders and possibly hundreds more smaller ones scuttled into view.

"Who speaks for you?" Bokaj spoke in a commanding tone.

A trio of spiders came forward, their bulbous bodies and horrid legs moving disgustingly as they approached us. Each of them had a base color of black and gray bodies, but they each had what looked like racing stripes down the sides of their bodies that were different colors. One was green, another gold, and the last red.

"We of the tribunal speak for these kindred children," the one in the center with red stripes hissed in the common language that we all understood, large fangs twitching. "You flies are brave to come so far into our territory."

"Your kind were able to take this land only because of the disease that claimed the surroundings," Bokaj accused. Then he pointed to us. "We have destroyed that plague and returned the jungle to its rightful state. Leave. You do not want any trouble with us."

"Laongal, can you and I convince other creatures to fight with us in this?" I whispered to the lion.

His eyes never strayed from the arachnids above. "I have friends who will come if I call, but I cannot promise victory."

"We might want their help if this goes awry." I turned my eyes toward the skies I couldn't see, and I pleaded with the Mother, *Mother, if you would be so kind and generous—send some help.*

With no tangible response, I turned my attention back to the conversation my friend was having with the spiders.

"...lands." The one on the right with sickly green lines on his sides spat, "You dare insult the rightful heirs to this portion of the jungle?"

"Hey, does anyone else smell food?" Muu asked and drew our attention. I took a sniff, and yeah, it smelled like Thanksgiving dinner. A finely cooked turkey with hot mashed potatoes, green bean casserole, and all the fixings. My mouth began watering as I took a step to follow the scent.

Teeth pierced the flesh of my right hand, and Laongal drew his lips back with my blood on his canines.

"What the fuck?" I was angry now. Things seemed so weird and fuzzy, and now I was hungry. Hormones? Those *fuckers!*

"That is their influence." Laongal swatted at Jaken and shoved him over. Then he leaped on to Muu. "All of you must stop!"

"Where's it coming from?" I shook my head blearily and began to look for the source.

"The lower portion of the webs. The small spiders there," the lion shouted, and suddenly, Bokaj was there and pointed his hands at a group of little brown spiders the size of chihuahuas.

"Fire in the hole," I grunted and released the pent up spell I had stored. This one was a Fireball with a caveat. Instead of the radial burst damage, the spell would cause a flash of flames to travel up to one hundred and twenty feet at the same level in a circle from the epicenter.

The spiders giving off that scent were caught in the attack, then all hell broke loose.

"Attack them!" the spider tribunal hissed loudly.

Laongal roared with all his might, and I cast a true Fireball at the tribunal of spiders. A living wall of smaller spiders rose up before them and took the brunt of the damage before disintegrating and falling away in ash.

A couple Astral Bolts hit the one with the green stripes, and then Yoh threw a Hellfire Arrow into the mix before another, then one final flaming, sulfurous arrow sped toward the largest of the spiders. His body crackled with flaming energy. Then there was a white glow, and his swords were suddenly drawn. He waded into the spiders flooding toward us.

The webbing was on fire by now where he had fired, and it spread easily due to the wind. James began to fight by Yoh's side, and I watched in awe as Muu took his new sword into a full out brawl.

The blade was thick at the base and came to about three feet in length before coming to a pronounced mushroom head. Where he cut and slashed, the spiders began to dissolve and turn to ash at his feet. Some managed to resist, but they wound up weakened severely and unable to keep out of the other's reach.

I'd have to ask about it later, but for now, we needed to focus.

I heard a dull rumble, and a slight tremor ran up my legs, "Fuck! Here come more!"

A large lioness bounded her way from off to our left and sailed over top of my friends to join the fray. Her claws and hisses caused a valuable opening for my friends to take advantage of and regroup.

More animals came.

A large gorilla-looking creature with funny looking ears and tusks in its mouth swung a broken branch that launched some of the smaller spiders in front of it. A few of those funny looking birds with the extremely sharp beaks and crazy-long wings dove from inches away from the webs. Then more joined the frenzy. Some of them became tangled, and a few of the spiders got there before we were able to do anything and tore into the poor birds.

More spiders the size of small dogs poured from openings in the webbing on the ground and rushed me. My right calf was on fire, and I looked back to see that one of them had managed to sneak up on me. An arrow sprouted from its disgusting head, and I decapitated it with Storm Caller. I nodded thanks to Bokaj and ate the ground between the charging spiders and me in long strides.

These smaller spiders fell quickly, as their HP was negligible at best. Still, they had no issues climbing over their dead comrades to get to me. Soon, I went down under a wave of spiders, and their webbing began to wind over me and secure me to the ground.

"A little HELP!" I shouted.

Muu was there almost instantly with his new sword, carving into the spider pile above me with ease. He tapped the weapon to the webs, and they began to dissolve in a wave of putrid-smelling grossness rolling down the sides of my body in rivulets.

"That's gross as shit, thank you." I sat up and punched my clawed hand through the abdomen of an either brave or stupid spider one inch from my neck on my chest.

"We need to consolidate our forces!" Jaken roared. His sword and shield danced around him as he carved through the waves of spiderlings coming at him with his large great sword.

One of the larger spiders, one the size of a minivan, dropped down on a gossamer thread from its bulbous back and tried to pull the tank from his feet with a web shot. Muu was on top of the spider's rotund body by the time it could tug again and was chopping at the webs that held the beast aloft.

He kept chopping, and although the threads had begun to show signs of wear, nothing was going to work.

Another pain in my right calf brought me back to my own predicament. A pulse that brought a wave of nausea rose through my body, and although I kept my breakfast, it burned something fierce. I lopped another head off and fell to my knee as another wave of spiders moved on me.

Yohsuke stepped in front of me and began to waylay the ever-loving hell out of them as they moved forward. James was there as well, and that gave me enough support to cast Purify on myself at 100 MP. The burning traveling up my leg cooled instantly, and I felt better. I lashed out with my great axe, unwilling to risk taking animal form and being swarmed—unable to cast spells that could be of better use. Motion caught my attention above us, and I was once more watching the scene between my friends and the large spider.

Muu stabbed down with both of his weapons savagely after trying and failing to sever the web. It must have worked well because the spider screamed in pain and rage as it fell to the ground on top of Jaken's great sword. The blood and viscera that fell on to him was pungent and more than a little disgusting.

Jaken shook the worst of the gore from his weapon and threw the great sword back into his inventory before calling his long sword and shield back to him.

"Crowd around, there's too many of them!" Jaken barked.

We fought our way to each other, and even though it was only twenty feet—the fight for each foot was brutal.

I watched in impotent rage as the lioness was swarmed by spiders a little larger than toddlers, stabbed multiple times and dragged into a large hole in the ground. The gorilla-like beast was fairing little better, his swings with his improvised weapon of a spider's limp corpse were slowing rapidly.

The birds had decided to flee or had been taken down because they were nowhere to be found any longer. Laongal was in the center of the circle that we had made, but even he was moving a little more sluggishly. He would dart out and swipe at a spider if one of us took too long getting back into the formation.

The battle had been going on for what felt like an eon, but I knew it had only been moments at most. Fighting was like that at times. It could be mere seconds and your perception of time seems to stretch forever. We couldn't afford that distraction right now. My breathing was more ragged than I would like to admit, and there didn't seem to be an end to the fucking things. Jaken and I were starting to wear down, but the others who had a higher dexterity score than us were having a slightly easier time.

I decided it was time to be a little more vocal about my disdain for spiders at that moment. I began casting Fireball and used my tinkering to make the spell a little more gruesome. It cost 400 MP overall, but hopefully, it helped.

"Fuck these assholes," I growled. "Fuck these spiders. Fuck anything unnatural in this jungle. We warned you. We warned you to leave! Now. *Fuck. Off.*"

I took both hands and cast the spell at all of the spiders and webbing.

"Maebe! Shield us!" I shouted. The Fae queen was there instantly with a shield of ice.

"Where was that stupid word!" she chided me, but I would handle her anger later.

The enhanced Fireball shot toward the spiders, and they burned as the spell careened over them. Rather than bursting and being over, this one moved into range at forty feet, then kept moving forward the rest of the range the spell had left.

The spell burnt through the spider walls that had burst into existence before the head spiders then kept going. Just as I thought it would reach them and we could crispy fry the bastards, the spell fizzled out.

"You overestimate yourself, little Druid." One of the large spiders spat and hissed at those around them. "Enough playing with your food! Kill them!"

The grab-assing was over, and the spiders came at us all at once. Maebe threw a dome of ice around us, just outside the circle. Some of the spiders traded places, little red spiders coming to the fore, and they began to spit venom on to the shield. It slid off at first, but then it began eroding. They didn't look like they would be stopping. As they began to eat through, other spiders began to try and climb on to the other side. These ones had large, metal-looking legs that chipped into the ice.

"How the fuck are they coming through already?" Yohsuke's voice shook a little as we watched in horror.

"I do not know, but the venom they use is draining my mana as it touches my shield," Maebe grunted. "This is going to be most unpleasant."

Mother Nature, please—send help, I pleaded silently. This was so not the way I wanted to go down. Sure—I had my friends around me, and that was awesome—but not by *fucking spiders!*

A rumble in the distance drew my attention from my would-be diners. I saw Jaken's lips moving fervently, his eyes closed, but what really got me was the fact that I was seeing trees move. Then bend. Then snap like a fence post hit by a car.

And all of those snapping trees were heading directly our way.

"Fuck, we got incoming!" Muu's voice sounded as panicked as I felt. My heart pounded wildly, and just before the tree destroyer broke into the portion of the jungle we were in—it stopped.

A bass, rumbling voice growled in disgust, "Take a forty-year nap and the rabble moves in. It seems that I must reacquaint myself with the scum. Leave, and I will not pursue you into that tiny hole of yours."

"Feh, illusions and petty magic will not fool us," The spider with a gold racing stripe stepped forward, but the others—the green and especially the red—scuttled backward quickly.

"Flee!" the red shrieked. "Flee, my children!!" The hissing voice sounded slightly feminine. "Scatter!"

"No, your fate is sealed now." An enormous head the size of an SUV tore through the final ten trees, and we could finally see what was speaking—a green Dragon.

The head swept from right to left and knocked all the spiders on its side away from us, the splatter of greens, browns, and red colors of blood and spider ichor clinging to its chin. It looked at us briefly before putting its head over the dome of ice and inhaling deeply.

The spiders began to flee now, all sense of unity they had in facing us gone. A stream of gray mist sprayed from the Dragon's mouth in a line so thick it could have passed as fog in a horror movie.

Where the mist struck, the spiders died almost instantly. The red striped one had curled up after it glanced her side and those who didn't make it to the underground tunnels stood no chance. They curled up, and the force of the blast swept quite a few of them into the webbing and beyond. The greenery here was already dead, but if it hadn't been—it would have died.

There were hundreds more spiders dead when the Dragon was finished expelling its breath weapon.

The only movement was the tattered strings of webbing swaying in a breeze that had been cut by some of the mist.

The Dragon smacked its lips almost lazily before poking its nose into one of the larger holes and inhaling deeply again. It sneezed. That would have been hilarious in its own right if not for the fact that the result was a large mound of upturned earth and spider remains.

"That should keep the miscreants from returning." The Dragon turned back to us, and I was able to get a better look at it.

It had green scales with horns of deep brown that struck out from the side of its head and looked like small trees or antlers that had some moss on them as well. The eyes were a deep brown. The Dragon was smaller than what I had expected from having met an ancient white Dragon. This one was possibly three-fourths the size of Winterheart.

"You may drop that failing shield, Fae creature." The Dragon still searched the area for prey before turning its head toward us. "I mean you no harm—I come as a friend. A reward."

"Uhm, what?" James's jaw almost hit the floor.

"I did not stutter, black Elf." The Dragon's head rested on the ground as it looked at James as close to in his eyes as possible. "I am Ampharia, an elder green Dragon, protector of this jungle and friend to the Lady of the Glade."

"And you are our... reward?" I tried to keep the uncertainty from my voice. Maebe had dropped the shield but kept her hands poised just in case.

"She was most insistent that I come and give any assistance that I could, and seeing as though you chose to act in my stead, I have chosen to heed her call." Ampharia snuffed at us a little. "You, little Druid, are to secret yourself away—right now—and call to her. She wishes to speak with you."

I nodded to the Dragon, then nodded to my friends. "I'll return to the mushroom village. Meet you there."

A couple of them looked like they wanted to follow, but Ampharia cut them off.

"Hello, little green, what do you call yourself?" Ampharia's voice sounded deeply curious. "Who is your sire? Your mare?"

"Uh, hello." Muu tried to sound bold, but I could tell he was a little thrown off by the questions. "My name is Muu Ankiman, but you can call me Muu if you like?"

I didn't hear the rest of the conversation because I had flown off.

It took a while to regain my bearings, but the large gap in the trees led me to the village we had taken as our base here.

I shifted swiftly as I landed. I walked into the center of the village and sat crossed legged. Since I was alone, I spoke out loud once again in the druidic tongue.

"You asked Ampharia to have me come and speak with you, Mother Nature?"

"I did." I turned to see that she walked here, among the mortals. Her toga was gone and replaced by a dress of leaves that flowed beautifully down her body. She looked younger, somehow. Some of the wrinkles and gray in her hair had lessened. Her violet and gold eyes sparkled as she regarded me.

"How can I further help you then, my lady?" I bowed my head respectfully.

"Continue with that, and I will turn you into a chicken," she warned lightly. Somehow—I believed her.

I raised my head and stood. She was still really tall, compared to myself, but it was a nice feeling. For once.

I couldn't help feeling helpless. Two times in as many days we'd had to rely on someone much stronger than us to help us do what we had set out to do. I felt useless. Like a kid again. Was I really worthy of being here?

"You're moping," she observed. "Why?"

I gave her the nice version of the thoughts going through my brain.

"Those spiders have had centuries to shore their numbers, and when the jungle was ripe for the taking? They acted. Though they are natural to their habitat, they have no place here. It is as much Ampharia's fault for being lax in her duties as a guardian of this place that this happened as you were stupid for going there so unprepared."

My shoulders fell. I got it.

"The Gods chose you for a reason. All of you. Hold your head up and accept that changes need to be made."

I sighed and tried to stop acting as if someone had kicked my puppy. I could mope or do something about it. It starts now.

"I wanted to let you know that Ampharia is the reward given to your party." She stopped and lifted a seed from the ground that hadn't been there before. "And this seed is your reward."

I stared at it in confusion, and the matronly earth goddess smiled before touching my ear lightly.

"Or rather, your reward is like this seed." She tapped it once, and I felt the little thing wobble, then it began to sprout. "Here, let us plant her here," she knelt down where we were and scraped out a hole for me to lay it in, "and watch. Now, your gift is the gift of new life. Much like the seed we just planted, you will grow, and hopefully, continue to do so. Especially with my blessing.

She held her hand over the spot we had planted the seed and water fell on to the soil. The soil parted slightly, and a sprout burst through the ground.

"As you grow, you will give new life to those around you, not just here but in your world too." The sprouting plant began to grow and thicken, slowly. "Though you may be a pillar in your own right, there must be a foundation as well as support. The center is not you, but your party and your ideals."

She waved her hands over the now ten-inch-tall plant that was still growing. Seven smaller plants sprouted in a circle around the original one and began to weave themselves around it in a circular pattern that lifted, supported, and protected the original plant, but something else I noticed was that they were all growing at a more rapid pace. Now it was a foot and a half, three feet, four, six.

We stepped back after Mother Nature tugged my sleeve gently.

"With the love, support, and strength of your friends—you all will grow faster." I turned to face her. She was smiling now, her dimples deeply creasing her cheeks, and it was a beautiful thing. "I bestow upon you the subclass of Primal Warrior. You are the first of your kind, as this tree will be the first of its kind. You will grow in unexpected ways, as will your friends. Also, the tail I withheld from you that should have been earned for reaching level 22. And another for having pleased me with trying your hardest to make up for your shortcomings."

She turned to face the tree, and it stood an easy one hundred eighty feet tall; its trunk was thick with crisscrossed wood that connected and was woven through the base trunk itself. It reminded me of a loosely woven wicker basket, but I had a feeling that it would take a good deal to harm this tree.

Mother Nature reached up to the lowest branch, and the tree seemed to relinquish it from the base like a plucked hair. She held the branch out to me. It was thicker than the meatiest portion of my forearm and a little over eight feet long.

"A final gift to the Ranger. There are people who call the eastern region of this jungle home." She allowed me to take it. "I believe that there will be a skilled bowyer among them. If you can convince her to work with an unknown material, this may be a worthy weapon for him."

"I think convincing a craftsman to work with new material would be within his realm." I grinned. I looked over the branch, which looked roughly the same as the tree itself, but it was more tightly bound and seemed springier.

I looked up to find her gone, but the evidence of her presence remained. My rump itched like crazy, and I looked to see that, true to her word, I now had five tails. I could choose what to do with my tails later. Right now, I wanted to see what the Primal Warrior was capable of.

SUBCLASS OBTAINED!

Primal Warrior – Druids, the chosen champions of nature and her wishes, have been known to take many paths. This is a trail that only you can carve. This subclass specializes in using aspects of animals to fight in newer ways.

Primal Instinct – The voice of animals is known to you, but now, so are their instincts. The shapes and forms the Druid takes can offer insight and guidance to the Druid now. The duration of Nature's Voice has been increased to twenty-four hours per casting.

Primal Aspect – While in their natural shape, the Druid can use aspects of their shape-shifted powers from their animal forms. Certain statistics or abilities may change depending on the aspect chosen and cast. Cost: 200 MP. Duration: 10 minutes. Cooldown: none.

These were so fucking wild that I didn't even know where to begin trying to explore them, so I decided to relax and wait for my friends to return.

I had gained a decent chunk of experience that put me more than a quarter of the way to level 26, but the lack of EXP compared to the carnage we had done was menial, and I was pissed about it.

For the first extra tail I had gained, I snagged a new ability called Vulpine Casting.

Vulpine Casting - The Kitsune brings their trickster nature to the fore to steal mana from a full strength spell. Once a day, the Kitsune may cast one spell for half the mana cost.

The fifth tail bumped my Charge ability up to a full thirty seconds of holding a spell. That's fucking awesome! It was weird that I couldn't pick anything else, but these were amazing.

I was about to look into my aspects when my friends returned with a small Dragon-kin who looked both reminiscent of Muu and Ampharia's true form. So I assumed that the Dragon could shapeshift. Which was pretty dope, actually.

"Yo... what's with the mysterious tree?" Bokaj asked as soon as he turned his attention from a conversation he and James had been having. "And what's with the stick?"

I tossed it to him, and he caught it deftly. "It's a gift from Mother Nature. She's pretty sure that a group of people live in the eastern portion of the jungle who might be able to make a bow from that."

Ampharia stepped closer to the tree and pressed a hand against it.

"This is from her." Her eyes closed. "It feels strong. A good napping tree." Her form shimmered, and her real body stood and curled around the tree with her massive head on her paws before yawning lazily. "This shall be my new nap spot. Wake me tomorrow, little Muu. We shall begin your training then."

"You got it, Dragon lady." Muu saluted lazily. He looked drained, the sword still in his grip.

"What's up with the sword, man?" I asked Muu.

"It's strong as fuck, it makes what it hits decay, and it's called Rotten Ruin," he said matter of factly. He held it out in front of me.

"That is a cursed sword." Ampharia's half-lidded eye focused on the weapon. "The Celestial Elf there can tell you more. Elsewhere."

We took our conversation into the building we called home and began speaking in the largest room.

"Is it cursed?" Muu asked, his eyes narrowed at Maebe uncertainly.

"Pass it to me, so that I might inspect it further." She offered her hand, but Muu pulled the weapon behind him.

"No," he said like a sullen child. We looked at him incredulously.

"What?" He looked at us nervously. "It's mine!"

"Did he use any other weapon in the fight?" Maebe asked.

"I saw him use his spear once," I admitted, "but he still had the weapon in hand."

"And Muu, do you feel the need to use any of your other weapons?" He looked confused for a moment, then stood his ground.

"Why would I?" He brandished the blade in front of himself. "Fighters have been known to use multiple weapons. Why not this one?"

Maebe turned to us. "It is meant to erode the will of the wielder so that they feel the need to only use this weapon, I believe. There are many cursed weapons such as this—I even have a few in my own vaults."

"Why do you have cursed weapons?" Bokaj looked sideways at her.

"Sometimes there are acts in war that require sacrifice." She raised her chin in challenge. "Sometimes those sacrifices are willing hosts to weapons of terrible and great power." She smiled wide. "Other times, I am an avid collector."

"I see." Jaken made a noise in his throat of thought. "So what do we do about this one?"

"Well, we could overpower him and take it," Muu instantly fell into a defensive stance at her words, "or we can help him overcome the curse in his own way. A sheath would be good for now."

"Muu, you any good with making things out of leather?" I asked.

He eyed me silently, then focused back on Maebe. His knuckles popped and strained around the hilt of his blade.

"Hey!" I snapped my fingers in front of him to get his attention.

His arm was moving before I could even think to dodge, and Jaken's arm was suddenly wrapped around the struggling Dragon-kin's throat. The weapon flashed dangerously close in front of me, and James was right next to me prying it from Muu's grasp using pressure points to try and dislodge his grip.

I stepped forward and whispered, "Sorry, buddy."

If anyone was going to knock my friend out, I wanted it to be me. Not for selfish reasons but because I knew that he would know I did it out of love.

I whipped my fist into his chin, once, twice, and finally a third time that put him down. We carried him to his bed, and Maebe held on to the weapon for a bit while Jaken and I tried to come up with a makeshift cover. Nothing could touch the blade and stay whole, so we opted to just let Maebe hang on to it for the night.

She stowed the item in her inventory with a slight shiver, then looked to me. "We truly do need to address your penchant for stupid ideas that can get you hurt."

"Oh, fuck."

Chapter Twenty-Three

Maebe had damned near chewed my ass straight off my body about my not giving her warning before throwing myself out there as stupidly as I had. By the end of it, she was fine, and I was fine. But there was an understanding that the next time I did some stupid shit—I would have my ass handed to me.

I climbed out of bed, dressed in some fresh clothes, then went outside to see what was going on for the morning. I walked outside to see that Jaken, James, Yohsuke, and Bokaj hadn't joined us yet.

Muu was sitting with his armor off in front of Ampharia as if he were meditating. In his hands was a globule of what could have been venom—or green apple jam—but I wasn't certain.

Rather than disturbing his training, I opted to shapeshift into my owl form and find my own source of training.

You flap your wings over much, Druid. A light, reedy voice spoke directly into my mind. I did my best to try and see where the voice was coming from, but the more I looked, the less I saw.

Who is this? I asked inside my mind. To avoid flying into something or being vulnerable, I landed on a branch with a loud rustling of feathers and the sound of my taloned-claws clacking into the wood.

I am the instinct of the owl form you are currently in. I am attempting to guide you on how best to fly. Your landing was not owlish either, the voice observed dryly. *It is not necessary for you to stop your flight. I will guide you. Take a small dive, then spread your wings and glide for a spell.*

Over the course of the next hour of flight, I learned how to fly silently and swiftly and how to better traverse the thermals that carried my body higher than I had been before. I learned to be more perceptive than I had ever been. I spotted multiple large rodents that, to the instincts in my mind, would make excellent prey. To me, nah, son.

Still, this was amazing too. I wondered how this could be applied in combat. If it could. I imagined it could. I'd have to check that out.

We had flown eastward. My reasoning being that the Elven village that Bokaj would need to go to should be scouted out, but the longer I flew, the more trees there were to be seen. There was nothing out here that I could find. After the second hour, I turned back toward the village we were using and began to fly.

I heard a loud crack and looked down just in time to see motion through a break in the trees. A small figure leaped from one medium-sized branch to another. I dropped lower to investigate further.

This is unwise for someone our size, Druid, the agitated voice groaned at me.

I ignored it and came closer to the scene playing out below me.

The trees thinned slightly, and I watched as a smaller Elf with deeply tanned skin in gray, green, black, brown, and tan tunic and breeches frantically leaped from one tree to another as a horned figure gave chase beneath it. It looked like a rhinoceros, but it had three razor-sharp horns working up the tip of the nose that were smaller as they went up.

The Elf looked younger—hard to tell ages on beings with such long-ass lifespans. He had a bow in his hand, and the quiver was strapped to his back, unlike my friend who wore his on his hip. I suppose this was okay since he was running for his life.

I dropped lower to try and get a reading on the animal giving chase. It was easily larger than my Ursolon form and didn't give the slightest fuck about the trees it was running into. It left huge divots and ruts in them where its gray, armored shoulders hit and shaved off the bark and wood.

Better do what I can, though that thing's hide is probably thick as fuck, I thought to myself.

This is not an intelligent endeavor for an owl, the owl warned me.

Pie, I retorted sarcastically then shifted to my fox man form slightly above a large limb that I was certain would hold me in the Elf's most likely direction of travel.

His eyes had been on the pursuing figure, so when I was just touching the branch with my toes, he turned, and we collided. By then, I had the place for Teleport in mind and cast it as we careened over the side of the branch.

The feeling of the jump that would bring us back to the village we were staying in was minor in comparison to the falling sensation that I felt in that moment. It honestly made me feel queasy.

We landed a moment later with a hard thud that really rustled my jimmies, and the kid groaned. I began to sit up while casting Regrowth on him. Then he put an arrow to my throat in an instant.

"Eathali, wick eir grein mahul, ard dulin twax?!" He shouted in my face, dwarfing everything around me and blocking out the sunlight.

His features were soft for an Elf's, his body lean but the angles were there too. I was sure he'd grow up to be a real lady killer—if he stopped picking fights with huge monsters and people like me. On closer inspection, I saw that his bottom lips pulled back to bare small tusks. A Fae-Orc then.

"Eathali ard dulani warnala ack var ni," I heard Jaken's voice trying to take a soothing tone but in a language I didn't understand. Some of the words were harsh, but the language itself had an almost-lyrical quality.

The child seemed to think for a moment too long for some of my party member's tastes because I heard a grumble of dissent, then James was suddenly in my vision. He reached down and snapped the arrow at my throat with his thumb and grabbed the child by the scruff of his neck and tunic.

"What was he saying?" I grumbled to Jaken as he helped me stand.

"Druid, with the green magic, where did you bring me?" Jaken translated.

He turned to the child. He seemed to know better than to fight the monk, but he wasn't happy, and he was beginning to panic.

"Lithuli, wilan ard dillir arckieri batu?" Jaken spoke then translated for us. "Cousin, where did you come from?"

Over the course of the next few minutes of tense conversation, Jaken learned the child's name was Set and that he had been sent on the trial to adulthood in his tribe when he had been interrupted by a cowardly Druid.

That last one stung. No lie. But hey—kids, right?

"I mean, of course I'm sorry for having interrupted him running for his life—I mean trial," I spat at him. "I saw a scared kid running from a beast that would have easily killed him before letting him put one of those lame-ass arrows in it."

Jaken translated for me, and the disgruntled wanna-be Ranger took a threatening step toward me with an arrow nocked. I thought about the spell I wanted to cast, and a large flaming great axe burst into life in my hands. I raised an eyebrow at him and watched the blood leave his face slowly.

Jaken said a few words, and he visibly relaxed and put his bow away. He mumbled something at Jaken, and the Paladin strode over to the boy and took him by the shoulder before leading him toward where we ate.

The Paladin spoke to Yohsuke, motioned to the child, then Yohsuke pulled out another plate and began piling food on to it. Looks like we would be taking the kid back home after all. Oh well. Could've been worse.

I could've had to watch that monstrosity gore that poor kid. I'm a dad. Didn't matter what was going on in my life, I wouldn't watch another kid die after what happened to us with Rowan.

Muu and Ampharia, in her Dragon-kin form, returned from the woods south of us, holding a good conversation.

"So, all you're saying I have to do is think of the venom coming from where I want, and then I can make it do whatever I want?" Muu asked excitedly.

Ampharia laughed loudly. "No. You still must focus it in one spot, but you can improve the potency by working with your venom. You truly are a special creature."

"Thank you, my mom assures me of the same," Muu responded, nonplussed. "So, since we can't train my venom any more, how can we continue?"

"You and I will hold mock battles, and we will discuss tactics," Ampharia explained. "Then if I feel you a suitable vessel—I may bequeath my blessing upon you."

"How long will that take?" Bokaj asked.

"As long as it takes," Ampharia responded simply, and she cocked her head. "Your impatience means nothing to a Dragon. Though Muu does seem to pick things up quickly."

"We have a plan, man." Muu clapped my other friend on the shoulder. "Believe me, I'll bust my ass for this."

Bokaj simply nodded and went to go speak with the kid while he ate.

"Don't worry about him. He's simply worried about a friend of ours," I told the Dragon as she watched Bokaj for a moment longer.

"Not my concern," she shrugged and walked off. Muu followed her dutifully, and that was likely the last we would see of him today.

"I must return to my people for a little while," Maebe said from behind me. "I have only been gone for a few hours, but something that requires my presence has occurred, and I must go."

I turned to find her standing in the doorway to the housing we all shared, her face unreadable.

"Will you be able to come back?" I asked softly as I walked toward her.

"It will be some time before I can. Days to a week, perhaps?" Her eyebrows furrowed. "My magics return swifter in the land of the Fae. I am stronger there. So it could be that long at most. I do not know for certain."

"Is being here hurting you? Making you weaker?" I asked softly.

"Not in so much as it takes me longer to recover my magic here. I can do it, I have been, but it can be taxing."

"Shit, I had no idea, I'm so sor–" She held a hand up to hush me.

"My aid was given out of personal interest and for the good of my people and friends."

"Okay, well I wish you luck with what you need to take care of, though I doubt you will need it." I tried to smile at her reassuringly. "Just be safe over there, okay?"

"I will." She pulled me closer to her by my hips. "I will miss you, Zeke."

"I'll miss you too." I kissed her softly. "Don't worry. I have the guys here to keep me from losing my mind too much and doing some 'pie'-level stupid shit."

"Good. Because if I return to find you hurt, I will lay waste to whoever hurt you." She kissed me fiercely. "I will go now. Please, give the others my regards and well wishes."

I nodded, letting her go reluctantly. I watched in curious, sad silence as she splayed her hand out in front of her and a circle of light burst into being beneath her feet. Her other hand flashed through a complicated sequence of motions before a rent in the air turned into a tunnel devoid of any light.

Maebe glanced back one last time, and I blew her a kiss. She blinked and looked at me oddly before nodding to herself and stepping into the tunnel. I blinked once, and it was gone. The others looked over at me, and I waved their looks away. I wanted to be alone at that moment.

Sure, I was moping, but who the fuck are you to judge? Oh, yeah... sorry about that, mate.

After an hour or so of obligatory sadness, I decided to go out and see what the others were doing.

"Just the guy we wanted to see!" James clapped. "You're gonna help lead us to the kid's village."

"Sounds fair to me. Where is it?" I looked to Jaken.

"He said it wasn't far from where you found him." Jaken leaned forward and pulled me close. "He doesn't want to teleport again. So we're gonna need to surprise him with it."

I smiled and nodded once before looking toward the tree line, "Who all is going?"

"The kid, me, Jaken, James, and Yoh," Bokaj said as he joined us. "Muu is staying behind, and I think we all know Maebe isn't coming."

"She said bye, by the way," I added. "Though I don't like leaving Muu behind."

"You gonna tell Ampharia to put her training on hold?" He raised a brow.

"Fuck no, let's get to getting."

We gathered closely around the kid, and he looked at us oddly. Jaken reached out and touched his shoulders. I saw that the others were all touching and activated the spell with the same spot in mind that I had gotten the kid out of.

The weird sucking and jumping sensation came and went, and the boy threw up uncontrollably. Poor kid. I cast Regrowth on him to try and help him. Luckily, we had landed on the ground and not the tree limb we had originally been on.

I surveyed the damage to the ground and trees around us. That creature had done a great deal of damage. Some of the trees had since begun leaning dangerously against the trees around them. I cast Regrowth on the closest one to me and watched as the injured wood began to grow back quickly. That was amazing! First time trying that, and it was a success.

Look at me, being all Druid-like.

The boy knelt on the ground and began to analyze the tracks that were there. He looked at us, determined, and raised his chin before stalking off. He pulled his bow off, then prepared an arrow.

"Eathali, padilon, Fae diwali liv mat filli fon. Omywio." He looked to Jaken as he spoke but was careful to speak slowly, then motioned for us to wait for him.

"He wants us to wait while he finishes his trial," Jaken translated.

"We gathered as much." Yohsuke shook his head. "Laggy-ass translator. He's gotta know that's not gonna happen."

"He's adamant," Jaken explained. "He told me that he was the youngest of the tribe to attempt it, but there's a lot of honor riding on this for him."

"So, then we follow at a distance, and try to make sure he stays alive." Bokaj motioned to the kid as he began to move on. "Say we give him a few minutes and then start moving?"

Two minutes had passed before we moved, and Bokaj picked up the boy's trail easily. He was definitely not leaving the trail that the armored creature did, but he wasn't nearly the invisible hunter he made himself out to be. Of course, I don't know that he had ever made that approximation of his skills.

I took my panther form and climbed up a tree, then padded through the limbs that connected and went in the same direction as the party. It was hard going at times, but I managed it well enough.

I half expected the voice of the panther to attack me the way that the owl's had, but it seemed content to be quiet and observe—if it was even interested.

The destruction stopped after about ten more minutes, doubled back, then reversed and moved on further along the trail with no damage to the trees. Well, there were some, but only when the trees were too close.

The foliage here in this area was much darker and thicker to look at than what we had seen initially. Our footsteps slowed because the boy's did. He was focusing heavily on the area in front of him. The brush and bushes began to shift and part as the horned head of the rhinoceros-like creature pressed through. There were flecks of blood along the side of its head and gore on its horns.

Shiiiiiit, I groaned to myself. The beast began to advance menacingly, and even I felt threatened by its presence.

The Belgar will kill that child, the panther's voice growled through my head. *It is fully grown and older. It can kill something his level easily. Unless you wish to take the child's remains to his family—I suggest you help.*

Well, shit. I prepared to leap from my spot, slowly sidling closer. To his credit, Set was cool under the creature's gaze, even if he was a mere thirty-five feet from him on level ground. His dominant arm began to draw the arrow back while the arrow and grip of the bow were still low at his waist.

I was suddenly aware of the others now. Jaken slowly crept from his trailing position forward to be within line of sight. Likely gaining line of sight so he could take the aggro.

The Belgar looked at all of us, and I shifted into my fox-man form to try and speak with it. "Hello, friend!"

The creature looked up at me, startled, "You speak, creature?"

His voice was surprisingly lyrical. Was that sylvan? Were each of the animal tongues that different in the realms too? Did that mean that I might not be able to speak with some creatures? I'd have to ask Mother Nature later.

"I do." I tried to smile and keep my voice light and cheery. "Tell me, how did a powerful Fae such as yourself come to be here?"

He snorted and pawed the ground. "I do not know. I found a drinking hole I liked and fell in. When I rose, I rose here. Then the little stick thrower attacked me." He tossed his head at Set. "I do not know the customs here, but that is a rude thing to do among the Fae. It is a challenge."

"And you cannot leave a challenge unanswered." I nodded sadly. "Well, that's unfortunate. I promised to get the boy to his people, and he seems to have it on the brain that he needs to kill you to prove that he's a good hunter."

The Belgar tossed his head back and laughed, "He can try! I will gore him as I have many others, and then I will kill all comers. You as well, creature—if you get in my way."

Oh, shit balls. I looked over at the kid, and James held him still. Though he struggled mightily, the Paladin barely moved.

"Tell you what, how about we play a game," I offered.

"There are no games," the Belgar grunted, unimpressed.

"Then a wager?" I offered a second time. The Belgar seemed to think a moment, then stayed silent, so I continued, "You know that you're capable of killing the child easily. So how about you give him an advantage. Let our Ranger help him. None of the rest of us will interfere so long as the two of them are fighting you. If you will agree to that, I will give my word, that should you win—none of us will attack you so long as you don't attack us."

"I can agree to this contest of honor. Stand before me challengers." I translated to the others. Set let the arrow slide back a little to relieve his arm.

I hope you know what you're doing, man, Jaken growled into my head.

They'll be fine so long as the kid stays on the move, and Bokaj can lay down the hate.

So, if it starts to get bad, we bring him toward one of you guys, and if he fucks up, you can join in.

I looked down to a tree across the path and saw Bokaj glance my way, and I gave him a nod.

Bokaj dropped from his position in the trees, Tmont's form slinking over behind him as he stood next to Set.

"I have no quarrel with you, panther. You may stand aside while I battle these two." The Belgar waved his head to the left for Tmont to stand aside.

"My place is with master," Tmont growled menacingly. "He will kill you, and I will help. Know that I bear you no ill will other than that you will be trying to harm my master."

"That is fair. Creature!" The Belgar looked my way, the eyes on the sides of his head looking my way. "What are these opponents' names?"

"They are called Set and Bokaj, and the panther is Tmont," I called down. "What is your name, so I can tell them?"

"I am called Teyatunga the Thunderous." He lifted his large head and snorted before stomping the ground with a resounding thud.

I translated the message for the two below us, and they nodded toward the creature.

Set looked at Bokaj and began speaking—Jaken translated actively—"Stay out of my way, and do not take my kill."

Bokaj just shrugged, slung his bow and stepped over to the tree I was on. He used Nature's Path, stepped through the trunk of the tree, and then stepped out on to a limb just above me.

"The one in front of you has opted to take your hide for himself, and Bokaj will graciously allow him to try with minimal support."

Teyatunga snorted and flicked his ears. "Fine. Say the words, creature."

"I, Zekiel Erebos, speak on behalf of this group. I give you my word of honor as spokesperson that not I, James, Jaken, or Yohsuke will harm you in any way during this fight or after should you be the victor—unless you attack us in any way. Purposely or otherwise."

"I, Teyatunga the Thunderous, meet this challenge as I do all others. I will stand by my word not to harm those who do not participate and hold you to yours with your stipulations. Fight well."

"He said to fight well," I called to Jaken, who translated to Set. He nodded to the Belgar and fired an arrow right at the creature's eye.

Teyatunga tossed his head to the side and snapped the arrow on his wide front horn, his ears flicking forward toward the enemy. The Belgar bellowed loudly and charged right at him.

Set rolled out of the way a second before the great beast steamrolled through his previous spot. He didn't make it out completely unscathed, though. His bow snapped as the Belgar's armored skin hit the end, and it was out of commission instantly.

Set cursed in a language I didn't understand and drew a small dagger from his inventory. He timed his stride with the next charge and ran up the side of a tree. The Belgar rammed into the wood, and the tree began to fall. Set leaped from the falling trunk and landed on the creature's back where he stabbed down as viciously as he could. The blade snapped in half and clattered uselessly to the ground with a soft clatter.

Maybe time to step in, bud, Jaken broadcast to all of us, but Bokaj simply shook his head.

Set placed his feet and hands inside the ridged plates of the Belgar's natural armor and held on as the creature bucked and thrashed wildly. It bumped the tree that we were in, causing me to lose my balance, knock my shoulder against the limb below me as I fell. Bokaj tried to grab me but wasn't able to keep me up from the momentum that shook me out of his grasp.

I collided hard with the back of the creature and the child clinging to him for dear life. The smaller horn on the top of the creatures head tore through my wrist and flung me sinfully from its back.

"Fuck, that hurt," I grumbled aloud.

The creature stopped and stared at me for a moment. It looked at my wrist and saw the blood that cascaded from it, dribbling as my health bar fell slightly.

"And so another has come," Teyatunga grunted. "Make this a worthy contest."

"You got it." I smiled grimly. This had gone according to how I had hoped it would.

With how much of a juggernaut the Belgar was in motion, and his destructive tendencies, that had been the exact result I was looking for—albeit I had hoped it wouldn't hurt so badly.

I cast Regrowth on myself and shapeshifted into my new Belgar form. I could see, but it was weird. Like the vision was split and angled to the sides of my head, though it was poor. Lines were blurry and fuzzy, but my sense of smell and hearing were sharper than my normal form. I flicked my ears toward the direction I had been facing and heard the creature pacing forward.

A deep baritone voice that had a musical quality similar to the creature I thought was still in front of me rang out in my head, *You are more nimble than he, shuffle to the side and press forward the opposite side of your shuffle with your head low. Let your horns do the work.*

Belgar instinct was trying to tell me how to run shit? This was going to be cool.

I followed the advice and shifted left before tucking my head and charging forward. I felt a clang against my armored skin and realized that I had missed my mark.

Prepare for impact! Your nimbleness was your undoing, lift your back legs, let the momentum of his hit carry your body around. You will be hurt, but you will be able to use that momentum to turn and charge his rear.

As I was about to ask with the fuck he meant by that, Teyatunga hit my left flank and flung my body around like I was a car in a bad t-bone accident. I tried to keep my legs beneath me as I landed, but one leg was a little more hurt than I'd be able to move with. It was next to lame.

I shifted back into my fox-man form, and my vision was instantly better. I saw that the Belgar was on his way to try and turn around, so I had time. I was at eighty-five percent health. Then suddenly, I was up to full health, and my leg was back in working condition. I looked at a flash of light above me and saw Bokaj nod to me and lift his bow.

Time to try something I hadn't been able to do until now. I activated my first aspect. 200 MP drained from my reserves, and my body was suddenly heavier, my fur hardened like armor, and my snout tickled slightly. My muscles bulged thicker, and I felt as if I'd be able to stop a truck.

Aspect of the Belgar – The Primal Warrior's body thickens, becoming sturdier and stronger like that of the Belgar.

+30 defense, +15 strength, Movement speed is severely lessened unless charging.

Oh, this was fucking sick! I lowered my body's center of gravity by bending my knees and prepared myself to meet him head on when an idea came to mind. There were no restrictions that I could see—could I stack aspects?

No time to experiment.

Fuck it. We'll do it live, I grunted and readied to rock and roll.

Teyatunga thundered toward me and lowered his head. I caught a glance of Set, and the kid leaped from the Belgar's back. I brought Magus Bane into my hand and switched from the bladed symbol to the hammer side and took a batter's stance.

"Ha!" Teyatunga was closing in now, only twenty feet away. "You think a stick will stop the Thunderous! I will shatter you both! Oof!"

Once he had stepped into my range, I activated Devil's Hammer and swung for the fences. The hammer portion of the great axe smacked into the side of his head as an arrow pierced his right eye.

Bokaj had given me a better target to aim for. The Belgar's health bar plummeted to fifteen percent, and though his momentum carried him further than my strike, his direction had changed from my ringing his fucking bell as hard as I did.

He careened through the trunk of the tree behind me about ten feet away, though he had hit it head on and it collapsed to the ground, his health had gone down further. Just barely there.

As I walked over toward him, Set just appeared above his head and spoke with his chin jutted forward.

"Ala putouri, Belgar—alar adanari ack me fratera." He took five of his arrows and threaded them between his middle two fingers. All that remained visible were the heads and maybe an inch or so of the shafts.

No time for dick jokes, man. Pull your shit together.

With a jump three feet into the air, the Fae-Orc child used the gravity of his landing to add strength as he punched his improvised weapons into Teyatunga the Thunderous's good eye. The Belgar stilled, and the life ebbed from him.

Set knelt in front of the creature's still corpse and put his head against the body. Upon closer inspection, I saw tears running down his cheeks.

"Jaken, did you hear what he said?" I asked as we began to move closer. I noticed that each movement I made toward walking was still slower.

I dropped Aspect of the Belgar, and I was immediately faster, but so much weaker. My fur returned to normal, and I knew that I would miss the added strength.

"He said, 'thank you, Belgar—your sacrifice for my brothers.'" I nodded. It was an interesting sentiment.

Thanking an animal for its sacrifice was a common thing that a lot of Rangers did, according to some of the games I had played and books I had read back home.

"Taking a life like that is hard, but it was his kill," Bokaj said from behind me. Despite having heard motion behind me, I still flinched. "Tell him to stop crying like that. He'll dishonor his opponent."

Jaken scowled at the Ranger, then knelt next to Set and began speaking to him in low tones. His head rocked back after a moment, then he looked at us.

"This was his first kill," Jaken said gravely.

What. The. Fuck. Who the fuck does that to a kid? Wait, was it done purposely? Did he come here on his own?

Before any of us could ask those questions, Jaken was already questioning the boy. It turned out that he *had* been sent here, and by his chieftain no less, to hunt the largest creature he could find. If the creature wasn't the largest in the area, and other hunters proved it wasn't, he would be cast out. The kid was an orphan. His parents had been shamed greatly, leaving him and his two little brothers behind when they fled the village.

"Fuck," James said with conviction more than any other emotion. "What do we do?"

"Only thing we can do, man." Yohsuke patted his shoulder. "We take him back to his people, and if they want to try and fuck with us, we take him and the kids back to Sunrise."

I looked at my brother, and the look in his eyes brooked no argument. That's what we would do.

"So, who wants to help me drag this big bastard to the village?" I smiled at the others.

I cast Aspect of the Ursolon.

Aspect of the Ursolon – The Druid takes on a larger, stronger form to better fight with.

+10 strength and damage output increased by 20%

My body grew, and my muscles thickened once more until I was seven feet tall. We tied a thick rope around the upper body of the Belgar, and between Jaken and me, we were able to drag it. I had to recast the Ursolon aspect spell every ten minutes, but that helped me get used the change that my body experienced each time. I did figure out that you couldn't cast an aspect with another one. It was one at a time. No mix and match.

Cool part was that there was no mana loss from the attempt, so that was nice.

It took us a couple hours, with a break every thirty minutes, but eventually, we made it to a heavily wooded portion of the jungle. There were large logs carved into spears dug into the ground facing toward our approach.

"This has to be the village," I grunted.

The strain of having to drag the Belgar's carcass was starting to truly wear on my body. Jaken's skin was just as slick with sweat as mine was.

Set ran ahead, shouting something that alarmed Jaken. "He's telling them not to shoot us. I can't even fucking see anyone—get ready for a fight if they don't like him that much."

Bokaj's voice rang through my head, *Two in the trees off to the left, six on the right in the bushes and shrubbery, and then there's one that we are about be on top of that is walking closer with the kid.*

How the fuck did you know that? Yohsuke asked back.

They hide well, but Tmont can smell all of them, and the one in front of us isn't trying to remain hidden, Bokaj responded readily enough that it seemed as though he had thought that question may come. Kudos.

"Welcome to our humble village," the person with Set spoke with a thick, musical accent.

His hair was light brown and long, even in a ponytail. His features were tanned, but not nearly as dark as Set's, and his light eyes were impossible to define in the low light in this area. His features were definitively elvish, as was his thin but muscular build.

"How can we help you?" the figure continued.

"We stumbled upon Set as he was fighting a Belgar that had stumbled into your territory," I looked the man in the eyes as Bokaj explained and motioned to the beast we dragged along. "A couple of us helped him, but he delivered the final blow."

There was a glint of hard disbelief. "I see. So he did not kill the beast on his own."

"He delivered the final blow," Bokaj pressed, but the Elf shook his head.

"The key to the Cocoalcata, the Moon Hunt, is that the hunter performing the trial fells the creature on his own."

"It's a fucking Belgar, man," Yohsuke spat. "It could have almost killed any one of us one on one. You expect a kid to kill it alone? On his first hunt?"

"Our laws are very strict," the man said.

"And just who the hell are you to decide whether a kid with hardly any meat on his bones and no one to teach him properly is able or not?" James strode forward angrily. He was close enough to reach out and touch the other man.

"I am Atuala, the spiritual leader of this village, and he in charge of communing with the moon goddess," the Elf said with a grin that said we had played into his hands.

An arrow shot toward James, in front of him—probably as a warning shot—but the monk didn't give a shit. He caught it deftly with one hand held straight out. Snatched it like one of those old kung fu senseis catching a fly with chopsticks in movies.

"I don't give a shit who you think you are," he hissed. "A normal person doesn't send a kid out to hunt the biggest and baddest creature he can find on his own."

"A normal person did not." Atuala shook his head. "The moon goddess did. I pass her word to the leaders of this village and its peoples. What happens from there is for the goddess to decide."

"I haven't heard of the moon goddess," Jaken said. He stepped forward and put a hand on James's shoulder.

"She has not deemed you worthy then. After all, you stink of an inferior deity." Atuala held his chin higher. "If you will wait I will send word to the chieftain and his counsel that you are here, and he will pass judgment on whether you may come in."

The priest—or whatever the hell he was—turned on Set and spat venomously in their own tongue.

"You failed your hunt. You are no longer welcome to walk among us. You are stripped of your name, your rank, and your people. Leave this place, or our people will offer you no quarter," Jaken translated for us through our earrings.

Jaken, you grab the kid and walk him back with me to translate. We need to try and get his siblings out of here, I told him. I turned on the others. *Don't say and don't do shit. This asshole doesn't need to know what we're planning.*

I received no affirmation from the others but the continued heated looks sent toward Atuala. Set was sobbing, trying to plead with the asshole, but to no avail. He reached out and tried to touch the Elf's hand and received a cold, back-handed slap.

Jaken was suddenly holding the Elf in his gauntleted grasp, "You touch the kid in front of any of us again, and all bets are off."

I heard the metal and leather straining as he gripped the shoulder. A look of pain flashed over Atuala's face.

Jaken let the other man go and took an arrow on his shoulder without so much as flinching. He tucked Set against his side, and the distraught child wept pitifully against his armor. He walked him back toward the tree line, and I followed. I caught a glimpse of a figure moving along with us.

We'll have a watcher with us, I warned.

Tmont has his scent. She can run a distraction for you to get the kid into the collar, Bokaj advised as he watched us walk away.

I hadn't even seen the panther leave her master's side, but I guess that she would have had to in order to scout for us. Had I been that distracted dragging that body?

Once we were out of line of sight, we spoke quickly and quietly with the boy. He was confused, but when Jaken said that we would do our best to get his brothers, Rogir and Velt, he agreed to go into my necklace. Before he went in, though, he described where they might be. A small hut built with a tiny roof between two tree roots.

After a mental call to Bokaj, we heard an angry yowl, and a man screamed. There were calls and shouts that sounded like they were heading away from us. I touched Set on his head and willed him into the collar. The boy turned into a dissipating cloud of smoke that funneled into the collar swiftly.

Once that was done, we walked back toward our friends to find them standing alone.

"He left to see about our entry," Bokaj mumbled to us. "I think we have someone close enough to hear us, so let's keep it soft and not mental. They would get suspicious."

"That's fair," Yohsuke grumbled. "Anyone else want to beat that asshole's fuckin' head in?"

All of us nodded. "Thought so," he grunted as a larger figure began to walk toward us with purpose.

"Greetings," a guttural voice called out as the owner came forward.

The large Orc man, his bald head covered in tattoos of trees and animals, walked toward us with an inquisitive look on his face.

"I am Wrokal, chieftain of this village, and I have heard that you sought entry with one of our former citizens after a fight with a Belgar, a creature of legend?"

"Set delivered the final blow," I said. I wondered how this guy would react.

His features hardened, "There is no one by that name anymore. That person was banished and stricken from our people's hearts and minds for failing his trial."

"Fine." Bokaj shrugged. "We had some work for your bowyer. We have a new material we were hoping he could take and make a bow out of."

Wrokal's features brightened immediately, "I would be more than happy to take a look at it." He motioned that we follow him.

As we began to move, Tmont slunk forward out of the shadows and joined us as though she had never left her master's side. Smooth, kitty. Real fucking smooth.

The majority of the village was in the trees. The houses were built on beams and supports that were grown directly from the trees themselves. It was a reminder of the city in the trees, Terra's Escape, that we had visited briefly in the Fae Realm.

The people—Elves, orcs, and Fae-Orcs—milled about, looking at us as we passed beneath them. There were some derelict and poorly made shacks that were on the ground close to the trees. A couple of them stuck out, but none like the little dugout between two roots that Set had described.

Wrokal led us to a hut in a tree toward the rear of the village itself. There had to be fewer than four hundred people living here, but still, the place was nice. Despite the fact that the people were backasswards.

The hut looked like it could have belonged to any craftsman, hell even a carpenter. There were pieces that looked like vices and some string hung in the sunlight across the room.

"What is this material you speak of?" Wrokal asked as he lifted an apron over his head and tied it behind his back. The muscles along his body were flexing crazily. "Show it to me, please."

Bokaj pulled the branch from his inventory and passed it to him.

"I have never seen the like before," Wrokal whispered as he took the wood from my friend almost greedily. "It has no name, what do you call it?"

My brain froze, and Bokaj grinned. "Wild Wood."

Oh, that motherfucker... oh well. It was accurate I guess.

"Yes, I can sense that is accurate," the Orc lifted the wood and actually used it to throw a portion of his roof away so that more light filtered in. "What kind of bow do you want? Short? Hmm? Maybe a longbow?"

Bokaj took out his Dragon Bone Bow and held it out. "Something better than this."

The bow itself was made of bones that looked bleached, the curved portion of the Bone Dragon's wings joined by a piece of leathery sinew acting as the string. It looked disgusting but cool as hell. It looked more like a short bow to me. Maybe?

"You want more power." He nodded as he touched Bokaj's old bow. "The weapon damage is surprisingly low. Though the ability likely kept it relevant for a little while. You could be hitting harder."

"That mimics my thoughts exactly, my good bowyer." Bokaj smiled.

The Orc began to sketch on a long leaf with a piece of charcoal, "A longbow, then. There will be a recurve, and the tension needs to be just so. The wood is supple, springy even. As if it wants and needs to retain its shape. Hmm..." He scratched his hairless head in thought. "The Belgar you brought, I will require portions of its innards and some of the sinew for the bowstring. Is this fine?"

"That's fine, but we won't part with the pelt for free, and we want the armored portions," I haggled.

"That is fine," Wrokal grunted. "My best skinner and tanner are working on it as we speak. I will send word to them of what needs to be done. With wood like this, all of my skill will be needed. I require five days." Before any of us could speak, he held up his meaty hand. "This is not negotiable. I will do my best work and nothing less. There are some craftsmen among us who have various trades and things to offer. You are free to move among us, come and go as you please, but you will check with my counsel before leaving and when you come. Those are my stipulations."

"We can agree to that," Bokaj answered quickly. The rest of us stayed quiet.

"Good, leave me to my work then, please." He began to measure and weigh the branch as we left the hut.

Jaken and I are going looking for those kids, we headed down the ramp to Wrokal's hut as I used our earrings to communicate. *You all go see what's what about some of the things to get here and keep us updated. Soon as we find the kids, we'll shout and meet up. Then g-t-f-o with them so that they're safe after the bow is made.*

Sounds good to me. Jaken cracked his neck. The others nodded to us as we broke away from them and began to explore in earnest. After looking for an hour and noticing that we had a tail on us, we decided to stop for the day and signaled to the others we were ready to meet.

The only thing of any realistic value to us were the herbs and medicines they had. I say medicines *loosely* because they lacked the tools and instruments to truly perfect the ingredients and distill the proper potions.

Yoh did find some good cuts of meats and more than a few vegetables that would help us last a while longer here.

After asking a nice Fae-Orc lady, we were able to find the counsel area. The counsel were elderly members of each of the races, nondescript really, but they took our comings and goings very seriously.

They really didn't want us there at night when they escorted us out. Like we couldn't get back in. But we would play along. For now.

We were escorted from the village, and after a half an hour walk, we teleported back to our own little slice of the jungle.

"So, I told the guy, I says—'hey. Fuck you.'" Muu said as we teleported into the middle of the village. The sound caused him to turn around, shrieking in surprise. The high-pitched cry going on almost comically long. Everyone stared at him, even Ampharia in her true form.

After a second he stopped and whispered, "You heard nothing."

"I really can't." I almost shouted incredulously. "The fuck was that?"

"What?" Jaken said loudly.

"I fucking hate all of you," Muu grumbled.

"What?" Yohsuke asked loudly.

Chapter Twenty-Four

Four days later, after one of us spent time searching from the ground and we had gotten a better map drawn for us by Set—we found the hovel.

The only problem was that the kids were never there while we were. They were always somewhere else, and no matter how hard we looked for them, they were nowhere to be found. There were signs of life, sure. The grass was laid in, and there were food scraps—barely—but the evidence was there.

That night, we ate peacefully, but in contemplation about what needed doing. It wasn't sitting well with any of us that these kids were suddenly missing.

"Could they have been adopted by someone?" Bokaj asked after having spent the day looking for them himself.

After conferring with Set, he shook his head. "No one would want them. The only way for them to regain their honor was for Set to prove himself as a hunter."

The boy looked upset, and I couldn't blame him—they had given him an impossible task.

"Hey, can't you go in at night Zeke?" Yohsuke asked.

"Yeah, you could go in owl form, and try to see if anything is going on," James added. "I'm not sure what it could be, but I'm sure if anyone could find them, it'd be you."

I nodded once and turned to Set. "Can you describe them?"

Jaken said a few words, and the boy motioned to himself silently before giving me two differing heights. Both smaller, almost in the toddler range. Fuck.

We had to try and find these kids. I had to try and find these kids.

"If Mae comes back while I'm gone—tell her 'Pie' for me." I took a running head start from where I had stood from our table and shifted into my owl form mid-leap. Since I was more familiar with the area, and the village was on my map, the flight there was much swifter than it had been the first time.

Scouts in the trees are watching your flight patterns, you need to go lower. As if you are hunting—there is a small, but venomous snake there near one of the guards.

I got the idea and dove for the rear of the slowly moving reptile. It must have been focused on something in the brush before it because my scooping it up by the tail caught it by surprise. The snake tried to strike at my legs, but with two sure flaps of my wings, I flung it into the guard.

The guard fell—silently to his credit—out of his perch tangling with the snake.

Much cleverer than I had expected, Druid. You are turning out to be a fine owl.

Thanks, I thought back dryly. I flew straight to the hovel and saw that there were indeed two children there, but they had nothing in common with Set. Deciding to take a huge risk, I shapeshifted and woke the larger one. He was a fully Elven boy, so I hoped he spoke common better than most of the villagers.

As I shook him awake gently, I made the universal motion for quiet with a finger pressed to my lips and a hard glint to my eyes.

"Rogir. Velt." I motioned to the place the other one slept before shrugging and pointing from my eyes to the ground. "Where are they?"

"You speak funny, why?" The boy asked strangely. I blinked at him, but he took pity on me. "They were taken to the pit as sacrifices earlier. We are next, but not for another week."

He seemed to be taking it well, the fact that he was a sacrifice.

"Sacrifice to what?" I asked.

"The Moon Goddess." he smiled. "She has taken the form of the great snake, Lothir. When she feeds, the goddess is pleased, and we can live our lives."

"Where is this pit?" I asked softly. My skin had begun crawling for some reason.

"It is behind the Chief's hut and close to Atuala's den. The pit is an altar. There is no telling when Lothir will bless us with her presence, but she will come soon."

"Thank you." I shifted into my fox form and began to slowly work my way toward Wrokal's hut. I walked up the ramp to the place and crept through the curtain that separated his hut from the outside world. As I entered the room, I felt that it was empty. I looked in the bed, and I saw that I was correct, but the bow on the table was what I had hoped to find.

On the table was a longbow made of the Wild Wood we had brought in, but this had been treated and strung tightly. Protecting the strung portion of the limbs on top and bottom were the somewhat hollowed portions of the Belgar's horns. The horns were still sharp, but they were truly attached. The string was thick to me, but it was no big deal.

Wild Bow

+12 damage, +10 to magical damage

Forester – when an enemy dies by an arrow fired from this bow, a tree grows from the remains almost immediately up to ten feet tall at a minimum, or higher depending on the corpse used as fertilizer.

Longbow made by Grandmaster Bowyer Wrokal Woodtusk.

I slipped the weapon into my inventory, then shifted into my owl form and hopped into the window sill. There I saw the reason for my earlier discomfort. The boy had been right. There was a large snake. Though I'm sure serpent was what he had meant. Its head was the size of a hummer, and the body itself was probably longer than a football field uncoiled. It was huge, and in the middle of its massive coils were three children. The chief and Atuala stood on a large lifted portion over the pit that just barely contained the serpent and his probable prey.

"Lady Lothir, we ask that you take this humble offering and speak on our behalf to the Goddess of the Night and Stars that we may have a good life, a good harvest, and healthy warriors." Atuala began to chant, and the Wrokal started to beat on a drum as if in a trance.

The giant reptile watched them in a bored manner before turning toward the three children. They were terrified, and I didn't blame them.

Even with all the other stupid-ass shit I did, I'd be reliving this one forever.

You are an idiot, Druid. The owl wasn't wrong. *Let us go to them.*

With grim determination, I let my body lean forward and fell from the window. I plummeted then arced my fall into a nearly silent glide that allowed me to brush my left wing over the back of Lothir's raising head. I banked and dropped heavily to avoid her gaze, then turned once more to land among the children who clustered together in fear. The scent of feces and urine was pungent here.

I landed and shifted into my fox-man form long enough to see the great serpent turn her head back toward us with her tongue flickering out lazily. I touched the children and cast Teleport as something gooey and wet hit my body. My muscles tensed painfully, but the spell was cast, and we were gone in a flash.

We landed next to the Wild tree in the center of the village, and I heard the others moving toward us. I tried desperately to move. To do anything. But my muscles were completely still. I noticed the paralyzed debuff under my health bar once more and understood why. This must have been venom from Lothir.

"It will not kill him, but it needs to be washed away from him so that he can begin to recover," Ampharia's great eye blinked over my body. My clothes moved toward her as she took a deep breath. "Lothir. What were you doing in the presence of the moon-cursed?"

I looked at her in impotent rage, and she chuckled, "Forgive me, a little paralyzing humor never killed anyone."

It took an hour for the others to try and figure out a way to get that goo off of me, but by the time they were ready to try it, the Dragon grew impatient and spat a great gout of—well, spit—on me, then used a plank of wood to scrape the fluids from my skin before Bokaj cast Purify on me twice.

It helped to loosen me up significantly, but it was a few more minutes before I was able to fully shake the effects of the venom.

By then, Set and the others had joined us, and Set pointed from Jaken to himself, then me and started to speak.

"He says that he wants to explain things from the children's perspective." We all nodded and Ampharia settled into a good position. As Jaken translated the events from their perspective, we simply listened.

"The children had been prepared by cleansing waters and ceremony before being taken to the pit. Each night the serpent would sit and stare at them, never moving, then leaving before daybreak. This was to be the final night that the ceremony took place and the serpent would eat them." Jaken looked as confused as I felt. "A snake shouldn't have that much trouble finding food, even just hunting at night. What's so different about this one?"

"The fact that this serpent is easily larger than even I am, though not as powerful," Ampharia informed the Paladin. Jaken's eyes widened as he looked at me for confirmation.

"It's true," an involuntary shiver rocked my body at the memory, "and that thing is going to probably eat more kids."

"It will eat more children," Ampharia explained. "Sit, I will tell you the tale."

We gathered on the inside of the building we took our meals in, and Ampharia took her Dragon-kin form to speak with us.

"More than a century or so ago, a large, beautiful serpent wandered this jungle. A fair and just creature, one that I had even counted as a friend. She was obedient to the balance of nature—life and death—and all knew that she was a favored child of Mother Nature. She had lived far beyond the normal years of a serpent of her ilk, but her mother's favor never once went to her head."

I looked at the others, they were taken in by the story. Jaken was even whispering the story to the children.

"At some point though, the praise from the creatures around her did begin to wear on her. They sought her out so that they might also gain the favor of the Mother. They treated her as though she was the one who was worthy of worship and love and not the Mother."

Ampharia's features darkened slightly, a sad look crossing over her. Her shoulders slouched slightly and drooped.

"She began to set herself up as a goddess. If the Mother was responsible for the earth itself and all that grows upon it—why should she not be the goddess of the moon, whose beauty lights the night? So, she beguiled others into building her alter—likely where that village is—and then taking sacrifices. The night of her first sacrifice came after two nights staring at the creature so that it could fill all of its last memories with her beauty. And on the third night, she struck. The blood that was shed over her vanity saw her cursed. No longer can she endure the light of day. It would turn her to stone."

"So what do we do?" James asked. "If she's as big as you say—there's no way we can fight her and have it be fair."

"Yeah, I'm all for leaving this one alone to come back and fight another day," Muu added.

"And the fucking kids, man?!" Jaken looked like he was about to burst a blood vessel. "What about the kids too? This thing needs to die to protect them. I don't care if it's not our fight—this whole fucking thing has 'our fight' all over it to me."

"Yeah, and we need the experience!" Yohsuke interjected. "Every little bit helps."

"Yeah, it does. Speaking of," I pulled the bow out of my inventory and handed it to its rightful owner.

"Yo, Forester looks tight!" Bokaj stopped and stared at it then a look of excitement dawned on his face. "I have an idea!"

Over the next fifteen minutes, he had a rough outline for us to try and follow. Half an hour after that, there was a flurry of motion on all of our parts. We couldn't risk more kids falling victim to a false deity, let alone a giant *fucking* snake.

This was going to take an insane amount of luck, but who knew if it would work.

This plan is... creative. The owl's voice echoed through my mind. *There is a vole on your right, thirty feet from the leftmost bush. It has stilled.*

After an hour of collection, I used Teleport to get us closer to the village while saving some energy. From there, we waited the half an hour needed for it to finish cooling down, then moved toward the village. We had left the children behind with the green Dragon promising to come back—successful or not, we were going to come back.

The villagers and guards were gathered at the back of the area, near where I had found the kids, and Lothir was on a warpath.

"Find theeeem!" she moaned. "My sssacrificess! My beauty needs to be reaffirmed in the sight of the moon!"

Bokaj was behind us, but he spoke to us telepathically, *No fucking around, guys. Hit hard, hit fast, and melt away. Guerilla warfare up in this bitch.*

A couple of us nodded. I summoned Coal and ordered him to stay close to Tmont, then I did my part and shapeshifted into my owl form before flying into the air. I watched as Jaken strode forward, and the people began to take notice of our presence.

Atuala stepped forward in front of Lothir and pointed accusingly toward the group. "It was you! The Druid who took our young children from us, was from *your* group!"

"Yeah—we don't like shit eating kids around us" Bokaj flashed a lopsided grin.

"And I bet that the poor snake there is hungry, right?" James shouted.

When no one answered, Jaken took that as the time to shout, "Hey, you big legless dick, come get some!" There was a bag that reminded me of a horror movie Santa Clause's sack over his shoulder that writhed and wriggled and he looked ready to fight.

Lothir hissed loudly and bowled over a couple of the villagers on her way toward Jaken.

A majority of them were intelligent enough to realize the ground was no longer safe for them to be on. Those ones fled into the trees. The guards began to try and fire arrows at us but stopped when they risked hitting Lothir from their current vantage points. Tmont rushed from her master's side toward where some of them had gone to flank us, and I sent Coal to go and join her in causing mayhem.

Yohsuke began to fire potshots with his Astral Bolts at her eyes. Then Bokaj began to do the same. When Lothir was close enough to lunge at Jaken—which she happily did—she got a mouth full of that bag full of jungle rodents, that was then hit with a Fireball Arrow. I felt Muu take the planned step off my back from where I circled above the great serpent's writhing form. She wiggled left and right, but Muu would have his fun.

As the dragoon began to drop, Lothir reared, and it looked like she would be able to dodge his attack, but a pair of green wings reminiscent of Ampharia's own burst from his back. They flared, turning him on his course slightly, then tucked around him, and he dove even faster toward her. His ice lance sank deep into her back just at the base of her skull. Then I shifted into my fox form before going Belgar and dropping face on that bitch. As I plummeted toward her, her jaws were forced wide as trees and tree limbs began to sprout out of her mouth.

Forester had activated in all the small animals we had killed with that one Fireball arrow just as we had suspected. I glanced against a tree, bouncing away from it a little, then connected with her right eye, goring the black orb. She hissed, and I heard a crack next to me. I shifted out of my Belgar form and into my fox-man form and did something disastrously stupid.

"PIE!" I roared as I pulled out Storm Caller and activated Wind Scythe and threw it above Lothir's head.

I used Blade Shift and teleported to my weapon just in time for Muu to rocket past me.

"Sup?" We greeted each other, then I focused my will to cast Aspect of the Ursolon. The expected changes washed over me like a warm shower.

I pulled Magus Bane into my left hand, brought it one handed above my head next to Storm Caller in my right hand. In my enlarged form, both weapons fit closely in my hands but not well enough. So, I took them back into each hand and readied myself. As I began to fall, I used what little time I had to check on my friends.

Muu was above me, duh, but James was fighting against warriors that had run forward to protect the wanna-be goddess. Bokaj was firing arrows into both the crowd rushing toward us and the gigantic snake. The snake wasn't getting too hurt, but the trees had hurt her quite a bit, and I hated to admit it, but Muu's attack had done some serious damage too.

Lothir's HP bar had fallen to forty-five percent, going down by slight, slight increments here and there. Jaken was in front of the snake, then on the side, his shield floating beside him, and his longsword was parrying blows from Atuala as Jaken slashed at Lothir with his greatsword.

Yohsuke was slashing at the scaled underbelly before him, then casting a random Astral Bolt into the crowd behind the serpent in an effort to try and help James.

Coal was sticking close to Yohsuke as well, but the damage he was doing was negligible at best. But he was trying his hardest.

Hey, you want a push? Muu's question brought me back to the present.

If you would be so kind. A feral grin stretched across my jaws. I heard a whistle behind me and looked up to see Muu behind me with his legs bent like he was about to jump.

I did the same with mine, and as soon as our boots met, he grunted through our earrings, *Now!*

He and I both pushed with all our might, and I shot forward and plummeted faster toward Lothir. Before I knew it, I was beside her neck and jaw. While her jaw was dislodged trying to work at either ejecting the growing trees or swallowing them, it was vulnerable.

I activated Cleave and struck with both weapons in unison. Lothir hissed in pain and rage and as she moved, I saw something of interest. A tear in the skin turned into a large wound that showed a pinkish, bulb-looking thing with a muscle behind it.

Muu! Hit her here, and don't let the insides touch you! He was high enough to have time to see her thrashing and my pointing at the wound.

I watched him pull his short spear from his inventory and line up his shot. He drove his arm forward, and the glint of moonlight off his bracelet was almost distracting. If I hadn't heard the whine of his spear piercing the air, I wouldn't have known he had thrown anything. It looked like it hit just below it, but when Lothir reared and shook again, I watched some of the same venom that had hit my chest begin to slowly secrete down the blade.

Get out from under her left side! I panicked and called to the others. *If that venom touches you, you're paralyzed and done for! That happens to any one of us, and we are fucked!*

"Got it!" Jaken called as he worked his way to her right side.

The great serpent didn't appear to be slowing down at all. Then it hit me.

Snakes are immune to their own venom, and I just made the playing field a minefield. Fuck!

I dropped to the ground in a dry spot—thankfully—and rolled to my feet. I turned and kept my eyes on Lothir.

Lothir's health was dropping lower slowly. Muu dropped back down on the top of her head with another monstrous strike—or he would have—if not for the arrow that pushed him slightly off track. So instead of hitting her head again, he hit ten feet back and did considerably less damage. I saw two arrows snap in Wrokal's chest as he lined up his next shot, then Tmont was on top of him.

Jaken, flatten your shield for me—I need a platform, I called to my friend telepathically, and he made a nod. The shield flattened as I put Storm Caller away.

I took Magus Bane in both my hands and kissed it softly. "Come on, baby."

I charged forward and used the shield as a platform to leap up from before Jaken put it back to use a split-second later. I was shy of my mark, so I dug my clawed left hand into the side of the snake and swung myself up on to her back. I ran up and over. Finally, the trees had been dislodged from inside her mouth, so Lothir was thrashing harder than before and was more dangerous now.

She tried to spit some of her venom at James, but he dodged out of the way, and the less controlled shot hit some of her followers. She hissed in frustration and reared up a little further. The motion shook me from my feet and over the left-hand side of her head.

I activated Devil's Hammer and smacked the counterweight of Muu's short spear with the hammer counterbalance on Magus Bane. The weapon shot into her head, and she screeched. Blood fountained from the wound and some hit me on my way down again.

I watched as a Volley, one of Bokaj's spells, hit Lothir from just in front of her face. She opened her mouth and arrows shot in. A Ki blast hit her full on in her good eye, and the arrows kept coming. Finally, I got an experience notification, and Lothir's body began to list to the side. I threw my axe away from me in the direction of Atuala who was still fighting my friends, then shapeshifted into my owl form.

As she fell, more of her people who had been trying to fight us began trying to crowd away from her, but some didn't make it and got crushed. Where she fell, roots began shooting from her body and into the ground, regardless of what was there in front of them. A couple of the people who had fallen when they were running from the fake god were impaled by the roots searching for the ground.

The grisly scene was enough to almost turn my stomach.

I turned to see Atuala trying to bury an axe into Jaken's back as he collected his weapons from where they had fallen. I threw a Winter Blade at him and watched as it severed his spine. The Elf dropped, and Yohsuke was suddenly there with his astral blade buried in his skull.

Bokaj called from his perch on a rooftop in the boughs of a tree, "Your leaders are dead. Your priest is dead. You can clearly see that your so-called god is turning into a tree."

The angry citizens watched him as he stood there with his arms wide for people to see him.

"Do you really want to continue to fuck with us?" he shouted so loudly that his voice was beginning to break. "We don't want to kill you all."

I turned and saw a good majority of the villagers putting their weapons aside. Some held on to them and gritted their teeth at the prospect of surrender. One of the Elves even readied a javelin and took a few paces back. As he took three steps forward to launch it, Coal leaped on to his back, and the projectile's flight arced way left of our Ranger. Coal savaged the back of his body and exposed neck.

The wet sound of tearing and chewing was audible all the way over to me. After the villager stopped moving, Coal stood and growled at all of the villagers around him. They backed away and began to put their weapons down as well if they hadn't already.

Jaken stepped in front of them and began to shout in Fae-Orc. I'd have to see if he could translate for us later, but the people began to gather what dead they could and started to drag them into a pile.

Well, with them doing that and the relieved look on his face—I could imagine that it had been something to that effect.

I had notifications, but I could look at those later. Right now, I wanted to check on my friends.

Everyone okay? I called out through our earrings.

Ouch, Muu groaned. I looked over at the still-growing tree coming from Lothir's corpse. I saw him hanging limply from a tree limb a few feet from the ground with his arm wiggling at us.

I looked over and saw James limping toward me. Yohsuke followed along behind him looking beaten up but alive.

Bokaj answered, *I'm good, man, but Tmont is hurt down there somewhere, and she's pissed. Can you find her?*

I held a hand up with only my thumb visible in affirmation.

I turned around and began to call for her, then cast Aspect of the Owl.

Aspect of the Owl – The Primal Warrior's mind isn't just the sharpest tool he has with this aspect.
Perception and sight increased 100%, +10 wisdom

Oh, fuck yes. This was a caster's wet dream right here.

I shook my head with my eyes closed and then began to look for the great panther in earnest. After a moment, I found her skulking in the shadows ten feet from a dead body. Her leg was pinned to the ground by a root that had shot through like an arrow.

As I approached her, she yowled at me angrily, "Do not touch it!"

"T, I have to so that I can heal you," I reasoned with her. I took a few more steps forward, and she swatted my way with a hiss.

"Your tails will feel nothing but my wrath if you do it!" she hissed at me, but I just growled at the threat.

I cast Ensnare on her and bound her so tightly to the ground that she could only yowl and spit piteously while I worked. I chopped straight through the root that pinned her as far from her leg as I could. After I pulled it and she threatened me again, I tapped her leg affectionately, and she cried out.

"Stop being a bag of dicks and let me help you already!" I pulled the root from her flesh as quickly as I could, but it took a couple tugs.

She panted, and her eyes looked bleary. Her HP was low when I pulled the root fully from her. I focused myself and used my Charge Spell ability. A full twenty seconds later, I cast Regrowth on her, and her health began to climb at an alarming rate. Expected, but this was the first time I had used that ability with a heal. Awesome results.

By the time I had finished healing her, Bokaj had jogged over and began to see to her himself. She didn't have the highest health, but her pain tolerance was low, so she was hamming it up for the attention he would give her. Typical cat.

Jaken was seeing to Muu, and the villagers had decided to give us a very wide berth as we saw to the aftermath. None of the villagers struck down by the roots of the tree had been so lucky as Tmont. We didn't ransack their corpses in front of their community.

Winning the hearts and minds—yay us!

Lothir had dropped nothing but some scales that Muu took immediate possession of. After we were finished, Jaken looked to the people once more.

"Aratu ack voli tolith cati, oro balistora, Lothir. Filtera ros eva ack deister Radiance. Por tullin ro mer dilt." He looked at me and nodded. "Ready whenever you are, man."

"The fuck did you say to them?" Yohsuke asked with an odd look on his face.

"Anyone who demands so much from you, god or Lothir is not a god. Mine is Radiance, and all she wants is peace. For her, I will make it."

"Did you just Paladin threaten a whole people?" Muu asked in awe.

Jaken's response was a grim nod.

EPILOGUE

Once we returned to the village, we told the kids and Ampharia what had happened. Turned out, those crazy wings Muu had were a part of her gift. Crazy right? I thought so too.

All of us had leveled up a good deal. Who knew killing a fake god and a few dozen of her people would result in a huge amount of experience. I felt dirty, though. Really dirty.

How had those people not realized that they were victims from the one thing they thought they could trust? I would likely never understand that, and at the risk of sounding callous beyond words—I didn't dare try.

All of us had received an interesting notification though for a change.

SECRET QUEST COMPLETED!

Filet the False God – As a little snake, she had been much adored by the land itself, but as she had grown—so too did her hubris. You have taken part in slaying the great false god Lothir.

Reward: 8,000 EXP, and the gratitude of the real Gods.

Woah. That level of experience, plus all the experience from the fight took me up to a grand total of eleven *thousand* experience gained! That meant that I had gone up to level 29! And some change, of course.

"Did you guys get a boon?" James's voice sounded uncertain, and it stopped me from placing my stat points for the moment.

I shook my head, and so did everyone other than Bokaj.

"So wait, you two got a boon?" Muu asked with a disappointed look on his face. "A boon from who?"

"The Gods," Bokaj whispered. "Does this mean that they can bring Balmur back from the Hells?!"

"It does not," a small, melodic voice behind us answered sadly.

We turned to find a small green figure—no not a Leprechaun—with an orange beard and fiery mane of hair sitting in one of the chairs behind us. Okay, maybe a Leprechaun.

"I come on behalf o' the Gods to let ye know that they cannot be goin' inta the Hells for ye. Sorry, lad." His sad eyes were for Bokaj in that moment. He wore a small leaf toga, kind of like Mother Nature's, and his features were very decidedly Gnome adjacent. "I'll be actin' as their mouthpiece here. Ask for yer boons, lads."

"Tell me where the strongest, nicest black Dragon is located," James stepped forward and blurted.

"Nicest black Dragon—boy do ye not know what yer kin are like?" The little man snickered and closed his eyes. "He be in the great swamp, northwest of here on an isle off the coast. Hasn't cared to move in decades. Last I heard."

James took out a little notebook and jotted it down with a quill he pulled from his inventory.

The little man looked at Bokaj next. "And ye want to know how to get into the Hells, don't ye laddy?" Bokaj kept his mouth shut and nodded. "Ask the question, boy. The boon cannot be given this freely."

"Tell us where, on this plane of existence we can find entry to the Hells without dying or being banished there, please?" Bokaj looked the man straight in the eyes.

"Since ye asked so nicely." He closed his eyes once more, then began to speak, "High Elves, in their great, walled city up north. There are some who may know of a way. The other, maybe less preferable. It's a city of the Drow, and they have the same level of knowledge. No matter what ye decide—know that yer close ta bein' strong enough to stand a chance in the demon realms, but yer gonna need to be careful."

He hopped down from his chair and walked toward us, then dissipated in a swath of clovers that blew away in a ghostly wind.

Okay, he had to be a Leprechaun.

"So, we have our heading and half our Dragon blessings," Muu tried to say lightly. "That just leaves getting a little stronger, then going to visit some assholes to see about a trip. That's like, three things left."

We nodded grimly. We were closer—damn sure not close enough—but closer. We had our heading. We had a plan.

"Looks like we're close to going into the Hells, boys." Bokaj nodded his head to all of us. "Let's get this show on a roll and get our fucking Rogue back."

Afterword

We hope you enjoyed Into the Dragon's Den! Since reviews are the lifeblood of indie publishing, we'd love it if you could leave a positive review on Amazon! Please use this link to go to the Axe Druid: Into the Dragon's Den Amazon product page to leave your review: geni.us/IntotheDragonsDen.

As always, thank you for your support! You are the reason we're able to bring these stories to life.

About Christopher Johns

Christopher Johns is a former photojournalist for the United States Marine Corps with published works telling hundreds of other peoples' stories through word, photo, and even video. But throughout that time, his editors and superiors had always said that his love of reading fantasy and about worlds of fantastic beauty and horrible power bled into his work. That meant he should write a book.

Well, ta-da!

Chris has been an avid devourer of fantasy and science fiction for more than twenty years and looks forward to sharing that love with his son, his loving fiancée and almost anyone he could ever hope to meet.

Connect with Chris:
Twitter.com/JonsyJohns

About Mountaindale Press

Dakota and Danielle Krout, a husband and wife team, strive to create as well as publish excellent fantasy and science fiction novels. Self-publishing *The Divine Dungeon: Dungeon Born* in 2016 transformed their careers from Dakota's military and programming background and Danielle's Ph.D. in pharmacology to President and CEO, respectively, of a small press. Their goal is to share their success with other authors and provide captivating fiction to readers with the purpose of solidifying Mountaindale Press as the place 'Where Fantasy Transforms Reality.'

Connect with Mountaindale Press:
MountaindalePress.com
Facebook.com/MountaindalePress
Krout@MountaindalePress.com

Mountaindale Press Titles

GameLit and LitRPG

The Divine Dungeon Series
The Completionist Chronicles Series
By: Dakota Krout

A Touch of Power: Siphon
By: Jay Boyce

Red Mage: Advent
By: Xander Boyce

Peaks of Power: Beginnings
By: Paul Campbell Jr.

Ether Collapse: Equalize
By: Ryan DeBruyn

Skeleton in Space: Histaff
By: Andries Louws

Pixel Dust: Party Hard
By: David Petrie

Fantasy

The Black Knight Series
By: Christian J. Gilliland

Coming soon!
The Lost Sigil: Insurrection
By: Raymond Beckham and Darius Cook

Appendix

The Good

Zekiel Erebos (Zee-key-uhl Air-uh-bows) – Marine who loves gaming as a civilian with his buddies who are still in. Class: Druid. Race: Kitsune, has a tail.

Yohsuke (Yo-s'kay) – Zeke's best bud/brother from the Marine Corps. Overlord, yeah, you read that right. Class: Spell Blade. Race: Abomination (half-breed Drow and High Elf).

Jaken Warmecht (Jay-ken) – Zeke's friend who typically needs help catching up in the games the group places together. Class: Paladin of Radiance. Race: Fae-Orc.

Bokaj (Bow-ka-jh) – A friend from the gym who loves video games and is in a pretty wicked band! Class: Ranger. Race: Ice Elf.

Tmont (Tee-M-on-t) – A panther with a taste for tails who happens to not just be a walking bag of assholes, but is also Bokaj's pet. Mainly that first one though.

Balmur (Ball-mer) – Bokaj's best friend and another good buddy of Zeke's who loves to game! Class: Rogue. Race: Azer Dwarf (Fire Dwarf). HIS BEARD IS A FLAME!

James Bautista (Really?) – Another Marine that Yohsuke and Zeke know and game with often. Class: Monk. Race: Dragon Elf.

Muu Ankiman (Moo Ahn-key-men) – Dragon Beast-kin with green scales and Zeke's roommate on Earth. Liiiiittle crazy, but he's okay. Class: Fighter. Race: Dragon-kin (it's shorter!).

Kayda (Kay-duh) – A pretty little bird with a shitty past and, hopefully, a bright future. Recently turned into a Storm Roc. Very protective of a certain Flame Wolf.

Coal – A Flame Wolf that Zeke is taking care of for a bit on behalf of the Primordial Flame Elemental. He's got a good temperament, a little heated at times, but he's a cool pup.

Sir Willem Dillon – Owner of the tavern in Sunrise Village (the starter town) and Paladin of Radiance. The first guy the group meets and doesn't try to kill. (Or do they? MUAHAHAHA—No really, do they?) Jaken's trainer.

Dinnia (Dih-nee-uh) – An Elven Druid who takes pity on poor Zeke and brings him into Mother Nature's good graces. Zeke's trainer.

Sharo (shah-row) – Another panther who assists his partner in crime Dinnia in training her student. Not a walking back of assholes.

Kyra – Queen of the bears and good friend of Dinnia's. We like her.

Marin (mare-in) – We, uh... we don't talk about her. 10 out of 10 though. Kick ass dire bear.

Tarron Dillingsley (Tair-run Dill-night-slee) – Gnomish enchanter who—let's face it shall we?—sucks as a teacher for various reasons.

Rowland – Blacksmith in Sunrise who decides he likes the travelers, especially the one with the tail—no bias.

Maebe (may-buh—soft buh—if she hears you talking shit, I'm not responsible, yeah?) – Unseelie Queen of Winter and Darkness, who somehow gets thrown into the mix. Also Zeke's girlfriend. I know, right?

Thogan (ThO-gun) – Champion of the Unseelie Fae, and a rather clingy Dwarf with a rough complexion.

Titania – Queen of the Seelie Fae, who has a predisposition of being a raging bitch to anyone and everyone she doesn't like. Like outsiders.

Craglim (Crag-limb) – Rowland's cousin. Racist piece of shit—but he's a good fighter.

Zhavron (Zah-vrun) – Orc Fighter with a sordid past. Muu's trainer in all things fighting. A little intense at times.

Pharazulla (Far-uh-zu-la) – A Bard of some renown, though a bit of a stuck-up asshole.

Vrawn (Like brawn, but with a V) – A lovely orcish woman with a soft spot for our local Druid. She's built like a busty, brick shit house.

Sam – Mayor of Sunrise village. A fair man whose Bear-kin wife and half Bear-kin children believe in him wholeheartedly. Prefers to hunt for the village rather than govern.

The villagers of Sunrise – Great people whose recently went through a lot of bullshit. Go easy on em, yeah?

Set – A decent little Fae-Orc kid, dooped into hunting a Belgar.

Ampharia (Am-far-ee-uh) – An elder green Dragon friend of Mother Nature's who comes to Muu her blessing and teach him how to fight Dragons.

Natholdi, Granite and son (Nath-ol-dee) – A good, humble Dwarven family that both Muu and Zeke love dearly. Newest additions to the Light Hand Clan.

Farnik Mugfist (Far-nick) – Leader of the Mugfist Clan and good friend to the party. Loves a good cup of mead and song.

Shellica Light Hand (Shell-ih-cuh) – Leader of the Light hand clan and a Grand Master Enchanter. Crazy as shit with a diabolical wit. Zeke's trainer, unfortunately.

Fainnir (Fay-near) – Newly named son of Granite and Natholdi Light Hand, and the first of a new generation of Dwarven Mages.

The Bad

War – Galactic conqueror who probably suffers from only child syndrome. Probably needs a hug, or he will keep trying to take over the universe.

Minions of War – Not the lovable minions everyone loves. You know, not the yellow ones, or that fish from that one Will Ferrell animated movie. These guys seek to undermine the strength of the Gods by eroding the world around them slowly. And serve the other assholes in this list.

The Generals – A Number of War's better warriors capable of taking out the strongest people open the planet—and together they did. Dick move.

Rowan – I'm not gonna say much about this guy—read the book then you'll know what a dickbag he is. Haha, *was*—sonofabitch is dead now.

Pastella (Pahs-tell-uh) – Crazy Elven woman with a taste for torture and violence.

Children of Brindolla – A group of misguided citizens who believe they are the only ones who can truly save their world. They found themselves on the receiving end of an ass kicking—but was that all of them? Too many questions, not enough asses to kick.

Decay – A Greater Fiend possessed by a minion of War who held his own against the party *and* Maebe. Fell due to a brilliant plan and a little bit of finesse. Okay, the plan was half-cocked and the finesse resulted in some bullshit—happy now?

Spiders – Just a bunch of overgrown pests that needed an ass kicking. Nightmare fuel FOREVER.

Lothir (Low-thear) – Big ol' wanna-be snake goddess who has a village of Elves, orcs and Fae-Orcs under her command and demands sacrifices to restore and keep her beauty. All of that means that she's coo coo for Cocoa Puffs.

And The Ugly

Insane Wolves – Think crazy wolves, but you know, crazier and angrier for some reason. Due to proximity to a minion of War, the minds of these animals have eroded to nothing but the drive to kill and eat anything that is not them, or another wolf.

Undead creatures – As you can imagine, due to proximity to a minion of War, these poor bastards rose from the dead in order to protect their alien masters. Even the stronger versions are worthy of a small bit of sympathy—they sure as hell didn't get any, but they are worthy of it.

Bone Dragon – I mean, pretty self explanatory, right? It's a Bone Dragon! No skin, no muscle—all bleached bones and hate for the living.

General of War (Blight) – The asshole who did some truly terrible things, sent us on a supposedly one-way trip to the Fae Realm, and got his ASS kicked. Yeah. That guy.

Ursolon (Ur-soul-on) – Think of a giant, striped bear with an anger management issue the size of North Dakota. Yeah. Now go fight one.

Werewolves – The heroes in some tales—but not this one. Oh no. These guys suck, big time! Hairy, needy pieces of crap.

Alpha Werewolf – The jerk in charge of the other jerks above. Bigger, badder, stronger, and usually *way* more cunning and ruthless.

The Wild Hunt – A flock of assholes (read demons) who patrol the realm of the Fae and take out anything they believe doesn't belong there.

Order of the Prime – A bunch of human wizards bent on controlling the elements and restoring mankind to their rightful place as rulers. Some real xenophobic asshats, these ones.

Spiders – Oh, I mentioned these already? Because there were a lot of them. With fangs. And all the feet. Seriously, I need to book an appointment for therapy now.

Belgar (Bell-gahr) – A rhino-like Fae creature with a surprising sense of honor and code that it lives by. Big as shit and it will run over anyone in its way through.

Teyatunga, the Thunderous (Tay-uh-tuhn-guh) – The only Belgar the party has met, honorable, but a bit of a dick. Not a nice guy.

And other random jerks too unimportant for now to mention – they know who they are. Bunch of assholes.

Made in the USA
Middletown, DE
26 April 2019